The Companion

"A darkly compelling vampire romance . . . the plot keeps the reader turning the pages long into the night."
—*Affaire de Coeur*

"Bestseller Squires charts a new direction with this exotic, extremely erotic, and darkly dangerous Regency-set paranormal tale. With her ability to create powerful and tormented characters, Squires has developed a novel that is graphic, gripping, and unforgettable."
—*Romantic Times* (4½-starred review)

"Travel through Egypt's deserts and London's society with two of the most intriguing characters you will ever read about. You will encounter a dark world that is intense, scary, and sexy, and a love that will brighten it . . . powerful and passionate . . . captivating . . . Squires has a wonderful ability to keep her readers glued to the edge of their seat."
—*Romance Junkies*

"A vibrant, riveting, and sometimes just plain scary novel that should satisfy anyone—including the man in your life—who enjoys paranormal tales . . . Squires's saga is off to an intriguing start."
—*All About Romance*

MORE . . .

"Squires does a fantastic job of taking an old tale, vampirism, and spinning it into a new and fresh tale with characters who intrigue and captivate."

—*Fallen Angel Reviews*

"An unforgettable, sensual, and erotic novel that takes you places you've never gone before . . . will make you believe in the power of true love."

—*Romance Reader at Heart*

"[*The Companion*] delivers sensual love scenes, an intriguing plot fraught with danger, adventure, and the unexpected which will leave readers anxiously awaiting the next enthralling tale from this immensely talented author."

—*Rendezvous*

"Squires has just taken the traditional vampire novel to a whole new level with *The Companion*. With her riveting and compelling writing, she has woven a tale of love amidst the most desperate of circumstances and created unforgettable characters . . . fans of the genre will be fascinated . . . *The Companion* will capture your interest from the first scene until the last . . . readers who like a strong historical novel as well as one with a definite bite should add *The Companion* to their wish list. It will be a keeper for sure!"

—aromancereview.com

"Squires has demonstrated a talent that few can surpass. Her descriptions and historical details are flawless. Her characters exceed their potential and the plot keeps you quickly turning the pages. Squires has joined the company of authors whose books are classics. Look for this book to become a classic in its genre too. *The Companion* is a gem. Obviously, everyone needs it."

—*Coffee Time Romance*

"A totally absorbing novel...the characters are brilliantly conceived and perfect for the gripping plotline. The author gives the reader a unique twist on what vampires really are, a tortured hero to adore, the only heroine who could possibly be right for him, a truly horrific villain—and a fascinating story that carries the reader through one exciting adventure after another... Squires's prose grabs you from the beginning and gives you a relentless ride through this complex, beautifully written book."

—*New and Used Books*

"A riveting story, the first of what I expect to become a fresh, unforgettable new vampire series."

—*BookLoons*

"A book to be savored, not torn through at breakneck speed... Squires is a talented author and *The Companion* offers the promise of more beautifully dark vampire novels to follow."

—*The Romance Reader*

ST. MARTIN'S PAPERBACKS TITLES
BY SUSAN SQUIRES

The Companion

The Hunger

THE
BURNING

SUSAN SQUIRES

ST. MARTIN'S PAPERBACKS

THE BURNING

ISBN: 0-312-99855-4
EAN: 9780312-99855-4

Printed in the United States of America

St. Martin's Paperbacks edition / April 2006

St. Martin's Paperbacks are published by St. Martin's Press, 175 Fifth Avenue, New York, NY 10010.

10 9 8 7 6 5 4 3 2 1

To Jennifer Enderlin, who is probably tired of having books dedicated to her. But she has to put up with it again because she was such an important part of this effort. She said, "More," just at the right times. And to Harry, without whom these books wouldn't exist at all.

One

They ran their hands over his body. There were three of them. Their palms rubbed his chest, his hips and thighs, and the bulge of his biceps where his wrists were bound above his head. The nails scraped lightly, threatening. He knew what was to come. The stone bench on which he lay was hard against the bare flesh of his buttocks and shoulders, but the room was warm. They loved heat. It was a true luxury in the winter of the Carpathian Mountains. The only illumination came from the fire licking at the logs in the great stone arches. Above him, their faces were unreal in the flickering light. Their eyes glowed red. Now they would compel him. Their low moans filled the little room cut into the rocky heart of the monastery. He knew every crevice in its stone by now. This room held his torment and possibly his salvation.

"Test him well, tonight, sisters," one of them whispered. Her breasts brushed his belly.

"Is he worthy of our father's trust?" another breathed into his ear.

He felt his loins throb, tight with a need he dared not

indulge. He had no idea whether they compelled that need, or whether it belonged to him. A tongue found his nipple. He could not help but arch up into it. The chains clanked. A hand cupped his balls. He felt the scrape of canines at his throat. They wanted blood tonight. He waited for the pain. How would he bear their ministrations in the long hours ahead? Atonement. You deserve this, *he told himself.* A thousand years of torment would not atone for your crimes. You have one chance at redemption and they will help you to it.

He breathed as they had taught him. He focused inward, searching for an island of control. His shoulders relaxed. All emotion drained slowly away. The piercing of his carotid was a fact of pain, no more. One of them sucked at his throat while the others kept him roused.

But now he was ready for whatever they might do to him. He would become what was required. No matter the cost, he would atone.

CHEDDAR GORGE, WILTSHIRE, MARCH 1822

"I won't live forever, Ann." Her uncle Thaddeus frowned up under his white, beetling brows at her and folded his newspaper. "My heart isn't good."

"Nonsense, Uncle. You are too cantankerous to die." Ann Van Helsing sat in her personal chair and smiled at her uncle. He wasn't cantankerous, but it always made him sputter when she told him that he was. Tonight she didn't want to hear her uncle talk about dying, even though his skin looked like parchment these days, and his breath grew labored at the slightest provocation. Here in the library, the cheerful fire snapped, nearly drowning out the tap of branches against the window and the bluster of the wind. *Persuasion,* the latest novel by Miss Austen, lay open on a small table with delicately carved legs. Ann held her wooden page turner poised above it. She couldn't touch the pages directly. Too many people had handled them at the lending library. But the library was comfortable. The moment should not be marred with talk of death.

"Young lady, you will not put me off this time." Her uncle put his paper aside and heaved his bulk out of the red leather wing chair across from her. "And I am *not* cantankerous."

Ann bit back her smile and looked up at his dear, worried face. He only had her best interests at heart. "Well, could we agree on . . . hmmm, 'of indifferent temper' perhaps?"

He wouldn't return her teasing, though. "You know what very likely awaits you after I die." His eyes darkened and his voice was tight with emotion. "You must be provided for."

"I am set up quite nicely. My father saw to that. I have money and property aplenty." She said it lightly, as though that were what he meant. Indeed, Maitlands was her father's gift to her. It had come to him with his marriage to her mother, and since it was not entailed to the Brockweir title he could dispose of it as he pleased. Her uncle, who held both the title and all the entailed lands, acted as her trustee, but that was in name only since she had come of age.

"That is not what I meant." Her uncle rocked on his heels and put his hands in the pockets of his trousers, his unruly brows creased in thought. Ann said nothing, hoping his thoughts would take a cheerier turn. Then he cleared his throat. "This young cousin of yours seems a pleasant chap."

Ann shot him an astonished look. "That eel? Too slippery by half, Uncle, to say nothing of the fact that he has jowls. You can't deny he has jowls."

Her uncle wisely chose to avoid the issue of jowls. "You're just not used to town bronze, Ann, locked up here in the country as you've been. He's been on the Continent for the last six years. Nothing like a Grand Tour to give one town bronze." He cleared his throat again. "He seems interested in you."

"Well, I am most definitely *not* interested in him." She saw her uncle start to respond and lifted her brows. "You know you will only set up my back, Uncle," she warned.

He bit his lip. "People think you fragile because of your looks," he muttered. "If they knew your willfulness . . ."

She sat back in mock protest. "I am the very *soul* of meekness." He did love her, no matter how much trouble she was. She smiled.

"I've invited him to stay at the house," her uncle said flatly.

Her urge to smile evaporated. "You what?"

"I . . . I think you should see more of each other." He would not meet her gaze.

"I do not want that smooth-mannered . . . dissembler roaming freely around Maitlands Abbey," Ann sputtered.

"He belongs at Maitlands. If your father had not settled it on you, Erich would have inherited it. He is the last of the Van Helsings. I suspect he has very little. Can you not share Maitlands with him just for a while?"

When he put it like that . . . "You have more claim on Maitlands than he does. It is your home. And you can invite whoever you wish to stay."

"I do not want Maitlands," her uncle said quietly. "I shall to Hampshire after I've seen you settled."

Settled? What was he thinking? "You're not thinking we will make a match of it . . . You *know* I can never marry! After what happened to Mother?"

"I know, Ann. I know." He made shushing motions with his hands. But he had not given up. She could see it in his eyes. "But not all marriages are . . . physically intimate."

The hair on her arms rose. The very thought of physical intimacy with that fat flawn of a man with a fish mouth and protuberant eyes and an air of . . . of supercilious condescension underscored by something far less appetizing she could not name was more than she could contemplate.

"He can stay, Uncle Thaddeus." She couldn't refuse. But there were limits. "But don't think I'm going to be put on display for evaluation like the prize heifer at the village fair." She shook a finger at him in mock warning. "I will never marry. *Especially* not Erich Van Helsing."

"Just be polite."

She chewed her lip. "You have no idea what you ask." But she smiled at him. "Only for you. And in order to recruit my strength, I believe I shall retire." She blew her uncle a kiss and headed out of the library. Erich Van Helsing under her roof and underfoot was going to be a trial. She trudged up the stairs to the fourth floor. There, under the eaves, was the nursery, the only place where she felt secure. She closed the door gently, so as not to make the knocker bang, and put her back to it as though that would keep out the fact that her uncle was indeed frail and that she was going to have a nightmare houseguest.

At least she had the refuge of the nursery. She looked around. The single bed, covered with a colorful counterpane, was set under the dormered windows now being rattled by the wind. The small dresser held jars and brushes. Bookshelves from floor to ceiling along the inside wall insulated the room against the rest of the world. Two slightly careworn dolls sat on the windowsill. Her nurse, Malmsy, dead now, had hooked the rugs. Everything was familiar. She walked to the dolls and touched one, feeling only the wash of her own childhood. She missed her Malmsy, who had held her since she was an infant. Malmsy was the only one whose touch was not a torment to her, the only one who had ever hugged her. Of course, her nurse had died before the full effect of Ann's affliction came on her. Would even Malmsy's touch have been torture once Ann turned fifteen?

The sense of loss that haunted the edges of her mind

washed over her. Human contact was denied her. She sat heavily on the tiny stool in front of her dresser. It still almost fit her, though it was designed for a child. The face in the mirror looked as though she didn't belong to this world. White-blonde hair floated around delicate features; straight nose if small, dainty lips. The gray eyes looked as though they saw ghosts, which, of course they did in a way, at least if she touched anything. The skin was pale, almost translucent. All in all, she looked too fragile for the world. Also true, as it happened.

Her uncle was right about her future. No matter how she tried to hide her fear from her uncle with shrugs and smiles, things were bleak. Her curse, the curse of all her female line, was to know things about people from touching. Touching people brought on a shower of their past, and their emotions and the raw, contradictory core of their nature. The experience of touching shocked whoever she touched almost as much as it shook her. Even touching things yielded impressions of all the people who had handled that object in the course of its life. If she wasn't careful, all the shouting information just overwhelmed her until she couldn't think at all.

That curse had driven her mother mad, and sooner or later it would close in on Ann's mind as well. She was likely to end in a cell with chains around her neat ankles and dirty straw on the floor, screaming until she was too hoarse to croak.

Her quiet life here, under her uncle's protection, had staved off the inevitable. But if he died, Squire Fladgate would find a way to commit her. She was the stuff of nightmares for the village, the different one, the one who knew things no one should know. Everyone in town was sure their secrets were not safe as long as Ann was at Maitlands Abbey.

And if she married? The madhouse for certain. She

shuddered at the thought of a man touching her, showering kaleidoscope experience over her. Madness overtook her mother on the very night Ann was conceived. It was the first time her parents had tried to have conjugal relations. Her mother was found, naked and drooling, the next morning. She'd died in an asylum the following year, shortly after Ann was born. And her father had all but committed suicide in guilt. He volunteered for Wellington's vanguard at Salamanca—a self-imposed death sentence certainly, but one that still allowed him to be buried in sanctified ground.

No. Ann would not marry. She would never touch another man if she could help it. And the villagers were wrong. She didn't want their secrets. Her uncle was wrong too. There was nothing Erich Van Helsing could do to "settle" her.

Couldn't she just live here with her uncle forever? A small voice inside her head whispered that it wasn't fair to him that he must live here, away from his own home. But it wasn't as if he had other family. He had not married, lest he conceive a girl child afflicted with the family curse. Better sterility and lonely death than to produce offspring like her.

Ann grimaced. There was no avoiding it, someday she would be alone, friendless.

She slipped off the dress she had made to tie in front. She had only four dresses old enough to be comfortable. It was too wearing to break in a new one, because the experience of the weaver who had made it and the shopgirl who had sold it would assault her until it was broken in and they faded. She unlaced the short corset she wore so she could extricate herself without the aid of a dresser. She took up an aged linen night shift and slid it over her head. Its soft folds enveloped her as she crawled under the counterpane quilt Malmsy had made for her. Tonight she would not think about the future.

She only hoped she didn't dream.

LONDON, MARCH 1822

Stephan Sincai sat alone in the coffee room of Claridge's
Hotel as the sun set, with half a dozen newspapers scattered
over the table in front of him. The other denizens of the
hotel were in the restaurant. He could hear the clatter of
dishes and the din of convivial conversation. In the restaurant
Stephan's dour visage cast a silent pall over the room. Or
perhaps it was the electric vibrations in the air that always
accompanied one of his kind. Humans always sensed the energy. The coffee room was deserted by night, a better situation for his purpose altogether. The windows at his elbow
had a view of the corner of Brook Street and Davies Street in
the daylight. Now the night glass only cast back his reflec-
tion. It had not changed in . . . in forever; black eyes, black
hair that curled to his shoulders, high cheekbones, and a full
mouth with a set that had created harsh framing lines.

It had been three days since the murder in Whitehall
Lane. The London papers were still full of it. The authorities
knew nothing of the perpetrator. "It was if he had disappeared into thin air," they said.

He had.

But the English authorities would never guess that. What
did they know of the powers conferred on him by the parasite in his blood, his Companion? He looked like any other
man. Just as the Chancellor of the Exchequer looked like
any other civil servant. They weren't. They were vampires.
Stephan was born to it, the Chancellor was made vampire by
that renegade Kilkenny. It was all Stephan's fault. He stared
at the face reflected in the dark mirror of the window. He had
murdered the Chancellor of the Exchequer because his mission was to make right what he had set loose upon the world,
and eradicate the cell of made vampires that was threatening
to take over the English government. He had twisted off the

creature's head and then called the power and disappeared into thin air as only his kind could.

No one would ever know what he had done. His Companion was beyond their comprehension. It was the true vampire. It required that his kind drink human blood, and when the hunger was on them, they could not refuse it. But in return it granted the power of translocation and incredible strength, heightened senses. He could compel a weaker mind, and the parasite that shared his blood repaired its host endlessly. He was immortal to all intents and purposes. That made him evil incarnate to humans. Was he? He could not answer that tonight.

He pressed down a memory of the horror he had committed. Killing was his task. He was the Harrier. He must complete the task in order to atone for his crimes against the Elders. And there would be more killing to come. He only hoped he was equal to it.

Stephan jerked back to the papers and scanned the small articles, the news from the provinces. No, in England they were called "counties" and they all ended in "shire" but no one ever pronounced all the syllables; a lazy country, really. He must have read a hundred papers in the last three days. The boots brought him armloads of them every night.

An itch ran up his veins. He would have to do something about that. It wouldn't do to let himself get too hungry. Just a sip. Enough to steady himself and not enough to hurt whoever became his donor. His control still wasn't perfect, and he needed to keep up his strength. He prayed his efforts would be enough. His sanity and the balance of the world depended on it.

Stephan snapped a page of the paper and folded it back. He couldn't even afford the fear that he might not succeed. He was allowed no emotion in his life now. He pushed his wine aside and spread out a regional news sheet from the

cathedral town of Wells just south of Bath. He started at the
back, scanning . . .

There! His eyes snapped back to the tiny article. An animal attack, it said. The body of the unfortunate Mr. Marbury
was drained of blood. He read it twice. Did they not talk of
wounds? There should be two puncture wounds. They did
not. Perhaps they didn't want to frighten the local populace.
The body had been found in Shepton Mallet to the west of
Wells. It was the second death in the area. They were searching the woods for wolves.

Now he read the rest of the paper carefully and found
what he was looking for. An outbreak of what the report
speculated was influenza was spreading in the area around
Cheddar Gorge. It brought about a strange lassitude and made
the sufferers unusually pale. The paper wondered if it was a
result of insect bites. There was a preponderance of insects
after flooding on the river Axe. The paper didn't say why the
authorities thought it was insect bites, but Stephan could
guess. He was sure the sufferers would exhibit two puncture
wounds.

Deaths? Epidemics? Lord, Kilkenny's creatures were not
even being circumspect!

Stephan snapped the paper shut and consulted a map he
had purchased in Jermyn Street. He picked out Bath, Wells,
Shepton Mallet, and Cheddar Gorge. Well enough. If they
had a shred of sense they would kill farther from home, but
they would be feeding closer to their nest. That meant Cheddar Gorge was his most likely target.

He folded the map and rose, leaving scattered papers and
the remnants of his meal. He must get word to Rubius. He'd
scribble a note and let the Eldest know that he had found a
nest of Kilkenny's vampire army. He would have the note
taken by courier with all possible speed to Horazu, where
the villagers at Tirgu Korva would deliver it to Mirso
Monastery. It would cost a fortune, but he did not care. He

always had plenty of money. He was getting closer to his goal, and that of Rubius.

First he would feed. Then he must get to a livery directly and see what could be had in the way of a horse. He was for Cheddar Gorge. With luck he would find Kilkenny there and at least a part of the army of vampires he was making. Kilkenny, the root of all evil. He dared not even indulge the hope that he could complete his task and return to Rubius and Mirso, for hope was an emotion, and he was not allowed those. Not anymore.

Two

Ann sat at one end of the long table in Maitlands's principal
dining room at her uncle's right hand and across from her
cousin. She had refused to entertain Van Helsing in the
intimate parlor where she and her uncle usually dined. She
didn't want him spoiling it. The servants spent the day cheerfully removing dust covers from Maitlands's grand dining
hall and polishing everything in sight. A huge fireplace roaring at each end heated the hall. The skeleton crew at Maitlands these days deplored the fact that so much of the house
was shut up. Well, the grand dining hall was being used tonight, though their three voices echoed and it took a hundred
candles to light it. Ann glanced up to the disdainful glare of
Brockweir ancestors hanging in their heavily wrought golden
frames. If one looked closely enough, the eyes of some of the
elegant women dressed in the style of bygone days glittered
madly in the light of the crystal chandeliers. The room was
all red walls and gleaming wood, silver service and sparkling
goblets. She had brought her own silver, of course, and her
own glass from the everyday dining parlor.

Ann was uncomfortable. The chair she was sitting in had not been used in a long time. Still she could feel the whispers of other nights around her. The room had hosted crowds. The tinkle of women's laughter and the boom of the gentlemen's guffaws played themselves out for her ears alone. A man who thought he was very important had sat in this chair last. It had creaked with his weight. But there were other, fainter echoes here, even back to . . . her mother. Her mother had once sat here.

Her attention was jerked to the present by the sound of Van Helsing's voice.

"What a fine example of Grinling Gibbons sterling," he exclaimed, gesturing to the massive epergne at the center of the table. His pale blue, bulging eyes were practically toting up the value. His blond hair would soon thin and his chin was decidedly weak, almost lost in his jowls. His lips were fleshy rather than full, the opposite of sensuous. In some ways they seemed . . . flaccid. She imagined that his kisses would be overly wet, and shuddered at the thought. His ridiculously padded coat covered a waistcoat that looked as though the buttons would pop at any moment. But truth be told, it was not the fact that he was overweight, or that his face reminded Ann of a fish, that made her cousin so distasteful. It was his expression. She couldn't quite put her finger on it, but there was something just not quite . . . right.

"The Ambassador of India gave that to Ann's father during the time he was secretary to Lord Woolsey," her uncle noted, as he slurped the lobster soup noisily. His color wasn't good tonight, but he was making a heroic effort to entertain their guest.

"A valuable heirloom, then." Van Helsing smiled. How could a smile look . . . greasy?

Ann pushed the whispers of the chair into the background. "I have been thinking of relegating it to the closet," she said with too much insouciance. "All those dreadful tigers pursuing the elephants . . . relatively bloodthirsty . . . and with the palms and monkeys and the flowers at the base it seems busy, altogether rather tasteless." Ann sipped her soup, then glanced up to see she had discomfited Van Helsing by questioning his taste. Inside he wasn't sure he belonged here. Good. He didn't. Let him realize it on his own.

Her glance stole to Polsham, standing ready to signal their lone remaining footman, Peters, and Mrs. Simpson, who had cooked the lovely dinner, and her helper, Alice, to bring the second remove. Polsham was suppressing a smile. He didn't like Van Helsing either. She raised her brows. His face shut down to impassivity. That brought a twitch to her own lips. Her cousin had not endeared himself to the servants with his overbearing, self-important nature.

"A shame, I'm sure," Van Helsing murmured. Then, recovering, "I did not see any finer example of exotic themes in my travels through the capitals of Europe. Have you been, Ann?"

A hit direct. He must know she couldn't travel.

"Ann has never been more than an afternoon's ride away from Maitlands, Mr. Van Helsing," her uncle said, motioning for Polsham.

"Ah, well, there is much to be said for the country, of course." He said it as though it were a lie, as indeed for him it was. Polsham, Peters, and Alice paraded through the door holding huge covered trays. Ann noticed Alice glancing fearfully at Van Helsing. Had she been crying? Van Helsing's voice droned on. "Still, Venice, Paris, Vienna, Madrid . . . now that Old Boney has been clapped up, the Continent is England's playground once again. You really should go, Miss Van Helsing."

"I have no desire to go traipsing around Europe," she said dampingly. True, given her current circumstances. "My books give me a window on the world." Polsham and Mrs. Simpson and Alice whipped the covers off the trays in unison, revealing pheasant, a butt of ham, and buttered crabs. *Dear me,* thought Ann, *Mrs. Simpson does want to impress the little prig.* Silence reigned as Mrs. Simpson retreated, only to reappear with a tray covered with various dishes of vegetables. She arrayed the dishes around Uncle Thaddeus, while Polsham poured claret for the men and ratafia for Ann. Alice had hurried away and had not reappeared.

"I think his lordship will be especially partial to the parsnips tonight and the creamed leeks," Mrs. Simpson murmured, before bowing herself out as Ann's uncle chuffed his thanks.

Ann resolved to seek out Alice and see just what had been happening. She suspected the worst, even though her cousin had only been in the house for an afternoon. The men dished themselves huge helpings of everything. Van Helsing looked up. "Miss Van Helsing, are you not partaking of this feast? Let me help you to some pheasant."

Ann bore his ministrations to her plate with as much civility as she could for her uncle's sake and wondered how she would stand the rest of the evening. At least the boor would probably lose himself in his food for the next half hour.

Even such a slender respite was not to be.

"Books . . ." he mused. "Hardly a substitute for reality. Still, many young ladies are fond of novels, and escape from reality is just the point of those sorts of books." He smiled in condescension. "I'm sure you read novels, Miss Van Helsing."

"I read everything," she said, stung. "Including novels."

"You mean everything fit for a young lady's mind, do you not? Surely your uncle guards you from anything which might offend your sensibilities."

Her uncle waved a fork. "Not necessary, my good fellow. Ann reads what she wants, newspapers, London and Paris magazines, political tracts, war journals, sermons, philosophers, poets . . . The lot of 'em. Always asking Polsham to bring her some book or other from the lending library in Wells or Meyler's in Bath. Writes letters even to the publishers in London. What I don't pay for the delivery of the post! The poor fellow can hardly carry the load of parcels up to the door."

"A bluestocking, Cousin?" The expression on Van Helsing's face could only be called a smirk. Ann so wanted to slap him.

"Bluestocking? A term made up by insecure men to denigrate an educated woman. Surely you are not insecure, Mr. Van Helsing." She made her voice deliberately sweet.

It didn't fool her uncle. "Now, Ann, don't badger your cousin. Van Helsing—"

"Excuse me for interrupting, but please call me Erich, both of you. I am family, after all." Erich turned that greasy smile on both of them.

Her uncle grinned back as though he didn't see how insincere and cloying that smile was. "Very well, Erich, tell me where you got that showy chestnut you've been riding."

Don't say anything more, Ann ordered herself, as the men talked horseflesh. *You've already been rude.* She even kept her opinion of Van Helsing's showy chestnut to herself. She'd just bet this little toad had been after Alice. Her uncle kept him mercifully engaged through the meal and invited him to retire to the library after supper for some of the fine local cheese with his port.

"Why don't you join us in half an hour, Ann, my love?" her uncle said as he heaved himself out of his chair. He wobbled a bit.

"Your cane, Uncle Thaddeus," she whispered, though she could not hand it to him or take his arm to steady him.

"Yes, yes, my dear. You worry too much." But he grabbed his cane.

Van Helsing took his arm in what he thought was an ingratiating way. He looked like a fat vulture. "Let me help you, sir."

They were gone. Ann sank back in her chair. She really must have a talk with her uncle. Family or not, "Erich" was insupportable. Would her uncle eject him once he had been invited? Unlikely. They were stuck with him. What if he *was* badgering Alice? Lord knew Alice was no better than she should be. Mrs. Simpson worried that she was cavorting with the boy who was the boots down at the Hammer and Anvil. But Ann didn't like the look she had cast at Van Helsing. She'd have to find a way to protect Alice from him at the very least.

Polsham brought her tea. She forced herself to calm and smoothed her dress over her lap. It was her best. Her uncle had insisted on it. In truth, she liked to dress up. She would have a hundred dresses, all the latest stare of fashion, if she could. This one had the big sleeves and slightly lowered waist in fashion a few years ago. It had been recut from a dress she had had since she was seventeen. Still, the silver toile brought out her eyes and set off her complexion. She wore it with the pearls her father had given her before his death nearly ten years ago.

She smiled secretly and touched the pearls. No one thought she had traveled. But she knew the shop in Amsterdam where the pearls had been strung and the aqua-blue waters where a brown, naked boy had first cradled them in his hands after an afternoon of diving.

She lifted herself out of her reverie as the long clock in the corner chimed the half hour. Time to face the lions in their den, or in this case, the library. Polsham and company began clearing the table even before the dining room door had closed behind her.

The door to the library was open. She paused as she heard Van Helsing's voice. Her uncle sat next to the fire, his back to the door. He was always cold these days. She couldn't see Van Helsing. "I'll make no bones about it, Erich, Ann's an odd duck, and you should know it."

"Young females are strange creatures in general, I find."

Oh, do you? thought Ann. She was about to enter and stop this ridiculous conversation, when a dreadful premonition dawned. She stopped dead. Was her uncle going to tell her cousin about her? It was none of his business. She stood in the shadow of the door, just out of sight.

"It's more than that, I fear . . ." Uncle Thaddeus cleared his throat, but could not go on.

"Don't worry, my lord," Van Helsing said. "I've heard what they say in the village."

"And what do they say?" Resignation laced her uncle's voice. Ann wasn't sure she could bear hearing what the villagers said about her.

"That she's a witch who knows what you're thinking," Van Helsing said calmly. "That she has a pact with the devil that allows her to see into a man's soul. Nonsense, of course."

Her uncle got up and paced the room. *Laugh*, Ann pleaded. *As though it were too outlandish to be true. That's what I would do.*

"I told you Ann is special, Erich."

No! Don't tell him!

"And now you'll say what the villagers think is true." Van Helsing chuckled. "Well, whatever you want to put about. I understand. Beautiful girl, rich into the bargain. Of course you want to discourage fortune hunters."

"Ann can't sustain the usual courting and the usual coarse relationship, Erich." Her uncle's voice was firm, commanding. "She . . . she doesn't like to be touched."

"What woman does?" Van Helsing chuckled. "Not the way we men want to touch them." There was something in his voice that was . . . threatening. "Men and women are cut from different cloth, Lord Brockweir."

"No, it's more than that. Since she turned fifteen . . . well, she can't abide touching."

There was a brief silence. Ann wished she could see Van

Helsing's face, then was glad she couldn't. "I want only your permission to worship your niece, Lord Brockweir." His voice dripped false sincerity. "From afar. She is an angel. Should I be fortunate enough to engage her affections, I would treat her like a delicate hothouse orchid, to be treasured and protected."

Don't believe him, Uncle! I don't even need to touch him to tell you everything about him is a lie. She saw her uncle raise his brandy glass in salute.

"Then may your suit prosper, young man. I shall do what I can to forward it."

Uncle! Betrayed! She turned and ran upstairs. She'd been betrayed.

Stephan rode through the night, south from Bath. Even though he was bundled to the eyes, the daylight had been difficult. But there was no time to be lost so he had ridden straight through. Now he was tiring in spite of his strength. His horse was fresh, though, having been changed out in Bath, and he cantered in long easy strides along the wide road under a moon playing hide-and-seek with the clouds of a coming storm. Stephan could smell rain.

His mind drifted. He had called Kilkenny the root of the evil he sought to rectify. But that wasn't true. Stephan himself was the evil, because Kilkenny was made by Asharti, and Stephan was responsible for Asharti and the crimes she had perpetrated upon the world.

It had started with Beatrix. He had found Beatrix, a beautiful natural-born vampire, haunting the streets of Amsterdam at seventeen, abandoned by her mother, with no knowledge of what she was or how to go on. She was ripping throats to get her blood. He had taken her in. What else could he do? A born vampire was rare and treasured. He made her his ward, tamed her, educated her, nurtured her.

Perhaps even then he loved her, feral kitten that she was.

And then he realized that with Beatrix he had a chance, perhaps his only chance, to do something about the injustice he believed was inherent in the Rules handed down by the Elders of his kind. The Rules said that vampires made by ingesting vampire blood must be killed. Rubius, the Eldest, said it was because the balance between vampire and human must be preserved. Of course, you couldn't go about the world making vampires. But if a vampire was made by accident one shouldn't let them die. That was murder in Stephan's eyes. Rubius said that made vampires went mad because they were not born to the burden of eternal life and physical and mental power, and the need to drink blood to sustain their Companion.

Stephan didn't believe it, naïve as he was then. What he did believe was that if he could find a made vampire about the same age as Beatrix, he could nurture them both, and love them both, and prove that made and born could be equally valuable members of their society. Then Rubius would change the Rules.

Fool! In so many ways.

He'd found the second half of his experiment when he had chased off after Robert Le Bois on the first Crusade, trying to overtake him before he sacked Jerusalem. He had wanted to stop the carnage. Le Bois liked carnage . . .

JERUSALEM, 1191

"Do you want her, Sincai?" Robert Le Bois had his beefy fist wrapped in the long dark hair of a young Arab woman. She was the most beautiful creature Stephan had ever seen, long straight nose, wide, full lips, and dark eyes lined with kohl. Her body was perfect, and imperfectly concealed in diaphanous scraps of cloth that fell from her shoulders and

were girdled at her hips with a beaded net. "I've tired of her, as have the men in my regiment."

"I hardly see how you've had time for carnal activity with all the killing you've been indulging in, Le Bois." Stephan examined the girl closely. She smelled of cinnamon and ambergris and he could feel the slow vibrations that surrounded her. She was a newly made vampire, and the right age too. He glanced to Le Bois. The brute had infected her with the Companion from his blood and then followed that up by forcing her to drink more vampire blood to get immunity. Otherwise the infection of the Companion would have killed her.

"These Jews and Infidels have no importance, Sincai. I rid Jerusalem of vermin, in the name of God." Le Bois laughed and downed a goblet of mead even as he wound his fist more tightly in the girl's hair.

"Why did you make her?" Stephan asked, his voice tight. "You know the Rules."

"They last longer that way." Le Bois tossed his metal cup across the room, where it careened across a game board, scattering dice and provoking a howl from the drunken players. "Don't be an old woman, Sincai. I know the Rules. I'll kill her when we finish with her."

"I don't think the intent of the Rules was that it was acceptable to make vampires if you killed them later, Le Bois." Stephan sipped warily from his own cup and glanced around the room. He had failed to overtake Le Bois. By the time he got to Jerusalem, it had fallen. He had found Le Bois and his inner command holed up in a mosque. The tiles of rich blue and green lining the walls were chipped where broadswords and pikes had been tossed carelessly aside. Any valuables had already been carried away. Outside, the streets were running with blood and echoing with the wails of the vanquished. He and his men were horrified. Twelve hundred Jews burned alive in a synagogue, men maimed, limbs severed, dying in their own blood. All in the name of Christ.

Still, Le Bois had achieved the goal they had all crossed two thousand miles and fought countless battles to accomplish. Why could he not like the man for it?

Le Bois narrowed his eyes. "Soft on made vampires, are you, Sincai? I heard that about you. You should be ashamed."

Stephan shrugged. "What do you care what I do with her?" The girl's eyes were not frightened, they were dazed. He wondered how long these beasts had had her.

Le Bois smirked and shoved the girl away. She fell on her knees at Stephan's feet. "All your talk of Rules, you'd better obey them. Rubius wouldn't like to find you'd let her live."

Stephan didn't look at the girl. "I don't need a nurse-maid, Le Bois." He leaned down, and without taking his eyes off Le Bois, he pulled the girl to her feet by her elbow, then he touched his temple with one finger in salute and turned his back on Le Bois's belly laugh.

That was how Asharti came into his life. God, what a simpleton he had been! He had thought Asharti was perfect for his experiment. Or his rebellion, as Rubius would have it.

And what had come of that rebellion? He had tried to nurture them equally as his wards. He had tried to show them both that they were valued. But he had failed. Failed because he fell in love with Beatrix, and that pushed Asharti over the edge into jealousy and excess. One could call it madness. Evil shot across the world propelled by Asharti's need for power until the universe had been nearly overset, all balance between human and vampire lost . . .

When had he known what she was becoming?

CASTLE SINCAI, TRANSYLVANIA, 1104

He pushed into the chamber he had left so recently, angry at Asharti before he even got there. The steward of the castle had reluctantly reported that the boy who chopped wood for the cook had to be turned off. He had fainted in Asharti's chamber, no doubt due to the wounds in his neck and the insides of his elbows, and had to be carried out.

Stephan knew at whose door he should lay that blame. He told the steward, Rezentrov, to find the boy and care for him. It was Stephan's job to confront Asharti. She had become increasingly wild and rebellious. She cared for none of the history of their kind he tried to teach her, and none of the Rules.

The door to Asharti's chamber burst open and banged against the wall.

Stephan had no idea what he had expected, but certainly not the scene that met his eyes. She had another strong young man in the bed he had so recently vacated. The naked boy lay on his back. Asharti straddled his loins, moving in rhythm to his thrusting even as she sucked at his neck. Her hair cascaded in a curtain over her face, her rich brocaded robe concealed her lush body. The boy moaned, somewhere between anguish and ecstasy, as Asharti began to grunt with her release.

"Asharti!" Stephan barked.

She did not look back at him. But she did withdraw her fangs and sit back as her own release made her shudder. She took in a long, slow breath.

"Stephan. How nice to see you twice in one night."

"Get off him."

She obliged, wrapping her dressing gown around herself and falling into the pillows on the great bed. The boy gasped for breath. There were ragged wounds at his groin. Stephan knew how they were made. Asharti was amusing herself by torturing this boy, just as she had amused herself with the cook's assistant. Stephan strode to the bed and felt the boy's throat for his pulse. It beat erratically.

He scooped the boy up in his arms. "Rezentrov!" he

called. The steward had been trailing him fearfully. Now he peered in through the doorway. "Take him down to the kitchen. Bind his wounds. Get him some wine and see if you can get him to eat something. I'll be down shortly." Rezentrov called for assistance. Stephan deposited the young man outside the door and closed it. He turned on Asharti.

She was watching him, a smile hovering about her mouth. She was curled like a cat in the bedclothes.

"What do you think you're doing?" he snapped.

"Amusing myself." There was not a shred of remorse, not even consciousness of her sin, in her manner or her voice.

Stephan clenched his fists. "You will not feed among the staff. I gave you specific orders. Do I not provide for you? I took you and Beatrix to feed only yesterday. And no one was hurt," he added pointedly.

"You provide as much as you can, Stephan." She looked up at him from under her lashes. "But some of us have larger appetites than others."

"You could have killed him, or the cook's boy."

"What is that to me?" She snuggled into the covers.

"The Rules say—"

"Outdated concepts for old men. Surely you aren't one of them?" Her manner was insolent under the feigned concern. "Why, I thought you wanted to disprove the Rules."

"Those that are misguided, yes. But you know as well as I do that only our discretion preserves our anonymity. That anonymity prevents war between human and vampire. It preserves the balance. I won't talk of morals since I'm sure that would not sway you. But toying with them is immoral."

"You are so timid, Stephan. They are nothing. We are powerful. We can take anything."

He took a breath. He had to believe she could be coaxed out of the . . . hardness that made her indifferent to suffering. "Taking is not the way to satisfaction, Asharti."

She narrowed her eyes. "Taking is the way of the world.

As I know, to my cost. No one will ever take from me again, Stephan. It is I who take now."

He did not deny her pain. Had she not suffered? But she must not turn that experience into a compulsion to give pain as it had been meted out to her. Could he stop the cycle?

"Just as you do," she added, her eyes narrowing in spite. "You take from me while you worship Beatrix. From her you want love. From me? Sex. But I'm used to having that taken from me, so that works out nicely, doesn't it?"

"No, Asharti. It isn't like that." But it was. He did love Beatrix. He might want to love Asharti, but how could he when he could see so clearly the growing blackness in her soul?

She laughed—that throaty, contralto laugh. "Lie to yourself, Stephan, but not to me."

Lying to himself was the one thing he could never do. His fault. His responsibility, that she had run amok, spreading evil and made vampires across the world in a vain quest for power so that no one could hurt her ever again. He had not killed her, even when he knew what she was. He had spared her twice, once in Transylvania, and once in a Paris cathedral. So he was doubly cursed with the blame for her sins. If he was lucky, he could atone and gain the peace of taking the Vow of abstinence at Mirso. If not, then this hell of guilt would go on forever.

Stephan turned his horse into the tavern yard of the village of Cheddar Gorge in the pouring rain. The creature's coat steamed in the night air. Both he and Stephan streamed water. Stephan dismounted and handed the reins to the lone ostler who darted out from the portico. Then he unstrapped his valise from the saddle and turned into the inn. He refused to be tired.

Conversation stopped as he stamped his feet and shook

his dripping locks in the doorway. He looked up and found the locals, men and women, staring at him. The tankards the serving girls carried dripped foam onto the scrubbed floorboards. He stared back and eyes around the room glanced away. The landlord cleared his throat and moved forward, rubbing his hands together nervously. Low conversation started again, though it had a self-conscious tone.

"Can I be of service, sir?" The man had gray, curling locks that hung about his ears.

"A room," Stephan muttered. "And some dinner."

"Yes, yes, of course. Molly, show the gentleman up to the room vacated by Mr. Van Helsing." He beckoned to a slatternly girl with a squint.

"No need. Just take up my bag." Stephan handed his valise to the boots and unfastened his cloak.

"And have you eaten?"

"I'll dine in that parlor." Stephan nodded toward a doorway as he shook out his cloak.

"Very good, sir." The landlord obviously recognized the quality of the cloak or the cut of the coat beneath it. Or maybe it was the gold signet ring. "I'll send Molly in to stir up the fire. Some hot ale for a cold night?"

"Brandy," Stephan said shortly, and strode through to the private parlor. He lounged in front of the fireplace as the girl poked up the logs. A boy of twelve or so brought in the brandy, bowing. The occupants of the coffee room made freer with their conversation with Stephan locked in the parlor. They couldn't know he still heard them so clearly.

He chose a venison steak and roasted potatoes from the bill of fare. The brandy warmed him, and he settled down to listen. He thought the town would be talking about the epidemic of "influenza," but that was not what was on their minds.

"So, young Van Helsing's makin' headway," a man's voice said, with a cackle.

"Moved in under the very roof," another agreed. "I calls that progress."

"'E's welcome to that one," a woman guffawed.

"Think 'e knows what she is?" the first voice queried.

"Think 'e cares? The money, woman, the money's the thing."

"I wouldn't be foolin' with no witch," the woman said.

"She ain't no witch. She's a loon, pure and simple. It's them eyes of hers and that white hair that makes you call her a witch. But that's just . . . sooperstitious, that's what."

"An' there's the little matter of knowin' things she cain't know," the woman returned. "That's witch, that is. I wouldn't have a wife like that."

"I would," the first voice chortled, "if she came with that kinda land and money. Husband would have it all. Once he's in, he just commits 'er."

"Shoulda been locked up a long time ago, I sez. We'd all be safer."

The landlord served Stephan's meal himself. The clatter of trays overwhelmed the conversation in the taproom. When the landlord bowed himself out, Stephan shut out the closer conversation and listened for others, fainter but still discernible. A discussion of cows. The curate at Winscombe was going to marry.

There . . . "My cousin's man, over to Shipham, come down with that influenza. Can't seem to get on his feet." This might bear fruit.

"Whiskey with lemon, I alays say."

"Now his sister's laid up. Nasty-looking bites, she has, in the neck, just here. Doctor says as how it's insects, but they look more like rat bites to me."

"I ain't heard of no influenza what starts with rat bites," someone warned.

There was a pause. "Could we be talkin', you know . . . plague?" the first whispered.

Stephan knew it wasn't influenza. It wasn't insects or rats. No. You might call it a plague, though. He was on the right trail. They were here somewhere. They would need a secluded place. With the number of afflicted victims, there was more than one. Three or four, perhaps. He ate his dinner mechanically. The joy of food was long gone, diminished by his awful purpose into merely the necessity of sustenance.

He might not be up to four. But if he tried to pick them off one by one, at the first death the others would scatter and he would lose his chance. He had no choice. He must find them together. But first he must find them.

Abandoned houses. Or . . . wasn't this area known for its caves? Uncomfortable, but who knew how uncouth these vampires were? Perhaps they liked caves. He pushed back his plate and rose. Tomorrow he would see an estate agent about abandoned houses in the area. He could comb the properties in the early evening and search the caves by himself in the wee hours.

There was still time tonight. The ostler would know about the local caves. And he would tell Stephan about them whether he wanted to or not, under compulsion. The vampires would be out hunting tonight, but he would know their lair if he found it. Perhaps it was best if he located it while they were away. Then, when they came back in daylight, he would be waiting for them . . .

Stephan pushed back the fatigue of a long ride. Time to begin the hunt, while he still had eight hours of darkness left to him.

Three

Ann paced her nursery, her heart thumping in her chest. She couldn't blame her uncle. He was trying to provide for her future, however misguided he was. But she could blame her cousin. Van Helsing could have no love for her. She had not seen him above half a dozen times. That meant he wanted what she had, not who she was. He'd have heard tales growing up of the money sunk in the Funds. Twelve thousand a year and no mortgages. The fact that she and her uncle lived so modestly only meant the land was in good repair, the latest improvements made to her tenants' houses, and most of the income ploughed back into the Funds. Oh, she might be called comely, if one could get beyond the look she had of not being quite connected to the world, and the eyes. But her appearance was simply more of what she had, not who she was. Actually, her eyes were the feature of her appearance most "who she was." That was probably why Van Helsing was uneasy meeting them.

It didn't matter. She could not marry. She could not even touch a man, let alone take a husband. Surely her uncle didn't believe Van Helsing would be content with a marriage without a conjugal relationship! She'd . . . she'd talk to her uncle tomorrow, have him send Van Helsing away whether it was good breeding or not to do so.

She caught her breath. She was actually panting. She felt out of control, as insane as people all thought her. There was only one remedy for that. She needed calm.

Ann grabbed a knitted shawl and a candle and turned to the ornate fireplace. She ran her hand over the intricate carving of the right panel. The panel clicked and opened silently onto darkness. Ann breathed. Here was the antidote to the dinner and Van Helsing's conversation with her uncle. She ducked into the dark passage she knew so well. Down through the walls of the house she tiptoed on the old stone stairs, careful not to touch the narrow walls of the passage or brush against the entrances to several other rooms at Maitlands as she passed. No one used this passage anymore. No one but her even knew of it. At last the floor leveled out. A stone arch with a jagged-toothed design in the Romanesque style signaled the end of the tunnel.

She stepped out into the immensity of the stone crypt that underlay the original abbey. The smell of old stone and damp earth and the dust of centuries enveloped her. The darkness was hardly dispelled by her tiny candle. The nearest round arches that held up the ceiling loomed above her. She had explored every corner of this hidden sanctuary when she was little. So she knew that if her light reached far enough, it would reveal the stone coffins, some with effigies carved in their lids, that lined the edges, and the side chapels where the walls had caved in and the earth fell into fans of wet loam. Several great fireplaces lined the walls. She had no idea whether they were there for heat, or whether they had once served some more sinister purpose. There were altars in the two small chapels that remained and carved fonts for anointing the dead. Nothing here held terror for her.

This was her secret place. Above her the ruined arches of the abbey when it had been taken by Henry VIII were Gothic because they were newer than this crypt. The standing walls aboveground were still attached to the part of Maitlands Abbey that was occupied, as if in silent reminder that all on this earth was transitory. The Brockweirs had no need to build a Gothic folly on the grounds to evoke tristesse and passing time. The building carried its own ruins. The intact portion had been transformed many times, its Gothic stone softened into comfort by succeeding generations who forgot about the crypts below the ruins. Ann only found them because of the secret passage.

Her footsteps echoed in the immensity as she crossed to the stairs that led to another narrow passage. Now she was creeping along under the knot garden, toward the wilder part of the estate. After what always seemed an eternity, she saw the stairs to the stone door in the monument that stood beyond the cultivated gardens of the estate, out past the meadow, next to the woods. She climbed and pushed against the door. On spring hinges it opened to her touch as though it were new and not hundreds of years old. She stepped into the night. The stars spread out in twinkling chaos after the rain as they wheeled above her, the constellations only an artificially imposed order. Behind the stars was the cloud of the Milky Way.

Calm. How could you not be calm in the face of such implacable immensity? She looked back at the impassive stone men in robes looming above her. Were they priests? Their inscription had been lost to time and weather. The door to the passage was in the base of their statue. They understood immensity. But she did not reach out to touch them. Their stone had been carved by human hands.

She turned to the woods marching up the slope to the Gorge. The Gorge was filled with trees and stones that had never been touched. Trees held only the passing of seasons, the occasional trauma of storm or fire, but no emotion; no betrayal or dismay or anger. There was a faint . . . satisfaction in trees, the almost imperceptible joy of growth. But up there, hidden in the sheer stone above the river, was her very favorite place. A place of stone. The stone of caves was even quieter than trees.

She started through the woods.

Stephan Sincai strode up through the forest behind the town toward the gorge that cut sheer sides through the Mendip Hills. They were more than hills really and the road that followed the gorge sloped up steeply. Best to keep off the road if possible. He struck out through the trees. The forest was mixed with deciduous trees and conifers, unlike his native lands in Transylvania. The night was nearly moonless and shadows of deep and deeper black were all that revealed the presence of the trees and boulders. But Stephen walked surely through the maze. The night was his time. The smell of rotted leaves and the green spice of needles filled the damp air.

The ostler said the hills were filled with caves, most without an entrance to the outside. Not promising. But there was one larger cave, discovered long ago, with many branches and side passages. Stephan would start there. He strode through the darkness, stiff with purpose. He would not think of the horrific job to come. It was the price. The price he longed to pay to expiate his crimes. Asharti was his fault, her evil laid at his door. He might have turned her toward goodness if it hadn't been for loving Beatrix.

Beatrix . . . for a while he thought she loved him in return. He began to see life as more than an endless series of jaded encounters with human cupidity and cruelty. He'd found that the world held possibility when he saw it through her young eyes. Then came the realization.

In the darkness of the barn, with the breathing of the animals all around, Stephan opened his eyes as Beatrix approached. The green smell of new-cut hay mingled with the aroma of horses. And beneath that, the musky scent of their lovemaking in the stall. As he sat, the blanket fell to his waist, exposing his bare chest and shoulders. When had she left him? He must have fallen into exhausted sleep. There was a hard core of despair in his belly. Beatrix thought he did not love her because he had tried to love Asharti. Asharti hated him because she knew in his heart he loved only Beatrix. Making love to Beatrix had not erased her hurt.

There was no happy exit from this tangled experiment he had made. Now Beatrix would leave him. Asharti, too. That did not matter. What he cared about was Beatrix. He looked at her dark, innocent eyes, now drenched in pain and decision.

And it came to him—an epiphany that wrote the story of a bleak future in his heart with acid ink. Beatrix was bound to go. She was an innocent, who loved him when her view of the world was narrow, and he could fill all her ideas of love. But first loves didn't last. She had outgrown him.

Beatrix stood in the doorway, mustering her courage to tell him. She did not yet know that she was bound to stop loving him, even though he would never stop loving her. "We're leaving, Stephan. Both of us. I just came to let you know."

He nodded. "I understand." He held himself tight against the pain. There was hope for peace in her heart, if not in his. He had to try to help her to that peace. "You will come to hate me before you forgive me. At least I hope you can forgive me. But first, be sure to forgive yourself."

"She has nothing to forgive herself." Asharti's sharp voice came from behind them. Beatrix turned abruptly. Asharti was dressed for traveling.

"You didn't trust me to say good-bye?" Beatrix asked.

"I didn't trust him, sister." She motioned to Stephan. "Let us go now."

"Be your own person, Beatrix," Stephan whispered. "If you need me, I'll come."

"Bea will not need you." Asharti sneered. "I'll teach her what she needs to know."

Beatrix stood, paralyzed, staring at him. Her eyes filled.

"Come, sister," Asharti barked. Beatrix turned. Time stopped. Stephan wanted to stop her, but what use? She didn't love him. He had no right to ask her to love him. He was old and soiled. She was fresh, with a thousand lifetimes ahead of her to experience the love she did not share with him.

Asharti stretched out her hand. Already her eyes were reddening. Beatrix walked to her. Asharti grasped her hand. Beatrix took a long breath. Stephan could see her call her Companion. Bile surged into his throat. He had no right to sully Beatrix with his love. She had outgrown him.

A whirling darkness enveloped the two young women. And then they were gone.

Stephan looked around him, not sure where he was or how he had gotten here. The town lights winked through the trees directly below him. Love was not for him. He had loved Beatrix for what? Seven hundred years? Give or take. Long after she had forgotten him. And eleven years ago he had pardoned Asharti for her crime of trying to take over the world through Napoleon when Beatrix asked it of him. But he had exiled Asharti inadvertently to the one place she could get the power she craved. That was his crime. During her exile, she had made an army of vampires and taken over North Africa. It was by luck alone that she was stopped before she could rule the world and turn humans into cattle, bred for their blood.

Now, perhaps, he could atone for his crimes. He had

trained to become Rubius's killer, And he would kill Asharti's leavings if he could. He might die. He did not care except that then his failure would leave the world infected with made vampires making other vampires, until there were no humans left to slake a vampire's thirst. But if he accomplished his task, then . . .

A woman's scream cut the night. It came from nearby. He knew what might provoke such a scream. Stephan slid quickly through the trees toward the sound.

It was still nearly a mile up to her cave. Ann moved quietly through the darkness. This part of the path wound up behind the village. The lights of the tavern were directly below her. She was never afraid, alone at night in the woods. Not anymore. The townspeople gave her a wide berth. There were no wolves this far south, and the scurry of small creatures did not frighten her. She had far more to be frightened of than a rabbit or a roebuck.

So she hardly noticed the stealthy rustle in the bushes beside the path until, coming round a corner, she was on them. She stopped stock-still. A figure in a rough peasant skirt and blouse lay sprawled on the wet leaf floor of the forest. It was a woman, her breast white and shuddering with hardly won breath. A figure crouched over her, his face nuzzled in her neck, a man by the bulk of him. For a split second Ann thought she was witnessing a lover's tryst, but something about the woman's staring eyes and the way her limbs were all askew told of something far less natural afoot.

The man lifted his head.

Ann gasped. The man's eyes glowed . . . red. It was not reflected light, for where was the source on such a dark night? He had *red* eyes and his canines were elongated. His mouth dripped with darkness. Ann recognized the smell of blood. She put her hand to her mouth.

The man lunged up, straight at her. Ann screamed. She couldn't let such a creature touch her! Fear washed over her. She turned and ran, feeling him reach out for her. She picked up her skirts and tore down the path, praying to God she would not fall. She could hear him behind her, feel his breath. It was as if he trembled in the air around her, vibrating in her chest along with her fear. She heard a growl and a heavy thud. A tree root grabbed her foot. She went down, turning in her fall to face the expected attacker.

There was no one there. But some way behind her, two men rose from the forest floor facing each other in a crouch, half attack, half defense. One was the man she had seen. His eyes were no longer red. No canines showed as he drew back his lips in a snarl. His skin was pale, his hair a light, straight brown. He was lean. The muscles on his forearms revealed by his rolled shirtsleeves were stringy. But he was still a monster. He hissed at his opponent.

Where had that one come from? He must have tackled the monster who pursued her. The man straightened and she saw that he was big, his shoulders broad, his hair a dark mass curling to his shoulders. Well dressed. His eyes looked black in the darkness. At least they were not red. Some part of her realized that he was handsome, perhaps classically so at first glance, but then one had to reevaluate. His cheekbones were high. His nose was a little prominent beneath a broad forehead, his lips . . . Ahhh, lips said so much about a man. These were full, but drawn down in a grim line. The commas etched around them made him look hard. Those deep lines kept his face from being the kind you would see upon a statue. All this was an impression in a single moment of fright and relief.

"What do you want?" her attacker hissed to the tall man.

"You know what." The voice of her savior was a deep rumble in his chest. He spoke with a faintly guttural accent, but it wasn't German. Could he be a match for the monster?

"You are the Harrier." The man hurled it as an accusation. What did he mean?

At that, the tall man stood straight. He did not confirm or deny the charge. "I am your destiny," he said. His voice was implacable, his demeanor sure.

Ann shuddered. Such words *should* be nothing more than melodramatic. But Ann could not imagine anything colder or more certain. If the monster could be dispatched, this man would do it. But then the big man's gaze strayed from his enemy to her, riveted itself upon her face in the shadows.

"Not tonight, you aren't," the monster crowed, even as a darkness whirled up from the forest floor and engulfed him. Her rescuer jerked his attention back to his enemy and lunged. But it was too late. The darkness dissipated and the creature was . . . gone. Nothing. No trace. She stood, paralyzed in shock, mouth half open and eyes wide.

The only man left on the path cursed. "Hell and damnation!" He turned on Ann. With an effort she managed to shift her gaze from the place that no longer held the monster to her rescuer's face. The guilt and old knowledge, the remorse she saw in his expression touched her. How could a man live with such emotions flickering inside him? What thoughts tormented him? She should thank him. Even as she hesitated, a mask descended over that rugged face. Emotion drained away. He seemed to collect himself and grow . . . distant. It was disconcerting.

A groan rose faintly from a spot down the path.

Dear God! The injured woman! She hurried past the man who saved her to crouch beside the figure on the ground. The young woman's breast was heaving, gasping for air. Her eyes stared up in terror; her hands twitched ineffectually at her side. What to do? Two puncture wounds on her neck trailed twin rivulets of blood. A rattle sounded in her throat. Ann wanted to take the girl's head between her hands, but she dared not.

"Breathe!" she shouted at her. "Breathe!"

Her command still hung in the air as the girl's last breath sighed away. The stare turned glassy. Ann let out a small sound of shock or despair. She recognized the girl. It was Molly who worked in the tavern. No better than she should be, Uncle Thaddeus had said, but no one deserved this. Ann felt the stranger's presence above her. Somewhere she heard shouts. She turned up toward him. "She's . . . dead."

He said nothing, but looked up, behind Ann.

Ann turned and saw a crowd of men carrying flaming torches, pistols or cudgels at the ready, coming up the path from the tavern below.

"You there!" Squire Fladgate, the doughy justice of the peace, called. "Stand where you are. Who screamed?"

"I did," Ann said, mustering what composure she could.

The crowd of men in work clothes clustered around Ann and the body of the girl, and the stranger. Their faces were demonic in the flickering torchlight as they stared at Molly. "The Van Helsing chit has done it now," a voice from the center of the pack called.

The squire eased his bulk onto his knees. "We thought it was Molly who screamed. She was working at the tap one minute, and the next minute . . ." He touched his fingers to the girl's throat, then shook his head. "She's dead."

"I alays know'd the Van Helsing girl was a killer, the mad ones alays are." This was Mrs. Bennigan. She had reason to hate Ann. In the disturbing onset of her powers Ann had blurted out the woman's infidelities when Mrs. Bennigan was shaking her for knocking over a tin of nails in the iron-monger's store.

"Mad? She's a witch pure and simple, and she killed Molly!" Ahhh. Mr. Warple. He had his reasons for hating Ann, too. By the time Mr. Warple brushed against her she no longer blurted things out. But he must have seen in her eyes that she knew he suffocated his sick wife with a pillow when he couldn't stand her moaning anymore. Ann didn't blame him. She knew he did it to spare his wife the pain, as much as to escape the yoke of her sickness. She knew too that he suffered every day for it. But that didn't make him love her for knowing it.

"Hanging's too good for her."

"Oughta be burned!"

The voices clamored around her. All of them wished her dead or gone. Ann shrank back. They mustn't touch her! She had to get out of here! "It wasn't me," she whispered. "I didn't kill her, I swear." But her voice was lost in the shouting. Angry faces closed in around her. She could hardly get her breath.

"You might hear her out." The commanding voice from behind her silenced them as if the man had waved a wand.

Eyes shifted from her to the stranger and back again. She looked up. A hard look had come over the stranger's face to replace the pain and remorse. That was even more frightening.

"Tell them," he ordered.

And somehow, she did. "There . . . there was a man leaning over Molly as I came up the path. I . . . I surprised him. He looked up." Would they believe what she had seen? "I think . . . I think he was biting her."

"Nonsense," Fladgate said. "I see no man." He heaved himself up awkwardly. "And these bites could not have caused her death. See? They bleed but a little."

"You'll find her drained of blood, I think, if you examine her," the stranger said.

Ann stared at the stranger. Drained of blood? She turned back to Molly. Yes! Dear Lord, her flesh had sunk as though the capillaries that supported it were . . . empty.

"It's her. The witch did that. Who else could?"

"She did it with her evil eye."

From the rear of the crowd came a commotion. Uncle

Thaddeus pushed his way to the front, gasping. "Uncle," she cried, and clasped her hands to her breast to keep from gathering him in her arms. "You shouldn't be here. You don't look well." His face was gray.

"I won't let you harass her, Fladgate," he gasped, his hand to his chest.

"We don't need your help, Brockweir."

"Then why did you come to Maitlands?"

"Because Molly was missing, man, and we thought your ward might know something about it. Your ward turned out to be missing, too. Quite a coincidence. Now we find it wasn't coincidence at all. Your niece committed a murder," the magistrate decreed.

The crowd yelled in agreement.

"No she didn't."

The cries were halted in mid-yell. The stranger's voice had that effect; oddly compelling. An uneasy silence fell over the men.

Fladgate cleared his throat. "And what have you to say to the matter?"

The man stepped up behind Ann, though he did not touch her. She could feel his body, threateningly close. "I witnessed the whole. She tells the truth."

"Where's this man, then?" one of the men in the front row of the mob challenged.

"He ran off that way." The stranger pointed down the path.

"Whyn't you stop him?" The man who challenged was the worse for drink.

"The girl was still alive. It seemed wrong to leave her." He was lying. He hadn't cared about Molly, but Ann certainly did not want to point that out.

"So you are saying that this killer just disappeared?"

"You have two eyewitnesses to corroborate that fact," the stranger said.

And Squire Fladgate accepted it. Ann couldn't believe it.
They had waited for years for an excuse to commit her or
worse, and here it was. Yet the squire backed down. He didn't
ask who the stranger was, none of them did. They didn't ask
how he came to be there. They knew she liked to walk in the
woods at night. The whole town talked about her idiosyn-
crasies. But shouldn't they be curious about a stranger?

Would they let it go? The squire shook himself and
peered at her. "She could have been in on it with him."

"Then why would she have screamed?" the stranger
pointed out.

"Coulda been Molly what screamed," someone in the
crowd shouted.

That clinched it for the squire. He whirled on her uncle.
"Bring her to the coffee room at the Hammer and Anvil tomorrow at four sharp for questioning. You'll be held responsible for any crimes she has committed, Brockweir," he warned.
Then he tapped his nose. "Or maybe I should take her into
custody while we investigate."

"Lock 'er up!" the crowd yelled. "She did it!" And, "No
one's safe if she's loose."

Ann looked wildly around. They could not lock her up,
could they?

Her uncle mustered his resources and drew himself up. "I
shall keep her in at night, Fladgate, if you men need to feel
safe from a slip of a girl that can't weigh seven stone."

"Locks?" Fladgate challenged, glaring at Ann.

"I'll lock her in the nursery on the fourth floor." Her uncle coughed and bent over. Ann stretched out a hand. Then
he straightened, cradling his left elbow. "Fair?" he gasped.

"Fair," said the stranger behind her, though it was certainly none of his business. And it was as if that was the last
word. The mob turned back, muttering. Fladgate ordered
two of them to carry Molly's body down the hill. Why

hadn't they suspected the stranger of making up the man who ran away with her? Why did they suspect him of the killing, too?

But she could not stop to speculate. Her uncle was looking paler and grayer by the moment. "Come, Uncle," Ann said. "You should get home to the fire."

She turned to throw a thank-you at the stranger, but he was nowhere to be seen. He seemed to have melted into the shadows. The unreality of the evening washed over her, taking her strength with it. Her knees half buckled. But she couldn't give in to weakness. Uncle Thaddeus had to make it down the hill. She looked around and picked up a branch of elm he could use as a staff. He couldn't lean on her.

"Here, Uncle," she whispered. "Let's go home." She held out the staff. "Can you make it?" He was gasping still, and his skin looked clammy.

He nodded, clutching his arm to his side. "I can make it back to the carriage. Jennings will drive us round to the house."

They made their tortuous way down the branch of the path that led to the tavern. Jennings was walking the horses up and down Cheddar's only street. From inside the tavern raucous voices relived the adventure, well lubricated with ale and brandy.

Jennings gathered Uncle Thaddeus into the carriage and then stood back as Ann climbed up. "Get us home and then go straight for Dr. Denton, Jennings," she whispered.

The blackness drained away, leaving Stephan farther up the Gorge. There was still time to search tonight. He watched the torches of the mob wind down toward the tavern.

Damn his weakness! He should have lunged for the vampire immediately. It was sheer softness on his part that he hadn't liked to kill the creature in front of that girl. The only way to kill a vampire was not pretty. He could have suggested her mind forget the memory afterward. Only it didn't work sometimes, if the mind was horrified enough. Sometimes the memories came seeping through, destroying sanity. How had he allowed her to influence him? Was it that she was so tiny and ethereal? Her great gray eyes and that halo of white-blonde hair made her look fragile, unable to sustain such a brutal shock.

He shook his head in disgust. What did he care for her sanity? His duty was to eradicate Callan Kilkenny and the vampires he was making. He had shirked his duty. True, he hadn't wanted to kill them one at a time, but better that than that the one tonight go back and tell his fellows the Harrier was hot on their trail. Would they remove from the area? Would he have to wait until more cases of "influenza" showed up in some other far location?

Still, they had been in this area for some time. Perhaps they were waiting for something, or there was something about this place important to them.

He drew himself up. He'd continue to look here until he was sure they had gone. And no more soft moments, no distractions. He forced himself to think about the struggle if there were many, the blood, his and theirs, the horror of decapitation, the danger to his life and his soul . . . That was his future. He was the Harrier. He belonged to Rubius. His only thought must be to complete his task and get back to Mirso Monastery.

Ann was shaking uncontrollably by the time they reached the wide gravel drive in front of the portico at Maitlands. Her mind reeled from red eyes to drained blood, from staring death to the compelling stranger who had saved her from the mob and disappeared into thin air. Her hand to her throat, she felt the hammering of her heart. Monsters, all the dangers of so many people who might touch her, the threat of incarceration, death.

It was only her uncle's unsteady breathing that kept her tethered to reality at all. He was not well. She wanted to touch him, to check his pulse or comfort him. But that wasn't possible.

The carriage crunched to a halt. Ann threw open the door. "Polsham!"

Polsham hovered on the portico, wringing his hands. "Miss, we were so worried . . ."

"Never mind that now. My uncle is unwell. Help him into the house." She motioned to Peters, just coming through the great door. "Jennings, away with you. Don't take no for an answer from Dr. Denton."

"Just so, miss." Jennings craned around to see his passenger alight heavily into Polsham's arms. He snapped the reins and clattered off as Polsham and Peters supported her uncle into the house and laid him on the chaise in the front drawing room.

"His cravat, Polsham, loosen his cravat," she worried, practically dancing on the pale Aubusson carpet in her anxiety. "It's his heart. I know it is."

Indeed, her uncle seemed hardly conscious. His eyelids fluttered and his breathing was ominously shallow. *Dear Lord, if you really do watch over us, please don't take Uncle Thaddeus.* "Get the smelling salts, Peters." The footman took off at a run.

A part of her whispered, *What will you do if he dies?* But she pressed that part down. Polsham chafed her uncle's wrists but it did not seem to be doing a bit of good. *God, how will I forgive myself if he dies?* Her uncle had come out tonight to face a mob on her account. It was her fault he had stressed his heart with anxiety and with climbing hills.

He wouldn't die. Of course he wouldn't die. Dr. Denton would save him.

It seemed hours before she heard the crunch of wheels on gravel and heard Jennings hail the house. She rose from kneeling by her uncle's side and hurried to the door.

"Dr. Denton," she greeted the spare, elderly man holding a leather valise. He had known her since she was a child and so knew to keep his distance. He was one of the few people in the area that would come to Maitlands. "In here." She gestured toward the front drawing room.

"Well, Brockweir, what have you been doing with yourself?" Dr. Denton greeted his patient in a jovial tone.

Uncle Thaddeus gave a weary smile. "Denton . . ." he murmured. "Come for last rites?"

"Nonsense, man. A little faintness. We'll have you right as a trivet in no time."

Ann watched the doctor listen to her uncle's heart, ask him to breathe, tap on his chest. There had better be some miracle in that bag of his. He spooned out some tonic. Her uncle made a face as he swallowed it. At last the doctor rose and motioned her into the hall.

"He is gravely ill, Miss Van Helsing. I shall not disguise the truth for you."

Ann tried to breathe. "Is there nothing we can do for him?"

"Rest, of course. Have your servants carry him up to his own bed. And give him one of these tablets twice a day." He handed her a paper of pills.

Ann stared at them. Her hand was shaking. The paper rattled. "What are they?"

"A crystallized tincture of foxglove."

"But that's poison," she protested.

"Only in large doses. It stimulates the heart, you see. Fatal for you or me, but just what your uncle needs. Scottish fellow discovered its properties from some gypsy woman."

Ann watched his wrinkled lips. She heard his words. But she could not quite comprehend. "Will it cure him?"

Dr. Denton smiled. It was a sad smile that, small as it was, refolded the creases in his face. "Nothing will cure him, my dear, except a new heart. It is only a matter of time."

Ann tried to swallow, but she couldn't. "How . . . how long does he have?"

"Tonight, a month from now, a year—who knows? The Lord above may, but I do not."

She gathered herself. "I shall do whatever you say, of course, Dr. Denton."

"I'll be back in the morning to check in." The doctor took his hat and cane from Peters.

"Jennings will take you home, Doctor. Thank you for coming."

He merely nodded as he shuffled out the door. His shoulders seemed more stooped than when he arrived. It occurred to Ann that he might see his own fate coming on the heels of his old friend's affliction. There had been much death and much mystery tonight. The world seemed a colder and much more frightening place than it had even this afternoon. And that took a lot, considering her usual relationship with it. She took a breath and turned back to the drawing room. "Polsham, Peters, let's get my uncle upstairs, and then you two can go to bed."

She saw him safely disposed in the great bedstead of his room, and sat beside him, determined to keep watch over him. Still, she must have dozed, for she had an impression of dark eyes and broad shoulders that made her gasp and jerk awake. She looked wildly about her, but she was alone except for the still form of her uncle.

Her mind returned as a compass does to true north to the stranger who had braved the townspeople for her tonight. He was compelling. He was a mystery. He was frightening. And she couldn't help but wonder if she would meet him again in the woods.

Four

Nothing. Stephan had checked the great main cave and several smaller branches but there had been no trace of the vibrations his kind gave off. The ones he sought were young, thus their vibrations would be slow and distinguishable even to humans. Of course, they could be out hunting. But there had been no smell of blood anywhere in the cave, and he could sense even the faintest trace of that. *The blood is the life,* he thought automatically, in the mantra of their kind. The ones he sought were infected with vampire blood by Kilkenny, who was infected by Asharti. They would pay for Asharti's crimes.

That gave him pause. Were they guilty of her crimes? He clenched his jaw. Of course they were. They were like her, greedy for power, self-involved, taking no responsibility for what they did. Their careless feeding proved as much.

He had to believe that. Because in some way it was his crime they paid for with their lives. He pulled the shutters closed on the windows of his room above the tavern and twitched the heavy draperies meant to keep out cold across them. The sun would rise soon. He could always feel the sunrise. A few hours' rest, and he would muffle up and brave the light to see an estate agent. He hoped the nest felt safe enough to stay in the area, or had a compelling reason to do so, even after the vampire who escaped tonight reported Stephan's presence.

He shed his coat and waistcoat and used a bootjack to remove his boots. He must feed lightly and regularly during the coming days to maintain his strength, and yet not take too much blood from anyone. He didn't want others to suffer for his needs. That was what he had tried to teach Beatrix and Asharti, as well. He'd been successful with Beatrix at least. One of the tavern girls, perhaps? He'd leave her with a sensuous memory rather than any recollection of her offering to him.

He lay upon the bed in breeches and shirt. His mind drifted to the girl who had lured him from his purpose tonight. Curious. She was so delicate. Yet she had pushed past him to tend to the dying girl. That showed a certain amount of courage. Judging from their accusations, she must be the one the villagers in the tavern had talked about. Were her looks the only reason they called her a witch? True, her eyes looked right through one. He felt she knew things about him that no one should know. Frightening, and yet . . . attractive. His was a life of secrets, burdens almost too horrible to bear. What would it be like to connect to someone again? A woman?

His body responded to that thought, as it did so easily these days. But he could never indulge that arousal. The loss of physical satisfaction was part of his atonement. And what was this girl to him, after all? She wasn't Beatrix. He had his purpose. That energy must be saved. Look what had happened the time he lost control! He wrenched himself onto his side, refusing to remember that time, and set his mind to contemplate the exercises he had learned at Mirso. But his mind was not obedient tonight . . .

MIRSO MONASTERY, DECEMBER 1819

The wind tore off the snowy peaks behind him as he guided his sturdy mountain horse up toward the luminescent towers growing out of the mountain. He felt the cold, but his soul welcomed it. Outside should reflect inside, should it not? Warmth was denied him. Love was denied. And rightly so. Had he not challenged the Rules laid down by his kind? And was not the fruit of his labor evil, an evil that those he had known forever had been forced to fight, down to the bloody last? Even now there was no guarantee that the balance between humankind and vampires was preserved. He had caused measureless suffering.

His soul was dead. He had no more will to go on living in the world, shouldering the burden of his crimes. Any life left to him was at the place where he began so many years ago.

Stephan raised his gaze again to his goal rising out of the mountain ahead and touched his horse with his heels. The moon came out from behind the clouds and lit the stone spires. They seemed to glow from within. The translucent onyx that formed the battlements and towers of the monastery was dotted with occasional squares of light. Mirso came alive at night. Others would call the sight otherworldly, evil, frightening. To Stephan it was home.

He had grown up at Mirso Monastery, abandoned by his mother, taken in by Rubius and the Elders as a treasure, since children even then were rare. He was not a treasure. A spectacular failure of judgment, unworthy of the love of the only one he had ever cared for . . . that was what he was.

Rubius should never have sent him out into the world. He

might never have caused all the suffering. The Eldest said he must experience the world before he could renounce it. The world was not for him. It never had been. He wanted to forget in ritual chanting and abstention what his mistakes had cost the world.

Would Rubius take him back after his transgression? Stephan felt a chill but not from the wind. Pray to whatever gods will have you that you're allowed to stay, *he thought. It was the only refuge left him.*

It was nearly an hour before he came to the great doors, heavy beams studded with iron straps in a defensive plaid. He dismounted as the snow swirled around him. The huge round iron ball held by iron strapping waited for him to knock. It would take more than human strength to lift it, but that was the point, was it not? Inside the gates the rasp of the huge bar he remembered sounded. The gates swung open. A monk stood there in black robe and rough rope belt, his hands tucked in the opposite wide sleeve, face hidden in the shadow of his cowl.

Stephan set his lips. "Stephan Sincai to see Rubius," he bit out in the old language. The words were taken by the wind.

"I know who you are," the figure said, then turned on his heel. Stephan followed. The monk seemed to float across the great empty courtyard, covered in several inches of snow. It was all as he had remembered it, the towering stone walls, the fountain burbling in the center, a mere pile of rocks in a simple stone circle. That fountain was the beginning of it all, though. Mirso had been built around it. The Old One had contaminated it with the parasite in his blood that his kind now called the Companion. The water in turn infected humans so many eons ago that only Rubius remembered it. Only a few lived through drinking that water, but when they did, their blood provided immunity to others who were infected. From that simple source, their race had been born.

Perhaps it was a curse. Sooner or later the weight of years or their own sins always got the better of them, and they needed refuge. They all ended at Mirso Monastery.

He followed the monk in through the doors at the far end of the courtyard, up the circular stone steps that wound around the inside of the main tower, and into the small receiving room, where the monk left him. The room held only a straight chair with a carved back. Suppliants for an audience with Rubius did not deserve comfort.

"Rubius will see you."

Stephan jerked his head up. He had not heard the monk enter. He was slipping. He rose and ducked through the low door at the far end of the bare room.

Rubius's quarters were a stark contrast to the Spartan feel of the rest of the monastery. Tapestries hung on the walls, Turkish carpets covered the stone floor. A fire snapped in the grate and joined candles set about the room in casting a warm glow over padded leather chairs, a sideboard laid with brandy and sweetmeats, and Rubius's collection of artwork. He glanced around to the familiar pieces: an Etruscan stone fertility goddess, Roman glass from the first century, Greek vases in black and red, a Chinese jade horse. His collection had grown in the centuries Stephan had been gone. He recognized a da Vinci, a fine Byzantine triptych, a Mayan calendar from the New World. That brought back painful memories. Stephan let his gaze wander over the room for a moment before it rested on the old man in the center.

"Hello, Rubius."

The old man nodded. He was an incongruous head of vampire society, a fact lost on Stephan in his youth. Overweight, white haired, with a full beard and a ruddy complexion, he looked more like a jolly Saint Nicholas than the chief representative of what humans thought was evil incarnate. Rubius was the last alive from those who first drank at the Source.

"Sincai." He motioned to the brandy and raised his brows.

Stephan nodded, his breathing uneven. Rubius poured out a glass and handed it to him. Stephan downed it, hoping it would steady him.

Rubius poured his own glass and motioned to a chair. "Why are you here, boy?"

"You know that," Stephan managed to croak. He did not sit.

"But I want to hear you say it," Rubius said softly, studying him.

Stephan took a breath. This was it. Push down pride. There was no pride to be had after what he had done. "I beg to be allowed to take the Vow."

"I find that most interesting," Rubius said, almost in a whisper. It was as if after all these years of only speaking to his own kind with their acute hearing, he had lost any desire to do more than murmur. He put down his glass and laid a finger aside his ruddy nose. "One who broke our Rules, nay, tried even to demonstrate that they were wrong, now wants to avail himself of our most precious Rule of all."

This was it. Rubius wouldn't let him in. The emptiness that sat in his belly threatened him with insanity. "I was wrong," he said. No pride. "Made and born vampires are not equal."

"Your little experiment with the Arab girl nearly destroyed our world, boy!" The whisper was outraged. "Wrong doesn't begin to cover the situation."

"No." Stephan's voice was bleak in his own ears. He acquiesced, knowing acquiescence would not be enough. Rubius was not going to let him in to Mirso.

"What were you going to do? Challenge the Elders for authority when you proved our Rules were wrong?"

"I . . . I don't know. I thought made vampires could be valuable citizens . . ."

Rubius waved that naïveté away with one hand. "Pride.

Rebellious pride. We raised you, boy, taught you, considered you precious. And you repay us with treachery." He had begun to pace, his bulk moving with surprising grace back and forth in front of the fire. *"And even when your experiment went wrong and the bitch tried to kill Beatrix, who was born, and rule the Continent through that human general, what was his name?"*

"Bonaparte, Eldest." He kept his voice flat. It wasn't hard.

"Even then, you let her go."

"I thought exile—"

"Don't excuse yourself!" Rubius rounded on him. He clasped his hands behind his back and paced. *"Look where it led. She found an Old One, took his blood. She was almost so strong none of us could stop her. Made vampires everywhere,"* he muttered. *"Khalenberg and Davinoff, Urbano and the others have had a time of it trying to find them all."*

"I volunteered—"

"How could we trust you to go?" Rubius almost spit the words across the carpet.

"You couldn't." That was the worst pain. He hadn't been allowed to make amends.

There was a long silence. Rubius rocked back and forward on his heels. *"Well. Now you want the refuge of the Vow."*

"You will find me a humble and eager Aspirant." Stephan kept his gaze riveted on the carpet at Rubius's feet.

"Will I?" Rubius mused.

"I swear it," Stephan said, unable to keep the emotion from the edge of his voice.

"There is a price," Rubius whispered. The look in his eyes was speculative, and . . . triumphant. That look frightened Stephan. What kind of price?

It didn't matter. *"How . . . how can I serve you, Eldest?"*

Abruptly Rubius turned away and eased himself into the

leather wing chair that sat beside the fire. He gestured to the chair's mate. Stephan sat stiffly. Rubius stared into the fire. The light flickered across his ruddy face. "I have a task for you, boy," he said at last.

"You have but to ask." Yes! He would prove himself. The old eyes bored into him.

"You will become an instrument of justice even as you have been a force for chaos. You will set right what has been loosed upon the world through your crimes. For that atonement, you will earn the right to work toward a quiet mind. You will be granted refuge at Mirso."

Stephan breathed. "Yes. Let me set it right."

"But to do that, you must be trained."

Stephan straightened in the chair, then went down on one knee before Rubius, head bowed. "I will be a willing student, Eldest."

Rubius put his hand on Stephan's bent head. "You make that promise lightly, but your way will not be easy. Still, the promise is made. I shall hold you to it."

Hope fluttered in Stephan's breast. "You shall not have to compel my obedience."

"Let me introduce you to your teachers, then." A door snicked open.

Stephan raised his head. Three beautiful women drifted through the door. One was dressed in red, one in black, one in shimmering white. They wore simple dresses in the style of Rome. But no matron of Rome would have dared wear them. Courtesans perhaps, in the privacy of a secluded villa meant for pleasure, but not matrons. Silk by the clinging look of it hung from their shoulders, leaving their arms bare, and plunged between their breasts to be clasped at their waists in gold filigree. Their hair was all long, black, and loose about their bodies, but the hair of the plumpest one curled softly rather than being straight like that of the other two. Their skin was the white of those who have never seen the sun.

Their eyes were dark pools . . . of what? Stephan saw desire, purpose . . . avarice?

"My daughters, Sincai." Rubius waved his hand.

Stephan could not help but register his surprise.

"You thought I was sterile? I am the father to many of you, somewhere back in time."

Stephan wanted to shudder. What did one become after so many years of life?

"What do you call yourselves these days, my dears?" Rubius asked the women. He turned confidentially to Stephan. "Women are always changing; names as well as dresses."

"Deirdre," one said. She was taller than the others, and her face was long, just as her body was lean. Her breasts were small and her arms showed the muscle in them.

"Freya," the second said, a petite and lithe version of the first.

"Estancia," the shorter, third one intoned. She was plump like luscious, ripe fruit. But her eyes were that of a bird's—inquisitive, callous.

"This is Stephan Sincai. He will be your next student." He turned to Stephan. "They can increase your power tenfold. It is the Hidden Way. Not even the monks here know it."

"What . . . what is this power, Eldest?"

Rubius frowned. "I will tell you. Then you will ask no more until they are finished with you."

Stephan held his breath.

Rubius fixed him with his ancient stare. There was something sly, calculating about him. Stephan quieted his heartbeat. All depended on his acceptance of this training. "The way to power is through suppression," Rubius said at last. "We all have the power in us. It must be drawn out. Then if you suppress that energy, it increases in strength. Think of a volcano like that one in Sumatra in 536. What was it called? Krakatoa. The magma is suppressed by the lava cap until it explodes. You will learn to control and direct that *power. You will become a powerful killing machine roaming the world, cleansing it of any who are made vampire."*

Rubius must have seen his horror. The old man's eyes narrowed. Behind him, his daughters exchanged sly looks. *"Did you not say you longed to be with those who eradicated Asharti's army?"*

"Yes, Eldest." Stephan's mind boiled. That was a specific task, horrible but limited. This seemed . . . like purgatory, indefinite, taking a continuous toll on his soul.

Rubius again placed his hand on Stephan's head. It was heavy. *"Do you agree?"*

Stephan took a breath. This was his only chance to atone. If his penance seemed more onerous than he expected, that was only right. Had he secretly wanted to escape the full consequence of his failures? *"I embrace it."*

"Go then. Your training begins tonight."

Stephan rose. Two of the daughters drifted forward and each took one arm. Deirdre cocked her head and looked at him quizzically. Her eyes were flat and hard. She was the oldest. He could tell by her vibrations. They were pure and high, almost beyond feeling. That meant she was far more powerful than he was. *"Your training will be rigorous,"* she said. And she smiled. A ripple of fear trembled through him. But it did not matter. His was the crime. His soul was already tattered with it. He deserved whatever lay ahead. At this point he had one hope of salvation, and it lay beyond whatever these women had planned for him.

They escorted him through the door. He did not look back. It shut behind him.

Stephan pressed his temples with his thumbs. No good to think about it, unless to invoke his lessons. He knew his way. If that way was sometimes hard, it was no more than he

deserved. He felt the sun beating on the shutters. Sleep. He
needed sleep before he rose and went in search of an estate
agent. That did not mean that sleep would be soon in coming.

Ann turned over in her bed, gasping. The dream still felt so
real! She was drenched in it. Images, feelings, still trembled
in the air around her. Her night shift clung to her damply.

She had been in a dark place. She could only dimly make
out the face above her. It was the face of her nameless rescuer, the pain in his expression now replaced by heat. That
was the only thing she could name it. She was almost burned
by it. And she *wanted* to be burned. She could feel his breath
on her face. The air was close in the room. He reached out to
touch her. And she didn't warn him away. She didn't shrink
from his touch. She put her own hand up to cup his cheek,
knowing what would happen.

Nothing happened. No drenching roar of experience. His
skin was smooth, hot to the touch. She had never felt another's
flesh like that, slowly, calmly. He pushed her gown from
her shoulders. Heat pooled between her legs at his touch. She
was burning inside. And then somehow, as it is in dreams, she
was naked and he was naked and she was feeling his body all
over, touching skin and the curling hair on his chest, and soft
nipples that roused themselves under her fingertips. And he
leaned down and lifted her head. His lips brushed hers . . .

God! What was she thinking? She opened her eyes,
blinking.

Light leaked into the room from the outside. Her narrow
nursery bed was disheveled, quilts tossed about, a pillow on
the floor. The room looked small and ordinary. She stilled
her breathing. She had had these kinds of dreams before. It
was no doubt a result of the solitary life she led. Or an example of her sinful nature. They could be banished with a

force of will. She steadied her breathing. But had they ever been this intense, this real?

She got up deliberately and threw back the curtains from the small windows to let light bathe her in reality. She could hardly credit the things she had seen in the forest last night now. What was real was Uncle Thaddeus being carried up to his bedroom, the doctor's grim pronouncement, her sitting with him through most of the night. The stress had caused her to have disturbing dreams. Hardly unusual.

Looking out the window, she couldn't see the sun, but she realized it must be noon at least from the shadows in the garden far below. She pulled on her dressing gown and hurried out into the hall. She must see how her uncle did. She came flying down the stairs and almost bumped smack into Van Helsing. She lurched back before she could touch him.

"Oh, ho! Cousin, how do you do this morning?"

"Uh, well . . . well. Thank you, sir," she said, gasping. She'd almost forgotten him.

"Erich, please," he chided her. "Do you breakfast? We could go down together."

At close range she saw that he did not clean his teeth properly and hadn't for a long time. His teeth were stained, his gums lined with soft whitish grit. It made his breath smell. She took a step backward. "No. That is, I must check on my uncle."

Van Helsing raised his brows. "I daresay he's out hunting or some such. He seems to be an early riser."

"My uncle has had a heart attack . . . Erich," she said coldly. "He is not out hunting."

"Oh. Well, I don't suppose he'll be joining us, then." Van Helsing saw her shock. Immediately he pulled an expression of utmost sadness across his face like a curtain. "Do you need anything, Cousin? Can I go for a doctor? You can count on me in your hour of need."

"No, nothing," she said tightly. Then her temper got the

best of her. "But you can stay away from the servants, if that wouldn't be too much to ask."

"What?" His look of surprise turned ugly. The fish eyes narrowed and gleamed with malice. It was as though he had removed a mask. Ann took a step back involuntarily.

She swallowed. She had to follow through for Alice's sake. "I think you've been importuning Alice, and I . . . I won't have her persecuted."

"That slut?" He sneered. "She quite threw herself at me. She started the game."

He didn't even pretend to deny it! "It is a woman's prerogative to call halt."

"She said she liked it rough and then didn't have the courage to follow through." Here he leered at her. "When a man is roused, it ain't so easy to call halt. You might remember that."

Ann sucked in a breath to steady her voice. "You will leave this house, sir."

He laid his finger aside his nose and cocked his head. "Brockweir invited me. And he's in no condition, apparently, to tell me to go. So I'll be staying. And I wouldn't worry about the kitchen slut. Unless you want to take her place?"

Ann was so deeply shocked she could hardly think what to say. "I'll . . . I'll have the servants—"

"And I'll have them clapped up in gaol for assault." He took a step forward, looming over her. His breath made the room seem stifling. "And don't think about the magistrate. Who would believe a word you say? You're a loon. Everybody says so."

All at once the mask slipped back in place. He blinked, smiled. His shoulders relaxed. "So, I'll be off. Back in time for dinner." He turned and skipped down the stairs.

Ann stood, shaking. It was worse, far worse than she had even imagined. And the most horrible part was that he was right. She'd have to send Alice away from here. She glanced down the hall toward her uncle's room. Her only option was to convince her uncle to throw him out. She strode toward the door. When she opened it and saw him lying there, her resolve faltered. His countenance looked remarkably gray. Only his eyes showed signs of life.

She steadied herself and smiled at him. "You gave us quite a fright."

He smiled tenuously. "I'll be up and about in no time." Ann doubted that. His voice was a throaty shadow of itself. His face looked sunken, somehow, among the folds of flesh.

"Whatever possessed you to come out after me last night?" she asked tenderly.

"They came looking for you here when Molly was missing."

They would of course. The villagers blamed her for every calamity, from failed crops to stillborn calves.

"You were not in your rooms. I was afraid . . ." He drew his brows together. Even that seemed an effort. "I know you like to roam about at night, but you must stay inside. You saw how dangerous it is."

He didn't know how dangerous the house had become. "Of course," she soothed.

"I'll have Jennings lock you in the nursery. Best for everyone." He raised his hand off the counterpane an inch or two to stop her protest. "Now, that's not too much to ask."

It was, but she couldn't argue with him or worry him in his current state. She couldn't tell him about Erich. She was alone in this.

"They'll all feel better about you . . . leave you alone," he murmured. He began to drift. She could see it in his eyes. "Let Erich take care of you, since I can't."

"Yes, Uncle."

"Nice boy . . ." And he drifted off to sleep.

◆ ◆ ◆

Ann took on Alice's aunt, Mrs. Creevy, to watch Uncle Thaddeus when she couldn't be there. The woman needed the money, so she accepted the position, though she made signs against the evil eye when she took her first payment, in advance.

Then Ann went down to the kitchen to see Alice. She couldn't let a dependent of hers be abused in her own house. She engaged the help of Mrs. Simpson and they caught Alice as she came in with a basket full of fresh-laid eggs.

"Miss Van Helsing wants to talk to you, Alice," Mrs. Simpson ventured.

"Wot? I ain't done nothin', I swears." The girl's swollen eyes widened.

Ann smiled. "Of course you haven't done anything wrong, Alice. I'm afraid some wrong has been done you."

Her eyes went frightened for a single moment before she looked at the ground and shook her head. "No. Nothin', nothin' ain't been done to me."

"Won't you tell me about it?" Ann cajoled. "I can help, you know."

At the expression of sympathy, the girl's eyes filled. "I can't, miss. He'll . . ."

Ann took two steps toward her, before she met the invisible barrier she always placed between herself and others. She softened her voice again. "My cousin can't do anything to you while you are under my protection. I'll send you away . . ."

"No, don't do that, miss. I swears, I aren't that kind. I never woulda . . .'cept . . ."

Ann held out a hand and made soft, shushing sounds. "You mistake, Alice. I meant that I'll find you a safe place, and I'll pay you full wages, and as soon as he's gone you can come right back to your job here." She should just leave it at that. But she wanted to know. What had Erich done? Raped the girl? She doubted he'd have had to rape Alice.

"I"—Alice sniffed—"I thought he just wanted . . . well, you know. I likes a bit of that meself. But then . . ." Here she started to cry in earnest.

"It's all right, Alice." Ann wished she could put her arm around the girl's shoulders.

Mrs. Simpson guided Alice to a chair. She sat with difficulty and let out a little moan.

Ann's brows drew together. "What did he do to you, Alice?" She had to know.

The girl's coarse features were lost behind the handkerchief she held to her mouth. "Oh, I couldn't never tell you that, miss."

Ann made her voice as soothing as she could. "Yes you could, Alice. You can tell me anything. Mrs. Simpson will help you pack. And Jennings can take you . . ." Where? "Don't you have family here about?"

"You been awful kind to me, miss . . ." Alice peered from behind the hanky.

Ann smiled. "And whatever you tell me won't make a particle of difference in how much I like you, Alice, and how much I value your service. I'm responsible for this household now. It is my job to know."

Alice hiccupped wetly, her red face contrasting in an unfortunate manner with her brassy blonde hair. "Well, he said he liked it from the back," she began tentatively. "And I didn't think nothin' of it, 'cause sometimes they do, and then he didn't want my quim at all but the other place." The words wouldn't stop now, and neither would the tears. "And I told him as how I couldn't take him without oil or summat to ease his way, tryin' to be accommodatin' like, and all, and he says he'll get juice another way, and he jes slams into me, and me cryin' and beggin' him to stop. And all the time he's

tellin' me he's gonna make me bleed . . ." Her voice trailed
away into a kind of keening.

"Beast!" Mrs. Simpson muttered and knelt beside Alice.

Ann straightened, and bit her lip, as if that would control
the anger in her breast. In some ways she was surprised that
someone like Erich was more than just talk. But apparently
his depravity knew no bounds. "Mrs. Simpson, does she
have a place to go?"

"A cousin over to Wedmore."

"Help her pack. I'll send Dr. Denton to attend her before
she goes." This was the man her uncle wanted her to take as
husband? Her stomach churned. At least her odious cousin
would not be able to persecute Alice any more.

Ann stomped through the house, unable to still her emotions as she stocked Uncle Thaddeus's room with lavender
water and smelling salts and several changes of clean linen.
The doctor came and pronounced her uncle improved. Ann
sent Dr. Denton to the servants' quarters for Alice, who was
bundled off with Jennings shortly thereafter.

By mid-afternoon her uncle's color looked a little better.
He told her that he'd let Erich have use of the Maitlands
hunting lodge, down near Winscombe. Ann hoped Erich
would spend lots of time there. She dared not disturb her uncle with telling tales on Erich at the moment. She'd have to
keep the wretch at arm's length until her uncle could become a support to her.

In late afternoon, Ann sat beside her uncle in his own favorite chair as he slept, mending one of his nightshirts with
tiny stitches. The chair whispered of him, and she realized
his health had been failing for some time but he had been
loath to tell her of it. The thread she used murmured about
the many lives behind the hands that made it, some who suffered, some who loved. The shadows lengthened. The fire
crackled with oak logs that had cured all winter. Ann tried to

put down the anxiety that seemed to suck at her. Her uncle would get better. He must! Dr. Denton was wrong. Everything would go back to the way it was before last night.

The long case clock in the hall downstairs began its sonorous striking. Ann jerked her head up and pricked her finger. Her uncle was supposed to present her to the town hall and Squire Fladgate for questioning at four! Surely she could plead her uncle's illness as an excuse. But sure as she failed to appear, there would be a mob of them pounding on the door and upsetting her uncle. His heart might not take another shock. There was only one way to prevent that. She had to go herself.

She took a huge breath. The last time she had faced a crowd was at Malmsy's funeral, eleven years ago. The outside, daylight world was filled with people who could shower her with their sorrows or secret guilts just by brushing up against her. Her mind wasn't strong enough for that. She put her hand to her forehead. But she had to go. Although at Malmsy's funeral she had had her uncle and Dr. Denton with her, to protect her. Could she face the squire alone?

She rose and rang for Polsham. Jennings would be back from Wedmore by now. While he ordered the carriage, she went upstairs to the nursery and put on her pelisse. God give her strength. She was going to do it.

Stephan was just preparing to go out when he heard raucous voices outside in the yard. The Hammer and Anvil seemed to be the noisy heart of the village. It was hardly the ideal place to get any sleep in the daytime. He finished tying his cravat in a simple style and twitched the ends in place. Then he thought he heard the word "witch" uttered in the shouting. He ducked over to the window and cracked open the shutters. Squinting against the fading sunlight, he saw the ethereal girl from last night alight from a carriage and gaze around her with frightened eyes.

"Touch 'er, Jemmy, dare you," a heavy lout urged a weasel-faced lad.

"Touch 'er yerself, ye coward," Jemmy returned.

"She knows yer secrets if ye touch 'er," a wizened old man cackled.

"Bet you a bumper 'o ale ye won't do it," the lout declared.

Jemmy got a calculating look in his eyes. "Make it two." They had crowded round the girl, who crouched back against the carriage. The throng of men was growing.

"Done!"

Jemmy lunged for the girl, who shrieked as he clamped a hand on her arm. They both stood there, a frozen tableau, as the men around them gasped and stepped back. The girl's eyes were round as saucers and they weren't seeing anything, at least anything of this world. She began to tremble. Jemmy trembled, too.

The driver leapt down from the box, cutting about himself with the handle of his driving whip. "Back, there," he shouted. He was a formidable bruiser. He cut his way through toward the girl. The crowd melted back, as much from fear of what was happening before their eyes as from fear of the whip. He grabbed the frozen Jemmy by the shoulder and pulled him away. The girl collapsed in a heap. Jemmy staggered, barely able to keep his feet.

"Miss Van Helsing, are you all right?" the driver asked. His voice was gentle, but he did not reach to pick her up.

Damn it! Would no one help her? Stephan swung the shutters out. There, the landlord of the establishment came out from the taproom. Shielding his eyes, he yelled, "You there, disperse that crowd and assist that woman!"

Five

Ann looked up at the shouting and saw him leaning out, squinting as though at the midday sun. His hair hung about his shoulders, making him look like some kind of a foreign prince, exotic. He seemed very angry. What had he shouted? She could hardly think. She was still suffused with Jemmy. She tried to breathe. Images and feelings doused her. All Jemmy's short life echoed in her mind, the abuse, the fear, the sly, defensive hatred of the world. His assault on the first girl he coveted, his love of cats, the petty thievery, the dull resentment. The complexity of him made her reel. What did you think about people when you knew everything about them? And everything they knew about everyone else . . . Her gaze stole to the heavy lout. His name was Harris. He supported Jemmy under one arm. Jemmy looked as dazed as she did. His eyes sparked fear, and hatred.

The landlord hurried forward. Ann held up a hand in defense. "No," she murmured. "I'm fine." The portly man reached out to help her up, but Jennings held him back.

"Don't be touchin' her, Mr. Watkins. You know better than that."

Ann smiled up at her groom. Jemmy's life and experience retreated just enough for her to steady herself. She pushed herself up on the steps of the carriage and stood there swaying. Her eyes rose to the window above the doorway, but the stranger was gone.

Squire Fladgate stumped out into the yard. "Well, girl, what's all this, then? You're late. Inside, inside." He motioned to her impatiently. She walked carefully toward the door. The men in her path fell away. No one wanted to touch her now. Squire Fladgate peered at Jemmy. "What ails you, man? Are you drunk?"

"'E touched 'er," Harris growled. "She put some kinda spell on 'im."

"Nonsense," the squire sputtered. But he looked uneasy and moved out of Ann's way.

She straightened. She must answer their questions, else they would persecute her, and through her, her uncle.

Squire Fladgate settled himself in the taproom behind a long trestle table. It had a low ceiling, and a huge rock fireplace. A fire crackled cheerfully there. The settles and chairs were a bit scarred from years of use, but the room was a comfortable one. "Well, sit down, girl."

Ann eyed the furniture and thought about how many people had sat there. "I . . . I think I'll stand, sir," she whispered, "with your permission." The other men sat down or stood near the fire. The crowd continued to grow.

"Hummmph. Well. As you wish." The squire spread his hands and touched his fingertips together. His voice was stentorian when he cleared his throat and began. "We are here to look into the matter of Molly Flanagan and her death"—here he raised his brows and stared at Ann—"which was most strange."

A murmur went around the room, a sort of delicious fear.

"It has been established by Dr. Denton that Miss Flanagan died, uh, exsanguinated."

"Whot's that, Squire?" This from Harris.

"Drained of blood."

A sound of dismay seemed to rise from no one and everyone. A girl with very red eyes serving tankards of ale let out a wail and ran from the room. No doubt a friend of Molly's.

Ann tried to focus on what the squire was saying. She had to shut Jemmy out if she was to prevent herself being clapped up in gaol. "And you think I did this?" She pressed her hand to her forehead, trying to think. She'd been planning in the carriage what to say but it had all been whirled away by the maelstrom of Jemmy's touch. Just as she felt she might fade to nothing or get herself mixed up with Jemmy and never be able to distinguish herself from him again. *Please, God, don't let me look insane.* What defense had she?

"You were found at the scene. You are known to be of strange habits."

"Molly outweighed me by two or three stone, and she was six inches taller." That was what she planned to say. She remembered now. "How could I subdue her?"

"Bewitched her," Harris said. "Put her under your power like you done Jemmy here."

Actually, there wasn't much to say to that. Jemmy was sitting on a bench, holding a tankard of ale with both hands and gulping as though he was dying of thirst. Everyone in the room could see he was dazed.

"I did not bewitch her." She forced her voice out to make herself sound surer than she was. "I saw a man bending over her." She couldn't tell them about the red eyes and the wolf teeth or they would think her mad for certain. "He was sucking at her neck."

"We only have your word for that." The squire waved her testimony away.

"And mine." The deep voice behind her made the whole room turn.

"And who *are* you? I did not get your name last night," the squire said pointedly.

"Stephan Sincai," the stranger said. He was standing in the doorway, leaning on the frame. He looked utterly relaxed, yet filled to overflowing with latent power, like the fastest horse in the county when he was trotting lazily. The very air was energized with his presence.

"And where would you be from?" No one in the room liked foreigners, least of all the squire, especially when they challenged him. He was used to being in charge.

"Does it matter?" Sincai didn't seem the type who felt obligated to answer questions.

The squire puffed himself up. "As justice of the peace, I have a right to know who I am speaking to." He suddenly reminded Ann of a bulldog, all jowls and outraged dignity.

"I come from just east of the Danube River."

"Danube! What country is that?"

"It has been many countries. Dacia, Wallachia, Hungary, Romany."

"Well, what is it now?" The squire was growing angry.

"Let us call it Transylvania."

"Damned gypsy is what he is," Harris muttered. "Can't trust 'em. They steal you blind."

Ann turned on him. "And you would know about that, would you not, Mr. Harris?" She felt as though she was on trial here for being strange and they would end up not believing this Mr. Sincai by making him out to be fearful and strange, as well. "You are such a fine justice of the peace," she spat at the squire. "What have you done about the robberies in Winscombe? Have you found who knocked that young man on the

head and took his seal ring and . . . and a fine silver watch? Or
that old woman's pearls? Ask Mr. Harris here. He bullied
Jemmy into accompanying him on the expeditions. Or better
yet, you'll find the watch under Mr. Harris's mattress, because
it's engraved, and no one will pay him for it."

Harris had gone dead white. He rounded on Jemmy.
"You're the only one who knows!"

"Not anymore," Ann said calmly.

Squire Fladgate looked as though he might burst a vein.
He knocked over his chair as he got up. "Watkins, Stanhope,
take those men. We'll see about this." The landlord and two
others seized hold of Harris and Jemmy Minks.

"Jemmy was led astray," Ann said directly to the squire.
She didn't want Jemmy clapped up. She understood the deep
doubt and shame about himself and his bastard lineage that
made him so susceptible to Harris's bullying. "He's had a
hard life. Without Harris, who frightens him, I doubt he'd be
in trouble." The squire licked his lips at this fresh evidence
of Ann's strange powers. "He deserves a second chance,"
she said.

Jemmy didn't know whether to protest or thank her. Instead he glanced fearfully at Harris. Ann could have kissed
him for that look, for it confirmed all she had said.

"We'll see," the squire harrumphed. "Whether it's true
or not, this doesn't absolve you, young woman, from the
murders."

In fact, she had just given them even more reason to
fear her.

"There have been several other murders like this one," the
dark stranger named Stephan Sincai drawled behind her.
"Winscombe, Shepton Mallet. Rather large men killed some
distance from your fine village. Miss Van Helsing is an unlikely candidate for such crimes. Perhaps you could check with
the authorities in those towns before sending her to gaol?"

One can't be grateful for murders, she thought.

"How do you know about these murders?" The squire was suspicious of the man.

Ann turned to see what he would say. His eyes flicked over her in dark disregard. Why did he defend her if he looked at her like that?

"Taverns all around here are full of talk about them." Sincai flicked at a speck of lint upon the dark perfection of his coat.

"Seems strange that you'd just happen—"

"Do not even think about accusing him," Ann warned. "He was the one who rescued me from the one you're really looking for. So just you look into those other murders, Squire, and in the meantime, I am going home." She turned to the door. "Jennings?"

Stephan Sincai blocked her path. She looked up at the dark, brooding face as she waited for him to move. She felt herself flushing. He stepped aside, bowing slightly.

"Thank you." But her voice did not hold all the thanks she owed. There was no time for that at this point. She must leave immediately, before the momentum of the situation changed again. She strode out to the carriage, Jennings trailing in her wake. The last of the gloaming had deepened into night. Jennings took the reins from the ostler. Ann climbed into the carriage and shut the door. Slapping reins gave the horses the office to start. The carriage rolled forward.

It was over. Tears welled up from somewhere and overwhelmed Ann. She didn't look back. She didn't care whether they arrested Harris. She didn't even care if they arrested Stephan Sincai. She was going back to Maitlands Abbey and its sheltering hills and never leaving them until they carried her out in a coffin.

The room erupted in startled speculation as the Van Helsing girl left. Harris was dragged from the room. The squire called for order. Stephan Sincai melted from the doorway. What had come over him that he had felt compelled to get involved? The girl had nothing to do with his mission. She was a distraction. Defending her exposed him to the small society of Cheddar Gorge and needless risk to his purpose. She was vulnerable. What difference did that make? She had courage. She'd dared the squire to detain her. He shook his head. Irrelevant.

Time to focus. Estate agents. He had a name from Watkins. Pillinger. He was scheduled to meet the man at six in front of the town hall. It would probably take days to explore all the houses to let hereabouts. It was far more likely that the nest would be set up in a house with comforts than a cave. He would get a list from Pillinger, so he could make solo visits in the dead of night to the more likely candidates. Perhaps Pillinger could satisfy his other need. Let's hope he was a red-blooded young man. Stephan strode out into the night, leaving the contentious denizens of the taproom behind to speculate on just what had happened to Jemmy.

It took some days sitting by her uncle's side, reading to him between his bouts of sleep, for Jemmy to subside within her. Her nights were spent in her nursery disturbed by sensuous dreams all featuring Stephan Sincai. Jennings locked her in religiously at night. She dared not use the secret passage. Monsters and townspeople lurked outside, waiting for her to venture out. Ann's only satisfaction was that her uncle seemed to be recovering, and that she managed to avoid her cousin. He hardly seemed like a sportsman, but he had been spending all his days at Bucklands Lodge and nights with brandy in the library. So she hardly expected to see him when she left her uncle's room late one evening.

But Van Helsing was tripping up the stairs. "Cousin!" he called. "I have been meaning to speak with you."

"Really?" Ann stopped on the landing so she would not brush him as he passed. "Do you require anything for your comfort?" That should daunt him.

He smiled slyly and cocked his head, undaunted. "Yes . . . I do," he said. "I require something quite particular. Would you join me in the library?"

Ann felt a shiver go down her spine. *Nonsense,* she told herself. *If he so much as looks as though he might get frisky, you can just ring for Polsham.*

"Of course," she murmured, and followed him down the hall. The library sported a cozy fire. The smell of burning pitch and, more faintly, old paper and leather bindings, was comforting. Van Helsing made directly for the decanters on the sideboard.

"Well . . ." he began, pouring himself a glass of the peaty, amber whiskey. "I thought I should declare my intentions before I approach your uncle."

"Declare?" she murmured. One didn't declare an intention to ravish people.

"I think I can relieve both your minds in this current sad circumstance. I intend to ask your uncle for your hand in marriage."

Ann's thoughts changed gears only slowly. He meant to offer for her. When her uncle was ill, and he'd practically threatened her physically in the very hall outside? When he'd injured a girl who was under her protection? "I can save you the trouble, Cousin. The answer will be no."

"I realize we have known each other only a short time." He waved a hand as though she hadn't spoken. "But your uncle could die at any moment and he would want to see you properly disposed of."

"Dis . . . disposed of?" Ann's outrage almost closed her throat.

"He wants to ensure that you are provided for after his death. It would be a kindness to him to see you married."

Ann drew herself up to all of her five feet. "A kindness he will have to do without. Marriage is impossible for me." That was blunt enough if a direct refusal was not.

Van Helsing got that sly look again. A hint of a smile lurked around his mouth though it did not touch his eyes. "But it isn't really up to you, is it?" he asked softly. "It's for your uncle to say. A girl like you . . ."

What on earth did this man think he was doing? "I assure you I am of age. My uncle has no right to 'dispose' of me. You must have *my* permission, not my uncle's, Cousin."

He shoved at a log with his toe. Sparks shot up the chimney. "I don't think so," he mused. "No, I'm quite sure the whole thing can be arranged without your permission." He threw back a gulp of whiskey and turned to her. The light in his eyes made Ann gasp. "In fact, it might be more interesting that way."

Ann almost shook with rage, but her voice was her own when she said, "I shall never marry you, Cousin."

She did not wait for a reply, but hurried from the room. The man must be kept away from her uncle. She ran upstairs to where Mrs. Creevy sat by the fire crocheting while her uncle read in bed. She nodded to Mrs. Creevy that she could go. As the woman passed her, she said, "Please see that my cousin is not allowed access to Lord Brockweir." Mrs. Creevy's eyes grew big, but she dipped in a graceless curtsy and nodded as she left the room.

"What's that, my dear?" her uncle asked. His eyes were tired. She gathered herself, swallowed, and then breathed in once and out. It would never do to upset him.

"Here, let me read to you, Uncle Thaddeus," she said, gently taking the book from him. It was a book of sermons. Dry stuff. But what did it matter? She sat in his chair. The feeling of him sitting there countless times past washed over her. She wouldn't think about what might happen if he actually died. Not only would she be bereft of her only friend, but also her only ally. The town all thought her crazy. Would they care about her right to refuse Erich's offer if she was safely tied up in the marriage knot, so someone would be responsible for keeping her locked up at Maitlands or somewhere decidedly less comfortable?

Mrs. Creevy came in with hot chocolate for her uncle and soon after that he slipped into sleep. She left him to Mrs. Creevy and crept up to the nursery like a fugitive in her own house. Polsham drifted up after her and locked the door behind her. She had forgiven the servants' abashed performance of this task, giving them absolution by saying it was for her own security.

As soon as the door was locked and the house quiet, she slipped into the passage beside the hearth and wound down through the house and out into the garden. She cared not what she met tonight, monster or mob. She had to get out. The house was a prison with her cousin as chief gaoler. Running into the woods, she leaned against her favorite trees, gasping. The thrill of sunlight, the satisfaction of growing, the wild abandon of tossing leaves in the wind, sank into her through the rough bark under her hands. Such pure feelings trees had; untainted, untrammeled. They soothed the tumult in her breast.

When she felt calmer, she pushed herself up and wandered farther into the woods, up toward her cave. Stone would be even calmer.

Erich, as he wanted to be called, wanted her money, but he wanted her person, as well. She dared not even think about what would happen if a man wanted to claim the full rights of marriage with her, let alone the hateful Erich and his abnormal proclivities. All that touching . . . not to mention probably being naked. No. Conjugal relations were denied her. She must never know the act of physical love, even with a man she found congenial, or it would be the end of her. She would never have a child. Lord forbid! Even if she

managed the dreadful act itself with a partner she did not
find repulsive, how could she risk having a girl-child who
would share her disability and her curse? No. It died with
her. Her own uncle had refused to marry in order to avoid
producing someone like her.

That settled on her shoulders. A mistake, an aberration—
that's what she was. And more than that, a burden. She had
ended her parents' lives. She had twisted her uncle's life into
one of sacrifice for a niece he would never have wanted to
beget himself. And now she might end with a man she hated
raping her into madness with the full blessing of society.
She started to run again. She raced up the path and then off
through the trees toward her special cave. A scent hung in
the air, spicy, like cinnamon. What was that?

She almost bumped into him.

Gasping, she took two hasty steps back. "What . . . what
are you doing here?"

Stephan Sincai simply stood there. His black cloak
blended into the darkness. He seemed strangely alive. His
form loomed over her, tightly muscled under his clothing.
She had never been so aware of a man's body beneath all the
fabric. In the light from the moon peeking through the trees,
she saw how strong his face looked, how . . . bleak. He was a
man who struggled with himself. There was pain in his past.
He might have committed who knows what sins. But his expression said he struggled with it. That was something she
understood, and something someone like Erich would never
understand.

"I might ask the same," he rumbled. The accent was . . .
appealing.

Why she felt the need to answer him she couldn't say.
"I . . . I needed to get away."

He simply raised his brows, as though to say his reason
was the same.

Now she remembered why she should not simply turn

and run. He had come to her aid. Twice. She cleared her throat. "I'm glad I ran into you. Or almost. Well, I mean, I'm glad I encountered you. I never got a chance to thank you properly for . . . for the other night . . . and in the village . . ." That sounded so incoherent. The sensuous fabric of her dreams about him suffused her with a blush.

"It was nothing." His face was quite inscrutable.

She remembered that he had seen the episode at the tavern when Jemmy touched her. He'd witnessed her using information she couldn't know in her defense. "I'm not a witch." Was that true? Why should she feel compelled to tell him that?

"What are you?"

Was that a smile lurking around his mouth? How different a smile from her cousin's! She lifted her chin. "I . . . I have a disability." That should make him stop his questions.

He frowned. "What kind of disability?"

How rude! She bit back her first retort. She was, after all, in his debt. Should she tell him? Could she? No one had ever asked her straight-out like that. "I know things about people if I touch them. Objects too, though the effect is fainter."

"That would be useful."

Useful? He couldn't know that she knew *everything* about a person, that the whole being of that person drenched her until she did not even quite know herself from the other. And she couldn't tell him. She managed a rueful smile. "Useful. I can't honestly say that is the first description that comes to mind."

He nodded there in the dark in the middle of the forest. "Yes, well, perhaps you wouldn't." The cinnamon scent was his—like the lavender water men used for shaving, but spicy. And underneath the cinnamon was some other scent, fainter, harder to identify. The air held some sort of vibrant expectancy, as though anything could happen. She wasn't sure what she wanted to happen, but she didn't want him to go.

"What brings you to Cheddar Gorge?" Inane! She made idle conversation as though they met in the village street, when what she wanted was to get away, from Erich, and the future, and all the dreadful possibilities circling her like wolves. She should want to be away from him as quickly as possible. But she didn't.

He seemed to consider her. "I am looking for a suitable house to lease."

Perhaps she could be helpful. "Mrs. Simpson says the Sheffields want to let Staines."

"It must be a vacant house."

"Oh." That made no sense. "I assume you've seen Foxdell near Rooks Bridge? It has been vacant for years. It would need renovation."

"I want something closer to Cheddar Gorge or perhaps near Winscombe."

"Oh." She knew of nothing near Winscombe except Maitlands's hunting lodge. Then she smiled. Why not? Erich obviously coveted it. The prospect of throwing a spoke in his wheel was appealing. "Hmmm. One of my more disreputable ancestors built a tidy little hunting box about three or four miles outside Winscombe. Bucklands Lodge. It hasn't been used since my father died. My cousin has been renovating, so it should be in fair shape. I could see my way clear to renting it out."

He inclined his head. "Should I see your agent?"

"Henry Brandywine is my father's steward. Mr. Watkins at the Hammer and Anvil can give you his direction."

He looked around as though someone else was present. "I should escort you home."

"I am not ready to go home."

"Do you think wandering in the woods alone at night is wise?"

"I go out often. I have a special spot I like to visit." She expected him to protest.

But he said only, "Then I shall leave you to it." He walked carefully around her.

Well! She found herself gazing after him, cinnamon slowly fading in the air.

So, she was the one who left the candles in the cave and had made the fire. He'd found what must be her lair earlier this evening. It was not well enough provided to be the place where vampires hid by day. There had been no traces of food, or bedrolls, nothing but the candles at the entrance to a remote branch off a branch off the main cave, a torch in a rough rock holder, and a stack of neat kindling gathered from the forest. And a book and a crocheted pillow. The book was by Jane Austen. Hardly fodder for hardened creatures planning to create an army in Asharti's memory and destroy the balance of the world.

No, the only lair he had found tonight was Miss Van Helsing's. Strange girl. No wonder one had the impression she looked right through one. She could do just that if she touched you. Dangerous for a man with secrets. He must steer clear of Miss Van Helsing.

And yet, he was drawn to her. It felt almost like alchemy.

Nonsense, he told himself sternly. It was because she was an outsider among her own people. It was because she knew secrets and had secrets of her own. Those were things he understood. He felt a certain kind of kinship. That was all. For all her otherworldly attributes, which he, of course, did not doubt for a moment, she was curiously down-to-earth. It must take courage to live with the gift she obviously thought a curse. And she tried to use it well. He had seen her compassion for Jemmy Minks today even though she knew the worst of him. Was that just her naïveté? Perhaps. But it spoke well of her. He shook off his thoughts of her. *No distractions, remember that.*

Her hunting lodge, however, would be his next exploration. It was near Winscombe, scene of two killings and a bout of the "influenza." He would cover himself, put on his colored glasses and venture out in the light to arrive just before dusk. They were young. They couldn't stand daylight. He could catch them together before they could leave the nest. He turned at the edge of the forest, but the girl had disappeared. He wondered how many there would be. Likely he was not up to this task Rubius had set him. But he had no choice.

Six

Ann sat the next night in her cave curled in her warm cloak, reading by the light of the torch. She resolved to come here every night. She felt safe here. No one knew about this little pocket off a disused branch of the Cheddar cave. The walk up the Gorge from the house had been nerve-wracking. Who knew but what she would meet that creature who killed Molly, or townspeople patrolling the woods? But she had met neither. She had not even met Stephan Sincai, though she could not have said that would be unwelcome. Even as she had tended her uncle today, and managed to avoid Erich, Mr. Sincai had crept into her thoughts. Why had a man who looked so impassive helped her, not once but twice?

It did not matter. She would not meet him again. And he could not save her from what she feared most now. All she could hope was that her uncle would recover enough to let her broach the subject of refusing Erich, and that he would send Erich packing. That might only be a reprieve for her sanity, but she needed that reprieve.

It was good to be back in her refuge again tonight. It

always amazed her that other people were frightened of caves. Somewhere close she could hear the drip of water growing stalactites and stalagmites, and farther away a small stream gurgled on its way through the cavern, but other than that it was quiet. The cave demanded quiet in return. Sounds were punished with echoes. The cave room she had chosen for her own had a ceiling which disappeared into the gloom beyond the reach of her candles. It was closed at one end except for the crevice that disgorged the stream and the opening at the other end was only big enough for her to duck through, but there was also an opening in the rock to some honeycomb channel above. That meant a fire could warm the space, and yet the smoke was drawn out. Her army of candles, the fire, and her torch made the cave almost inviting. The floor was coated with soft sand, comfortable for sitting on a quilt, and Malmsy's crocheted pillow made a fine back rest against a large rock. This was her cocoon.

She yawned. Sleep had been elusive what with worry over her uncle, anger at the vile Erich, and those dreams about touching Sincai . . . They were pervasive tonight. So she had put on a cloak and half-boots and, with her night-dress and hair down, fled to the cave. She'd have to go soon lest she fall asleep and fail to return before the servants rose. No one must know she could still escape her nursery.

She didn't want to return. Her house had been invaded by the enemy. But she couldn't abandon her uncle.

With a sigh, she closed her book and made a move to go.

Stephan stumbled from the open door of Bucklands Lodge. His chest heaved for breath. One had gotten away. The one he'd surprised in the forest. He hadn't gotten them all. That meant he'd failed. He staggered across the small garden. His boots squelched with his own blood. The smell of blood was everywhere; his, theirs. There had been five. He had barely been a match for four. They'd come after him before he could prepare. He hadn't been able to use the full power the Daughters had taught him at Mirso. He'd had to fight them, and that distracted him. Failed. He'd failed. Pain drenched him. Safe. He needed somewhere safe to heal. It might take a while. His vision blurred. He shook his head. He couldn't lose consciousness, not before he found refuge. Where? He couldn't go to the tavern, spreading blood for which later there would be no wounds of explanation.

Quiet. Secret. That's what he needed.

He knew where.

With his last strength he called to the one who shared his blood. *Companion,* he thought, *lend me your power one more time tonight.* A red film descended on the world bit by bit. He felt the darkness gather, slowly, around him. *Companion!*

As the blackness whirled around him, his vision went from red to black. The pain from his wounds was joined by the exquisite pain of the power ramping up past endurance. Then he knew no more.

Ann was gathering her cloak around her and about to blow out the candles when she heard a growing hum behind her. She jerked around, startled by the unfamiliar noise. There, by the doorway to the cave, a whirling darkness grew out of nothing. Ann gasped. What was that?

The darkness melted away, leaving the figure of Stephan Sincai. She put her hand to her mouth to stifle a cry. He was covered with blood. Horrible wounds gaped over his body. He took one step, then his eyes rolled up into his head and his knees buckled. He fell to the sandy floor.

Ann heard a small sound like a frightened animal would make and realized it came from her own throat. God in heaven! What was that darkness? How had he appeared so suddenly? Her brain layered questions frantically, without answers, as she stood, staring.

The sand under his body began to darken. Blood. Dear Lord, he was bleeding to death! He might be dead even now. That was enough to move her. She rushed to stand over him.

Close, the wounds were horrifying. Her gaze roved over his body. His shirt was shredded, his breeches in tatters. He wore no cravat and what was left of his shirt was open. His neck was cut so deeply she could see the white of bone. But his neck was not the only place bone was revealed, and in his belly it was something worse. She raised her hand to her mouth to prevent a shriek from escaping. Her stomach heaved and she bit her lip to take her mind off the nausea. The whirling darkness now seemed less important than the fact that she was about to watch someone die right in front of her for the second time this week.

She stood there shuddering while some part of her grew calm. She hadn't done anything for Molly but watch her die. What kind of person did that make her? Was she human at all anymore? She didn't want to be the thing she was becoming; remote, detached. Was that not the first step to real lunacy?

She knelt beside Sincai. Her hand rose to her mouth.

You're going to touch him, aren't you? a part of her asked. *Isn't that your mother's road to craziness? Was it not prolonged touching with a man that ended her in an asylum, hoarse from screaming, rocking herself with unseeing eyes?*

"I'm not going to have conjugal relations with him," she whispered aloud. Her voice hardly shook. The cave threw her whisper back to her, magnified and hissing. "And if all roads lead to craziness, then I might as well be of use." She threw off her cloak, gathered the flounce from the bottom of her nightdress and ripped.

His neck—God, his neck must be her first concern. And she couldn't just wrap it with the fabric. She'd have to pull the flesh together. How? She peered at the wound. Perhaps she had been mistaken about the bone. Thank the Lord! She licked her lips and gathered a ripped section of the flounce. Very well, she'd lift his head with it. That would close the wound. Then she'd tie the cloth about his throat.

The worst part was that all her sacrifice would be futile. He was a dead man. No one could sustain such wounds and live.

It didn't matter. If she didn't try to help him, she would know she wasn't connected to the human race anymore, and all else in her life would flow in consequence of that moment.

She held one end of the strip of cloth in each hand and worked it back and forth under his head, sliding it down to his neck. She didn't even have to touch him. She lifted. The neck wound closed. Then, holding his head up with the sling of cloth in one hand, with the other she made a pad and pressed it in place, careful not to brush his skin. She could feel him through the pad, just an echo of . . . of strangeness. She'd never felt anything just like it. Blood began to soak through the pad, but the wound wasn't practically gushing as it was before. She pushed down the dreadful thought that perhaps he had not much blood left to lose and tied the cloth tightly around the pad. She watched carefully to see that he could still breathe. Only when his chest continued to rise and fall, however slightly, did she turn to his other wounds.

Now what to do? Oh, dear. Her stomach sank again. It must be the belly wound. She breathed raggedly, trying to suppress the nausea as she let herself examine it more closely. It gaped, revealing what could only be intestines. What could she do about that?

Bind it together as you did his neck, that's what, she told herself firmly. What use was there here for some squeamish miss? She made a pad. She'd have to touch him. She had to lean over him and push a strip of cloth under his body to tie the pad against the wound. She watched from somewhere else as her hand reached over him. She could practically feel the flesh of his bare abdomen. It would be sticky from blood in places. She knew what to expect. There would be a rush of experience. She would know his essence, good and bad. She'd work through it. She could do that. She'd slide the hand with the makeshift bandage under him as far as she could go, then pull back and push her hand under him from this side to grab it and pull it through.

As in a dream, things speeded up at the last moment. Her hands clenched even as she thought about pulling back. It was too late. She pushed the strip of her nightdress under him. The flesh peeking from his tattered shirt seared her.

Death! Murder!

Blood. Terrible strangeness. Evil? Sometimes he thought himself so.

Three women in Mirso Monastery. How he longed to go there!

Ann struggled against the onslaught. She pushed her hand under his body and reached for the strip of cloth.

Guilt! Guilt no one could bear. Guilt for the fate of the whole world.

Guillotine. Sacrifice for the one he loved.

Blood.

Love unrequited. Lifetimes of it. Beatrix.

War. Fighting. Indian natives? Jungles. I am their god.

Chanting. Someone called him Dalai Lama. Massacre.

Hope. Asharti. Beatrix.

Faster now the images came. Back and back, more and more experiences cascaded over her. She couldn't breathe.

Ships.

Starving.

War.

Painting.

Hate.

Tenderness.

Murder.

Women.

Fierce.

Strength.

Lust.

Blood.

Blood.

Always the blood.

She felt herself falling over him. Blackness descended, pitying blackness.

Stephan breathed. He was not in a bed. Beds were soft. He must be lying on the ground. Where was he? He should open his eyes and see. That seemed like so much effort. Why was that? Oh, Kilkenny's vampires.

He had done what was required. Not the way he'd been taught, exactly. But did that matter? They deserved what they got. Did they? How did he know? A flash of blood and bone and scattered heads and limbs flitted through his brain and lodged there. Because they were made by Asharti, and Asharti was evil. They broke the Rules. And if he had to live with that image in his brain it was only one more element of his atonement. Perhaps someday when he had taken the Vow, the image could be encysted with chanting and meditation until it did not burn so much. What had happened in the hunting lodge was only one more horror in two thousand years of frequent horrors.

Awareness rose slowly, like a tide, inside him. It had taken all his Companion's power to kill four of them. That was why the healing was so slow. But the pain was less now. He just couldn't breathe. There was a weight on his chest.

It might be the weight of failure. He hadn't gotten them all. One had escaped. And none had been Callan Kilkenny. He couldn't go home to Mirso until he got Kilkenny and killed all his minions. How could he succeed if he couldn't do as the Daughters taught him? He wasn't ready! He needed help. But there was no one else. Kilkenny was building another army, like Asharti's.

Whose fault was that, all of it?

He breathed. His. The weight of it sat on him.

But there *was* a weight on his chest aside from guilt. He opened his eyes.

Bloody hell! There was a girl collapsed over him. The one people thought crazy. Her long white-blonde hair was spread over him. She was wearing nothing but a night shift. Blood soaked the thin linen and made her hair sticky. She must be hurt! Had he hurt her somehow? He got up on his elbows and lifted her gently off his chest.

Then he sat, cradling her in one arm. Tiny flames guttered in candle stubs scattered about the cave. He leaned over and grabbed one to examine her for wounds. Her face was smeared with drying blood, but he couldn't find a source. He pushed her hair back from her face. Lord, but she was beautiful! So tiny, so delicate in his arms. Her features looked too perfect to be human; small straight nose, skin so translucent and fine he could see the veins in her temples. Fragile. That's what she was. But was she dead? He felt for the pulse in her throat with thumb and middle finger. It beat erratically back at him. She was alive.

His brain began to work. She was unconscious, but the blood was his. He pulled up one eyelid and waved the candle before her eyes. The pupil did not contract. He patted her face and, when that got no reaction, pinched her cheek. Nothing.

This did not bode well. He'd seen people dead to the world like this before. How had she gotten that way?

He looked around, trying to piece together what had happened. The book, the guttering candles almost burned to the socket . . . He remembered now. It was the girl who used this

cave. She must have seen him appear here. He'd lost consciousness immediately thereafter from pain and loss of
blood. He must have been a sight. He looked down at his
own body. His clothing was shredded. The gaping wounds
beneath were memories. Only lines and circles of pink, new
skin remained. Soon even they would disappear.

Swallowing, he felt some constriction at his throat. He
tugged at his cravat, before he remembered he hadn't worn
one. He felt the cloth about his neck. It must be a bandage. He
pulled at the knot. A bloody pad fell to the sand. He glanced to
the woman still in his arms. She had bandaged him. After
what she must have seen? That was courage, indeed. And
kindness. He couldn't remember the last time someone had
been kind to him.

He laid her out upon the floor of the cave. He would leave
her here to recover. He tried to sweep the cobwebs from his
brain. The vampire who escaped would go to Kilkenny. That
meant Kilkenny would come for him, or send others of his
army. Perhaps many others. But Stephan was willing to bet
he would come himself to see his nemesis eradicated. Not
what Stephan had intended. But perhaps not a bad outcome.
He had gone from stalker to bait. Very well. He was sum-
moning his own destruction. But it *was* one sure way of finding Kilkenny.

That meant Stephan needed to wait in Cheddar Gorge
and he couldn't afford suspicions about his nature to arouse
the townspeople. He remembered the girl saying she could
sense things about people if she touched them. She had certainly touched him. Would she know what he was?

If he was smart he would kill her right here. The pulse
beat faintly in the fragile stem of her neck. Rubius would do
it. The Daughters would kill her. A wash of failure swept
through him. He couldn't. He didn't know for certain she
knew what he was. He couldn't kill her on the off chance that
when she woke she would know he was a vampire. Enough

innocent people's deaths could be laid at his door. He couldn't afford another one.

He glanced around to the candles. They would soon go out. The torch she read by had already failed. She would wake in darkness, frightened. Could she find her way out? His gaze slid back to her. He felt in some way that he knew her, had always known her. He had an impression of goodness, sincerity, terrible loneliness, and yet underneath a strength that belied her fragile looks. He had met her three times, no more. What could he really know about her? And yet he could not shake the impressions . . .

Stephan sucked in air and blew it out. He was going to do something stupid.

He picked her up, along with a cloak lying in the sand, and kicked out the remaining candles. She felt so small cradled against his chest. A woman like this needed protection. She was warm against him in the cool air of the cave. The skin on her bare arm almost burned his palm. His power started to rise of its own accord. He knew why. His loins tightened in a familiar reaction. It was the curse of the training, that was all. He was surprised he still responded to her after he had expended so much power tonight.

Use the rising power, he commanded himself. He would take her out of here. She lived at that great house connected to ruins just outside of the village. *Companion!* The power rose around him. The cave went red, then black. Good thing she was unconscious. She wouldn't feel what happened next. A moment of searing pain, and the cave disappeared.

They appeared at the edge of the wood that lay between Maitlands Abbey and the road to Wells. He'd leave her here where others could see to her. He must do it soon before he had to practice the chanting to control his body. It was becoming insistent with a need he dared not fill.

But now leaving her did not seem so simple. It was near dawn. The sky was lightening. Already he could hear someone about in the stables and stirrings in the kitchen. He mustn't be seen in these bloody, tattered clothes. He glanced down to Miss Van Helsing, clutched against him. She was covered with blood, as well. There would be questions. He didn't want anyone asking her questions. He didn't want her to reveal how she had gotten bloody. He was hoping to hell she wouldn't remember.

His mind raced. He could remove her clothes and just leave her. Of course her reputation would be ruined. She might be a witch in people's eyes, but she was a chaste witch. There would be no limit to the scorn heaped upon her if anyone thought she was a loose woman, as well. Besides, her person would be smeared with blood. If she was found naked and bloody? Then there would be suspicions *and* her reputation would be ruined.

What did her reputation matter in the grander scheme of his purpose? But he couldn't . . .

Damnation!

He laid her down. His body missed the warmth of her instantly. He was fully erect now, just with the nearness of her. He hadn't touched a woman since he left Mirso. He had vowed not to take the chance. And here he was handling a barely clothed and beautiful girl. If he was going to be an idiot, best do it and be done with it, before she roused his power beyond the reach of his control. He eased her out of her cloak and flung it about himself to cover his torn and bloody clothing. He slid down the slope to the back of the house, where the kitchens were.

The woman who came out to throw a bucket of water into the yard was older, her years of work lined deeply in her face, her gray hair confined by a simple mobcap. She wore a knitted woolen shawl against the morning cold.

"Good morning," he said, stepping out from behind an

outbuilding corner. It was the root cellar by the smell of potatoes and carrots and raw earth.

The woman started. Then she looked him up and down. "If you want a handout, they'll be breakfast scraps at ten." He ran a hand through his hair and knew he must look wild in his tattered breeches and the borrowed cloak that was only three-quarters length on his tall frame. So he wasted no time. He brought up his Companion, just enough to put compulsion in his voice.

"I'm no one you need to worry about," he said softly. "Where is Miss Van Helsing's room?" He watched her eyes go unfocused as though she looked at something far away.

"She has the fourth floor, all of it. The old nursery," the woman muttered.

The nursery? Odd. "You were startled by a shadow this morning, nothing more."

She nodded slowly. He bowed and turned away before he let his Companion stand down. He strode back to where he had left the girl. She would be cold. He wrapped her in the cloak and gathered her against himself. His body responded almost instantly. He clenched his jaw against the feeling swelling through him. Then, setting his sights on the fourth floor of the great house, he drew the power once again.

They flickered into space in a low-ceilinged room, quite large, with dormered windows and simple, childish furniture. The coals of last night's fire glowed in a fireplace at one side. The servants would not dare disturb their mistress for some hours. That would serve his purpose. Too bad he could not order up hot water for the hip bath he saw in the corner. He laid her on the narrow bed in her cloak to keep the bedclothes from being stained. Then he took a poker, stirred up the fire, and laid on several logs. That would get this room warm. Even at the top of the house, it was cool here.

He turned back to his charge. Now he must steel himself

for the ordeal ahead. Control. Wasn't that what he was good at these days?

He went to the dressing table and poured water from a flowered china pitcher into a matching basin and found a soft cotton towel and some lavender-scented soap. He set the basin on her night table. He didn't light the lamp sitting there. That would attract attention. Behind him, the fire snapped and cast a flickering glow across the room as the logs caught. It was enough. He saw quite well in the dark. Sitting on the edge of the small bed, he made sure he had himself firmly in hand. Then, without looking at her face, he grabbed the neck of her shift and ripped it down the front to the hem.

Zeus above! Even mottled with dried blood, she was exquisite. She was delicately made, yet her figure was lush. Her breasts were heavy for her frame, tipped with rose aureola and small nipples. The curve of them made his loins tighten. And her skin . . . it looked like creamy silk. Her hair, so very blonde as it was, had come undone as he carried her, and now it splayed across the bed, echoed in only slightly darker tones in the triangle at the apex of her thighs. Her hips were generous for her size and the curve of her calves made him practically quiver.

He took a ragged breath and fought for control. He could not give in to the need that cascaded over him, pooling in his loins. *Tuatha, rendon. Melifant extonderant denering.* There. That was better. He had the control required, thanks to the Daughters.

He clenched his teeth and dipped the towel into the water in the basin. He was clenching more than his teeth as he started with her face. His erection would not be banished, but that did not mean he had to acknowledge it. The only reason he couldn't seem to suppress it was that he was weakened by his battle. That was all. He wiped the delicate features carefully, paying special attention to the blood that had seeped into her hairline. He half expected to find some kind of wound, some lump where she had fallen to cause her swoon. But he did not. There were no abrasions, no bruises even. Once the blood was wiped away, her skin was pristine. He worked down her neck. Such a tiny column; so vulnerable. Her pulse throbbed through the arteries there. It made the need inside him multiply. Blood and sex mingled together until he throbbed in answer to the blood pulsing in her veins. He wiped her shoulders, and, God help him, her breasts. He was breathing heavily now, his loins on fire. *Denering tuatha feralicenta perala.* He dipped the towel, wrung it out, began again. Over her ribs, across her flat belly, he wiped away the sticky blood. His blood. She was covered in his blood because she had tried to help him. Even though she hated to touch anyone. Even after she had seen him appear in a swirl of darkness. She must have seen him . . . What woman would try to help him then?

He held himself firmly in check as he daubed at the blood that had seeped into the hair on the mound between her thighs. Dip the towel, wring it out, go over her body one more time, the hips, the belly, her breasts. Dip, wring, neck and shoulders, face.

There. Her fine skin was ruddy where he had scrubbed at some of the thicker smears of his blood. But she was as clean as he could make her. The splotchiness would fade by the time anyone found her. He pulled her shift and her cloak from under her. Then, his loins almost painful with arousal, he lifted her in one arm and pulled back the quilt. He laid her in the bed and covered her. Now to remove all trace of his presence. He opened a window and tossed the rosy water onto the roof of the portico below. The towel and her torn and bloody shift were wrapped in the cloak. Those he would take with him.

He turned to look at her one last time. She seemed so frail and fragile in the child's bed.

Still he was puzzled by her condition. With no wound he could discern, why had she not awakened? The sun was rising. He had finished at the hunting lodge at what, midnight? The quilt barely moved with her breathing. Something was not right here. The only thing he knew for certain was that it was his fault. Somehow, she had swooned when she . . .

When she touched him! She said she knew things about people when she touched them. But it must be more than that. When that scrawny one at the tavern touched her the other day, it seemed to daze her. There was some sort of consequence to the touching for her and yet she had bandaged him. *Generous,* he thought. *A generous impulse. And courageous.*

He pressed his lips together grimly. He owed her nothing. She was stupid to touch him if it had some physical consequence. It was her fault she had passed out, not his.

Stephan clutched the bundle of gory clothes to his own tattered and bloody shirt. Someone would get her a doctor when they found her. Her people would know what to do.

Companion! The room went red. The blackness pooled at his feet and began to rise, more quickly even than usual. Desire still pooled in his erect member. The Companion fed off his sexual energy and ramped up their joint power to excruciating. He had to get out of here.

Seven

Stephan stood in his room at the Hammer and Anvil as the blackness drained away. With it, the terrible need the girl had engendered in him subsided as well, leaving him feeling empty and dry. It had been foolish to take her into the house. What did he care for her reputation? As for the fear that leaving her bloody would generate questions, he could have avoided that by just killing her. It had been stupid to let her live. If she woke knowing what he was, she would scream for the magistrates. Having the entire town storming after him with burning brands would make it inconvenient to wait where Kilkenny could easily find him.

He had been rash, all the way around.

He'd think what to do about that later. Now he must do for himself what he had done for the girl. He stripped off his tattered clothes and wiped his body with a towel wetted in his washbasin. But he couldn't get his mind off her, what she had done for him, what could be keeping her unconscious for so long.

He wanted to know. He didn't want to be the cause of yet

more distress. Especially since she had tried to help him.

He rolled his clothes up with hers. Tonight he would bury them somewhere in the forest. Now he needed rest. Suddenly, he was so exhausted he could barely stand. The first rays hit the closed shutters. He toppled into bed. Rest . . . he had to rest.

But the contact with the girl, undressing her, moving his hands over her body . . . He tossed in the bed, trying to forget. But his body remembered. Even now his member began to throb again. He could thank them for that. The Daughters and their training . . .

MIRSO MONASTERY, DECEMBER 1819

The small room in the bowels of the monastery was hot. A fire blazed in the huge gaping maw of the hearth. There were three chaise longues, upholstered and modern. They contrasted with the wide bench of rough-hewn stone centered in front of the fireplace. A large cupboard of carved wood, Tudor perhaps, sat next to the doorway. On the left hand against the wall was a long table laid with plates of hothouse fruit and sweetmeats, and several decanters of red wine. The walls and floor were stone as well, only partially covered by two thick Turkey carpets, one on each side of the stone bench, and several tapestry wall hangings. The room was comfortable only on the surface. Underneath, it was hard and unyielding.

Behind him one of the sisters, he thought Estancia, closed a heavy wooden door strapped with iron and studded with bolts that were blackened with age.

Deirdre drew herself up and clapped her hands, once. "Pay attention, Penitent," she said sharply. Stephan felt a snap of annoyance. It must have shown in his eyes, for she approached and laid a hand along his jaw. He went still. Her hand slipped around his throat just above his cravat. He knew she could snap his neck or tear out his throat without even exerting herself. She was that old and strong. Nothing he could not heal, of course, unless she resorted to actual decapitation. But there were even worse possibilities. A thrill of fear wound around him.

"Penitent," she whispered, so close now he could feel her breath as she caressed his throat. "Let us be clear. You have chosen your path. Your path is through us. We can banish you from Mirso forever. Or we can keep you here and work to improve your attitude. But you do not control here. We control your destiny."

This was what he feared most. The two others slid around their sister and put their hands on him, light threats in support of their sister. Stephan found himself sweating in the heat of the closed room.

"What happened to the willing acolyte we saw in our father's rooms?" Estancia whispered. She touched his hair, his ear. "You must submit to our tutelage."

Stephan clenched the muscles in his jaw against a shiver that wanted to go down his spine. He knew his job here. He knew what he wanted. He knew he deserved whatever was to come, no matter how difficult. There was no room for pride or disobedience. They were right. "Show me the way."

"Is that a command?" Freya asked softly, in his other ear. They were all clustered about him, their hands moving over his back, down his hip.

"No," he corrected himself. "I beg you to show me the way."

"And so we will," Deirdre said. "But first we must assess your vigor."

"We must know where to begin," Estancia echoed. Her hands moved under his coat. They pulled it over his shoulders.

"How much natural energy you have . . ." Freya continued.

Deirdre was unbuttoning his waistcoat. Estancia picked at the buttons on his breeches. The room was so hot . . . his head began to spin, whether with the heat, or from the proximity of their old and powerful vibrations, he didn't know. What did they mean, "assess his natural energy?" Why . . . why were they undressing him? Their hands moved over his body, underneath his shirt. Freya pulled at the ends of his cravat. Their power hummed in the heavy air. He swayed. They had him naked to the waist. Estancia pulled at his breeches. Deirdre pushed him gently onto the wide stone bench. It was warm on his bare buttocks. Deirdre sat beside him and licked his throat just under his jawline where she had touched him earlier. Her hands ran through the hair on his chest and plucked at one nipple. He felt his loins tighten. Estancia and Freya tugged at his boots. His mind was reeling as if he had drunk too much. Then he was fully naked. Their hands pushed him back on the bench. It was wide enough to be a bed of sorts. They stroked his belly, his thighs. The satin of their gowns caressed his skin. He knew he was fully erect and throbbing. They . . . they were going to make love to him? Deirdre brushed his lips with hers before she kissed him full on, thrusting her tongue deep into his mouth, pushing, searching. Even as she kissed him, he felt one of the others, the buxom one, Estancia, slide up against him and begin sucking his right nipple. She had slipped the silk from her shoulders. Her naked breasts pressed against him, her nipples nubby with passion. God, the third one, Freya, was cradling his sac, rubbing the stones gently together. He groaned into Deirdre's mouth as his cock throbbed harder. Freya stroked his cock directly. He lifted his hips, needing more. What was happening to him? He had never been so aroused. His senses overwhelmed him. Estancia's hand stole from caressing his hip to massage his balls, as Freya grasped his cock and slid her hand up and down. Yes! God, yes! How long had it been since he had had relations with a woman? But three women? He should . . . he should what? He couldn't think.

"You first, Dee," Freya whispered to Deirdre. "You are eldest."

Deirdre pulled away from his mouth, lifted her black silk skirts, and straddled his hips with her long legs. Estancia scooted up and began sucking his lower lip, her teeth just grazing it. Freya came round and sat at his other side, stroking his forehead or occasionally pinching his left nipple. Deirdre was sliding her wet slit along his aching cock. The heat, the overpowering smell of sweat and cinnamon, the hard, hot stone beneath his body, the ripples of sensation across his body where they touched him, the crackle of the fire, and the low sounds of the women as their own lust cycled up, all blended into one exquisite sensation so intense it was painful.

Deirdre slipped him inside her and began riding him. His hips thrust up in counterpoint. He wouldn't last long at this rate. He could feel sensation ramping up past his ability to control it. Even as he thought that, Deirdre whispered, "Not yet. Only when I say you can."

He felt a light shower of their will. It came from all three of them. He looked up and saw the red of the reflected firelight in their eyes grow more pronounced. Deirdre rode him harder. Estancia ran her tongue inside his mouth while Freya watched all, caressing his forehead with one hand and plucking at his nipple with the other. He teetered on some impossible edge of feeling, but he didn't fall. The pleasure was so intense it was almost excruciating. They . . . they were keeping him from his release until they could get their own satisfaction. A tendril of panic made his eyes widen, but he was powerless to do anything but thrust his hips and kiss Estancia's pouty, bowed mouth. They were totally in control here.

"Shusssh," Freya soothed, stroking his hair back from his

brow. "Be calm. Enjoy. There is much more to come."

And he was calmer, in spite of himself. He thrust his cock into Deirdre until she began to gasp and make small sounds in her throat. He could feel her clench around him. At that moment, they let him go, and he cascaded over his cliff edge into the ecstasy they had denied him. White exploded in his brain even as his cock pulsed in its own explosive ejaculation.

He lay there, trembling, hardly conscious.

"Let's see how long it takes him to come up again," one said from somewhere far away.

"I can't wait." Which one was that? A hand slapped his face lightly. "Focus, Penitent!"

He blinked in response. Estancia loomed above him, her red silk dress hanging over the gold filigree girdle at her waist, leaving her breasts bare. They were full breasts. Her skin was tawny, her nipples large and the color of chocolate with milk in it. She leaned over him. He knew what she wanted, though she said not a word. He lifted his head, reaching for her nipples with his lips. He ran his tongue around her nipple then sucked gently. She lifted her head and moaned. Her throat arched. "Harder," she whispered. He pulled at her breast then switched to the other as it dangled, heavy, above him. She squeezed the breast he had just left and rolled her nipple between her thumb and forefinger. As if she could stand it no longer, she straightened, pulled her red silk skirts apart, and straddled his shoulders.

Her buttocks were smooth and warm against his chest. He could smell the musk of her. She reached into the dark thatch at her groin and spread her nether lips. "Let me see your skills, Penitent." Stephan felt as though he was dreaming. But he did not question. He licked her, his tongue running up and down the moist folds of flesh until it found the nub of passion, already roused. Sucking and licking, he felt her moan above him as her hips jerked.

He applied himself assiduously. He was not surprised

when he felt himself tighten again. His erection throbbed to life. Freya, dressed in pristine white satin, moved toward him. "Look, sisters," she said, behind Estancia's moans of pleasure. "Already he rises." She straddled him behind her sister and slipped him inside herself. Then they were both bucking and riding him, using his mouth and cock together. He gasped and heaved. It did not take long before Estancia was shuddering and shrieking, her hands knotted in his hair, and Freya cried out in her own release. He came again in wrenching unison with them.

"He has potential," he heard Deirdre say as he sank into a stupor, heat and sex and sweat and female musk overwhelming his senses at last.

That wasn't the end, of course. God! Stephan ran his hands through his hair, sweating even two years and a thousand miles away from that night. They hadn't made love to him. One couldn't call it that. They had used him. Had he not been willing to be used? He couldn't withstand the pressure of their need, that night or any other.

He pushed down shame. It had been necessary. They had shown him that. He only wished he had been a better vessel for their teachings.

"Again, anyone?"

Stephan cracked his eyelids. Deirdre lay draped, naked, over the chaise longue closest to the fire. The flames were only a flicker. The shadows and light moving over her face made her look like a demon. "He's finally spent himself, but I can bring him up again if you like."

"No, no, my dear. I couldn't." Freya fanned herself with her hand and fell into the other chair. She was lithe, an

athlete, with muscular calves and delicate muscles in her back. "Three is my limit tonight. Or was it four?"

Estancia spoke in a childish, high voice. "I must admit I haven't been so pleasantly exhausted in years." She came to stand over Stephan. She lifted his chin with one finger. "I think he has potential, don't you, sisters?"

"Potential for what?" Stephan managed to ask. "This is no kind of training—"

Estancia slapped him so hard his head snapped to the side. "Never, never question us."

"Come here, Penitent, and kneel." Deirdre's voice was steely with the command of her Companion's compulsion. Stephan felt every one of her thousands of years in the power that throbbed through him. He fought the urge to obey, but she was stronger than he was. He struggled off the stone bench, staggered over to the chaise, and fell to his knees. She leaned forward and glared at him. "You will not speak unless spoken to. We will tell you what you must do, and what you need to know." She rose and walked around behind him. "You will obey quickly, eagerly, and silently."

"That is part of the suppression of emotion which is essential to your training," Freya explained. Her expression was soft. Was that sympathy or something else?

"All he needs to know is that if he does not," Estancia said, "he will be punished." She distributed her ample figure over the third chaise. "Or we could let our father punish you."

Freya sat up from her chaise and slipped a silken robe over her athletic frame. "Don't threaten, Stancie. Stephan wants to obey. He wants to learn to increase his power and control it. He wants to atone and take the Vow and make peace with his past deeds and his soul."

It was true. He did. He bowed his head. This was part of his atonement, this submission to their training. No matter what kind of training it was.

"We shall see." Deirdre's voice seemed habitually hard, pitched low, almost masculine in quality. It matched her tall, angular body and her implacable eyes. "Very well, sisters. What do you think of him?" She shrugged on the wrapper that lay at the foot of her chaise.

"Easily aroused, even for one of our kind. He is highly sexed." This from Freya.

"Good stamina," Estancia acknowledged grudgingly. "Though he might not have expended himself in some time. We shall see if his endurance continues."

"But his control is not what we could wish." Deirdre tapped her finger to her lips. "I had to suppress ejaculation several times tonight."

"That's what we are here to work on." Freya shrugged.

"He must rid himself of emotions." Estancia was pouting again. "I can feel them simmering just below the surface. Rebellion, self-absorption. He is prideful." She was the only one who had not covered her nakedness with a robe except Stephan, of course. His clothing lay strewn around the room, but he did not think taking the initiative to retrieve it would be viewed with complacence by the sisters. He swallowed, trying to conceal the fear, repress the rebellion.

Deirdre slapped her knees and rose, "So, first we increase the sexual energy further."

Estancia gathered up his clothes. "Suppress to increase."

Freya took his boots. "Then frequency is the key."

"And then, when the power is sufficient, we go slowly, to be sure we don't have a repetition of the last one." Deirdre swung open the door.

"Rest," Freya said to him. "You will need your strength." She laid their dresses over her arm, along with Estancia's robe.

They trailed out the door. It closed behind them with a thud. He could hear the iron bar being lowered on the outside.

It could not keep him in, but it was a clear signal that he was not allowed out of this room.

Exhaustion welled up inside him. He felt stripped both mentally and physically. Could he give himself over to these strange and powerful women? But what choice did he have? They held out the promise of salvation, for him, and if Rubius was right about Asharti's followers, for his kind and for the world. He had to persevere. He had no choice. He bit his lip. He was coward enough to be afraid. It might be a long and tortuous route to the grail.

He had to get some sleep. Stephan rolled onto his back. Damn the Van Helsing girl! She brought on these memories. *The Daughters were right,* he told himself. They had increased his power, no matter how painfully. They had forged him into a tool to serve his kind. Not the best tool, but they had worked with such flawed material. They at least showed him the way to earn redemption. He thanked them for that. No matter how badly it ended.

He couldn't think about that. *Tuatha, denon, reheldra, sithfren,* he murmured to himself. He couldn't think about the Van Helsing girl. *Sithfren, hondrelo, frondura, denai.* There. He had control now. Better. Blank was better.

Eight

Stephan awoke as the sun set. He had slept like the dead, exhausted from his ordeal at the hunting lodge and the memories of his training at Mirso. The sweat of remembrance had dried on his body. He was himself again, however inadequate that was. He heaved himself up on one elbow. Kilkenny's army would be coming for him. The one who got away last night would bring Kilkenny himself, if he was lucky. How long? It depended on how far Kilkenny was from Cheddar Gorge. The North? Scotland? Ireland? A week at the least, perhaps more. That would give him time to recover fully from his ordeal. He must find blood tonight, perhaps from several sources since he would take only a little from each.

His thoughts strayed to the Van Helsing girl. They would have found her and called a doctor by now. Had she spoken to anyone of what she had seen? Was she still unconscious? What would the doctor say was wrong with her? That still puzzled him.

He sat up. He wanted to know.

Whatever he told himself last night, it was his fault she was ill. More suffering to be laid at his door. It was his fate to atone, to try, however vainly, to correct the wrongs he had wrought. Besides, if she had wakened he could compel her to believe what she had seen had all been a dream. In her weakened state, that would be easy.

He dressed hastily, shrugging on his coat and tying his cravat with careless fingers. He ran his hands through his hair but did not shave. Then he swirled his cape around his shoulders even as he drew the power and the darkness whirled up around him.

Stephan suppressed the grunt of pain as he flickered into the shadows of the great front portico at Maitlands. A man with luxuriant sideburns and a medical bag was just climbing into a carriage on the drive. The carriage door snapped shut and the driver Stephan had seen at the tavern flicked his whip over the horses' heads. They crunched forward through the gravel. He thought briefly about snapping into the seat beside the doctor, questioning him, using his power of compulsion to make the man forget.

Not wise. What if the doctor had a strong mind? In strong minds, sometimes a stray memory or some remnant of fear and suspicion lingered. No. He must let the doctor go. There were other ways to get the information he wanted.

He turned his attention to the house. Lamps glowed out into the darkening gloom of an early twilight. Clouds threatened rain. Farther down, the empty Gothic arches of the ruined section stared blindly out across the rolling lawns that gave onto a small lake, ruffled by the wind of the approaching storm. The water was empty of ducks now. Above him, he saw a shadow moving in a second-floor room in the right wing. Only a dim glow could be seen in Miss Van Helsing's childish domain on the fourth floor. Why did a grown woman inhabit a nursery? He slid along the house, silent in the night, his ears pricked for sound. Around the side was another long wing, this a more modern addition. The house was built in an L-shape. At the back were the kitchens. He heard clattering, sobbing.

Peering in at a window, he saw the older woman in the mobcap crying into her apron, her shoulders heaving. Stephan's heart dropped. Had the girl died? A dour-faced, middle-aged man dressed in slightly old-fashioned livery thumped her on the back.

"There, there, Mrs. Simpson. The doctor hasn't said there isn't any hope."

Stephan breathed again. She wasn't dead. But it didn't sound good.

The woman wailed anew. "An unfortunate turn of phrase," the man acknowledged.

"So still she is. It's like she's dead already."

"Coma. The doctor told Mr. Van Helsing she's in a coma."

"What's that? And when will she wake up?"

"I don't know," the man admitted. "Mrs. Creevy said nobody knows."

"And . . . and that devil saying we can't have anyone in to stay with her . . ." she hiccuped.

The man's face darkened. "He can't say anything of the sort. He's not master here."

"Yet!" the woman hissed. "Mark my words, Mr. Polsham, with Lord B. laid by the heels, and now Miss Van Helsing in such a bad way, he'll be calling the shots, sure as sugar is sweet."

"Mr. Brandywine will have something to say to that." But Polsham didn't sound certain.

"He's only Lord B.'s steward. He ain't here every day. And that creature saying, since he's her cousin he's the only relation she has living 'cept Lord B. . . ." she trailed off unhappily.

"I'll speak with him," Polsham said grimly. He handed her a handkerchief. "Don't you worry, Mrs. Simpson."

Mrs. Simpson took the handkerchief gratefully and blew her nose. "When I think . . ."—her sobs overtook her again and her voice cycled into a throttled squeak—"that she might wake up with no one there . . ."

"Do you need my support just now, or . . . ?"

"Go!" She motioned him with her free hand as she held his handkerchief to her mouth. "He's in the library."

Polsham gave her shoulder a final pat and strode off resolutely. Stephan melted into the full dark and listened to the footsteps retreating. He remembered the conversations in the tavern. The villagers thought this Van Helsing cousin was angling to marry the girl, in spite of the fact that she was generally thought to be crazy or a witch. The servants were obviously distraught at any thought of change, but it wasn't as if the cousin could actually make trouble. *It's not my concern in any case,* he told himself and pushed down the uneasy feeling in his gut. He had no business with feelings of any kind. The wind had risen further. It plucked at his hair. He glided around the end of the wing. A room shone light into the garden from the main portion of the house. The floor-to-ceiling bookshelves were clearly visible.

A plump young man stared into the fire, a glass of whiskey in one hand. His features had a dissolute look. The combination of protuberant eyes and a loose, wet mouth was particularly unattractive. He was dressed in the height of style, rather too high as a matter of fact. The padded shoulders of his coat, added to the fat he carried and height of his neckcloth, made him rather ridiculous. But there was an air of debauchery about him and a hard look in his eyes that was anything but comical. Stephan saw no resemblance to his beautiful cousin upstairs. Still he knew this creature's kind. They were constantly disappointed that the world didn't seem to know it owed them whatever they coveted. He'd wager there was a string of ruined women and broken men who had bought into some one of his schemes behind this one. Stephan didn't like the look of him at all.

Van Helsing downed the whiskey, and Stephan could see his hands shake. He seemed afraid of something. He started visibly as Polsham knocked and then entered.

"What is it? Dinner?" the cousin snapped, when he realized it was only Polsham.

"Shortly, sir." Polsham inclined his head to acknowledge the question, but the man's back was stiff with purpose. "I wanted to speak with you, sir."

Van Helsing's eyes narrowed. "About what?"

Polsham hesitated, but he mustered his courage and continued. "We . . . Mrs. Simpson and I . . . we thought someone should sit with Miss Van Helsing in case she wakes."

"Oh, you did, did you?"

His tone was belittling. Of course one like him had a mean streak.

"And who did you think would sit with her? Me?"

Polsham cleared his throat. "No, sir. That would not be seemly."

"You, then? I hear the cook's assistant has been bundled off and the footman gave notice this morning."

Polsham colored. "We could get a girl from the village—"

"As far as I can see, no one within a hundred miles of this place would come here, regardless of the pay, after what she did down at the tavern yesterday."

That was a facer for Polsham. He looked around blankly, trying to think of someone.

Van Helsing took a swig of the whiskey. "She's a loon, or worse. And let's not forget that she might be a murderer. You've already got the only idiot who would come to this house sitting up with your master." He topped off his glass from the decanter at the sideboard. "Likes her gin, but then, we can't be choosy."

"Mrs. Simpson—"

"Is the cook. She's busy. Especially now that she has no help, thanks to my cousin's interference." He took a gulp of whiskey. "Have the Creevy woman look in on Ann during the day. Mrs. Simpson can sit up with her at night. As long as it doesn't interfere with her duties."

Polsham looked grim. "I'll tell her, sir." He turned to go.

"Polsham!"

The man turned back. "Sir?"

"I want no one let in to this place. No, strangers, do you understand?"

"You said yourself no one would come here, sir." Polsham's voice was flat.

Van Helsing grimaced. "Just do it," he said impatiently. "You may go."

Polsham stumped out of the room. Van Helsing gulped the rest of his whiskey, turned back to the fire, and pushed at a log with his booted foot. Sparks fled into the chimney in a rush. His face was weak, but his expression was malevolent. He would be like a whipped dog who bit out of fear. Stephan suddenly did not like this Van Helsing having the ordering of the household. The servants were right to be worried.

Van Helsing straightened. Slowly, he turned toward the great windows that looked out on the manicured gardens where Stephan stood. Stephan melted into the shadows at the side of the window. Van Helsing frowned and walked to the window. All he would be able to see was black night and rushing wind through the trees.

Van Helsing's eyes widened in shock. His gaze darted over the landscape. Then he backed away from the windows. The cut-glass tumbler dropped to the rug, spilling its contents across the Aubusson carpet's arabesques.

The man knew Stephan was here. There was no question about it. How? And Van Helsing was afraid. "Polsham!" he yelled, then ran to the draperies and unhooked the silken tassels that held them back. As though that would keep Stephan out if he wanted to get in.

Did Van Helsing sense his vibrations? Why would that make him afraid? He couldn't know what they meant. Perhaps he got the sensitivity his cousin had at third remove. He didn't know what he was frightened of, but felt suspicious and uneasy.

Stephan slipped into the garden as a few random drops of rain began to fall. Damn! There were all sorts of things going on in this house. He took refuge under a huge old fir tree and stared up at the fourth floor with the dim light flickering in a single dormer window. The girl was in a coma. He tried to remember what he knew about comas. They could last a day or forever. He thought of her up there, small in her tiny bed, alone, dead to the world because she tried to help him. Somewhere thunder echoed.

None of his business. A distraction to his purpose here. He had enough guilt without adding this to his plate. Weren't his sins against his kind more important than whatever happened to a single slip of a girl?

If only the uncle weren't sick. With only servants to care about her . . . They couldn't protect her. And Van Helsing was right. No one in the village would come here.

Mrs. Simpson's fear that she would wake alone and frightened echoed in his mind.

Maybe it wasn't that bad. These people were just wrought up. The uncle would surely recover soon. Then he could take his place as her guardian. He would know how to get someone to attend to her. Or Mrs. Creevy . . . perhaps she was capable.

He clenched his jaw. He had his purpose. It wasn't to interfere with the domestic trials of people he didn't even know.

But he had to wait for Kilkenny. His purpose couldn't be executed at the moment. He paced beneath the heavy roof of needles under the tree. The scent of pine and damp air was pervasive. As if to echo the chaos of his thoughts, the world was outlined in white light. Thunder followed at the count of two. The clouds took that as their cue and rain spattered the garden in great drops. The wind made it gust against the house in flapping curtains.

Loki and Hel! He stared at the lighted room on the second floor. Van Helsing might know he was in the house. But Stephan wanted to assure himself that someone competent was there to at least supervise the girl's care. He'd just see about this woman, Creevy.

The room was lit by only two candles, one by the bed, and another by the chair. Stephan now stood in the shadows near the dressing room as the darkness drained away. The woman sitting in the chair hummed to herself as she crocheted some interminable and indeterminate item of mouse-colored wool. Her mouth had the sunken look of those who had lost their teeth. Her mobcap was not overly clean or starched. There was a glass of . . . gin—he could smell it—next to her on a small table. He glanced to the bed. The creature lying there bore little resemblance to the oversized, well-padded man he had seen in the forest. Oh, he was still large, but his flesh seemed loose, as though the tension of life that had held him together was dissipating. The effect was heightened by the grayish color of his skin. Stephan had seen that color before. It was the look of death, not necessarily imminent but inevitable. He seemed to doze.

A knock sounded on the door. Stephan stepped back into the deeper shadows.

Polsham stepped into the room. He glanced to the bed and then away, resignation clear in his expression. "Mrs. Creevy," he whispered. "A word?"

"No need to whisper, Mr. Polsham. 'E cain't 'ear you

when 'e's sunk so low. Twilight brings it on. Always does."
Her voice was a grating caw.

"You were there when the doctor made his diagnosis of
Miss Van Helsing?"

"Coma," she said, nodding sagely. "She mayn't never
wake up."

"But she *could* wake . . ." Polsham held to hope. Stephan
liked him for that.

Mrs. Creevy made a tsking noise and shook her head.
"Doubtful, that."

"Well," Polsham said, straightening. "She will require
care."

Mrs. Creevy raised her brows, incredulous. "Don't think
you can foist 'er on me! I got me 'ands full with this un." She
gestured to the bed.

"Surely he can't take your attention every moment," Polsham reasoned.

"An' if I rests my bones between bouts o' physical labor,
that's only proper, that. He's big, and when 'e needs 'elp hits
all I can do to drag' im about. What'd you 'ave me do?"

"Well." Polsham cleared his throat. "Miss Van Helsing
would not take much effort. She's such a tiny thing. Not like
her uncle at all. Between the times he might need you . . ."

A sly look came into the woman's eyes. "I expect I could
look in on her a couple times a day for double the pay," she
proposed.

Polsham froze for a moment before he said stiffly,
"Mr. Brandywine will oblige you."

"Well, I sees Brandywine before I sets a finger to 'er. You
got to get somebody else for nights." She sniffed.

Polsham looked grim. "I take it you couldn't convince
one of your friends . . ."

Mrs. Creevy looked at him as though he had gone mad.
"To this 'ouse?" Then she chuckled. "Alays one for a jest,
you are, Mr. Polsham."

"I'll send for Mr. Brandywine first thing in the morning."
Polsham turned on his heel and shut the door behind him.

Stephan frowned in the dark beyond the window. He had
thought to make this woman sit with the girl at night using
his power of suggestion. But would a greedy alcoholic be of
any use to her? He hated to think of her rough hands tending
to the girl's needs even once or twice a day! Polsham would
be reduced to convincing an exhausted cook to sit with her at
night. Mrs. Simpson would be asleep in minutes. Did not
people in comas sometimes have trouble breathing? Who
would watch and clear her throat if need be in the wee hours
of the night?

Stephan drew the darkness and reappeared under his tree.
It was raining steadily now. The wind shook sheets of rain-
drops to spatter over the lake and the lawns. The dim light of
the fourth floor glowed through the haze of water in the air.
He shouldn't get involved. What could he do for her? What
business had he in this house? The answer was clearly "none."
Her debauched cousin might sense his presence. He should
get back to the Hammer and Anvil.

He paced through the needles that carpeted the ground.
He was a match for her cousin. That one, for all his casual
cruelty, had a weak mind.

What was he thinking? *Damned girl! How could she be
in some cursed coma or other, with no one to watch over
her?* Stephan leaned his back against the great trunk of the
tree.

Damn.

He drew the darkness, saw the world of rain and the scent
of evergreen go red, waited for the moment of pain . . . And
he materialized inside the nursery on the fourth floor.

He'd just check on her before he went back to the tavern.

The room was dim, lighted by a single candle at her bedside. She looked like one of those marble figures carved in
stone atop their coffins, tiny, as befitted people of bygone

centuries, remote, her skin as white and smooth as marble. Her blonde lashes, three shades darker than her hair, brushed her impossibly pale cheeks. Her lips had once been blushing rose, but now they too were almost colorless.

His fault. It would be hours before Mrs. Simpson would come up from making and serving dinner. Perhaps he could just sit with the girl a while. He'd hear Mrs. Simpson coming up the stairs long before she got here. He could hide . . . where? He glanced around the room. Dressing room off to the side. Why didn't the girl have even a dresser or a maid-servant?

Then there was the problem of Van Helsing. The dissolute cousin might barge in if he sensed Stephan's presence. Stephan went still and listened to all the sounds in the house. Polsham and Mrs. Simpson in the far kitchen wing wrangled about what to do. Mrs. Creevy was snoring. He heard the clink of a glass from the general direction of the library and footsteps pacing on carpet. Van Helsing's sensibility apparently had limits. Stephan vowed to keep one ear tuned to the library.

He sat on the bed, half expecting the girl to waken. She did not. His fault. He had the urge to take her hand and chafe it lightly in his own. Wasn't that what one did with sick people one wanted to rouse? But there was a real chance that touching him had landed her in this predicament in the first place.

So he sat, willing her to waken, waiting for . . . what? Mrs. Simpson? A miracle? Confirmation of his guilt?

Mrs. Simpson snored over her book in a wing chair in the corner by the nursery wardrobe. She would not wake until morning unless Stephan lifted the gentle compulsion urging her to sleep. Van Helsing slumbered in an alcoholic stupor in his room. He had been hard to subdue, distraught as he was.

He was definitely upset about something. Dawn was still far away. Stephan sat on the bed watching the girl's chest rise and fall. He felt trapped like an insect in amber with time standing still around him.

The mess at the hunting lodge would be discovered sooner or later and the hunt would begin for the perpetrator. As a stranger in town he could expect questioning. Nothing he couldn't handle of course, but his life was complicated by the fact that he had to stay in the village if he wanted to be certain of meeting Kilkenny.

Kilkenny. Stephan's thoughts drifted from the innocent face of the girl. Asharti herself was dead by horrible means, but she had left her seeds behind. Kilkenny. What did he look like? Would Stephan know him instantly for the powerful force that threatened the world? Irish. The name was Irish. Red hair? A dusting of freckles and blue eyes? Would his expression be sly and debauched like Van Helsing's or hard and confident, announcing his plan to rule the world?

He ran his hands through his hair. Soon the guilt would end. Kilkenny would come with his army. Stephan would successfully summon his power and kill them, including Kilkenny, or he would fail and die at their hands. Death would not be unwelcome.

But if he failed, the world would be forfeit. Kilkenny's army would grow. The balance of human and vampire would be destroyed. Humans would be cattle, used for their blood, at least until there were too many vampires and both races ceased to exist. Armageddon. The Book of Revelations made real. If he failed there would be no atonement. A vision of Hell as an endless training by the Daughters in the bowels of Mirso flashed into his brain.

He had to get them all. He'd have to find blood soon, and make time to practice his focus. He must be able to draw his power up more quickly, and make the leap to that more potent level where accomplishing the task set him would be possible. He had to do better than he had at the hunting lodge. Emotions must be banished.

His body felt heavy, weighted down with the immensity of the task ahead. Yet, was it really the grand sorrows that ate at your soul or the small disappointments nibbling away at your expectations and your idealism that finally broke you?

Stephan rolled his head. Idealism . . . He had left that behind when his experiment with Beatrix and Asharti went awry. How naïve could one be? He had thought it was only the traumatic experience of being made that sometimes seduced made vampires to violence and madness. He had thought he could convince Rubius and the Elders to change the Rules.

He picked Asharti to prove his point. More fool he.

He had begun to pay for his crime two years ago, if any penance could ever atone.

MIRSO MONASTERY, SEPTEMBER 1819

Stephan sat naked on the bench staring at the walls, nearly numb. The room was hewn out of solid rock. The builders of this secret prison in the bowels of Mirso had not bothered to smooth them. The tapestries could not camouflage the rough surface. It poked through between them, around them. It was evident even under them. What hands had stitched those myriad threads? The tapestries showed stately men on horses, frozen in an eternal prancing gait, following packs of slavering hounds. The hounds tore at a deer who thrashed under their fangs.

In the corner of the room the rock was stained as though blackened by smoke. The stone appeared shiny. What had happened there? He rose, drawn by curiosity, and touched the sooty surface. It felt almost greasy. Pulling up the edge of the tapestry, he saw that it was rather a large stain. He followed it up and saw a spray of darkness he had not noticed on the dim ceiling through the shadows. On the floor, the stone seemed almost to be melted into a pool of black translucence. Could a simple fire have caused such intense heat? And what made the stone feel greasy? He turned to the hearth. The fire had gone out long ago. Somewhere it was daylight, but not here. The room was chilly now. A stack of split oak logs sat next to the andirons. He could build a fire, but the last thing he wanted was heat.

Awareness claimed him in a burst of recognition. He had let last night happen. Shame washed over him. Was he so easily lured to lust? How many times had he pleasured them? He lost count. His cock had been roused again and again, even if he didn't match them orgasm for orgasm. They were insatiable. But he? He was demoralized by despair and by guilt. That made it easy to lose himself in the transformation of physical pleasure. He should have had more spine.

But surely it was over. Last night would have quenched any thirst they might have for sex. They would leave him alone now. Wouldn't they? He wanted to start his training. The real training, not what had happened last night. The last numbness faded. Words from last night echoed in his mind. Obey. Eagerly. Highly sexed. Control. Punished. Banished. Sexual energy. Increased. Suppression. *The words crowded together into new combinations of meaning.*

That was what Rubius had said. "We all have the power in us. It must be drawn out. If you suppress that energy, it increases your power . . . Learn my daughters' lessons."

An awful realization drenched him. Rubius meant sexual energy. Last night was not an aberration. His daughters' lessons would use sexual energy, increase it, teach him to suppress it, use it to become Rubius's killing machine? He inhaled a raw breath.

In the corridor outside he heard steps. Several men approached. They carried something awkward. He smelled beef and charred vegetables and the yeasty scent of ale. The bolt at the door was drawn back. With a shock, Stephan recognized the monk who appeared at the door.

Brother Flavio glanced at Stephan and motioned to those who followed him. They carried in a tub, which they set in front of the fireplace, and went directly to build a fire. A line of monks trailed in with buckets of steaming water in either hand. They poured the hot water into the tub and turned to leave. One laid a towel over the side. The last in line had a plate piled high with food and a tankard. None of them took notice of Stephan's nakedness.

Brother Flavio said nothing to him. His eyes did not meet Stephan's. The monk's long nose and narrow face, his prim mouth and kind, dark eyes were as familiar to Stephan as his own. Of course they were. This was the man who had been his caretaker, his tutor at Mirso, as near as he had ever had to a father during the time he had grown to the point of manhood where all aging stopped so many centuries ago. Stephan watched the others go. Brother Flavio arranged the plates. In a moment he would finish. Stephan couldn't let Flavio walk out without some signal, even if it was only recognition.

"Brother Flavio, do you not know me?" His voice was raw.

Flavio still did not look at him. "I know you, boy."

Stephan looked up at him. His eyes felt raw from lack of sleep. He had frolicked in this man's wake as Flavio tended the monastery's flock of geese. He had provoked Flavio's smiles by teasing and pulling on the cord that tied the monk's robe. There was no smile now, only judgment. He was a criminal to Flavio, to his kind. And to himself.

"You are ashamed of me."

Flavio's shoulders sank. Stephan knew that it was true. "But you will make me proud again," he whispered. "You can still redeem your sins."

Stephan's throat constricted around any response he might have made.

Flavio straightened. He fished in the pocket of his habit and produced a bar of soap. "Eat and wash," he ordered, submerging into the role of servant/guard once more. "They will be here soon."

In fact, Stephan could feel the sun setting. He looked down at the soap. The strong scent of lye permeated the room, mixing with the smell of pitch oozing from logs in the fire and the scents of olive oil, cooked meat, and ripe fruit from the food. Flavio turned and hurried out as if afraid that he had already given the Penitent too much solace.

Stephan took a breath. In some ways this was more a moment of decision than his commitment to Rubius last night. Now he could guess the fearful road ahead. The weight on his shoulders of Flavio's judgment and his own was earned. The prospect of bathing and eating to make himself ready for them was unbearable. Would he refuse the only way back?

He wanted death.

But they would not reward him with death. Death was not atonement.

The steam of the bath filled the air and lay heavy in his lungs. It made the room feel claustrophobic.

Atonement was doing what was unbearable.

He raised his head, with effort. He stood, soap in his hand, and stepped into the bath.

Stephan jerked his head up at Mrs. Simpson's snort as she settled herself more comfortably in the chair. There was no point in dwelling on these memories. In fact, the emotions they raised in him told him that even now his training was not complete. He must push them down, concentrate on what his purpose was.

The candles guttered. It must be close to dawn. He blew them out. In the dark, the girl's small form looked even more vulnerable, more isolated. He glanced over to Mrs. Simpson. She would not be able to watch over Miss Van Helsing. What did it matter? The girl was in a state only once removed from death. And he had his mission. He would wait in his room at the tavern, preparing with chants and meditation. He had no obligation here. He was obligated to Rubius and his daughters who had worked so hard to make him what he was. He was obligated to his kind and their future, and his own future of refuge at Mirso.

He watched Mrs. Simpson's head nod onto her chest.

It would not do. He took a breath and let it out, realizing what he intended.

Then he went to stand in front of the old woman. He raised his power just enough to make the room go red, and shook her shoulder. She gasped awake and looked around, frightened. But as she fixed her gaze on him, he had her. The fear drained away.

"You do not need to sit with her. She sleeps the night through," he said, his voice low, commanding.

She nodded.

"You and Mrs. Creevy will see to her needs during the day." He watched her nod again. "Now go to bed, good woman."

Mrs. Simpson rose and tottered to the door. She came to herself and let herself out, murmuring, "She's all right. She's sleeping the night through. I'll just to bed now."

Stephan drew the wing chair up to the bedside and sat down. He would stay just a while more. And he'd be back tomorrow night. He wasn't becoming involved. That might lead to emotion. It was just something to do until Kilkenny came for him.

Nine

The shouting in the courtyard of the tavern woke him. Stephan's eyes snapped open. It was nearly sunset. He was stronger today. He had fed near dawn twice. The fulsome widow and the maidenly girl had both been rewarded with sensual dreams to take the place of their memory.

"Murders," a man yelled. "They's been murders!"

"What? What's that you say?" This was a chorus of voices.

"T-t-terrible," someone else stuttered. This one sounded young. Stephan got up and went to the window. So, they had found the horror he had left behind at the hunting lodge. He cracked the draperies and pushed the shutters out just enough to reveal the scene below. Ostlers and denizens of the taproom crowded around a boy of perhaps sixteen. An older man with gray hair and a ruddy complexion climbed down from a cart pulled by an unassuming horse.

"Van Helsing had Dick here deliver supplies to Bucklands Lodge."

Unfortunate that it was a boy who had come upon that

gruesome scene. The lad looked pale unto death. Stephan
knew he would be haunted by his discovery for the rest of
his short life.

"What is it, boy? What did you find? Murder, you say?"
The crowd was growing.

"Blood." The boy's eyes were saucers. "Heads . . . and
great gobbets of . . ." His voice slid up the scale, until he
broke off and buried his head in his hands, sobbing. The
older man put his arms around the thin, shaking shoulders.

"Now, Dick, it don't do no good to dwell on it." His own
voice was unsteady.

"Did you see it, Will?" the proprietor of the tavern asked
sternly, coming out to the yard and wiping his hands on his
apron. "Or did the boy get foxed last night, and start seein'
things?"

"Oh, it were real, all right," Will replied. "Dick come to get
me. Somebody got tore limb from limb. Several somebodies."

The crowd went silent.

"What could do that?" the proprietor asked quietly. "Tear
men limb from limb?"

"An animal . . ." Will said into the silence. But he didn't
sound certain.

"Who was it in the hunting box?" This from a tall, hawk-
faced man in work clothes.

Will shook his head. "Mayhap someone at Maitlands
would know."

Stephan grimaced. They might know who the men pur-
ported to be but not who they really were. The proprietor of
the tavern shouldered his way to the front of the crowd.

"Will, take Dick over to the squire's. Tell him I'm getting
a party of men up to go down there. He'll want to send to
Bow Street for the runners, I expect."

"Runners don't hunt animals, Mr. Watkins," a man
Stephan recognized as Jemmy said plaintively.

The proprietor, Watkins, looked grim. "An' if it turns out

it's animals, we'll thank 'em kindly and let 'em go home to London."

Unexpected that they'd send to London for help. But of course anything like this was far outside the provincial experience of a small town. Two days to get here if they came immediately. One up to London, and one back. They'd certainly be here before Kilkenny. There was no evidence to link him to the murders. Inquiries would be inconvenient, nothing more. Still, he was an outsider. If Bow Street runners acted without proof it could be inconvenient.

He felt the sun set. He needed to feed again to keep his strength up. He'd search out Pillinger. The young agent could more than spare a pint or so. Then, Maitlands Abbey called.

There was really no reason to be here. The budding branches clacked above him in the March wind. The lights of Maitlands Abbey's south façade winked at him across the wide swath of lawn. It was growing a bit rough in places. Apparently the place could not keep gardeners, either. The library blazed with light. A glow from the back said the kitchens were occupied. And one window on the fourth floor glimmered faintly. Maybe she had wakened. Perhaps she merely slept in her narrow bed with a candle at her side.

Why had he convinced Mrs. Simpson not to sit with the girl? It didn't matter. He had. He gritted his teeth. He could feel the tug from across the lawns. She drew him to her side.

The Harrier, implacable executioner of the Elders' will, was steadfast. He *would* be steadfast to his purpose. But in the meantime, he would keep the commitment he had made to watch over her. That was who he was. He drew the power, felt the wash of pain, and blinked into awareness in the darkness of her dressing room.

He peered into her room and received a shock. She lay,

pale and still, in the child's bed. Over her hung a shadow. It was Van Helsing. Stephan slipped back into the shadows. Van Helsing came to himself and looked around. Fear grew in his eyes. So, he must be feeling Stephan's vibrations, just beyond the edge of his senses. Well, let him feel this. Stephan ramped up his power. The room went red. He murmured, "You don't feel anything." Then he let his Companion slide back down his veins. Van Helsing shook his head. His attention returned to the fragile, insensate figure of the girl. He bent and lifted the corner of her coverlet.

"Oh, ho . . ." he whispered. "What have we here?" He threw back the coverlet.

The women had changed her shift. The worn but fine linen that covered her body was as thin as cobwebs. Stephan could see the outline of her breasts, the shadow of her nipples. Van Helsing cupped her right breast and thumbed her nipple through the cloth. His soft, plump hands caressing her skin made Stephan's flesh crawl. He clenched himself shut. No emotion. He chanced control of weaker minds only to protect himself. This was not his business.

Van Helsing's hand strayed to her throat, caressed her jaw, fingered her still lips. "Wake up, my delectable loon . . ." he whispered. "Do you not want to give me a kiss?" She lay silent, her thick lashes fringing her cheek.

Van Helsing chuffed his disappointment and flicked at her cheek with his finger. "You'll be doing your wifely duty soon enough, once you wake up." She offered no response. He smiled and straightened. Stephan hated that smile. "You'll spread your legs and your backside, too, my loon. I'll bet your anus is smooth and tight. I'll have to lubricate your back passage with your blood or my seed." The smile grew into a grin. Stephan could see that he'd gotten an erection. "Any I have left after you've sucked me." He bent as though to lift the hem of her shift.

The surge of power cascaded over Van Helsing and made

him gasp. His face went blank. Stephan was shaking in the darkness. "I have to go," Van Helsing muttered, coming to himself. He frowned and turned on his heel, leaving her uncovered.

The moment the door had slammed behind him, Stephan lurched from his hiding place. His Companion healed the half-moons of blood on his palms left by his nails almost instantly. He strode across the room and pulled the quilt up over her. Anger churned in his belly as he sat beside her. The coward! He dared to disrespect her when she could not defend herself? Thank God, she would never agree to marry *this* vile worm, not if she was the woman he suspected she was. This creature would hurt even a normal woman, just for the pleasure of being cruel. But for one afraid of touch, Van Helsing's idea of conjugal relations would be hell. The fear this girl had lived with all her life seemed very real to him at that moment. It had taken incredible spirit to live with fear like that.

Stephan sucked in air and stilled himself. He closed his eyes and let the familiar words wash through his mind as he sat down beside her. *Tuatha, denon, reheldra, sithfren.* He called the calm and control of the chants to suffuse him. Van Helsing was nothing to him. She was nothing. He opened his eyes, and his gaze filled with her. She was fragile, and so helpless. She deserved protection.

Stephan resolved to get to her nursery just at twilight tomorrow. He wouldn't bother to conceal his vibrations. Let's see if the brute wanted to stay and touch the girl then. Stephan wagered he could chase him from the room in seconds.

A horse pranced and whinnied on the gravel drive. He heard Van Helsing's voice.

"I'll be back with the runners."

So, he was the one going up to London after the runners. Good. He'd be gone for at least a couple of days. He couldn't be allowed to soil Miss Van Helsing with his unclean needs.

Ahhh, but what was churning up through Stephan's own loins even now? He felt her thigh against his hip, warm under the coverlet. Was he any better than Van Helsing? Their kind was far more highly sexed than humans to begin with, and after his training . . . He pressed down an incipient erection. He was good at that. It was the legacy of the Daughters . . .

MIRSO MONASTERY, DECEMBER 1819

Stephan sat naked on one of the chaise longues, waiting. The room was warm again. His body was dry. They would be here soon, he was sure. He tried to take comfort in the fact that they could not possibly use him as they had last night. Anyone would be satiated from such a session. Nevertheless, he strained to hear steps in the corridor, his muscles tensed. He stared at the strange stain in the corner of the room and waited.

The sounds were faint when they finally came. A shushing. The crackle of a torch. But he knew what it was. Bare feet against stone. They were accompanied by vibrations so old as to be nearly beyond sensation. So he was not surprised when the iron bar thunked open and the heavy oaken door swung inward.

Deirdre entered first, of course, tall and willow-lithe, dressed in black again; a loose silken fabric gathered at her waist and rippling about her ankles. She was followed by Estancia, her figure straining at the red of her own deeply décolleté gown. Freya was last. She put the torch in a holder in the corridor. She was wearing white, her well-muscled body taut as a bow string. Their dark eyes and pale skin, a certain wide shape to their mouths, proclaimed their relationship. Stephan felt a small worm of fear in his bowels. If not sex tonight, what?

"What are you doing sitting in our place?" Deirdre's voice was crisp and hard.

"Your place?" That, of anything she might have said, was not what he expected.

She took two strides and slapped him. His head snapped to the side. In shock, he surged to his feet. He felt her power ramp up. Red shone in her eyes.

"Dee, he doesn't know what's required." Freya grabbed her sister's arm. "He needs education, that is all." The red drained slowly from Deirdre's eyes. She turned away abruptly.

"Tell him, then," she rasped. She went over to the sideboard and selected a peach from Mirso's hothouse. Grapes, peaches, plums were heaped in summer bounty, glowing in the firelight. Estancia circled him, rubbing her breasts against him like a cat. Deirdre bit into her peach. The juice ran down her chin.

Freya sat in the offending chair and motioned to a place beside her on the carpet. She smiled. Stephan had himself in hand now. He approached and knelt. Estancia followed.

"You are a Penitent," Freya began. Her voice was kind. Estancia began running her fingers through his damp hair. "That means there can be no challenges from you. You do not speak unless asked a direct question. And when asked, you answer humbly and straightforwardly with eyes downcast. You indicate your gratitude for our training and attention by complying eagerly with all instructions, no matter how difficult for you."

"We can force you, of course." Estancia knotted her fist in his hair and pulled his head up to look at her. She too smiled. It was not kind.

"Stephan does not need forcing. He needs instruction," Freya corrected. "Stancie, let him go." Estancia unclenched her fingers and ran them once more through his hair. He bowed his head. "You may sit on the bench, or on the carpets.

*You will kneel in our presence. In our absence you may re-
lieve yourself in the chamber pot as you require, but when we
are here, you must ask permission. In our absence you may
stoke the fire. That is allowed. But you must never touch
yourself."* Here she looked sad. *"Do you understand?"*

*He nodded. "I understand." Could he do this? Had he
any choice at this point?*

"Tell him about the training," Estancia prompted.

*Freya looked at Deirdre for confirmation before pro-
ceeding. Deirdre had come to stand over them, watching as
she finished her peach. "I'm not sure you realize this, but
the Companion blesses our kind with much more sexual
drive than humans. Our partner's urge to life is uniquely
linked with its power, and expressed in sexual form. The key
to increasing our power is to stimulate our sexuality. That
is what we are about here. You will be subjected to intense
sexual stimulation without release. This will be alternated
with milking to strip you of your juices. The regimen will
increase your potency and you will experience an increase
in power. As you become even more highly sexed, the periods of restricted release will become shorter."*

*Stephan's stomach churned. Horror! What kind of train-
ing was this? The blues and reds of the pattern in the carpet
seemed to swirl together.*

"Tell him about the next phase—"

*"No," Deirdre interrupted. "Enough. He knows what is
required of him. No more is needed." She threw her peach pit
into the fire. "Get to your bench."*

*He could not move until the room and the carpet stopped
writhing.*

*"Do you need compulsion?" Freya asked softly. "It is al-
lowed to ask for compulsion."*

*He shook his head and made a supreme effort to stand
and stagger over to the wide bench, more a bed than a sitting
place. Estancia followed him. He fell onto the warm stone.*

"I should go first tonight," she proclaimed, running her small, plump hands over his chest, thumbing his nipple. He was shocked to feel his loins tighten, until he realized that she had drawn a bit of her power. She was forcing his erection.

"As you will. There is time tonight for all of us," Deirdre said. "Just go slowly. Remember what happened last time."

Estancia shrugged. She bent over him, her gaze roving over his body. He felt pinned, immobilized. Her eyes glowed with more than firelight. His cock swelled in response. Her hand strayed to caress it. The touch was like fire. She cupped his balls and squeezed in gentle threat. It made him suck in his breath. Deirdre came to stand over them, watching. Estancia rubbed him just behind his balls in slow circles. He suppressed a moan. Then she pulled her skirts apart—they were split to the waist—and straddled him. She grasped his cock and put it inside her. She was slick and ready. She began to ride him, her hands pushing against his chest. Deirdre watched. He lifted his hips, thrusting into her. He burned with need. Then Estancia slowed the pace and spread her most private lips to finger her own nub of pleasure as she pushed herself up and down over his cock. It wasn't long before she was emitting little yips of ecstasy. Her contractions almost brought him off, but just as the feeling ramped up to intolerable sensation, he felt Deirdre call her power. He teetered on the edge of release . . . and did not achieve it. Estancia collapsed on his chest and rolled away with a moan, her back to the fire. He was still hard and throbbing, his chest heaving and his body covered with a light sheen of sweat. He turned his head. His eyes met Deirdre's. He knew his need showed clearly. But he didn't care.

She shrugged off her black silk garment and lay beside him, one thigh over his. She did not touch his member, no matter that he willed her to it. Instead he felt that she wanted him to suckle her. He reached for her breast and licked, then sucked. Her nipple responded to his tongue by tightening. If *possible, his need increased. Deirdre presented her other breast. He sucked eagerly. She urged him up and rolled under him. He straddled her on all fours. Estancia got to her knees and stroked the muscles in his back, and down over his buttocks. Deirdre spread her legs. His cock prodded her entrance. He felt Estancia's hand slide between his buttocks. Her thumb rubbed at his anus. Deirdre wanted him inside her. Estancia pushed him down. He entered, fully, suddenly. He thrust inside Deirdre fiercely, seeking the mutual explosion he felt was possible. Feelings ramped up past all endurance, and then Estancia pressed her thumb inside him. Deirdre drew him down. He felt caught between them, transfixed as he continued thrusting. Deirdre drew her canines and pierced the vein just under his jaw. She sucked and rocked against him as she came. He was about to join her when he felt Estancia shower him with will. Again he was stoppered like a bottle. Deirdre contracted around him. Estancia withdrew her thumb. He thought his cock would explode. The need burned him, almost crossing over into pain. Surely soon they would allow him his release. Had he not been sufficiently restrained yet?*

"Excellent," Deirdre murmured. She had not uttered a sound during the pleasure she took of him. He collapsed onto the warm stone. Estancia moved away.

"Freya," she called. "Your turn."

And so it went. When at last they were done with him, he lay on the rug, barely conscious, but still aching with need. He had not been allowed release at all.

"He did well," Freya murmured as she closed the door.

"We shall see."

Stephan took the girl's hand as though it was a lifeline to the present. *Anchor me.* He didn't want to remember those times. He wanted to remember the control they taught him in the end, but not the torturous path to achieve it. But he couldn't help it. The dim room of the nursery seemed only too like the dim room in the rock roots of Mirso, lit often only by the dying coals in the fire. Pressing the girl's hand roused him. The feeling of flesh to flesh shot down into his loins. The memories crowded in on him. He couldn't thrust them away.

They used him to exhaustion that night and many others. He wondered if they would ever allow him a release. His cock was chafed and raw, even though his bath was laden each day with soothing oils. He slept away the daylight hours as one dead. But then gradually, he had begun waking early, waiting in dread for the bath, the food, and then the Daughters to appear. With no books to distract him he spent hours staring at the black and greasy stain in the corner of the room. Sometimes the stain seemed to pulse or grow. He began to make up stories about it; that someone had thrown acid on the stone, or that someone immured here in the bowels of Mirso had tried to burn the monastery down. He wondered if the Daughters had used this room before. Perhaps there had been an occupant of this room even when he had been here as a child, never suspecting the suffering occurring beneath his feet. Over time the burning need for release grew. They forced his erection sometimes, but sometimes they didn't have to, to his shame. He wondered how long he could go on like this, and whether he was any closer to his goal.

He dropped the girl's hand, afraid that was what was bringing on the rush of memory. But it didn't work.

Those first weeks were not the worst. There was the day of his failure, for instance . . .

MIRSO MONASTERY, MARCH 1820

He woke when daylight was still strong somewhere beyond the walls. He lay like a discarded doll on the carpet. But he had an erection. How could he, after what had happened every night? He got up and splashed water from the basin on his face. The bathwater from last night was cold. Perhaps he should immerse himself and hope that would cool his heat.

Or he could take himself in hand and do what they would not. He didn't care how raw he was. He would go insane if he did not do something. He paced the room like a tiger, distracted by the throbbing in his cock. He sat abruptly on his bench, head bent, his eyes clenched shut so he could not see his erect and needing member. They had told him straight out not to do it. He wanted to obey them. He did. He wanted what they had to give him. Salvation. But would they know? If his performance tonight wasn't quite what they could wish, he would plead exhaustion.

He stood, looking around wildly. The fire was almost out. He strode around the bench, and threw some logs onto the grate, then tried to still himself as he watched a flame lick out at the oak from the coals.

Steady. Just steady yourself, he thought. The fire caught. The logs went up in conflagration. It echoed the burning inside him. His eyes filled. He fell to his knees. His cock throbbed insistently, hateful thing that it was. He grabbed it and jerked at it.

It didn't take long. His semen sizzled in the flames as he spurted. The orgasm shook him like a terrier shakes a rat to kill it. When it was done, he collapsed against the hearth.

He did not know how long it was before he roused himself. It was still light outside. He could feel that. But darkness was approaching. He got to his hands and knees.

He could smell his semen. The hearth had several dark, wet stains on it.

God above! They would be able to smell it, too. Panic took him as he looked around for something to clean it up with. They gave him no blankets. There! Under the sideboard, a napkin had been left behind when the monks cleared *the wine and tidbits away last night. He scrambled over and snatched it up. Wetting it at his basin, he scrubbed at the stains on the hearth.*

Calm yourself. *The room must always smell of sex, though he couldn't smell it himself anymore. They would not be able to distinguish this smell from the other, more general one. He needn't panic. He threw the napkin on the fire and watched it burn to ash.*

The monks with the water for his bath and his dinner were early. Brother Flavio threw open the door and looked around. He had never repeated his recognition or his confidences with Stephan. Indeed he rarely spoke. But today was different. "We're missing a napkin," *he accused.*

Stephan made a show of peering around the room. "Have you tried the corridor?" *What could they care for a silly napkin? Still, anxiety ramped up inside him.*

Flavio sniffed the air and searched the room again. His eyes rested on the hearth. Stephan saw that the place where he had scrubbed at the stone had not quite dried. Flavio turned back to Stephan. His face went closed. He motioned the monks in. They changed out the bathwater and left a tray of mutton and cabbage with a sour cream sauce. Flavio frowned and then strode out through the door. The bolt thudded into place.

Stephan dove for the bath and scrubbed himself with soap until his skin was raw. He couldn't eat his dinner, so he left it on the sideboard. He sat on his bench and waited. He could smell nothing. Their senses could not be that much more sensitive than his. Could they?

When next the door burst open, the Daughters entered, already suspicious.

"Flavio says a napkin is missing," *Deirdre charged. They sniffed the air. Deirdre smiled.* "So. You have disobeyed us."

Stephan fell from where he sat on the bench to his knees on the carpet before them.

"He lasted longer than we thought he would." Freya's voice was reasonable.

"And you didn't eat," Estancia added. It seemed a nail in his coffin. Stephan's fear ramped up. He swallowed. He only hoped his offense was not enough to warrant banishment from Mirso. How could he have succumbed?

"Inevitable, but you must still be punished." Deirdre put her hands on her hips.

Freya looked sad. She turned away and went to pour herself some wine.

"Not until dawn," Estancia pouted. "We have time for our pleasure and he must be drained, after all."

"We will not use him tonight, Stancie. Since he is so eager to spill his seed himself, we shall indulge him." Deirdre motioned to Freya. Freya brought a bowl and put it down in front of him. They stood close around him. He could feel their power humming in the air. "Grasp yourself and spill your seed in the bowl," Deirdre ordered.

He wanted to shake his head, but there was no refusing them. He took hold of his cock.

"More roughly."

He obeyed.

Time after time, they brought his erection up and bid him handle himself until he came into the bowl. The final time, there was no fluid left and the orgasm was painful. When at last they released him he collapsed onto the carpet feeling stripped and raw inside and out.

"Stancie, call for the workmen," Deirdre ordered. Estancia slid out the door.

Freya knelt beside him. She picked damp strands of hair from his forehead and smoothed them back from his temple. "Let him rest, Dee, until dawn. He will need his strength."

Stephan's spirit was exhausted as well as his body. What had happened tonight, what had been happening for months now, could not be advancing to his goal. But he had no *choice. He was trapped in an endless process. These women could make him do whatever they wanted.*

Two monks came in carrying heavy manacles. He watched dully as they fastened them to rings at each corner of the underside of the bench. They coiled on the carpet like strange metal beasts. What were they for? They couldn't hold him.

Deirdre answered his silent question. "Of course you could break them. You could use your power to translocate and escape. But you will not. These chains will act as a reminder to you of the restraint you must learn. Lie on the stone, on your back," she ordered. Stephan heaved himself onto the bench where Freya locked the manacles on wrists and ankles.

"Leave him, Freya. We will come for him at dawn."

The door thudded closed, the bar slid into place. Still, he heard them talking. "He is becoming even more highly sexed," Freya noted. "His progress is rapid."

"I agree. That means we must be even more careful to go slowly," Deirdre said.

"But Father wants him ready as soon as possible." This from Estancia, petulant.

"We can't afford another failure." Deirdre's voice was always so implacable. How could anyone disobey her?

A door in the corridor clunked shut faintly. This was progress? And what did they mean, another failure? What punishment was in store for him? He should be afraid. But that was more than he could muster. They would do what they would do. Eventually, he dozed on the warm slab. The feeling of being stripped and vulnerable slid into his dreams and created nightmares.

That was why he was easily roused. Nearly two years, in the end, before he had ridden out of Mirso Monastery as the man he was now. *Still ill-prepared,* a voice inside him whispered.

But it didn't matter. He did what was necessary. He did what he could. He was steadfast.

The girl's room around him suddenly seemed too small. There wasn't enough air in here. He couldn't sit here all night and remember Dee and Freya. Stancie, God forbid! He staggered to his feet and looked around wildly. He should leave, right now, before these memories raked his bloody soul for another instant. But leaving might not banish them. Where would he go? The cool woods so like and yet not like the forests around Mirso? The tavern with its bawdy wenches entertaining their coarse beaux? Not likely to calm his arousal.

The nursery came in to focus as he spun around. Books! There were bookshelves everywhere. That's what he needed, to lose himself in a book as he never could at Mirso. He strode toward the shelves, scanned them frantically. There was a surprising variety. And not just a nursery's school-books. History, the Greeks, French and Italian languages, Marcus Aurelius, Cicero, Hegel's *Encyclopedia of the Philosophical Sciences,* Karamzin's *History of the Russian Empire,* Savigny, Dugald Stewart, Schopenhauer, Bell's *New Idea of Anatomy of the Brain,* Davy's *Elements of Chemical Philosophy,* and the modern poets—Keats's *Endymion,* Shelley's *Prometheus Unbound,* Wordsworth's *The White Doe of Rylstone,* and most of Scott's novels of course, including his latest, *Ivanhoe . . .* Who would have thought a young girl would have read so widely? They must be hers. He picked up a volume, any volume. It happened to be a book of poetry. *Childe Harold's Pilgrimage* by George Gordon, Lord Byron. He let it fall open and read a stanza. Not bad. The poetry was energetic, lyrical, and sometimes a little more. He read a section of Canto IV:

> Oh Time! The beautifier of the dead,
> Adorner of the ruin, comforter

And only healer when the heart hath bled:
Time! The corrector where our judgments err,
The test of truth, love—sole philosopher,
For all beside are sophists—from thy thrift,
Which never loses though it does defer—
Time, the avenger! Unto thee I lift
My hands, and eyes and heart . . .

A painful smile curved his lips and he wondered how old the poet was. He guessed very young. This Byron was quite wrong about time. It neither healed nor avenged. It slowly sapped the life from you with small transgressions and large, yours and others against you, that never healed but only festered. He scanned several other passages. Forgiveness. The hero of the piece cursed those who had transgressed against him with forgiveness. Did the author mean to make a tortured hero? Stephan shook his head. The puppy didn't know what tortured was. Tortured was when you were the one who required forgiveness and no one could forgive you, even yourself. Then there was only atonement . . .

The threat of dawn crept through the window of the nursery. Stephan was exhausted with memory. He should go now. He wondered if he could bear another night sitting by the still figure who nonetheless roused him so he had to practice constant control. He tossed the Byron to the floor. Apparently books could not command his thoughts, either.

He glanced at the girl. Her lips were dry again. He wet the cloth and mopped her brow, rubbed her lips with the contents of a small jar that smelled like medicinal ointment. How long could one go without food and water? She might just waste away, never again seeing the daylight that was her birthright. That brought a sere of pain. His fault. He folded the cloth neatly, and touched her jaw once more. He shouldn't want her to recover. She might know what he was. If she did, would he have the courage to do what must be done? If she recovered, she could be the next of his failures, and another lapse would keep him out of Mirso Monastery forever. If he disposed of her, he knew the guilt would stain him even further. He closed his eyes, once.

There was another possibility. Perhaps she would remember nothing when she woke. He resolved to brave the doctor with some questions before he decided what to do. With a grim set to his lips, he called the blackness.

Ten

The townspeople of Cheddar Gorge could not stop talking about the murders. Their obsessive discussion kept him awake. He sat in a chair when tossing on his bed became oppressive. With relish or with fear, with wrath or rampant speculation, the tavern seethed all day with the subject. They suspected him, of course. He expected that.

"What is 'e doing here?" a woman hissed. "I don't believe for a minute that he's looking for a 'ouse to let."

"'E ain't been 'ere two days and Moll gets murdered, gruesome like," a man declared. "And now . . . *this.*"

"Where was he, I'd like to know." This from the proprietor, Mr. Watkins. Stephan could imagine him wiping glasses behind the bar in the taproom.

"Jest you go ask 'im," the woman laughed. Her laugh was a caw.

There was a brief silence, then the whole room erupted in laughter.

"'Course, what did he know about the hunting box? It's over to Winscombe."

" 'E coulda asked about it."

"Ask Pillinger. 'E was takin' the gent around."

"I did ask Pillinger." This from the proprietor again. "He says he didn't show him the property. No reason to. It wasn't to let."

That stopped them. But only momentarily.

"*She* knows the lodge." Stephan recognized Jemmy's reedy voice. "She owns it."

Stephan gripped the arms of the chair and leaned forward. They suspected Miss Van Helsing? As though a slip of a girl could murder four strong men!

"I hardly think she could have done what I saw down there. They sent Mrs. Stoadright in to clean it up and she fainted." Watkins shut them up. "Don't know who they'll get to mop up all the blood, and . . . and parts."

"Well," Jemmy said reluctantly. "Don't nobody know what a witch can do. Look what she did to me. Stole my soul, just about."

"Don't start putting it about you got no soul, Jemmy Minks," the woman cackled.

"His soul was so small it wan't barely a handful," another cawed.

"Doc says she's in some kinda trance. Maybe it happened when she killed 'em." Jemmy's theory was a little shaky, but he had captured his audience again.

"Maybe she 'ad 'elp. She and that stranger was nothing short o' chummy up on the mountain the night Moll snuffed it," another put in thoughtfully.

"Under what you might call 'mysterious circumstances.' "

"He's strong looking."

"And those eyes."

"He don't never come out in the daytime . . ."

"Maybe . . . maybe they done all of them—the murders, I mean—together."

"Bow Street runner'll find out . . ." the woman said

doubtfully. "I gotta go. Don't want to get murdered my own self."

This was echoed by several others. There was the shuffle of a general exodus.

"Damn it, Peg." Watkins banged a tankard on the bar. "I can't evict him until the runner gets here to back me up. But he's murdering my trade at the very least."

Stephan couldn't leave yet. But the bathwater might begin to boil around him.

MIRSO MONASTERY, MARCH 1820

*The Daughters came for him shortly after sunrise with sev-
eral monks in tow, unchained him, and to his surprise led
him outside into the corridor. He had not been out of that
room for months. The procession wound its silent way up and
up through many stone staircases. They met no one else. This
must be an unused portion of the monastery. At last they
came to a single door, and went through it into a small stone
room. Stephan was breathless from the climb. He looked
around. Was this where he was to be punished? It had comfortable chairs, books, a chess set, the usual tapestries and
carpets. And it had no windows. A good place to spend daylight hours. Very normal, except for the ladder in the corner
that led up to a hatch in the ceiling. The monks put up their
cowls. They were wearing gloves.*

*They were dressed for going out into the sun. Realization
flooded him.*

*Deirdre motioned him up the ladder. Two monks followed
him. When he came to the hatch he opened it. Dawn light almost blinded him. He covered his eyes as he was prodded
from below and stumbled up, naked, into the day.*

*He was on a tower battlement of Mirso, high above the
main monastery below. The sear of sunlight on his flesh sent*

pain scratching over his skin. Stephan peered between his fingers and saw the Carpathian Mountains, their forested shoulders night-green, falling away to the valley below. The edge of the round area where he stood was crenellated stone and in the center were two massive wooden posts with chains affixed to them.

Fear curdled in his throat. They were going to bind him here in the sun, naked. Pain from the light increased. His eyes burned, and he felt his skin redden. But this was faintest dawn. The sun would not come out from behind the mountains for hours. When it did . . .

"Get along here," the monk said, and prodded him with a staff. "We don't want to be out here any longer than we have to." Stephan staggered toward the posts. They chained him there, hand and foot, and scuttled down to the comfortable room below. He could hear the Daughters admonishing them to merge their powers and keep him from using his strength or calling his Companion. They were to change out every two hours to ensure that they didn't lose focus. Their power hummed below him. Two started a game of chess.

Stephan clenched his eyes shut against the light. But when the sun came over those mountains, there would be no defense. The worst of it was he wouldn't die. The Companion would heal him, no matter the damage. But not before he had experienced what was for his kind the ultimate torture.

Night, precious night. From somewhere far away he felt the sun set. His heart beat, his nerves sent signals to his brain, horrible as those signals were, his blood pumped. The Companion had kept him alive. Now it would begin to heal him. He had lost consciousness periodically, but when he did, the monks below came up and roused him, gave him water. He must have been quite a sight at the end, for they looked grim

*For the last couple of hours the torture slowly waned, as the
sun dipped below the mountains and could cause no more
direct damage, but the hours at midday had already taken
their toll, and their searing pain still lived in his body . . .*

*The monks came up and loosened his bonds. He could not
open his eyes. They seemed to be sealed shut. Just as well. He
didn't want to see himself.*

*"Poor bastard," one of them muttered. Their hands on his
body made him want to scream, but his throat was so raw he
had no more screams left. "What could he have done?"*

*Masturbate. He had masturbated, he wanted to shout. But
his lips wouldn't work. They pulled his arms over their shoulders, and the pain brought blackness.*

Stephan pushed the memory of his torment away. He sat in
her room on the third night, staring at her, a book open upon
his lap. The dim nursery had begun to feel like a cocoon, the
long hours of night fraught with the danger of memory, yet
insulated from the killing behind him and the terrible trial to
come when he would chance all in a single contest with evil.

He wouldn't think about any of that. He'd think about the
girl. Her face, glowing in the light of the candle, sometimes
seemed his only connection to reality in the dim swirl of
night and memory. Why did he feel he knew her, that he had
always known her? Perhaps his feeling of knowing her was
what drew him to sit here, night after night. He thought back
to the first time he had seen her in the woods. The courage of
her rueful smile, her faint air of "otherness," all made him
feel a fascination even then. But it was when he woke in the
cave that he had begun to feel . . . affinity.

He knew with a certainty he couldn't explain that she
wasn't mad. But he wanted to know exactly what had happened between her and Jemmy in the courtyard. He wanted

to know what she experienced. Most of all, he wanted to know why she was locked away inside her body now. What had happened? What had he done?

The doctor had been unable to explain what caused it or the consequences, even under Stephan's compulsion. He said a coma could come from a blow to the head, or if someone was almost suffocated, or from shock. Stephan was betting on shock in this case. But whether she would recover, whether she would remember all, or parts, or none of what she'd experienced, was unknown. The doctor said it seemed to vary patient by patient. Dr. Denton was no genius. But these were the conclusions of the various and sundry medical books he'd consulted.

Stephan flung Miss Austen's novel to the floor. Not that it was not entertaining. It was, even skilled and insightful. But the book he wanted to read was laid out before him in a coma, unreadable. He thrust his hands in his pockets and slumped in his chair.

Her situation irked him, to say the least. What awaited her if she wakened from her coma? She had no parents living else her uncle would not be her trustee. Now her guardian lay downstairs with a weak heart and a tenuous grip on life. What would happen when even this one person who cared for her was denied her? Who would shield her from the slings and arrows of outrageous fortune and superstitious hatred then?

She might need shielding from a force much more particular. Van Helsing would return tomorrow, bringing the threat of a runner for him and another threat for the girl. He could keep Van Helsing out of her room, for a while. But if she recovered? With a lout like that in the house, was she safe? Without her uncle the servants were in no position to say him nay. And then there was the fact that she was suspected, however stupidly, of murder. Stephan chewed his lips.

Only his sharp hearing would have detected the low moan.

His eyes widened in shock. Her eyelids fluttered. He dove from his chair to his knees beside her bed and began to chafe her hand. She moaned a little louder. She was waking! *Thank whatever gods you choose,* he commanded himself. He would not be spared damnation, but at least his crime against her, whatever it was, might not be irrevocable. She was about to come to consciousness.

He jerked his hands away from hers. She would not like to wake to being touched. A stranger by her side? Not reassuring. Especially one whom she had last seen covered in blood and whirling darkness. But there was no one else. And he could not let her wake alone.

He mustered what he hoped was a reassuring smile.

Ann struggled up through layers of cotton. She had been aware of a presence near her for some time. It felt good. Safe. The air was filled with excitement and an exotic, spicy scent. She thought she felt a touch. That was just a dream, of course. Any touch would be excruciating. In her dream it was the stranger who was touching her. His dark hair, burning eyes, and full lips floated before her, just behind the cotton. She remembered his strong thighs. She had never noticed men's thighs before his. She found herself idly wondering what he would look like naked. His chest would have dark curling hair. She had seen men without shirts. She would touch that thatch of hair. She had never seen more of a man than that, though. What would the rest of his body look like? The skin on his hips would be smooth under her hand . . . She would touch him . . . everywhere.

But that wasn't possible. The dream seemed to recede, but so did the cotton. She let out a little moan of protest. *Come back!* Not fair. She wanted to touch him, but he was gliding out of sight. She had to look for him. *Come back! I want to touch you.*

Well, of course she couldn't see him! She realized with a start that her eyes were closed.

She tried to open them, but they were so heavy. The spicy scent of cinnamon from her dream still wafted around her. She wanted to say something encouraging to herself, but her words stuck in her throat. Maybe she would just rest for now.

But then he would be gone.

She tried again. Her eyes opened, though they felt dry and crusted, like a rusty hinge. The familiar sloped ceiling of her nursery hovered comfortingly above her. Safe. But what about the presence she had felt? Cinnamon and the smell of something else filled the room.

With an incredible effort, she turned her head.

He was there. Of course he was. He had been here all along. Somewhere inside, she was aware of that. He looked worried and relieved all at once.

"Miss Van Helsing, thank God!" He knelt beside her bed.

She wanted to tell him that he needn't kneel. But all that came out was a breathy croak. Her mouth was so dry!

"Let me get you water," he said, rising quickly. He turned back with a cup he had filled from her pitcher. He surveyed her for an instant and then leaned over, slid his arm under her pillow and lifted her head. How thoughtful that he didn't try to touch her. He held the cup to her lips. The water coursed over lips and tongue and down her throat like a gift from God.

"Little sips," he whispered. "There will be more when you want it." He was right. Even now she was too tired to drink more. He set her cup upon the night table and laid her gently down. He looked . . . worn.

"Are you all right?" she croaked. After all . . .

The room went into a spin. After all, he had appeared out of a whirl of darkness in the cave, wounded unto death, and she had touched him trying to bandage him. And then she had felt everything about him. Everything.

Her eyes went saucer-wide. He was a vampire, who had lived what, a thousand? Two thousand years? And she had been right there with him all down the ages, whether she wanted to be or not. She only remembered pieces. But what she remembered she experienced as if she had lived the events herself. And what experience! Wars, loves, hopes, fear, killing, and . . . very recently, pain and lust and terrible guilt. Through it all, there was the blood. *The blood is the life.* He drank blood. He was a monster, a vampire!

He started at her expression. Then faint sorrow and a resignation settled like weights upon his shoulders. They sagged. "I . . . am not like you. You remember that. But you need not fear. I will not hurt you, or anyone in the house. I will go to get Mrs. Simpson . . ." He turned away.

"Wait," she croaked. Her mind was turning slowly, but still the impressions and images whirled through her. He wasn't a monster. She had felt everything he was. He had a core of sympathy and goodness, however hard he tried to be unfeeling. Someone named Rubius, who looked like Santa Claus but was far more dangerous, wanted him to be unfeeling. But he wasn't. And he felt like a failure for it. He turned back to look at her in surprise. He wouldn't hurt her. She knew everything about him; all the bad things he had done, all the generous impulses, the selfless loving. She didn't want him to go. "I don't want Mrs. Simpson."

He glanced about as though he might find what she did want lurking somewhere in the room. "You . . . you need sustenance . . . some broth perhaps? Or perhaps you should sleep."

"In a minute," she whispered. He approached the circle of light, tentatively. How could such a powerful creature be tentative? "Talk to me."

He hesitated. Then he turned and pulled the wing chair

farther into the circle of light. He leaned forward, elbows on his knees, worry lines around his eyes.

"How did I get here?"

He cleared his throat. "I brought you."

She closed her eyes in acknowledgment. "Thank you." She creased her brows. "Now they know about the cave." Her refuge would be lost to her.

"I brought you straight to your rooms. No one knows you were out."

"How?" Ahhh . . . but she knew how. He must have translocated directly to the fourth floor. What a wonderful ability, to go where you want, immediate and unseen! The flash in his eyes said he was about to lie to her.

"Up the back stairs," he answered smoothly. "They were all asleep."

He wanted to protect her from the truth about him. Should she tell him she knew everything about him? Would anyone welcome someone knowing *everything* they had experienced, everything they were? Definitely not. That's why the villagers hated her so.

She wondered if he knew her in return. That was how it worked. She got all of them, but they always got at least a little of her. That was why her uncle understood her, and Malmsy. Now Jemmy understood her, too, for all the good it did her. He was now sure she was a witch. Maybe she was. Did Stephan Sincai understand her?

"Thank you, Mr. Sincai. I wouldn't want my uncle or the servants worried," she said.

Sincai looked at her strangely for a moment, then apparently weighed his words. "You may not realize that you have been unconscious for more than three days."

Three days! "Oh, dear!" She tried to raise herself on one elbow. "I must see to my uncle."

He lurched out of the chair but stopped himself from touching her. "Please, lie back. You're weak," he protested.

He needn't have bothered. Her weakness was only too evident. She fell back onto her pillows. "Three days," she breathed. "With only that dreadful woman to care for him . . ."

"Polsham and Mrs. Simpson have been assiduous in their attentions. I wouldn't fret."

"Is he well?" she asked, her voice a clear indicator that she was unable not to fret.

Sincai straightened. "If it will help you sleep, I'll check on him."

She took her dry lips between her teeth and nodded, fighting tears. What if her uncle died without her to watch over him? "Yes, please," she whispered.

He nodded, and without another word turned into the shadows. He seemed to melt into them, but she knew better now. He would go see to her uncle. He had said he would. And Stephan Sincai kept his promises. She breathed a sigh of relief. She could count on him.

She was so tired. She should take Mr. Sincai's advice and sleep. But not until she knew about her uncle. Who knew what might have happened with Erich in the house?

Still, her thoughts returned to Mr. Sincai. No one knew he was in her room. Surely the servants or even Erich would forbid something so scandalous as a strange man in her room alone with her at night. How had he been here just at the moment she woke? Could he truly have been here for three nights? He couldn't visit during daylight hours. Stephan Sincai slept during the day and stayed out of the sun.

How strange that she accepted all that about him! But of course, she always accepted the people she touched. It was impossible *not* to accept them when you knew all their fears, their secret desires, all the experiences, wonderful and horrible, that made them what they were. In fact, it was almost as if you had experienced them yourself. What deeper kind of understanding could one have? She could accept even the fact that Stephan Sincai was a vampire. But then, it was not his fault. He did not choose it, would not have chosen it perhaps, though even he wasn't sure of that. He didn't appreciate the thirst for life he had from the Companion in his blood. He lived so intensely! He drank blood because the Companion demanded it, but he did not kill when he drank. She looked back through the ages. Once he had taken too much and drained someone. But he was devastated by it. She could forgive him that. She wondered that she did not despise the drinking of blood. But she had felt what it was like, through him, and to him it wasn't horrible.

Stephan Sincai had killed, though, on purpose and recently, in a ghastly way. She had experienced that nightmare. The scene at the lodge flickered through her mind. It made her suck in her breath convulsively. He had done that? She felt the pain of his wounds, the excruciating guilt at his deeds, the certainty that he was damned for it, the suppression of his emotion. But he thought he was protecting his kind and humans, as well. Regardless of the cost to his soul, he meant to kill again.

She was too tired to think about what that meant to her. She returned to the fact that he might have sat three nights by her bedside. Why? What was she to a man like Stephan Sincai that he should do that for her?

Ahhh. The guilt. Guilt was his driving force. He was killing others of his kind to atone for crimes, crimes she didn't understand. Did he feel guilty for causing her illness? Was that why he sat here? For it was certainly the rush of his experience which blew out her consciousness.

She turned her head as he strode out of the darkness. He came bearing a bowl.

"Your uncle is resting peacefully," he said.

Relief washed through her. She took a deep breath and smiled at him. He tightened his mouth for some reason. He looked down at the bowl. "I brought you some broth from the kitchen. If you could . . . uh . . . take some, it would help you regain your strength."

She nodded. She did feel better. She might be able to push herself up to eat. And she owed it to her uncle to gain strength quickly. He set the bowl down and adjusted the pillows behind her. But the effort of sitting was too much. When he handed her the spoon, it trembled in her hand. He took it gently back and sat beside her. "Let me help."

She shook her head. "I don't . . ."

He held up a hand. "I won't touch you." He let a small smile escape. "Just feed you."

She let him. He was gentle with her. Surprising, considering how strong he was. He had lifted a boat out of a raging river once and rolled away the stone from a tomb in Jerusalem. Dear God! Was it *the* tomb? Had he . . . ? Had he been there? Her glance stole to his face.

The spoon paused on the way to her mouth. "Don't be afraid of me." he said. The voice was a low rumble, filled with pain. "Difficult with what you saw, I know. But truly, there is no need. I will not hurt you."

She rolled her lips between her teeth. *You know what kind of . . . man he is,* she told herself. *Man? Yes, man.* She searched his face. *A good man, in spite of almost impossible circumstances. A man of principle.* She took a breath. She nodded. "I know that."

He looked surprised. He examined her face. Then she saw him swallow once and offer his spoon again. She sipped the broth. It was a simple beef broth and only lukewarm, but it tasted better than anything she had ever eaten. He scraped the last of the bowl. She sipped the final spoonful and he set it aside. "Can you sleep now?"

She looked around at the dark nursery. *What if I don't wake up?*

"I'll stay with you and wake you at dawn, if you like."

Had he read her thoughts? But no, she knew he couldn't read minds. Was she so transparent? Or was it that one of his immense experience could guess what she was thinking? His experience was now hers in some ways. Could she use it as he did?

She slid under the bedclothes. He sat back in his chair and picked up his book. She could tell he was only pretending to read. That made her smile inside. She closed her eyes.

Stephan stole down to the kitchen well before dawn and washed the bowl. She was alive. She was awake and might be none the worse for wear in time. He had never felt so relieved. He hastened back up to her side. What he did not know was just how much she knew about him. She remembered what she had seen in the cave—she had asked him if he was well. Maybe . . . maybe she just remembered the wounds, not the fact that he had appeared out of nowhere. Maybe her touch did not tell her that he was vampire. Or she did not remember that part. What still amazed him was that she mastered her fear of him. How could she accept him, even if all she knew was how wounded he had been that night? No human could heal those wounds.

Now, as he watched her, standing over her, feeling the coming dawn outside, he realized he had another problem. He had been just watching over her until she wakened to make sure she was all right. As Mrs. Creevy and Mrs. Simpson came to tend her today, they would see she was awake. He was not needed anymore. That made him feel . . . lost somehow.

"Miss Van Helsing." Her eyelids fluttered.

"Miss Van Helsing. It is dawn."

She turned her face toward his voice even before her eyes opened. She smiled. God, how that smile seemed to shower moonlight over him! He loved that smile so much he had to clench himself against its influence. She opened her eyes slowly.

"You stayed." Her voice was musical, feminine, small, like she was.

"I said I would." He glanced up at the lightening sky from the dormer windows. He had not thought to close the draperies. The sun would rise at any moment. "And now I must go."

"I know," she whispered. "Thank you."

She couldn't know, of course, not really, not *why*. Could she? He turned on his heel and strode into her dressing room to conceal his disappearance.

Eleven

The fuss of Mrs. Simpson's tears of joy, the brusque handling by Mrs. Creevy as she helped Ann wash and change into a fresh night shift, and the visit of the doctor left Ann exhausted. The doctor proclaimed her well, but bled her nonetheless and recommended thin gruel and rest. Her cousin sent up word that he wished to see her. Mrs. Simpson, who brought the message, smiled in satisfaction when Ann said she was just too tired to receive him. The very thought of seeing him made her want to shudder in repulsion.

At least all the fuss kept the memories at bay. Well, they weren't really memories, or at least not her memories. They belonged to Stephan Sincai. Snatches of them floated in and out of her brain. He had advised Alfred the Great to build a navy. He spoke Chinese, and surprisingly, she understood it, too. No man would want someone who knew everything about him. She didn't want to frighten him away. And yet, to hold her knowledge secret seemed . . . underhanded. Finally, the frenetic activity of her brain just wore her out.

Ann slept in fits most of the afternoon. But she had

disturbing dreams of silken skin, and dark, burning eyes. When she woke, she was wet and aching between her legs. She felt swollen and sensitive. This was getting out of hand. She couldn't afford this kind of reaction to any handsome face that came along. Not when her life would be devoid of the simplest physical pleasure of touching a man. She remembered the feel of touching the flesh of his belly, even though he was wounded. She would never forget that sensation, though it cost her consciousness.

Would tonight bring Stephan Sincai?

Sleep was far away for Stephan. He was thinking about Maitlands. By now he was unneeded. He had no business there anymore. If he had ever had business there. He shouldn't stain another life. And now he knew that she was well, there was no excuse.

But *was* he unneeded? What about Van Helsing haunting the house? He was due from London today. Surely he would not dare try to take advantage of her during the day with the servants about. But at night?

Perhaps he ought to stand guard at night, just until she regained her strength. What would it cost him to spend some hours by her side? Of course, when Van Helsing returned, he might sense Stephan was here. But he could handle Van Helsing.

He was in danger of going to Maitlands tonight, and he knew it.

He shouldn't get involved in her life. She had recovered from her encounter with him. He had no further obligation. It did no good to dwell on her situation: friendless, or nearly, Van Helsing living under her very roof, the townspeople sure she was at best mad and at worst some supernatural evil. She wasn't evil. He knew that in his soul. She wasn't mad. But she was far from ordinary. He could sympathize with the fact that she was an outsider who would never be accepted. If only seeing her would not endanger his mission. Would she remember what she had discovered of him?

But wasn't she in danger, too? The townspeople of Cheddar Gorge wanted to believe she had done the murders that he owned.

Perhaps there *was* an obligation.

Or perhaps he should just be certain she did not recover her knowledge of him. He had nothing better to do for a few days.

Below him, a new guest arrived. Stephan, in his room on the first floor, heard the arrival quite clearly. He had expected the Bow Street runner to be a thug half a step away from criminality himself. But the voice of the man who presented himself to the landlord was, if not cultured, at least educated.

"My good man, I'd like to bespeak a room."

"All our rooms are either taken or reserved, sir," Mr. Watkins replied brusquely.

"Mr. Van Helsing said I might find accommodation here."

"Oh. Oh, of course. You're . . . you're not from Bow Street, by any chance?"

"I am. My name is Steadly. Ernest Steadly."

"Well, Mr. Steadly, you're most welcome. Give him room, there, Jemmy, Peg." The proprietor lowered his voice conspiratorially. "As a matter of fact, I'll put you in a room next door to one of the prime suspects. Boots! Boots there. Take Mr. Steadly up to number five."

Scurrying feet. "Guv'nor!" A reedy voice, no doubt the boots. "Turrible deed," he muttered as he started up the stairs. Stephan heard his step coming closer, and the faint clink of keys. A second step sounded behind him. "You'll want to take Sincai, then go get the witch girl up at Maitlands. Get confessions from them both, I expect. Probably in it together."

Just what Stephan had feared. He could take care of himself. The girl could not.

"Will you want rooms for your associates?" The boy halted outside Stephan's door.

"No."

"Well, we're pretty much the only place in the village that puts up travelers, aside from Mrs. O'Reilly, and she takes only two. I'm sure Mr. Watkins could accommodate you."

"I am alone, sir. I have no associates."

The steps froze. "Alone? How do you 'spect to take killers like the ones wot done that as folks saw at Bucklands Lodge?"

"I have my ways, boy." The voice was quiet and sure of itself.

"The village could muster a militia fer you." The steps continued. Then the voice lowered again to a whisper. "You want Mr. Watkins to gather the lads now?"

"No," Steadly said calmly. "I shall interview Mr. Sincai and then look in at the lodge, if you can provide me with a guide."

"A guide! Well, I 'spect Jemmy could take you."

"I would appreciate it." Stephan listened as the boots opened the door and showed Steadly in. "Perhaps you could ask Mr. Sincai if he is free to join me in the coffee room?"

Stephan opened his door and stepped into the hallway. "I'd be happy to join you, Mr. Steadly." The boots scuttled past him, pressed against the farther wall. He looked for all the world as though he was about to make the sign against the evil eye. It was a sign Stephan knew well, though he hadn't seen it in more than a century.

Steadly nodded, polite but watchful, and motioned to Stephan to precede him. He was a tall man, slightly past middle age, sinewy, with gray at the temples. He was dressed in a respectable coat if not a truly stylish one and his cravat was crisply starched if plainly tied. His eyes were a sharp gray Stephan could not say he liked in the present circumstances.

Stephan seated himself in the coffee room, one leg stretched out, exuding relaxation. Steadly stood, rather stiffly.

"What can I do for you, Steadly?"

"You may not credit it, but I am from—"

"Bow Street," Stephan interrupted. "No doubt about those dreadful murders. I've half a mind not to take a property here if people are going to be killed in such a gruesome manner. Tell me, do you suspect an animal?" That was more speech than he had indulged in since he'd come to England; more speech than he had made in years. And he had no doubt the landlord was listening. He would think it odd. Fine. He wanted suspicion cast his way. Better his than hers.

"Hard to tell, yet, Mr. Sincai. I shall know better after I have seen the site of the murders. I would like to know where you were on the night of March the eleventh, however."

"Me?" Stephan let himself sound incredulous. "You can hardly suspect that I had anything to do with these dreadful events!"

"I'm asking everyone, sir."

Stephan appeared to gather his wits. "Well, let me think back. Tuesday. I was with Pillinger the estate agent searching for a house to let down near Wedmore. I'm sure the agent can vouch for that." He wouldn't. But that's what Stephan wanted.

"All night?"

"Of course not. We saw the last property about ten. Then I rode back here."

"No one saw you come back?"

Stephan shrugged. "Ask them. I did not speak to anyone, if that's what you mean. The taproom was noisy. I went directly upstairs."

"Word has it that you sleep in the daytime, sir."

"Is that a crime?"

Steadly looked down for a moment, his smile tight. "No.

Of course not." He looked up sharply. "It would be nice if there was an explanation."

"I am sensitive to sunlight. An unmanly weakness, I know, but there you have it."

"I have never heard of that."

"Are you a medical man?" Stephan kept his voice soft.

"No." Steadly frowned. "No, I'm not."

"Well, then."

Silence stretched between them as Steadly considered Stephan.

Stephan smiled and raised his brows. He was baiting Steadly and Steadly knew it. The better to create an underlying animosity. "Do you have other questions?"

Steadly cleared his throat. "No. Not at the moment. But I expect you to make yourself available for questioning at a future date. Do not plan on leaving Cheddar Gorge."

"At your command," Stephan murmured. If Steadly expected him to leave the taproom, he was disappointed. Stephan stayed rooted where he was, looking openly up at the runner until the man cleared his throat once more, turned on his heel and retreated.

Well, that would keep the runner busy for at least another day. When he found Stephan had lied to him, it would focus all suspicion on him, and away from Miss Van Helsing. But there was nothing the man could do. There were no witnesses, no evidence connecting Stephan to the horror at the lodge. And he had only a few more days to wait here, visible, until Kilkenny came.

He tightened inside. Then he would fulfill his purpose or die in the attempt.

He glanced out the window and saw that the sun was sinking low. It would set in half an hour. Van Helsing was back at Maitlands. The runner was certain proof. So, he was for Maitlands to make sure Van Helsing stayed downstairs. It was a small enough thing he could do to make up for the fact that

Miss Van Helsing had suffered trying to help him. He found he wanted to see her. Easy to explain. He wanted to know she was truly recovered. And what she knew. Nothing more.

Mrs. Simpson came up to carry away Ann's tray, and recommended that she get some sleep. Ann acquiesced. But she wasn't sleepy. Tired, true, but she had slept all afternoon and early evening and now a thrill of anticipation kept her wakeful. Would he come? What if he didn't? What if she never saw him again? Her body seemed to quiver, somewhere deep inside, at the thought of him in the chair beside her bed.

She felt him more than saw him. The air in the room seemed to vibrate with energy. The scent of cinnamon, and more subtly, ambergris, came to her. His scent. She would never have realized it was ambergris before she touched him. She breathed out. She knew everything about him. Not that she remembered everything, still. But she would. She was sure of it.

"Hello," she said softly. After a brief hesitation he stepped into the room.

He examined her face with a frown. "Are you well?"

She nodded. His lips looked like they would be soft. The shoulders under his coat were heavy with muscle. She bit her lip. What was she thinking?

"You look very pale."

"The doctor bled me. That makes me pale, I expect."

"He *bled* you?" He was at her side in three strides. He reached for her wrist and she snatched her hand back in panic. He stopped himself, swallowed. "Apologies. I forgot myself." He clasped his hands behind his back.

Had he wanted to check her pulse? How . . . *like* him to be concerned for her. She wondered how many other people knew his generous impulses. Perhaps none. She took her own wrist and felt for the pulse. "A little fluttery, but perfectly strong." She raised her brows.

He let out a breath. "Bleeding! Quackery, pure quackery," he muttered. "I shall have to have a talk with the good doctor."

"Would . . . would you care to sit? You quite make one nervous, looming over one."

"No, no. I can stay but a moment. It is late." He stepped back, apparently so as not to loom. But that meant she could barely see his face in the shadows of the nursery. "Did your cousin come to see you today?" he asked.

"He sent up a note when he first arrived from London. But I was too tired to receive him." Again the revulsion showered her.

"Don't receive him," Sincai ordered peremptorily.

She raised her brows. What right had he to order her? "My own cousin?"

His mouth went grim. "Not until your uncle recovers. You are not . . . safe with him." The words seemed torn, as if even that elucidation of his motives was more than he was used to giving. And it was. What need did a man of his power have to explain himself? And . . . now she came to think of it, how could he know about the danger of her cousin?

She drew her brows together. "The days I was ill . . . did he come to visit then?"

"Yes."

She almost . . . almost remembered.

"Don't think of it. But don't let him visit."

"You are quite alarming me . . ."

"I . . . I didn't mean . . . Sincai trailed off, then seemed to listen. "He's having dinner. I'll let you know if he is coming up. And I can prevent his visit." Ann looked up at him. She knew exactly how he could prevent that. He could make her do anything he wanted her to do, as well. He had made women come to him often enough in his life. He had taken their blood and left them with an impression of a pleasant dream. She searched his memory, her memory, for a time when he had forced a woman to have sex with him. He could do that. But he hadn't. Not ever.

She smiled. She liked that. But then the smile evaporated. Why would a man like Sincai have to force a woman? Women would fall over themselves to draw his attention. He had experienced love in all its countless varieties. He was exciting. Why, his very presence filled the air with expectation, while she was a country girl of twenty-five years, a virgin who could never touch a man. The gulf between them seemed as wide as the river Axe when it spread itself across the plains below the Gorge at Wedmore. In some ways she wished she didn't know about him. She let her eyes drift away. She thought she heard Sincai clear his throat, but he said nothing. The silence goaded her to say *something*. "Couldn't you sit, only for a moment?" Her voice sounded small and uncertain in her own ears.

He cleared his throat, quite audibly this time, and sat on the edge of the chair. He took his hands from his knees and folded them in his lap then put them back on his knees. "You might wonder that I myself did not ask permission to visit. It is late and you are ill. I . . ." He trailed off. He wanted to ask her something, but couldn't bring himself to it. He got up and paced the dim room. The air fairly crackled with his agitation.

She didn't want him to go. The feeling washed over her unexpectedly. The gulf between them was real. Yet had they not exchanged their souls? She had got his at least. Telling him so might frighten him away from her. He was not a man who shared his secrets easily. And yet, if he did accept her friendship and then found out she had known about him all along, would he not hate her for dissembling and putting him through the farce of dissembling, as well? She took a breath. What she was about to do took all her courage. "I know why you come at night without asking leave."

"You do?" In the dim light he looked aghast.

She nodded, serious. She wanted to touch his brow and smooth away the anxious frown. Was he only worried that he'd been found out? Maybe he was afraid that if she knew him she would despise him. But of course that wasn't it. How could it be? She had no right to judge someone like him. He must know that.

Now how to explain that she knew about him without frightening him away? The explanation would expose her own secrets. Maybe vulnerability was the only way to win through. "I need to explain about the touching." Suddenly her throat threatened to close. Could she tell him? There were only two people in the world who knew the whole. One dead, and one, God help him, soon to be so.

She looked down at her hands. Somehow they had twisted themselves in the covers. "I told you in the forest that I know things about people by touching them." She looked up. "I touched you in the cave."

"You tried to bandage my wounds." He seemed puzzled over that. Did he not believe that someone would try to help him?

She took a breath. "I didn't know your Companion could heal them then."

He jerked up to standing, straight as a broadsword. "You know, then." His eyes burned her. He looked dangerous and distressed all at once. The energy which always hovered around him cycled up another notch. She should never have said it right out like that. She should have approached it obliquely.

She put her hand to her mouth. "I'm sorry. That is my curse. It isn't just that I know *some* things about people. I know it all."

"All?"

"Well, since you are so old and have had so much experience I can't quite encompass everything yet. There are gaps.

But I know about the blood. *The blood is the life* for your kind."

He turned away, ashamed. His voice drifted out of the darkness. "Will you tell Fladgate?"

"Why would I indulge their petty superstition?" He turned slowly back toward her. He was examining her, looking for signs of revulsion. That gave her hope. "I know what kind of man you are, and the experiences that made you. You grew up at Mirso Monastery, and fought in the Wars of the Roses. What hardships you endured on your Chinese expedition! I know the Mayans worshiped you as a god, and what you tried to do with Beatrix and . . . Asharti."

"Then you know my crimes." She had never heard a voice so bleak. "I am weak."

"Hmm," she mused. "You forget generous, loyal, idealistic."

"Weaknesses," he said bitterly. "No more. I have expunged them. I have one task now."

She did not say that his idealism and his generosity still lurked inside him, no matter how hard he tried to deny them. "Redemption is a worthy goal . . ."

He paced in the darkness beyond the light. "God, you must know about—"

"What happened at the Treasury and Bucklands Lodge? You are sent to dispose of Kilkenny's evil rogues. They threaten everything."

"And the . . . training?" His voice was a choking rumble.

She furrowed her brow, thinking. "Training in weapons with Alfred the Great . . . ?"

She felt more than heard his breath of relief. He wavered just outside the circle of light.

She smiled. "Do you want me to be afraid of you? You will be disappointed." Indeed, she felt . . . a kind of kinship. Did he not get some sense of her in return? But he was unconscious at the time. "If I am not frightened of you, can you not overcome your fear of me?"

His eyes widened, almost imperceptibly. Then he raised his brows and smiled ruefully. "Ah, you may be only a girl, but someone who knows everything about you? More frightening than a mere monster. You . . ." He cleared his throat. "You cannot read minds, can you?"

She shook her head. He would be afraid of that. "It isn't like that. If I touch you, I get your past experiences, your feelings about them. It's rather overwhelming. But I don't know what you're thinking now." There, she had told him. But if she was going to tell the truth, it might as well be all of it. "I suppose knowing so much about a person makes it easier to guess, though. Sometimes I could finish my uncle's sentences for him." That made them sound like an old married couple or two elderly spinsters. But that was what it was like, to know another person that well.

He looked taken aback. Still, after a hesitation, he stepped back into the light. "That's why you went into the coma, isn't it? You got all two thousand years."

She couldn't suppress a smile. "You were a bit of a surprise."

She thought she saw an answering smile in his eyes. Then he sobered. "How do you live with that kind of knowledge about everybody?"

"Badly." She sighed. "I can never touch a m—" She stopped herself. "I can't touch people," she corrected. "I wonder if the lack of physical contact has made me cold."

"You? Cold? No." A wistful look washed over his features. "But I know what it is like. Touch has become . . . difficult for me as well."

She chuckled. "Then what could be safer for us than someone who shares our aversion?"

He examined her face. Those unfathomable brown eyes— who would guess they could soften with affection? A flash of all the loves he had experienced lanced through her. Beautiful women, brilliant women, cruel women, and innocent women—he had loved them all. A shudder passed through her. *What am I thinking, to ask a man like this to . . . what?* What did she want of him? She looked at her hands, gathering her courage.

"Sometimes I think I will go mad if I cannot maintain some connection with the world. When . . . if my uncle dies there will be no one left who . . . accepts." That might be the definition of a friend. She faltered and clutched the edge of the quilt. "Who better to accept than one who is as strange as I am?" She saw his look of doubt. "We could . . . talk, even if only for a little while." She had asked too much!

"When Kilkenny comes, I will go to meet him." The voice had iron in it.

"I know." He thought it would be the death of him, or his salvation. "And until then?"

"I . . . I can spare some time." He cleared his throat. "Waiting is difficult."

"You could have the use of my library. Books pass the time."

He glanced around him, looking for another topic. "A nice collection. Yours?"

"Books are my friends." That sounded idiotic. "I saw you with a book when I first woke."

He looked at his hands and nodded. Then he pulled the wing chair into the circle of light and sat, gingerly, on the edge of the seat, as though he was about to rise and go at any moment. She couldn't help thinking that he was a wild animal she was coaxing to come closer.

"You can tell me about your favorite authors." She shrugged, lifting her brow. "Let's see. Lao-tzu, Aeschylus, Sophocles, Euripides. Confucius. You like Ch'u Yuan. Ovid—not Martial, I note. Antarah ibn Shaddad, Wang Wei, Bharavabhuti, and Li Po of course." Someone who knew everything about you could be convenient, too. She could show him that.

He looked startled. "Have . . . have you read them?"

"Well, the Romans, of course. And the Greeks, but only in translation. My Greek isn't good enough for reading the originals. I realize now they weren't very good translations."

"Then . . . then you read them through me?" His voice was hard. It was as though he was probing a wound as he explored just how much she knew about him.

"No, no," she assured him. "I only have your impressions of them."

"Oh. That's good." He wasn't sure of that.

She decided not to tell him what his impressions told her about him. He revered truth and defying tyranny (surprising for one so bent on a mission given him by the Eldest), and more surprising still, he believed in the forgiveness of Saint Augustine, just not for himself. She liked the man who could love those particular books. And what of the Chinese poets? In them, he admired tranquility, yearned for it. Hard, for a man with a mission like his to yearn for tranquility.

"I'd like to read the Chinese poets. Would a library in London have their work?"

He gave a half-chuckle. "No. Your powers are failing you."

She concentrated. What did he mean? "Oh. They're from the seven hundreds—Tang dynasty? And . . . and your copies were destroyed when the peasants burned your palace in India."

He took a breath. Each new demonstration of her knowledge would be frightening. "The last copies are in the Imperial Palace in the Forbidden City in Peking."

"I have never been to Peking." She sighed. "Nor am I ever likely to go. In fact, I really haven't been anywhere. You're very lucky in that."

"Everywhere is the same after a while. People are alike, and you take yourself with you."

"I would love a chance to discover that."

He smiled. It was such a tiny smile one would have

missed it if one were not looking carefully. "You have your books. They can take you places."

"Not the same," she said, though she had lied to Erich and said it was. "One sees things only through the author's eyes. All one's impressions are borrowed. I can sometimes feel other times and other lives through the things I touch, but that is still reality once removed. I want my own reality."

"Reality is overrated." He chewed that marvelous lower lip thoughtfully. "Still, it might be well for you to set yourself up in London."

"I could not leave my uncle." That might not be an issue for long and they both knew it.

"Not right away, of course," he added hastily. "But life in a less restricted society would be good for you. These people here are too provincial to appreciate you."

"You mean they know too much about me." She chuckled. Then she sighed. "For someone like me travel . . . living in London . . . well, it's just impossible."

"You hire a companion. Take Mrs. Simpson with you and Polsham, Jennings. A fashionable house in town . . . a select society . . ."

"And how would I avoid people touching me?" she challenged.

"You will be an eccentric," he declared, that wisp of a smile lurking at the corners of his mouth. "Wear gloves at all times and declare that touching others is simply too unrefined for your tastes. You will become all the rage."

She couldn't help but chuckle as she shook her head. "You make it seem so easy."

"It is."

She grew serious. "For someone courageous like you. But not for me." She looked around at the darkened room. "I couldn't leave my nursery. I can touch things here and not be . . . assaulted by everyone who's ever touched them."

He bowed his head and looked at his hands. "This is a refuge for you."

"You understand the need for refuge."

"Yes."

Sadness flickered in his eyes and was gone—now that she knew what to look for, she could see the tiny display of emotion. Was that all he had left after everything he had experienced?

"You have had much pain in your life," she whispered. "You deserve peace."

"No I don't, not yet." The hard edge was back in his voice. His eyes looked as though he was far away. He really believed that he didn't deserve refuge. He didn't think he deserved kindness from another, either. That was why he couldn't believe she had tried to bandage him when she saw him so wounded. What must it be like to hold yourself in such contempt? He came to himself with a start and peered at her. "You are tired."

She was. She was bone-tired. But she didn't want him to go. "Not really."

He raised his brows. "I'm going to read one of your books here in this comfortable chair. You are going to sleep."

Her eyes *were* heavy. She could hardly hold her head up. "You won't go, will you?"

"At dawn. If you wake in the night, I'll be here."

"And you'll come again?"

"If I can."

"Perhaps I'll sleep just for an hour." She smiled and scooted down in her bed and drew up the quilt. "I have several language books. You could learn Italian."

"You're slipping. I already know Italian."

"Oh, yes . . ." Her eyes were so heavy. "I had forgot . . ."

Twelve

Stephan watched her eyes close. She'd sleep the night through, of course. That was good. She needed sleep after her experience. At least Van Helsing would not come creeping up the stairs in the night. If he did, Stephan could send him to the right about. And Stephan was out of the way of the runner. He would enjoy reading and watching her sleep. Enjoy . . . he hadn't said that word in years, let alone experienced anything like enjoyment.

Did he really enjoy being around her? The fact that she knew so much about him was unnerving. The fact that she seemed to accept what she knew was, frankly, entirely implausible. Maybe she didn't know it all. He'd have to test her. She didn't appear to remember his time in training in Mirso. That was a God-sent favor. He wouldn't like to think that such an innocent . . . Still, she might know about other liaisons he had indulged in over the years. She said she knew about Beatrix and Asharti, and certainly part of his relationship with them had been physical. With Asharti it was only physical—a part of his mentoring program. He had been trying to show her that sexual relations could be tender and filled with mutual giving. It was obviously a lesson she had not learned. Another of his failures. With Beatrix the sexual relationship was secondary to the love he felt. She had loved him too, at first. But then she'd grown out of it. First loves never lasted, especially between an innocent and one who had seen and done everything.

He watched Miss Van Helsing sleeping. She looked like an angel, so white, so innocent. She thought he deserved peace. That was her own kindness coloring her vision of him. He didn't. If he completed his mission he might earn forgiveness, but not kindness. When had anyone ever been generous to him, kind?

Actually, it might have been one of the Daughters.

MIRSO MONASTERY, MARCH 1820

He came to consciousness in the room he had grown to hate, chained to the bench again. Someone was stroking him and humming softly. The touch was soft. It didn't hurt. He didn't hurt anymore. The terrible pain seemed like a dream. He opened his eyes.

Freya sat beside him, rubbing oils into his naked flesh. He raised his head and glanced down at himself. His body was whole, every hair, every inch of skin just as it had been. Companion, he sighed, and felt the thrill of life along his veins in response.

"That was hard, I know," Freya said. Her eyes were soft. "But you are better now."

He rolled his head around the room, but they were alone.

"The others will be here later. We wanted to give you a chance to rest. It will take a day or two to truly regain your strength." She took two fingers of cream and rubbed it over his shoulders and up over the swell of his biceps.

"Would you like to ask me questions?" she asked as she worked the cream into his skin. *"Dee and I disagree about how much information you should have. I think information makes you a more eager Penitent, and obedience is easier if you know clearly what is required. Dee thinks you should be kept ignorant. But she is not here."*

What could he ask? He had a thousand questions. He wanted to ask why they had punished him so horribly just for masturbating, but he was sure that would only make her angry. And now he came to think, he had more basic questions. *"Can this . . . this training really increase my power?"*

"Oh, absolutely," she said. *"You are already stronger than you were when you came. And this alternation of repression and milking will make you more powerful yet."*

He thought about that, about not being quite as exhausted, about waking earlier. Maybe they were right. *"How . . . how long will that go on?"* How long could he stand it to go on?

"Hard to tell. Your improvement will level off. Then we know we have as much as you will get, and we move on to the second phase."

"What is the second phase?" He was afraid to know. He was sure she wouldn't tell him.

"We teach you to control yourself instead of us controlling you. You must learn the discipline of suppression and focus. That is when we turn your raw energy into a refined force that can be directed and used."

"How will I do that?"

"Force of mind. Chanting and directed meditation helps. You'll be able to control your erections, prolong them, ejaculate only on command. You will be able to suppress pain, even the kind of pain you experienced today. It is a kind of Tantric discipline. We'll start small of course, inflicting wounds during sex because during sex your power is at its apex, keeping them open with our saliva to stop your Companion from healing them too quickly. Stancie likes that part.

You'll learn to conquer hunger, fatigue, heat, and cold and still perform. You need discipline in order to wreak vengeance on Asharti's army."

"How, how long will it take?" His voice was hoarse in his throat. The bleak prospect she laid before him was so chilling he began to contemplate the possibility that he might go mad before he could be made ready to fulfill his purpose.

She looked into his eyes. "A year, perhaps two. We are trying to go slowly."

Two years? Panic cycled up out of his belly into his throat. "How can we wait that long when Asharti's army may be rebuilding at this very moment?"

She glanced away, and he saw that she was staring at the stain in the corner of the room. "If we go too fast, we might ruin everything," she said softly.

Stephan swallowed. This might be the silliest question, but he was suddenly very afraid that it might be the most important. "What is that stain?"

She sat up, but her gaze never left the corner. He thought she wasn't going to answer. But she tore her gaze away and looked at him. "That is all that is left of the last Penitent we were training to be a Harrier." Stephan felt his eyes widen.

"Conflagration," she said calmly. "We tried to ramp up his power too quickly." She took a breath. "That cost us more time in the end than just progressing by easy stages would have done. Hard as it is to wait, especially for Stancie, we have to make certain we are successful." She stood and glanced over his body. "Of course, you can help us. That's what Dee never understands. Learn to control your erections and ejaculation, your response to stimuli. The more control you have, the less we have to force you, and the more quickly you progress. In the end you will have increased your sexual energy to a point where it is a dangerous weapon. You will use it by suppressing it, turning it into power, both physical and mental. You will be able to turn others' thoughts against them, amplified, until you *literally blast them apart. That is what Rubius wants of you. There is a price, of course. You must eliminate anything that weakens you or disperses your power. That includes ejaculations, emotions, pain, hunger—for food if not for blood. So we will teach you to eliminate all those things."*

Her speech stunned him. They were going to torture him to ensure that he was capable of enduring whatever Asharti's minions could produce. He was going to be changed, fundamentally and forever, by this process.

She softened. *"The training is painful, but the result is required. You may wonder why we are increasing your sexual power only so you will never ejaculate again. It is because when you are at your full power an ejaculation can damage, even kill, your partner."*

"I can hurt the woman I'm with?" It seemed too cruel a fate.

"It is not as though you may not lie with a woman. You will have such control that you will able to resist orgasm. You will also be able to resist all emotion, and withstand privations to which another would succumb. You will be a killing machine."

She must have seen the horror on his face. In truth, how could one bear such an existence? *"It is a great thing you do for your people, Stephan,"* Freya said, her voice low and vibrating with emotion. *"Your sacrifice will not be forgotten. Have the courage to obey. Help us make you into the instrument of our salvation."*

She turned at the door. *"We will be back in a few hours to begin again."*

Yes, Freya was kind to him, in a twisted way. Or it had seemed like kindness in contrast to the others. The hard edges of the Daughters' faces burned in his memory. Those faces, those bodies, were his world for nearly two years, whether he would or no. His initial revulsion suppressed as time went on in favor of the need to serve a purpose for his kind, to redeem his failures. He had embraced his fate if not enjoyed it. His mind skittered back over that time, before the final failure, when he had been sure he could achieve redemption. Had the Daughters always looked that hard, or had they become that way? Would his face look like that when he was as old as they were? It wasn't the years that etched themselves onto their faces. No, it was the degradation of the soul that wrote itself there. He stole a glance to the little mirror on the dressing table across the room where his own face was reflected in the shadows. He didn't look like that yet but he was willing to bet that he would someday, perhaps soon. It occurred to him that he might have set himself upon a path that would lead him to become what they were.

He turned back to the sleeping figure in the bed. She would never look like that. She glowed with goodness. She had been kind to him, regardless of the cost. She was the opposite of the dark emptiness he cultivated. And yet she understood. Sitting here staring at her in the wee hours of the night tethered him to a world that did not require killing and emptiness in order to deserve redemption.

But his torment was that her pale beauty stimulated his body. He was forced to chant to keep his erection at bay. He did not deserve a tether to the force of light and goodness. His reaction defiled her. If she knew that he lusted after her she would be horrified. Was he no better than Van Helsing?

What was he thinking? The fact that he would horrify her was the least of his problems. He could not afford a distraction from the grim purpose that was his lot. The hot need pumping through his genitals must be controlled, or he would risk failure on several fronts. So dawn, when it came, was filled with regret and relief. Time to go, before he disgraced himself.

He spared a glance at her before he drew the darkness. He would have a talk with the doctor today. There would be no more bleeding. And he would come again, danger or not.

Thirteen

Mrs. Creevy barged into the nursery, making Ann wake with a gasp.

"Lazy puss," Mrs. Creevy cawed as she bustled over to open the drapes and let the early afternoon sunlight pour through the dormered windows. "Time to get up."

Mrs. Simpson came trudging up the stairs and brought a tray in through the still-gaping nursery door. "How are you feeling, miss? Could you take some toast and tea? I've a bit of gruel here too if you thought you might."

Ann pushed herself up in bed. She was feeling stronger today. She smiled. The room still smelled faintly of cinnamon. "I'm much better, thank you, Mrs. Simpson. And I'm sure I shall be better still for some of your gruel."

Mrs. Creevy stood with her fists on her ample hips as Mrs. Simpson set her tray over Ann's lap. "Well! I expect you don't need to disrupt the entire household. So selfish, when your uncle is having a bad morning."

"Oh, dear," Ann exclaimed. "I didn't mean . . . I mean,

by all means, go to him. Do you think I could see him today?"

"He don't have energy for the likes of you." Mrs. Creevy huffed out of the room.

"Don't mind that one." Mrs. Simpson frowned. "I wish we didn't have to have her here."

"I'm sure she takes good care of Uncle Thaddeus." Ann applied herself to the gruel.

"No she don't," Mrs. Simpson said bluntly. "But Peters left us, and Alice is down to Wedmore, and that leaves just Polsham, Jennings, and me."

Ann looked up, stricken. "And I have been such a charge upon you all! I'm so sorry."

Mrs. Simpson smiled. "Never you mind about that. I'm just glad to see you looking so much better. Eat your gruel." Ann obeyed. "Perhaps you'd like a bath? Mrs. Creevy could help you. She wouldn't have to touch you."

"I can manage a bath by myself," Ann insisted. She looked over at the hip bath near the fireplace and thought about the four floors that bucket of hot water would have to be carried. "Could I come downstairs and take a bath in the little sunroom off the kitchen?"

"Of course, my dear. That way I'll be just by if you should need anything."

Ann smiled and took another spoonful of the gruel. "You are so kind, Mrs. Simpson." The older woman blushed.

"One gets kindness by being kind, Miss Ann, and you have always been that."

Ann ate in silence for a moment. "I wonder you can shop in the village with all the speculation there about me."

That hit a nerve. Mrs. Simpson shrugged. "What people don't understand don't sit well. Can't change that."

"Are they still talking about Jemmy touching me?" Ann scraped the bowl with her spoon. When Mrs. Simpson didn't answer, Ann looked up. The old woman's eyes were wide. Ann raised her brows in question.

Mrs. Simpson cleared her throat. "I don't want to frighten you, Miss Ann, but there's been murders."

Of course. She smiled up at Mrs. Simpson as she set her spoon in the empty bowl. "Well, at least they can't think I did that."

Mrs. Simpson's face fell.

"They *do* think I did it?"

"Some of 'em." Mrs. Simpson looked apologetic. "Some of 'em think that dark fellow did 'cm. And some of 'em think you two done 'em together."

"Dear me!" They suspected Mr. Sincai! They couldn't do anything about it. He would just disappear. But that wasn't an outcome she wanted, either. "Do you think Squire Fladgate will want to question me?"

"Mr. Van Helsing fetched a Bow Street runner," Mrs. Simpson said in a stage whisper, as though that were the worst news in the world. "He's looking into the matter."

"Really? I have never met a Bow Street runner. That will be an adventure." She began to plan how she could throw suspicion away from Mr. Sincai.

"You're a brave one, you are, Miss Ann. But you shouldn't ought to worry. Mr. Van Helsing gave orders not to admit strangers."

"Did he now?" Ann felt anger rise for the first time since she'd awakened.

"He did." Her cousin stepped up behind Mrs. Simpson. Suddenly, he sniffed the air and then his head snapped back to her, his eyes narrowing. "You may go, Simpson."

Mrs. Simpson looked rebellious, but Ann gave her what she hoped was a reassuring look. No good could come of Mrs. Simpson challenging her cousin. She could handle Erich Van Helsing. But a thrill of repressed revulsion washed through her and she remembered that Mr. Sincai had told her not to receive him. Mrs. Simpson took the tray with a sniff and left the room. "I'll be back in half an hour," she promised.

"Come calling?" Ann asked sweetly. She would not show a single chink of fear in her armor in front of this bullying cousin.

"Apparently, I'm not the only one. Have you been receiving strange men, Cousin? We'll have to put a stop to that." He loomed over her bed.

Ann felt as though she had been slapped. How did he know?

"Your secret lover leaves a scent."

Ann stared him down. "Mrs. Simpson brought me some new perfume."

"Don't lie to me." Erich sneered. "You have no idea what you have let into your bedroom." He peered at her. "I do. I should think in your condition you couldn't spare what he wants of you."

Ann flushed. "I have no idea what you are talking about." But she put her hand to her neck for reassurance that there were no twin wounds there. She had not looked in a mirror in days. Was that why she had such erotic dreams about him?

"And I think you do," he marveled softly. Then he straightened and his voice grew hard. "He murdered four men."

"Men?" she asked pointedly. "I think *you* have no idea what is happening hereabouts."

"*Au contraire,* my simple cousin. I will tell you exactly what is happening. Your mystery visitor is called the Harrier. He is the ultimate evil. He has been trained to kill innocents and he does his job most effectively. But his days are numbered."

"And will *you* dispose of this 'Harrier'?" She tried not to let her voice shake as she said it.

Erich shook his head, chuckling. "Not I."

"I hardly think a Bow Street runner will do the job."

Erich turned and ambled over to the fireplace. "No. But

given the proper tools, he can make life very inconvenient for the brute."

Several things connected themselves in her mind. She opened her eyes in surprise. "You were fixing up the hunting lodge . . . *You* let them in." The conclusion was inescapable. "You work for Kilkenny."

"How do you know—" Erich's head snapped around. His startled look gave way to smirking realization. "Of course. You have an inside source. I'm surprised he would tell you."

If he expected Ann to tell him anything about Sincai, or how she knew things, her cousin was doomed to disappointment. "Well?"

He shrugged. "Anyone who can't go about by day needs an agent. They pay quite well."

"In return for your soul." How could her own cousin work for evil incarnate and stand here in her bedroom looking so ordinary?

He laughed outright. "You're a simple creature." He looked her up and down. "But rich and not bad looking, if one fancies the exotic. I will enjoy plowing your every last orifice."

Ann felt a chill run down her spine. "I want no husband."

"I don't care whether you want one or not." His voice grated on her. "I want your portion. I've grown accustomed to living well these days. But one must provide for the future. My . . . employers might not want my services forever. I need some reliable income and some standing in the world. Your father took care of any chance I had to inherit this place."

"Is that why you're so bitter?" Ann asked. She hadn't been sure until this moment that Erich knew that Maitlands would revert to the Crown if she died without issue. She had always wondered about that provision of her father's will. But the land was not entailed and it was his to dispose of as he pleased once he had it through her mother's dowry. Her father had made certain the provisions of the will got about before he left for the Peninsula. He said it was to protect her. But Erich had been on the Continent. Had her father specifically written about it to him?

"Bitter, why should I be bitter? I am the last male Van Helsing, and yet he leaves me nothing? Instead he leaves it to a mad female who has no idea how to enjoy it! Not bitter, I'm . . ." He didn't finish the sentence, but pressed down the anger in his voice and continued in a lighter vein. "I've grown fond of Maitlands Abbey. I shall like being master here. After you have fulfilled a suitable stint servicing me, I shall have to find a place to care for your sad malady. Who will blame me?"

"An asylum." Ann kept her voice steady as her heart raced. His rape could go on as long as he liked. The asylum was a foregone conclusion. It might be a relief.

He shrugged and smiled. It was not a pretty smile and that had nothing to do with the condition of his teeth.

"My uncle will have something to say to that," she said, hating that her throat was full.

"Your uncle is not long for this world." He shrugged again. She hated him more.

"I'm of age."

"The world thinks you're mad. Or a witch. They'll tell themselves they're doing the right thing for you, and coincidentally, they'll be relieved to have another be responsible for you. I'll have Maitlands in spite of your father."

What he said was true. She glanced around, frantic. "There is one who will protect me."

"The *Harrier*?" Van Helsing barked out a laugh. "He is single-minded, and his mind isn't on you, my simple creature. Besides, he will be disposed of."

"Kilkenny?"

But Erich only smiled. "I made arrangements while I was in London."

"What kind of arrangements?" she pressed. If she knew she could warn Sincai.

"Several kinds. A special license, for one. It should arrive any day."

"I will never marry you," she hissed.

"Of course you will, my dear," he said lightly. "And by the by, I would advise your amorous visitor to keep his distance. The next time I sense him here, I'll call in reinforcements. I know the ways of his kind. I can put him out of the way permanently."

Ann ran through what she knew of Stephan and his kind. Could Erich and Kilkenny decapitate him and separate the head? That would be what it took to kill him. She shuddered in revulsion. Or they could drug him. Drugs depressed his Companion's power. Could they accomplish that against his will? "I advise you to keep *your* distance," she returned fiercely. "Go, or I'll tell the runner you were the one who murdered the creatures at the hunting lodge."

"Would he believe that the man who came to fetch him was guilty of the crime?" Erich only pretended to muse. "He is more likely to believe it of your cinnamon-scented suitor. Now fair cousin, adieu. Think about your prospects. I know I shall. We shall talk again."

Ann watched him saunter out the door. Inside she was shaking. Maitlands was starting to feel more like a prison than a refuge. Her threat about Stephan Sincai coming to her defense was all a lie. He would never risk his mission to defend her. And what did she expect him to do? Kill her cousin? She shuddered at the thought that she would be responsible for murder.

Her only refuge now was her uncle. She wanted to go to him. But she had another problem. Stephan Sincai might come back here tonight, and Erich could well have the runner and some villagers waiting for him. If anyone could take care of himself it was Sincai. Couldn't he? Her cousin wouldn't really resort to drugs or decapitation. But if he knew Sincai's weaknesses, that was bad. And if Sincai defended himself, people would die. She could not have those deaths on her conscience, either. She must warn him so he could disappear. Regret shot through her. She would never see him again. She would be even more alone against her cousin than she was now. But that didn't matter. His safety did.

Ann threw back the quilts and tottered to the wardrobe. It seemed unbelievable that her cousin could be involved with the vampires at the hunting lodge. But he had not even bothered to deny it. She shed her night shift and laced up a half-corset. Then she pulled a round-collared blue kerseymere walking dress over her head. Stockings were rolled up and feet shoved into some sturdy walking shoes. Had he brought Kilkenny's army here? Or had they just discovered him and used him for their own foul purposes? Easing herself down the stairs by clinging to the banister, she called for Jennings. She had to get into the Hammer and Anvil and warn Sincai.

Where the hell was Kilkenny? Stephan lay on the bed at the Hammer and Anvil in his shirtsleeves and breeches. The sun was still high outside the shutters. It had been six days. Shouldn't Kilkenny have arrived by now? Surely he would seek Stephan out first thing. And Stephan had not troubled to hide himself. He could not sleep for an itching anticipation of Kilkenny's arrival. Or was it that he was looking forward to another night in the company of Miss Van Helsing? At least she might keep away the memories . . . And at the thought they came welling up again. No! he thought, sucking in a breath. But it was too late.

After Freya's adjuration to sacrifice and courage he tried to use his purpose as a shield against his fear. From that time of his first punishment, they fed him by hand, touched him as he relieved himself, caressed him as he bathed. He tried hard to control his sexual urges with what he thought were mixed results. He was obedient. He licked them, sucked their breasts, penetrated them as required. They handled him tenderly, roughly, sucked him, and they penetrated him as well. Now his baths included anal cleansing rituals to which he submitted docilely. Almost every day one of them would suck his blood, usually from his carotid. They were careful not to take so much as to weaken him. It became a normal part of sex.

Dee was pleased that his fear of punishment had such good results. Freya only smiled.

During the daylight hours he lay chained to his stone, often erect and needing. But he understood that as a part of his atonement now, and accepted it. If he had a wet dream and they came in to find his semen spilled over his belly, they took it as a sign that it was time to milk him, and he would be made to come until he was dry in the next session.

Their schooling had its effect. His sexual energy increased. Often they did not have to rouse him artificially at all and he had enough control that he could pleasure them for hours without their aid in restraining his release. Freya whispered more than once that she was proud of him. Months went by and still they coaxed him to greater levels of performance. The periods of restraint and forced ejaculation grew closer together, until one day, after a night of ejaculations, he dreamed that he was burning like he had in the sunlight but from within. He woke to semen on his belly.

He waited for them, staring at the stain on the wall, knowing he had crossed some line.

The monks arrived. Brother Flavio, glancing to him, stopped to stare. His eyes softened. "Well, boy." Fear and pride chased each other across his features. "I'll get them."

"My, my," said Stancie said, "just what I've been waiting for."

Freya brought the towel from the bath and wiped his

belly. *"Congratulations,"* she said softly. *"You have made it to the second phase."*

"Now we can strip you every night," Dee remarked, as she loosed his wrists.

"And I can start your lessons in a new kind of control." Stancie's eyes gleamed.

"Don't be afraid, Stephan," Freya soothed as she unlocked his ankles. *"You are up to it, I know."* They led him to the bath. He stepped in and they washed him, more tenderly than they were wont, though just as thoroughly. They drew him up when they had finished and he stepped out of the bath. He was fully erect now from having their hands upon him, and they took him, each in turn and two at once, on the bench and on the carpet as he controlled his ejaculation.

"Excellent performance," Dee remarked as she took a break for some wine. *"I shall have to tell Father how well you are coming along."*

"Can I have him now?" Stancie pouted. *"I've been waiting."*

"Yes, yes," Dee said impatiently. *"Though I'm sure you'll have to bring him up."*

"Perhaps not," Freya said, sitting down by his side where he lay on the carpet and stroking his hip gently. She ran her tongue over his lips, and then let him sip from her glass of wine. He suckled at her breast as Stancie pushed his legs apart and fondled him. Soon he was filling her hand. Stancie straddled him and began to ride him, but then she changed her angle and slid her full breasts up along his chest. Her nipples teased his own. Freya continued to whisper to him. Now she was saying nonsense words in some rhythm and Stancie was riding him hard. He knew what would happen here. Freya had told him. He could bear it. He knew he could. Suddenly he felt a little whoosh of power and Stancie, instead of biting his carotid, bit his chest and dragged a

furrow down it. He jerked away from the pain involuntarily. Stancie began to lap at the wound. The pain threatened his erection. But Freya said sharply, "Listen to me, Stephan. Listen." He looked up at her and was captivated by her eyes, red sparks winking in their depths. The nonsense syllables she whispered seemed to have a power of their own. He focused on her voice. "Tuatha denon. Beluorga lefin. Argos pantid." *She whispered them over and over again. They were teaching him the Tantric chants at last. Stephan felt himself harden to bursting in spite of the pain. Stancie licked at the wound, keeping it open.* "Come now," *Stancie commanded as she began to contract around him.* "Come!"

And he did. Stancie shuddered and cried out, a sound of ecstasy that cycled into pain. Stephan spurted on and on. The pain seemed to urge him on until there was no more fluid in him.

The room was quiet. Stancie rolled off him. He gasped for breath. He had never experienced an ejaculation like that. It felt as though he had pushed his soul out through his cock. He lifted heavy eyelids. Freya and Dee were leaning over Stancie and exchanging startled looks. Stancie seemed only half-conscious.

What had happened here?

At last, Dee straightened and looked over at him. She heaved a breath. "Well, we will have to make some adjustment in our schedule. From this moment, your ejaculations are dangerous to your partner."

That was the first sign that he had changed forever. After that, they switched to schooling him only in restraint and the suppression of pain. He learned the chants, long strings of words in languages long dead that sometimes seemed to have meaning and sometimes seemed like nonsense. They helped him to concentrate, though.

Stephan ground his face into his pillow to steady himself. That was when they started teaching him the disciplines. Of course they opened wounds. But there were other torments, too.

"How many nights since he has eaten?" Deirdre asked, as she popped a walnut into her mouth and sipped her wine.

Stephan knelt, light-headed, belly hollow, and watched them eat. The smell of the beef tormented him. They left the food there during the day with strict orders that he not touch it.

"A week, I think," Stancie said, her mouth full. "He's had no sustenance, unless you count the female juices he has swallowed." She laughed.

"Then it is time he learned other disciplines. Freya, take him up to the battlements."

Not the sunlight, Stephan thought frantically. But no, it was night. He was safe.

Freya slipped a tiny chain around the head of his cock like a leash and headed out the door. Each tug as he followed tormented him. He thought he might faint as all the blood in his body threatened to pool in his erection. He stumbled up the stairs after her, afraid to know what was ahead.

It was winter again. He didn't know the month. The stone of the battlements was covered with a light dusting of snow. And the winds tore down from the mountains and plucked with icy fingers at his naked body, swirling the dry flakes up around them. His erection should have shrunk immediately, but it didn't. He was as hard and needing as ever. What was happening to him? Freya stopped to put on furs and soft boots. She twitched up the hood around her head and led him out into the open. There, on the battlements, was a glowing cauldron of coals with several iron rods stuck in it. Deirdre and Stancie joined them, similarly attired.

Brands? No, *thought Stephan*. They can't do that. *His chest heaved as icy breath surged into his lungs. But of course they could. And his Companion would heal it, so they could do it as often as they liked. And there, there was a block of ice, smooth from being melted and refrozen. The ice had a hole about the size . . . About the size of a man's cock.*

Freya motioned for him to kneel, too far from the cauldron to collect any warmth from it.

"Let me hold his leash," Stancie said eagerly. "Dee, you hold the rods."

"Stephan," Freya said, her voice taken by the wind. "This is an exercise in stamina. You must learn to hold the power of your erection in all circumstances. Use the chants to help you. We will alternate between the ice and the brands. You control the pace. You will ask for the brands, tell us where to place them and press your flesh into them. You will hold your erection through the branding and then find your release in the ice. Is that clear?"

Oh, it was clear all right. Could a man, even a vampire man, do this? Did they know what they asked? He nodded. Looking down, he saw his nipples peaked and hard from the cold through the dusting of dark hair across his chest. And in spite of his fear, his cock bobbed with the pressure of the fluid bottled up inside him, red and swollen. Stancie jerked on the delicate chain around its head rhythmically until he thought he could come right there in the cold.

"You can do it, Stephan," Freya said. "Or we wouldn't ask it of you."

"Sithfren, hondrelo, frondura, denai," he murmured.

Dee took a brand from the cauldron. It glowed orange and dull red, steaming when the flakes of snow impaled themselves on it. "Where?" she asked, but it was more of a command.

He thought the chants, willing them to protect him from the fear. "Left breast."

She strode forward and held the brand a few inches from his chest. Chanting, his breath heaving in his chest, he leaned forward into it. The sear of pain made him grunt sharply, but he held himself against the brand. The smell of burning flesh fouled the clear, cold air. At last Dee withdrew the brand, leaving Stephan gasping. He wanted to vomit. As he leaned over, he saw the initial seared into his flesh, black and smoking. R was for Rubius, no doubt. He sucked in the jagged, cold air and watched it pale, then turn pink with new flesh.

Only when Stancie said, "Excellent," did he realize that his cock still stood to attention. Filled with revulsion, he looked around at them. What was he becoming that his need transcended even that kind of pain? Freya motioned to the block of ice. Stancie loosened the chain around the head of his cock. He crawled to it on hands and knees.

"Put your rod in it, Stephan," she instructed. "Work it until you come."

He leaned over the block with both hands braced. He couldn't do this.

"Yes you can," she whispered at his shoulder.

With one hand he placed his cock inside the icy hole. The ice brought its own kind of pain. "Your chants, don't forget your chants," she reminded.

He let the words flow through him and began to move his hips. The chants carried him away, until the sear of cold was just another friction on his cock, and all there was, was the boiling need inside him. His hips banged against the unyielding ice. He heard moaning and some part of him knew that it was him. And then his seed boiled up out of his balls and shot through his cock into the ice. He imagined it freezing as it pooled in the ice. He hunched over the block of ice, *proud and shamed as the chants drained away. Slowly he withdrew his cock, his chest heaving, the cold creating goose pimples over his body. He looked up at them through the shock of dark hair that had fallen over his eyes. Freya was smiling at him. Stancie looked smug. Dee brought up a rod.*

"Bring yourself up," she commanded, "and tell me where to place it."

Unbelievably, his loins began to throb. Were they making him erect, or was he doing it himself? God help him. "Hip," he croaked. "Right hip."

He fainted several times during that long night, whether from hunger or cold or the pain of the brands he wasn't sure. But they had always roused him. The respites they gave him were only from the hot irons or the ice, not from the hunger or the cold. Toward dawn, the dizziness came on him again. He reeled as Stancie ordered him to the block of ice. Could his Companion even heal when he was this tired, this hungry, this . . . empty? And how in hell could he have an erection in this condition? But he did. His cock was swollen and corded with vessels, leaking a drop of clear liquid which should be freezing on it, if not for the heat he was generating. He dragged himself across the snow. It melted around him, in spite of the predawn cold. The heat from the burn on his thigh seemed to be working its way inside him. He raised his head, sweating, and looked around. He could see everything, even more clearly than normal; the texture of stone, the crystals of ice in the snow. They gleamed and glowed. As a matter of fact, everything was glowing. He looked around again, as though from far away. Dee was inside getting warm, but Freya and Stancie had halos of light around them. Or maybe it was him. He looked down. He was . . . glowing. And he felt strong. The whoosh of his Companion running up his veins was so intense he hardly recognized it. He had a core of heat burning inside him. He stood and as he rose the rush of power inside him made him feel strong. He was bigger than they were, bigger than the night or the brands or the ice. He could do anything.

And then the world went black.

The next day, he was wakened from the sleep of the dead by the bolt on the door clunking back. What had happened last night? Fear fluttered in his center, not molten power. Whatever had happened, it frightened him more than the prospect of their endless training. He might be changing, somehow. And he might not be able to go back to what he was. Ever.

He was surprised to see Stancie slip in and sit on the bench beside him.

"They want to go slow. But there is no time and you may be getting close." Her eyes held a gleam that was a little maniacal, though at least they did not glow red. "You need to be schooled more rigorously." She ran her hands over his body, and grasped his organ. "Are you ready to take the next step?"

He nodded slowly, even though the last thing he wanted was an after-school tutor.

"Then I shall teach you, and you will obey me." She left him chained to the bench. "First I want my pleasure. Your regular training might be enough for Dee and Freya, but not for me."

Not enough? What kind of creature was she, that those nights of sex did not satisfy her? But already her power had coaxed his erection. She sat astride him, and all thoughts were pushed from his head by his need to restrain himself. How in the hell could he be ready to come after last night? She had shuddered twice and cried out when she lifted herself off him, and let her skirts swing down over her hips. She knelt beside him, caressing his cock slowly, as she whispered in his ear.

"If you do well, I'll feed you." He had forgotten that he still hadn't eaten. *"Think about lava, pooling in your loins,"* she breathed. She took his cock full in her hand. He couldn't help but moan. *"I'm going to work you, hard, but you won't come. You won't let yourself come."* Her hand slipped up and down his shaft, demanding, as she whispered encouragement in his ear. The feeling ramped up inside him until he wasn't sure he could bear it. *"You have a molten core, ready to explode."* Stephan began murmuring his chant. He was in imminent danger of spraying the ceiling with his semen. *"That's right,"* she whispered, but she pulled on him even harder. *"Do you feel the lava inside you, backed up from your balls into your belly?"* He was chanting frantically now inside his mind. *"Do you?"* He nodded. *"Good. I want you to feel that lava. It wants to be released, but it can't be. Does it burn?"* Again he nodded, though he did not stop his chanting. God, but it burned! She scrubbed the clear fluid he was leaking over the tip of his cock. *"I'm going to teach you new chants, Penitent. Now listen to me."*

Stephan took a deep breath and turned his head. Her eyes were red. She was helping him. "Bletherdon, hargarden, slitenger, shuit!" *she said.* "Now say it after me."

"Bletherdon, hargarden, slitenger, shuit!" *he whispered.*

"Again!" she commanded. *"With more feeling. The words are the chute through which your power flows."*

"Bletherdon, hargarden, slitenger, shuit!" She pulled on him to match his pace. He felt the burning in his loins, but the feeling of invincibility he had achieved last night was nowhere to be found. Again and again he said the meaningless words as she rubbed him, his back arched, every muscle in his body tensed against the lava that churned inside him.

"Enough!" she said sharply, after what seemed like hours. He collapsed against the stone, sore and exhausted. She rose and looked down at him, her mouth a small moue of disappointment. *"We still have much work to do. But I do no*

despair." He lay there, chest heaving, sweating, frustrated.

Just leave me alone, *he thought.* Mother of Mary, just go.

*"Not a word to the others, or I'll ensure you are pun-
ished," she tossed back over her shoulder. The energy that
burned inside him ramped down only slowly. He stared at
the stain in the corner, and wondered if it was his destiny to
be a second stain on the stones of this room.*

*And so it went. Nights with the three of them, days with
Stancie. They wanted that glow of power again, he knew.
But he couldn't produce it. They worked on his stoicism. He
tried to suppress all emotion other than a desire to be the
perfect tool for Rubius. He ignored increasing amounts of
pain for them. There were wounds, periods of starvation, of
sleep deprivation, and sessions with the brands and the ice.
He chanted for Stancie in the daytime as she worked him.
He ached and needed constantly. In moments of weakness he
didn't care about being the perfect tool. He wished he
would explode and be done with it. Let the burning inside
him become manifest and end his suffering.*

In the room above the tavern he was clenching his fists in his
pillow, sweating, sleep far away. Could these memories not
let him be? What good were they now?

Downstairs he heard a commotion.

"Please send for Mr. Sincai."

He would know that voice anywhere. What was she doing
here? He shot up off the bed.

"I'll do no such thing, Miss Van Helsing." Mr. Watkins
huffed his disapproval of such hoydenish behavior.

"Then I'll go up and search your rooms myself until I
find him."

Stephan thrust his arms into his coat and reached for
boots and boot pulls.

"Miss Van Helsing!" Watkins was outraged.

"Cousin, don't . . ." Van Helsing's voice. Stephan pulled his boots on. Her cousin here?

"Don't touch me!" A note of panic in her voice.

Stephan ripped open the door and ran down the stairs, achieving insouciance before he emerged on the landing. "Did someone call?" he drawled.

The scene before him was a tableau of startled faces. Van Helsing loomed over his fair cousin. She cringed away from him. Steadly, the runner, stood behind Van Helsing. Stephan spotted the bulge at his hip—probably shackles. Stephan set his teeth. The landlord had both fists planted firmly on his hips. Several denizens of the taproom had circled round to watch the fun. All stood frozen, staring up at Stephan.

Van Helsing was the first to recover. He drew back from what was obviously an attempt to grab Miss Van Helsing's arm. "Just in time, Sincai. This is the man, Steadly."

"I'm well aware of Mr. Sincai, Van Helsing."

"Then you know he did those murders."

"What I know is that he was not where he said he was on the night of the fifth."

"Then let me disabuse you of your doubts." Van Helsing sneered. "I saw him in Winscombe on the fifth when I went to get supplies."

Stephan strolled down the remaining stairs. "So we were both in Winscombe on the day in question?" he asked politely.

"*I* have an alibi for the time of the murders." Van Helsing smirked. "I returned to Maitlands, as the servants can attest. Do you have an alibi, Sincai?" He looked pointedly at his cousin. "Perhaps you were with Ann?"

"Yes," Miss Van Helsing said instantly, at the same moment Stephan said, "No," with equal emphasis.

"He was with me," she insisted, looking daggers at Stephan.

"Perhaps you were both involved," Steadly mused, looking at the girl. "They say you have . . . powers."

"Miss Van Helsing had nothing to do with the affair at the hunting lodge." Stephan's voice was firm and steady.

"I tend to agree, since the act took uncommon strength," Steadly observed. "And I am not normally a credulous man. Still . . ." His eyes flicked here and there, as though remembering the scene at the hunting lodge, and his face lost all color.

"Take them both in for questioning," Van Helsing suggested. "There is a second cell behind the town hall."

Stephan knew he had no choice at that point. He couldn't let Miss Van Helsing be imprisoned for his crime. "Alas, you have found me out." He sighed. "I confess the whole."

She looked at him, incredulous. "Don't do this."

Van Helsing wore an expression of triumph. Steadly looked self-satisfied. "Come with me, then," he said in his best stentorian tones, as though he was judge and jury.

Stephan inclined his head.

Miss Van Helsing began a protest, blinked twice, and fainted.

Immediately Mr. Watkins and several of the onlookers darted forward.

"Don't touch her," Stephan commanded. His voice held all the compulsion he could muster. All stopped in their tracks. Stephan grabbed a towel from the bar and pushed past Van Helsing. He knelt beside the girl and flapped the towel over her. The breeze lifted the curls from around her face. She had never looked more ethereal. "Get me water, man." The landlord leapt away as though he had been stung. "And you, boots, get me a pillow."

"Who put you in charge?" Van Helsing complained.

"Be quiet and stand back," Stephan ordered. "Miss Van Helsing?" he asked softly, continuing to flap the towel to give her air. Why had she come here when she was so weak? Had she wanted to warn him of Steadly and Van Helsing? She must know they couldn't hold him. What did it cost him to spend a few hours in a gaol cell? As soon as night fell he would escape.

Miss Van Helsing's eyelids fluttered. The landlord held out a tankard. Stephan smelled that it was filled with water. The boots scampered up with a pillow. "Miss Van Helsing?"

She blinked and looked up at him with those clear gray eyes. He saw them soften. With effort she raised her head. He slipped the pillow under her neck and held her up, then lifted the tankard to her mouth. She made a face as her lips touched the metal. Could she feel the others who had drunk from it? But she sipped. He pulled it away as she sighed. Then the worried frown came back to perch between her brows.

"Don't be concerned," he said, his voice pitched low. "Jennings will take you back to Maitlands." He looked up at Van Helsing. "Stay away from her, or you will answer to me."

"Go now, Mr. Sincai," she whispered fiercely.

He tried a little smile, hoping it was reassuring. "Right here?" He glanced around, then shook his head. "Can you sit?"

She nodded and he pushed up on her shoulders with the pillow to help her. "He knows," she whispered, only for his ears.

"I see that. Jennings," he called, and the man materialized from just outside the tavern door. "Take Miss Van Helsing home." Jennings touched his forelock. Stephan slid the pillow downward to help her stand and steadied her with it.

A mulish expression crossed Miss Van Helsing's face. "I won't go until I know where they're taking you."

"Well, come along then," Steadly said. He took the heavy shackles from his belt. They clanked ominously.

Stephan shoved up the sleeves of his coat and held out his wrists. Steadly clamped the cold, thick iron around them. Miss Van Helsing touched her fingers to her mouth in dismay.

"Go now. I'll be fine."

Again she set her lips. "I am up to this, Mr. Sincai, I assure you. I don't know why I fainted. A momentary weakness."

"Shall we?" Steadly gestured to the door. Stephan led the way, followed closely by Miss Van Helsing with Jennings hovering over her and the tavern's denizens trailing behind them.

Day was winding down. The sun shot deep red-gold rays between the leaves of the trees as it set behind the half-timbered town hall. Stephan squinted against its feeble light and felt his cheeks burn in reaction. Uncomfortable, but he wasn't naked, and it wasn't noon. He was old and he could stand a little sun these days. The party wended its way around the back of the hall and through a narrow wooden door strapped with iron. Inside, a lamp on the wall flickered and smoked, but shadows lurked everywhere. There were two stone-walled cells with rusty iron bars, obviously rarely used.

But what was most amazing was that one cell was draped with braided garlic and woven garlands made of some leafy branches with small white flowers. Stephan suppressed a smile. Wolfsbane.

Ann stared at the garlic and the wolfsbane hung over the cell. What was this? She searched her memory. Those would not hurt Stephan or keep him locked in the cell. The thought that garlic or wolfsbane would harm vampires were mere myths that had grown up around his kind. So, Erich didn't know as much about vampires as he pretended. Had his "associates" deliberately kept him from separating myth from fact? Perhaps they didn't trust him as much as he let on. She glanced to her cousin, whose face displayed a self-satisfied smirk. He thought he had trapped Mr. Sincai. She mustn't disabuse him of the notion. She took a breath and let it out. Sincai would be free as soon as they were gone. A few hours with the stink of garlic in his nostrils was the worst he would suffer.

She glanced to him and saw the tiny suppressed smile.

Mr. Steadly opened the cell door with a spine-scraping shriek and motioned Sincai in. He strode through the cell door, forced to duck to accommodate his height.

"Comfortable?" Erich asked.

Sincai sat on the hard wooden bench and stretched a leg out in front of him, folding his arms across his broad chest. Steadly slammed the door and turned a large key in the lock. Erich stepped forward and looped a large silver crucifix on a leather thong around the bars and tied it.

Ann carefully arranged a blank expression on her face. Another myth. Stephan had once been a Jesuit priest, and kissed a crucifix a dozen times a day. It could not harm him.

"That should keep you," her cousin announced, and turned to the runner.

Squire Fladgate sailed across the yard like a frigate with all sails spread. "What's this? Van Helsing, Steadly? Why wasn't I consulted about this?"

"We have a runner from Bow Street here, Fladgate," Erich said, and waved a dismissive hand. "That should be enough authority for you."

"Not in Cheddar Gorge, young man," the squire puffed. "Here *I* represent the Crown."

Erich barked a laugh. "Well, then. We have caught your murderer for you. Are you saying we should let him go?" Several in the crowd guffawed.

"Well, no. No, of course not." The squire realized he was not in command of the crowd. More, he had made himself an object of fun. "Just that we should make it official. I shall conduct the trial on Tuesday."

"So you shall," Erich said magnanimously, clearly in control.

"Why this folderol, Van Helsing?" Steadly frowned at the strings of garlic and flowers.

"Indulge me, Steadly." Erich grinned. "You saw the room

at Bucklands Lodge after the murders. You don't think a normal man could have done that, do you?"

"No." That word said it all. The whispers from the crowd that pressed in at the doorway behind him contained the echoed word "vampire." Ann turned to see several villagers make the sign against the evil eye. She had seen that sign often in her life. Stephan would be outcast now. He would have to leave the village even if by some miracle he was acquitted of the murders. The crowd at the door dispersed as though they were leaves blasted by an autumn wind.

"Come, Cousin," Erich said, motioning her to the door with exaggerated deference.

She glanced to Sincai and felt the small reassuring smile as much as saw it. She couldn't muster a smile in return. This would be the last time she would see him.

When Ann and her cousin got to Maitlands, Polsham and Mrs. Simpson were hauling loads of garlic and wolfsbane up the main staircase to the first floor.

"Ah, I see the delivery has arrived," Erich said, throwing his hat and gloves onto the table in the grand foyer. "Haste, haste! It's full dark. I want my room entirely covered."

"We're done with your room," Polsham said, barely civil. "These are for the nursery."

"Then I'll take dinner in my room." Erich hastened up the broad stairs. "Bring in a bottle of brandy, as well." He didn't seem so confident now that night had come on. What had he to fear? Sincai was probably long gone by now.

The drive home with Erich had been excruciating, what with his gloating and reliving the expression on Sincai's face when the shackles had been applied. She had huddled in the corner of the carriage. The only consolation was that he had not brought up the special license. How long would it take to arrive from London? Anxiety had given way to despair.

Now Ann was truly exhausted. She tottered up the stairs after Polsham and Mrs. Simpson and stopped in to see her uncle. She daren't tell him about Van Helsing's threat of a special license. She was most afraid he would agree with the plan. Nor could she let on that the entire town was afraid of Sincai. She didn't want to worry him. Her uncle seemed to be a little better, though with twilight his spirits too had sunk and he could only murmur his thanks for her sitting with him.

When at last she left her uncle, Mrs. Simpson followed her up the stairs, tut-tutting, plainly frightened by her cousin's odd proclivity for garlic and wolfsbane. She gave Ann her mother's crucifix to wear and brought a bowl of barley soup. Soon enough Mrs. Simpson and her nervous chatter were leaving with the empty bowl. Ann huddled in her bed, an empty ache growing within her. Dark eyes, wild dark hair, and the sense of strength she'd gotten from him already seemed to be fading. There seemed no escape. She couldn't leave her nursery or her uncle. But if she stayed, her cousin could well carry out his threat. He probably waited for marriage only to keep the goodwill of the servants and the townspeople. After he married her . . . Horrible images of her cousin's wet mouth over hers, his tongue slimy, his soft hands kneading her, came to roost behind her eyes like carrion birds and would not leave. And then there was the madhouse. She felt it lurking just out of sight. She had seen her mother there, rocking in dirty straw, scratching her flesh until it bled.

There was no one to help her. Her uncle sick, Mr. Sincai no doubt already gone, the servants cowed by her cousin—she had never felt so alone.

Fourteen

Stephan stood in the woods above Maitlands Abbey, a deeper shadow in the night. The wind through the trees around him shushed in whispers he could not quite understand. The bark of the great birch he leaned against was smooth against his back. What he didn't understand was why he was about to translocate himself into the fourth-floor nursery below him. Kilkenny would be here anytime, perhaps with others. The time to test himself was nearly at hand. He would die or find redemption. Stephan couldn't stay at the tavern anymore, the most obvious place for Kilkenny to find him. But he could spend his nights at the hunting lodge. Surely the one who had escaped would start his search there. It was isolated, a perfect place to battle to the death, away from human eyes. He was sure no one would go within a mile of the place with all the whispered stories circulating in the villages round about. Days he could spend in Miss Van Helsing's cave. He had a plan. He should be focused on his mission.

Yet here he was, in the dark and the rising wind, staring at a nursery, knowing he would go. Van Helsing might know he was there. But the weasel couldn't stop him. If he accosted Stephan, why, it was just a matter of raising his Companion and drawing the compulsion and Van Helsing would remember nothing. The man had a remarkably weak mind.

Weak? Who was weak? Weak enough to stand here, knowing what he would do.

Why had this slip of a girl gotten so far under his skin?

He clenched his teeth. He was not one to shirk the truth. It was because she knew him. She knew what he was and she was not appalled. She knew everything about him. Well, except for his experience with the Daughters, and that was just as well. She . . . forgave him. He did not deserve forgiveness, but she gave it anyway, naturally.

She was strong enough even for that. She had tried to bandage his wounds, at great personal cost. She was strong enough to try to save him today, from what? A few hours in a cell?

Ah . . . she knew his weaknesses. And she thought Van Helsing might know them, as well. There was a time when he would have wanted to kill anyone who knew the few ways to best him. Strangely enough, with her, it seemed a comfort that someone knew.

And understood. The thought astounded him. Still, she was an outcast, like he was. She had special abilities that made her different as he did. She was hated, as he was. Part of her ability was to see the good in people, even after she knew the worst. And she knew the worst of him. Would she recognize that as a fabulous advantage?

It was he who was weak. He felt something for her. He wasn't sure what. Friendship? It wasn't the all-consuming passion he had felt for Beatrix for nearly seven hundred years. Miss Van Helsing affected him physically, but that was just his training with the Daughters getting the better of him. Whatever it was, it ate at him, wouldn't be banished. It made him . . . ache. Maybe because he had never experienced just this feeling.

Feeling? God, but he couldn't allow emotion now. That would weaken him for the coming battle. He was a poor tool at best. He could not afford to weaken himself further.

He swallowed and tried to think about the power he had found at Mirso with the Daughters. He would need that power now, every ounce of it.

MIRSO MONASTERY, SEPTEMBER 1821

"Wake, Penitent." Her small, petulant voice reached him in his half-conscious state. He couldn't call it sleep. He turned his head.

Stancie stood just inside the doorway with a glass ball in her hand, about the size of a Seville orange. It caught the light from the fire. What could that be for? He was beyond fear. What would happen would happen. He felt only a mild curiosity.

She set it on the sideboard. "We are going to try something different today." But as usual, she started with her own pleasure. She fancied licking first today, and then one frantic riding of his cock. But there was a sense of expectation about her. When she had finished with him, she knelt beside the bench and began the torment and whispered instructions. He felt the molten lava inside himself. His cock was an aching steel rod, his balls heavy as iron. He muttered the chants as the boiling inside him ramped up. She lifted his head, urging him to chant with greater vehemence. He watched her rub him with increasing urgency.

"Watch the glass ball," she hissed into his ear. "Focus all your heat on that ball." The glass burned at its core. Was that reflected firelight? He stared at the glass, feeling the

burning inside himself echoed there in shades of dull red.

On and on she urged him, long after she would normally have let him rest. His body was taut as a bow string, every muscle tensed. He could feel Stancie's power ramping up farther and farther as she kept him from ejaculation. He was not even sure ejaculation was possible at this point. Sensation had gone beyond the sexual into something different, more painful, more intense. The glass ball flickered with a more incandescent orange.

Suddenly, there was another hum besides that of Stancie's power in the room. The pain of his sensation receded. He still arched his body. Stancie still massaged his cock. The ball began to emit small white flashes. The molten core of him seemed to melt outward, enveloping the entire room in a haze of burning light. The power glimpsed so long ago on the battlements shot through him.

The glass ball burst into blinding white light. An explosion went off inside his head. Somewhere he heard shrieking. Was it Stancie? Was it him?

Then the light was gone. He collapsed. Blackness enveloped him.

When he woke the three of them were in the room. He felt far away, empty.

"What you did was dangerous, Stancie." Dee's voice was steel-hard and disapproving.

"You could have killed him, or yourself," Freya protested.

"You are both too timid." Stancie pouted. "He needed a stronger hand. I gave it to him. And look . . . he has done it."

"You could have ruined everything, like you did the last time," Freya accused.

"You two would take years to make him ready. Father was growing anxious."

Stephan cracked an eye. He was lying on the stone bench.

But no chains bound him. They clustered round the side-board. Dee stared at something on the floor, then looked back at him. He lowered his eyes. "Come," she said. "Come and see."

He struggled up. He was so weak, his knees barely held him up as he staggered toward them. They parted. There was a pool of molten glass on the stone.

Freya answered the question he was not allowed to ask. "You did that, Stephan. It means you are nearly ready."

"And your training has entered phase three," Freya said. No one had mentioned there was a phase three. Dread and fear welled within him. Would he ever be ready?

"It means you, Stancie, will let him alone during the day," Dee ordered crisply.

Stancie smiled and nodded.

Stephan stood, chest heaving, trying to lock out the memory. A storm was blowing up. He looked up through the trees and saw the moon at the center of a luminous ring being eaten by the rushing clouds. His body was electrified with memory, filled with energy that expressed itself in a throbbing in his loins. Or was it memory that affected him so? Of a sudden, all he could think about was the girl's body under his hands, her clear gray eyes that knew him, and did not turn away. *Tuatha, rendon, melifant, extonderant, denering.* He whispered the chants without thinking. Slowly he fought his feeling, got control, suppressed the erection. His test was at hand. He had only one chance for redemption and refuge. He could not afford to jeopardize it.

He gazed down at the dim light issuing from the gabled window he knew was next to her bed. There were so many reasons he should not go down there. He could not deny he was becoming involved with her. She roused him physically and emotionally. Sexual impulses were dangerous in his current state, except as they were used to draw the power. He could never trust himself with a woman again. He would never know physical love. Not after what had happened . . . He jerked his mind away from that. The girl couldn't experience a physical union, either. They were a tragedy or perhaps a farce. In fact, they were perfect for each other. But the emotional connection he felt for her endangered his mission even more than the physical attraction. Emotions were something he could not afford.

He must *not* go to her. His night vision made out the garlic braids and the wolfsbane garlands in Van Helsing's room. The stupid creature had barricaded himself in his room, at least in his own mind. There was no threat of discovery from that quarter.

Very well. Stephan realized the decision was already made. He was powerless to resist the attraction. He drew the power.

Ann sat huddled in her bed, her fears running circles in her head.

She felt him more than saw him. Cinnamon, with a sweet underlying structure of scent, wafted through the room. She lifted her eyes and saw a whirling pool of black. She had not seen that since the first night in the cave. But it didn't frighten her now as it had then. Stephan Sincai stepped out of the evaporating darkness.

Relief and something more drenched her. She could not say just how she felt.

"Hello," he rumbled softly. She would know that voice until the day she died. "Do I disturb you?"

"Is it safe for you to be here?"

He gave half a grunt. "You think Van Helsing will venture out of his room?"

"You're right." She smiled. "I'm glad you came."

He looked as though he was not sure he was glad. "I had to thank you for your courage in coming to warn me today, unnecessary as it was."

"I thought Erich . . . but it turns out he doesn't know very much about you after all."

"Unlike you."

A silence stretched between them, until she felt something would snap. "Please, won't you sit?" What had changed? Why did she not feel at ease? She had felt more natural around him than anyone else in her life. But now there was some new element she couldn't quite identify. All her erotic dreams came back to her. She could practically feel his body inside his clothes. She couldn't afford to indulge those dreams. She would never touch a man in that way. Except her cousin, and that only against her will.

"What is wrong?" he asked sharply.

She shook her head quickly and smiled. "Nothing."

He drew up the wing chair. "You can't lie to me, you know. I think I got something of you when you got all of me."

She clutched her knees to her chest. So, he had figured that out. Part of the problem, she could confide. "Erich sent for a special license. He means to marry me. You . . . you know how impossible that is for me."

A fierce expression flashed in his eyes as his brows drew down. Some would find him frightening. "You're of age."

"And friendless. Who would say him nay?" She tried a smile. It didn't work. "The village wants me under some-one's control or locked up. Even my uncle wants a way to *provide* for me."

"Then go to London, now, tonight. I'll set you up with a lady companion, rent you a house. I'll come to see you are settled as soon as I—" He broke off.

They both knew that he might not survive his confronta-tion with Kilkenny.

"When will he come?" she whispered.

"Tonight, tomorrow night. He could have been in Ireland, or France. But soon." His voice was bleak. He leaned forward, his elbows on his knees, head hanging.

"Perhaps afterward . . ." She knew he would never forgo the task that would buy him peace, no matter that it would require killing, no matter the wounds he suffered, no matter the outcome. She would never ask it of him. He was doing what he could for the future of his kind, and he so needed the refuge it would buy him. She understood about refuge.

He nodded, briskly. Then he peered at her. "Here I am keeping you from your sleep. And I should go to the hunting lodge. That's where I'm most likely to meet him."

She nodded. She couldn't say anything. Her throat was knotted around a huge lump.

He did a surprising thing. He reached out and laid his hand next to her foot under the quilt, just laid it there, quietly, not touching her. They both stared at that hand. It was strong, and square. No one in Cheddar Gorge but her knew how strong.

After a long moment, he rose in one smooth motion. "You control your own fate, Miss Van Helsing. Refuse him." His eyes went red as they rested on her in an expression half puzzled, half regretful. The darkness swirled up around him. When it dissipated, he was gone.

The lump in her throat turned into a sob. Tears rolled down her cheeks. So close and yet so impossible. The future had never looked so bleak. Did he realize she was about to lose the very kind of refuge he sought so single-mindedly? She found herself thinking, not about her predicament, but that Stephan Sincai was gone, perhaps to die, and they would never touch.

Stephan shimmered into view just outside Maitlands's hunting box, Buckland Lodge, with all sorts of emotions churning in his breast. It had taken him three translocations to get here, and he had pushed his Companion ruthlessly for power. It wasn't speed in getting here that drove him, he knew, but speed in getting away from Maitlands and Miss Van Helsing. The draw he felt for her was growing stronger. He could not afford to indulge it. Lord knew he was an imperfect enough tool as it was, without damaging his powers further.

The lodge was situated in a grove of sycamores on slightly higher ground that looked out over a sea of grasslands that sloped gently down to the river Axe. As garrulous and rushing as it was coming out of the Cheddar Gorge, down here the river spread itself in lazy splendor among the reeds. There would be waterfowl aplenty for Brockweir guns as well as foxes, hares, and the more traditional pheasants. Now a wind that promised storms tossed the tall grasses in dancing abandon. Stephan looked up at the lodge. It was old, a Tudor affair with brick work and half-timbered plaster, sheltered by a stand of ancient trees. The first floor overhung the ground floor, giving it a slightly menacing look appropriate for the atrocity he had committed here.

Stephan stepped up to the front door, his cape swirling around him in the wind. It was a heavy affair of iron-strapped wood with a lock meant for a great iron key. After the squire sent down women to clean it they had locked up so it wouldn't become a place for thrill-seeking young people to picnic or provide refuge for petty human criminals. But they hadn't stopped at that. No, they'd nailed the door shut with great six-inch spikes. Several were still scattered on the portico.

A flash of failure overwhelmed him. He hadn't been able to use his new power properly against the nest. He'd been forced to fight the creatures with conventional means. He had been stronger than usual. The training had given him that much. But he'd barely escaped with his life, and he'd not been able to kill them all. Now he was feeling emotions over the damned girl. His power would be weakened even further. How could he win against even more of them when Kilkenny brought his army back for vengeance?

Stephan pulled at the door until the nails shrieked, the metal of the lock protested and gave way. The minute it creaked open, he could smell the blood. It still lurked in cracks and crevices and corners. Stephan wondered if he could bear to wait for Kilkenny here. He roamed through the house. The dining room was empty. A flash of how he had last seen it snapped through his brain; filled with shards of furniture and broken glass, blood and severed heads. He had not been able to use his full power that night, to his shame, but he had caused carnage enough. Or almost enough. They must have taken the wood out back and burned it. Through the overwhelming smell of blood, Stephan had the scent of burning wood . . . and cinnamon.

Dread crashed through him. He pushed it down savagely. Emotions were not allowed, now least of all. Wishes, though—one was allowed to wish, wasn't one? He wished with all his heart there were not too many of them. He stepped into the front parlor silently. Among the dust-covered furniture he stopped where he could see the front door, swinging wildly on its hinges in the wind. He went still, that he might feel the vibrations of the newly made and count them.

What he felt instead was that hum at the extreme edge of consciousness indicating very old vampires.

He took a breath. His heart galloped in fits and starts in his throat as a tall, graceful figure slid through the open doorway.

"Hello, Deirdre," he said with outward calm. He was the Harrier now. He did not have to kneel to her. "What are you doing here?"

She was dressed in a heavy wool cape, black, lined with black satin. She pushed back the hood from the dark mass of her hair. Behind her, Freya stepped out of her shadow. Freya too wore a black wool cape, though hers was lined with shimmering white satin. Their eyes were hard, cold as they looked him up and down, saying nothing.

All the reasons they could be here darted through his mind. He sent a phrase of the chant through his thoughts to banish fear. Could they mean to help him, knowing he would be overwhelmed? They did not look like eager warriors . . .

"I can smell the stink of emotion on him, Freya." Deirdre's voice cracked out, clear against the howling wind.

"It's a good thing we came." Even Freya's voice was unforgiving. And why would they forgive him? His last failure at Mirso had cost them a sister's love.

"Why are you here?" Stephan repeated, making his voice reflect his will, implacable.

Deirdre eyed him up and down. "To clean up the leavings, when you fail."

That hit him hard. They were so sure he would fail? He wouldn't ask for their help. He couldn't blame Rubius for needing insurance. But to send his own daughters out into the world, away from the protection of Mirso? Rubius too must think he'd fail, and be desperate, indeed.

"I'll try to do you out of a job."

"Like you did with the ones who were staying here?" Freya's words slapped at him.

Guilt bent his head. He took a breath and raised his eyes to theirs. "The one that escaped will bring Kilkenny here, where I can get at him."

Deirdre's expression of disdain was like an arrow in his heart. "Don't tell me you let his second in command go by design."

The one that got away had been Kilkenny's second? How did they know that? And . . . now he came to think on it, how did they know where to find him? It had been only two weeks since he had written to Rubius about coming to Cheddar Gorge. It would take far longer for the note to get to Mirso and the Daughters to travel to this remote corner of England. Unless . . .

"You don't think Father trusted you, do you?" Freya asked, apparently reading his question in his face. "After what happened at Mirso?" She looked . . . disappointed in him.

"So you were sent to follow me from the first," Stephan said matter-of-factly. He felt once more like the humble Penitent not allowed to speak in their presence. Their certainty he would fail was like a knife in his belly. He could not let them see that. "Why didn't Rubius just send you to kill Asharti's remnants in the first place?" he asked.

"We are his daughters," Freya said, drawing herself up. "He does not want to risk us."

"Freya," Deirdre snorted. "How can you still be naïve after all these years? The truth is, Harrier, our talents are not for killing. No, we are the way to make more weapons like you. He does not want to endanger his capacity to create Harriers."

Freya sniffed. "It is a measure of his desperation that we are here at all."

"Your power in its current state will get many, but not all," Deirdre said. "Our job is to assess the degree of your failure and know how many more of you to create."

"Well, you've had a long trip for nothing." He got himself in hand and managed insouciance. "I'll kill them all. You should have more faith." He took a breath and made his voice light. "You're staying at the Hammer and Anvil? I trust you find it comfortable. You should perhaps return there, unless you have some final words of wisdom for me."

Deirdre smiled. He had never seen her smile. He didn't like the sensation now.

"Here are my words," she almost whispered. "Prepare yourself for your task, if you are to have any chance to return to Mirso." Then her eyes went red.

For an instant, Stephan thought she was going to take

hold of him, tell him to strip and give him a lesson in obedience and control right there in the drawing room of Bucklands Lodge. But the blackness only whirled up around her, followed an instant later by Freya's own power, and they disappeared the way they had come.

Stephan was left standing in the darkened room alone. His stomach churned. They would not have gone far. They would want to know when Kilkenny and company arrived. Stephan had enough control not to move. He did not pace or run his hands through his hair. He simply stood.

Why had they revealed themselves to him? To shake his confidence further? To ensure he would not succeed? To punish him for what he had done . . . ?

He pushed the thoughts, the memories away. *Sithfren, hondrelo, frondura, denai.*

Air into his lungs, air out. He breathed. Better. He couldn't be afraid when Kilkenny came. He couldn't doubt himself. Damn the Daughters! Damn the Van Helsing girl. He had been indulging in emotion entirely too much lately.

He turned and sat in a huge wooden chair, one of the peculiarly uncomfortable carved Tudor thrones. It suited his purpose admirably. He wanted to be uncomfortable. He would sit here until dawn or until Kilkenny came, drawing his power, practicing his control. Preparing.

Ann's mind was in turmoil after Mr. Sincai disappeared. She couldn't possibly sleep under the circumstances. She had to think what to do about Van Helsing, about her uncle, about Mr. Sincai . . .

He came to her bedside. He was naked. She saw his chest and shoulders clearly, but his nether parts were in shadow. He was bulky with muscle, dangerous and strong. His long dark hair swirled about his shoulders with a life of its own. He didn't say anything. He just stared at her. He was sweating slightly. His skin was damp. His nipples peeked out through a light dusting of dark hair. His eyes burned her. He was going to touch her . . . everywhere and she wanted that. As a matter of fact, she had a peculiar, full feeling between her legs and his touch might cure that. Or make it worse.

How had she come to bed naked? But she was, and he knelt beside her on the bed. He pressed his body alongside hers, touching the whole length of her, and feathered her neck, her lips with kisses, until she began to throb between her legs. She knew she would be wet there, but that was not a thing to regret. His hands roamed her body, touching her with an exquisite, firm, strangely masculine touch. She couldn't describe it, but it wasn't what she expected at all. She wanted more. *Needed* more. She lifted her hips against him, wondering what would happen next. But he just kept touching her, kissing her, until she wanted to scream. Her nether parts were clenching. She put her own hand down to stop them from doing what they were doing, but somehow, as she searched for the place that itched with need, she couldn't find it. She kneaded her mound, trying to press away the throbbing. Then a wrenching sensation contracted her whole body.

With a shock, she woke, gasping. Her hand was between her legs, even as she throbbed with . . . what? What had happened? She jerked her hand away. Her thighs were wet. Her fingers smelled of her own musk. God, had she damaged herself somehow? Was that . . . Wait! She knew of such things. It was called "the little death."

She had rubbed herself to ecstasy while thinking of Stephan Sincai. A blush suffused her whole body. Wanton! She could not have the touch of a man, so she touched herself in her sleep? Pathetic. Sterile. Everyone she knew would call it sinful. Sadness came and sat on her shoulders. Not so much, unfortunately, because of her sin, but because that was all she would ever know of what made her a woman. Stupid girl! If that was all it was, she could live without that.

It was still night. The draperies in her bedroom had not been drawn and branches tapped and scraped against the glass in the wind. Rain beat in staccato sheets and shimmied down the pane, making the world seem unreal. It must be near morning. She hardly felt strong enough to move. Weak flesh! She had drained her resources pleasuring herself when she should be thinking about her cousin, her uncle, not about Sincai. She could practically feel Van Helsing down in his room, polluting the refuge of Maitlands. Soon it would be daylight, and Erich would come to her room whenever he pleased or be waiting for her when she went to visit her uncle. She wasn't sure he'd even wait for marriage. What was to stop him from taking her here, in her bed, in whatever disgusting way he pleased? It wouldn't be anything like her dream about Sincai.

She had to leave this place. Not permanently—how could she contemplate that? But just for now. She rose and threw on her cloak, drew on her stout half-boots. She was for her cave.

The key turned in the lock of her door. Erich threw open the door to the nursery without even using the knocker she had installed long ago to warn her of intruders to her privacy. She hadn't heard him on the stair. "So," he said, eyeing her. He slapped a rolled paper against the palm of his opposite hand.

Ann turned and pulled her cloak around her. She felt the blood drain from her face. "How . . . how dare you enter without permission, sir?"

He strode to the center of the room, glaring at her. The snap of the rolled paper cracked at her senses. He glanced about the room. "And how do you get out, my willful loon?"

"Get out? Oh, you mean my cloak." She swallowed. "I was cold."

"What a poor lie. You were going out, even though your door was locked." He looked around again, more carefully. "Let's see, my loon, how you escape."

To Ann's horror, he went to a bookcase and began running his hands over the carved wooden edge. "Speaking of lunacy, whatever are you doing?" she croaked.

He whirled on her. "Where is it? There's a secret passage, is there not?"

"You, sir, are a guest in my house, and you will leave my private chamber at once."

Erich glared at her. Then his stare seemed to waver. Her heart fell into her shoes as she realized he was staring over her shoulder at the fireplace. "Priests' holes . . . They're always near the hearth, aren't they? An old pile like this might have one. They'd need a plan to get the children to safety from the nursery in case of . . . wasn't one of the Brockweirs a Jacobite sympathizer?" He strode past her to the fireplace. "Bonnie Prince Charlie and all of that."

"You will leave immediately, sir," she commanded with what authority she could muster as her knees weakened. He was going to find it. Even now he ran his hand over the stone carving . . . the knob at the center of the rose . . .

The door sprang open.

He spun, maniacal triumph writ large on his face. "I knew it!"

"And so?" Ann felt calm coat her, though the center of her boiled with anger and with fear. The secret door had been the only thing that kept her refuge from being a trap.

"So I shall have Polsham nail it up at both ends." Erich drew himself up and went still.

"Polsham takes his orders from me." But Erich seemed so sure of himself.

He let a slow smile spread over his features. It just didn't reach his eyes. Ann had never seen a smile just like that. "Not any more, my own private loon." He held up the rolled paper. "The special license," he announced. "And I received your uncle's blessing today. Your retainers know that with a quick trip to Mr. Cobblesham tomorrow afternoon to make arrangements and two witnesses, by Thursday afternoon we shall be locked in holy matrimony."

"And my fortune will be yours."

Again the smile. "And by Thursday night, your body will be mine, as well."

Ann's eyes welled with tears. "You can have my fortune. I won't make any trouble for you. But . . ." The word stuck in her throat. She tried again. "But . . . please don't touch me."

"A husband not claim his rights? Your high-handed treatment hasn't inspired restraint."

"I won't be high-handed. I won't be proud." Her voice sounded small even to herself.

"No you won't. But I still plan to do some plunging. Quite a bit in fact."

"I'm not crazy, you know. But I will be if you carry out your plan." She said it straightforwardly, as sanely as she could.

He approached. He was only six inches taller than she was but still he loomed over her. She could see the slime on his teeth, smell his foul breath. She daren't cower or run to the other side of the room. That kind of behavior would incite a bully. "I don't care," he said between gritted teeth. "In fact, that guarantees I can put you in an asylum. Your fifteen thousand a year will set me up nicely." His pale blue eyes gleamed. "And no one blames a man deprived of a wife in the prime of life for taking his solace where he may."

He tapped her forehead with the rolled license. She felt the men who had prepared it, the one who had rolled it and got a faint, distasteful echo of Erich himself. He was . . . weak. She knew that of course. He had . . . secrets. She couldn't tell what they were.

He turned and headed for the door, yelling for Polsham.

She let out a breath when he disappeared, but he shocked her by putting his head back around the doorjamb. "Don't think your Harrier friend will save you. He'll be out of the way in a day or two. We'll just protect our rooms at night and let nature take its course."

He was gone.

Ann collapsed where she was on the floor, as though all the air had been let out of her. She was too horrified to sob. She looked around at the nursery as though it had become Katmandu or Peking. Her refuge had been transformed into a prison. What could be done? What could she *do*? Her uncle was now on the side of her persecutor, through the best of intentions for her welfare. She couldn't upset him when he was so ill. The servants were helpless. Mr. Cobblesham had never been an intellectual light or a beacon of courage. He hadn't even kept the chimney sweeps from taking children from the orphanage as climbing boys and virtual slaves. He wouldn't help her against someone who would in the next days become a powerful patron.

Who might help her? Not Mr. Sincai. He had made it clear he had his own concerns. She would probably never see him again. Mr. Sincai wanted her to leave for London. It might as well be Katmandu or Peking, it seemed so impossible. She wanted her refuge back, and that meant ousting Erich somehow from Maitlands.

The squire! Squire Fladgate had the power to revoke a special license, didn't he? He could not want an outsider to have Maitlands, especially one likely to be as pushy as Erich. After the episode at the gaol, he would have no love lost for Erich. Was he concerned enough to try to throw a spoke in Erich's wheel? She would have to find out. It was her only chance.

Fifteen

Ann hadn't slept a wink. The sun was full up and still she paced. But if she was to leave the house at all Ann had to do it now. Right now, so she might catch Erich off his guard. She hurried to the nursery door and peered out. The staircase was empty. She heard voices, faintly. Erich was engaging Polsham to board up the secret passage.

She lost no time but darted down the stairs. If she could make it to the stable . . . Another flight, past Erich's room, and she was on the first floor. She peered over the railing from the hallway overlooking the great arched staircases that ran down to the hall below. She shuddered to think about the echo her footsteps across those great marble tiles would make. Surely Erich would catch her! She couldn't go out by the kitchen. The voices came from that direction. They were arguing now. Good for Polsham! The French doors in the library . . . they gave out onto the terrace. She scampered down the stairs as fast as she could and took an immediate right through the dim Grand Salon with its dust-covered furniture, into the long library, and let herself out in the morning light.

Once Maitlands had required a staff of fifty, what with gardeners and grooms, footmen and undercooks and such. Now it was silent. The fish pond at the center of the formal gardens was cloudy and dull. The hedges themselves, once so neatly trimmed, had sprouted leafy prongs of disarray. Maitlands Abbey was dying.

She pulled up her skirts and dashed across the flagstone terrace. A tiny voice said that maybe having her gone would be better for Maitlands, that she was the reason there were no servants to keep it up. She swallowed hard and ran for the stables.

"Jennings," she gasped as she put her head in at the huge barn, now holding only carriage horses and her uncle's aging hack. "Jennings, are you here?"

He stuck his head out of the tack room, soap and a rag in his hand. His broad, solid face was creased in concern. "Miss? What's wrong?"

"Could . . . could you harness my cart for me? I must leave immediately on an errand." She struggled to get her breathing under control.

"Why, let me take you in the barouche, miss. It would be much more seemly." He was dressed in polished boots, buff breeches, and shirtsleeves. His bottle-green uniform coat was hung on a peg next to the tack room door.

"Not necessary." She managed a smile. She did not want to drag Jennings into this. If Erich won out and became master of Maitlands, his involvement would have consequences. "The cart will do, and you know very well I'm a good driver." She had her own harness. Jennings kept it clean. That's how she knew he was utterly trustworthy. She sensed it through the leather.

He must have seen the look in her eyes. He nodded briefly, threw the soap and the rag on a stool, and retreated into the tack room to retrieve the harness. In less than ten minutes, Ann was scrambling up into the cart and taking the reins.

"Thank you, Jennings," she murmured.

"Be careful, miss." His voice rose to follow her, since she was even now slapping the reigns over the Haflinger's creamy mane and tail. The cart clattered out of the stable yard.

The squire's residence was on the far side of the village about three miles on. But she was betting she did not have to go so far. The woods flashed past the pony's brisk trot. They would have discovered Sincai's escape by now. The squire might well have been called to town. She might even meet them on the road as they came to inform Erich.

But there was no one on the road to Maitlands. With anxiety rising in her breast, she urged the Haflinger to a canter. The cart jolted over the road. She slowed him only when she reached the outskirts of Cheddar Gorge. She allowed him to trot by the Hammer and Anvil and up to the town hall. People in the street pointed and whispered. She tried not to notice. She needed the squire. She must focus on that.

Pulling up in front of the hall, massive and solid with its hewn stone walls, she leapt from the cart and patted the pony. "Good boy, Max." The pretty blond beast was blowing. "Boy," she called to an urchin nearby. "A shilling if you walk my pony up and down." He rushed up, hand out. Max threw his head up and down twice and blew out a whicker through his flaring nostrils.

Ann went round back of the hall. A crowd there muttered around the open door to the two gaol cells. She could hear their fear talking.

"Just disappeared, he did." This from Jemmy.

"The cell door was still locked, I hear," Mrs. Scrapple cawed.

"All that garlic and such didn't keep him in. What was Van Helsing thinking?"

"What was 'e that 'e could get out through a locked door? Maybe Van Helsing was right." Mr. Watkins sounded unsure, but there were several grunts of agreement.

The crowd turned. She stopped. Silence fell. "Is Squire Fladgate here?" she asked in a voice she hoped wasn't tremulous.

"Do you have information?" The familiar stentorian tones carved a path through the crowd as they parted, heads pivoting. Squire Fladgate's paunchy figure stood at the open door.

"I need to see you, sir."

"And I need to see you, young lady." He strode forward. The crowd fell away, muttering.

Ann swallowed. "Can we talk somewhere private? At the inn perhaps?"

"Did you have anything to do with this?" The squire frowned.

"With . . . ?" Ann looked around at the reflected accusations.

"With Sincai's escape."

So. Erich was right. They thought she was his partner. That would make her job more difficult. "Has he escaped?" she asked, craning to look around the squire's bulky form.

"You're a bad dissembler," the squire accused.

"How could I have gotten him out of a locked cell?" she asked, trying for incredulity.

"Ye're a witch," Jemmy screeched. "Ye can do magic."

"You think I got him out with magic?" She chuckled. "Surely, Squire, you don't believe that. You are an educated man."

The squire flushed. "He got out of a locked cell somehow. The key has been in Mr. Steadly's possession here all night." He nodded behind her.

Ann turned. The Bow Street runner had come up behind her. His eyes were dark blue and cold. His mouth was set in a grim line. The crowd leaned closer. "Perhaps we can talk, miss?" He reached out and before she could pull away he took her arm just above the elbow.

Crashing sensation engulfed her. Steadly was under suspicion by his department for taking bribes. That was why he had been sent to what his superiors considered the hinterlands on this wild-goose chase. Their suspicions were true. His life flashed before her; an impoverished childhood, being taken in by a philanthropist, educated, rejected by his patron's friends because of his background, finding his place in Bow Street, disillusion that corruption prevailed even there, joining the corruption, his shame and his relentless rejection of that shame. It all cascaded over her. She watched his eyes grow big.

With a supreme effort, she wrenched away and staggered to the side.

"Girl, where do you think you're going?" The squire pulled her back.

Self-congratulation! Bitterness at his wife's death. Angry confusion that he did not know how to talk to his son who was up at London doing the town and in dun territory. Determination not to let his position in the town be compromised by this incident.

Ann let out a cry. The squire let her go as though he had been burned. She careened through the crowd, bumping against first one and then another. Mrs. Scrapple hated her, hated Mr. Watkins, hated everyone. Jealousy bathed Ann, and . . . failing health. Mrs. Scrapple would die within the month. The ostler at the Hammer and Anvil thought Ann would make a fancy piece, and imagined her lying with her thighs spread in the hay. He wanted to take her but knew he couldn't do it. His body always betrayed him, to his shame. It made him hate women.

Sensations showered over Ann. She thought she would faint. Breaking free, she stumbled into the lane behind the hall, gasping. Nausea overcame her and she leaned on her knees, head down. The small sounds she heard in her ears were her own. "Leave me . . . alone," she pleaded.

No one crowded around her now. Ann couldn't hear anything as she tried to keep her mental balance. At last, she looked up. Mrs. Scrapple's face was red and crumpled. Sound filtered in. The woman wailed. The ostler stood, shaking and pointing at her. Others in the crowd milled restlessly. A general murmur grew in anger. Finally she focused on the squire. His face was slack, his eyes unfocused, his chest heaving. Then his gaze turned to her.

"Y-y-you," he accused. He swallowed. "You should be locked up. You are a menace."

"I . . . must talk to you," she panted. It was useless. She knew it even as she spoke.

The squire drew himself up. "Get in your cart. Your uncle must control you until we can find a more permanent solution."

Ann's heart froze inside her. Permanent solution?

"Get my horse," the squire croaked. When the ostler did not move to obey, Jemmy leapt into action and fetched the beast. The crowd surged around to the front of the hall, leaving Ann a wide berth. Ann tottered in their midst.

"Jemmy," the squire ordered. "Drive the cart. Get in the back, woman."

Ann heaved herself up in the cart and fell onto her elbow, images of all that touching still careening around inside her. *A tumbrel,* she thought. *The cart feels like a tumbrel carrying a prisoner for execution.* The squire heaved himself into the saddle of a chestnut gelding.

As they passed the Hammer and Anvil, Ann smelled a whiff of cinnamon. Stephan? She wasn't sure. It was . . . different. The sweet ambergris undertone was more pronounced somehow. She pulled herself up to peer over the side of the cart. There, in the doorway of the tavern, stood two female figures, one tall, one shorter and compact. They were dressed in dark, plain dresses, but the drape of the fabric said it was expensive. Both figures wore gloves and veils. She couldn't see their features. But their heads followed the cart as it passed. Ann repressed a shudder. A certain electricity vibrated in the air around them.

Kilkenny's army looked to include female vampires, as well.

Of a sudden, it hit her. Kilkenny must be here! His army was gathering and Mr. Sincai was in danger! She must warn him. She raised a shaky hand to her forehead. But she would never have the chance. She'd be locked up until she could be married to Van Helsing. The vibrant feeling in the air subsided as the two dark figures were left behind.

Most of the town made the trip to Maitlands. The squire paced the cart on his hack. The crowd behind them strung out, their excited whispers a menacing murmur. Steadly stalked at the rear as though to make sure she could not escape. The way had never seemed so long. Ann could hardly think, let alone decide what might happen when they got there.

Jennings and Polsham and Mrs. Simpson were waiting for the procession of cart and horses and crowd on the portico of Maitlands. The servants were obviously frightened, whether for her or for themselves, she couldn't tell.

"Get down," the squire ordered.

She climbed from the cart and steadied herself against a wheel. Jennings came to hold the pony's head. The squire motioned to the door. Ann stumbled up the shallow stairs and pushed through the entryway under the classic pediment and into the foyer.

"I should like to see Lord Brockweir," she heard the squire announce to Polsham.

"I am afraid he is indisposed, sir," Polsham muttered without real hope.

"Will you make me search the place?" the squire threatened.

Polsham made no further objection, but opened the door wide to whoever wanted entrance. The squire pointed to Watkins, Mrs. Scrapple, Steadly, and the Reverend Mr. Cobblesham, who had joined the crowd somewhere along the way. "You four come with me. I require witnesses." He motioned Ann ahead of them.

Polsham led the party upstairs and opened the door to her uncle's room. Mrs. Creevy screeched, dropped her knitting, and scuttled for the dressing room door, slamming it behind her.

Ann watched her uncle gather himself and push up to sit against his pillows with obvious difficulty. "What do you mean by this, Fladgate?" He came to her defense without hesitation. She loved him for that.

"Your niece, sir, has been wreaking havoc with her witching ways."

Her uncle didn't even look at her. He speared the squire with his gaze. "Did you touch her? You know better than that, Fladgate."

"We can't have this menace in our town, Brockweir. I charged you with locking her up."

"I lock her in at night. What more can you want?" Her uncle glanced at her with a look that was meant to be reassuring.

"I'll order her incarcerated until a suitable asylum can be found."

"Lord, man, she's a slip of a girl! What harm can she do?" Her uncle flushed in anger.

The squire's brows drew together in fear and disapproval. He glanced nervously to Ann. "Lock her up, Brockweir. Bars on her windows, all doors bolted, or I'll clap her in irons in the cells in the village." His outrage ramped up. "She doesn't wander, day or night, do you hear me? And that's just until I can think what to do about her."

"You won't take her from me, as long as I live." Uncle Thaddeus's face turned almost purple. He heaved himself out of his bed.

"Don't bestir yourself, Uncle," she said, lunging forward to kneel beside him.

"You're lucky I'm letting *you* lock her up, Brockweir," the squire hissed. "I could throw her in gaol this minute."

Uncle Thaddeus drew a great breath to reply, and froze.

An awful drawing sound came from his throat, without any intake of air. His face purpled. He clutched his chest with his right hand, eyes bulging.

"Uncle," Ann cried.

A murmur of horror rippled through the crowd.

"Do something," Ann shrieked. "Get Dr. Denton."

Mr. Watkins whirled and scrambled to the door. The rest of the crowd seemed stunned.

"Uncle!" But it was too late even then. The old man collapsed against the pillows, eyes still staring. But they didn't see her at that point. They did not see anything. His hand slid, slack, from where it had clutched his chest. His mouth hung open but it no longer contracted, looking for air. Her uncle seemed to simply fold in upon himself until he looked small, like half the man who had been in their midst a moment ago. "Uncle . . ." Ann's voice drained away.

The crowded room was silent. Steadly stalked up to the other side of the great bed and put two fingers to her uncle's throat. "He's dead."

Ann reached forward and grabbed her uncle's hand. Some idea of forcibly bringing him back into his body trembled in her, giving her courage in spite of all she had suffered that day from touching. But no cascade of painful knowledge overwhelmed her. She had no sensation beyond that which she got from touching objects. A faint impression of Thaddeus Trimble, Viscount Brockweir, passed over her and was gone; his last moment of pain and regret that he was going to leave her in the middle of such difficulties. How typical that he had given his last thoughts to her. Sobs took her. She would never see him again, ask his advice, know his love. She was now alone against the village and—

"Such a crowd," the hated voice observed behind her. "What's the occasion?"

"Lord Brockweir has passed on," the squire intoned.

Tears spilled down Ann's cheeks as she rose and carefully placed her uncle's hand across his chest and closed his eyes.

"Well, well." Erich rubbed his hands together. "A sad event, but not unexpected. Did all of you come to witness his passing? Mr. Cobblesham might have been considered sufficient."

"We *came* to see your cousin locked up until we can decide what to do with her." The squire glanced to her uncle. "But now—"

"I shall see your wishes executed," Erich said with businesslike efficiency. "If there is anywhere in the village I can procure some iron bars and locks . . ."

"Dedham, the blacksmith, will oblige you."

Ann felt absent from it all, as though it did not concern her. All she could think of was that this discussion was going on over her uncle's body as though his death didn't matter at all when it was . . . everything. It changed everything. The world would never be the same without Uncle Thaddeus in it.

"Still . . ." Squire Fladgate hesitated. "Since she inherits, she is mistress here."

They talked about her like she wasn't there.

"Did she not tell you?" Erich put on a fair imitation of astonishment. "We are betrothed."

"I perform the banns tomorrow," Mr. Cobblesham confirmed.

"You're going to marry the witch?" Mrs. Scrapple asked, incredulous.

· "Who else can protect her?" Erich stepped forward and

faced the crowd. "And who better to protect you from her?"

The squire had a grim set to his mouth. He had no love for Erich, but he thought Erich was right. He would not interfere. Mrs. Scrapple had a self-satisfied smirk on her face.

"Not before I talk to her," the runner barked, "about Sincai's disappearance."

"What?" Erich's face went white.

Steadly shook his head. "Your foolish preparations were superstition only, man. Garlic and flowers and crosses couldn't hold him in that cell."

"That should have worked," Erich muttered, chewing his lip. "Someone let him out."

"I agree," the runner said softly. "And locked the door after him. Are you sure you want to marry her, under the circumstances?"

Now it was Erich's turn to look grim. "Very sure."

The runner shrugged and made for the door. "I'm getting a few men together to search for him, but she'd better be here tomorrow for questioning."

"Get up to your nursery," Erich ordered Ann. "Polsham, bring a hammer and nails. We'll need to block her door until the blacksmith can get here."

Mr. Cobblesham moved to the bed to murmur the last rites. Squire Fladgate took Mrs. Scrapple's arm and led her away. Erich pointed toward the door and followed after Ann.

Ann turned at the threshold and stared once more at her uncle, now drained of color. *Good-bye, dear friend,* she thought. The tears came unbidden. They rolled down her face and left salt on her lips. *You gave up a life of your own to protect me. Love was all I had to give in return.*

She turned and trudged up the stairs to her rooms. *Go to God, Uncle.*

Sixteen

Stephan sat in the darkened sitting room at Bucklands Lodge feeling the sun arch across the sky outside. A candle gleamed on the small writing desk in the corner. It was the room's only light. The draperies were pulled tight against the day. Kilkenny and his crew did not appear last night. Perhaps to-night. He had been thinking about the Van Helsing girl. It must mean he was tired. He had practiced raising his sexual energy, suppressing his reaction to it, controlling the conse-quent power all night. There had been no glow of power. It *must* just be that he was tired. Now, when he called on the sexual energy, the image that came to mind was Miss Van Helsing's ethereal white hair, her clear gray eyes and pale, almost translucent skin. Indeed, the easiest way to raise the energy was to imagine her soft flesh under his hands as he washed her. This way lay madness, and failure.

She wouldn't leave Maitlands Abbey. She wouldn't stand up to Van Helsing. She'd be married to the devil, perhaps today—certainly by tomorrow, and more trapped than ever. The brute would get her money and the right to dispose of

her person. And if he took her virginity? She was right to
fear madness. And no court would say him nay. There was
no one to protect her.

Stephan paced the room in front of the cold ashes of the
fireplace. Bloody hell! Here he was feeling anxious about
the girl. He couldn't afford feeling *anything* right now. Nor
could he stay his mission. Stopping Kilkenny meant changing the fate of the world, most likely. It meant redemption.
He couldn't sacrifice that to help one single girl.

But maybe if he settled her problems he could banish the
emotion she caused in him.

He'd go in the daytime. Kilkenny and friends wouldn't be
here until twilight at the earliest, if they came at all tonight.
He stopped pacing in front of a desk in the corner of the sitting room and pulled a quill and an inkbottle over to some
sheets of foolscap. He scribbled about half a page on three
different sheets and signed his name to each one, then folded
them and warmed a stick of wax over the candle flame. He
let it drip onto each paper then pressed his ring into the
gooey mess. He would prod her to have the courage to go.
He'd provide everything else, money, introductions, all the
arrangements. Besides the draft on his bank, he could give
her coin of the realm when he saw her. He always traveled
with a great deal of money. Who would steal from the likes
of him? He grabbed another envelope and filled it with ban-
knotes from his purse.

He pulled on gloves and hat then fished some dark blue
spectacles from the pocket of his coat. Even in late afternoon the journey would be uncomfortable.

He shimmered into view in the garden under the Gothic
arches that marked the ruined portion of the abbey. Maitlands was a hive of activity. Half the workmen in the county
must be swarming over the fourth floor. Long ladders leaned

onto the roof gutters. Shocked, he saw that metal bars had been placed over the nursery windows.

"'At's it then," a man in dirty nankeen breeches with enormous forearms yelled from the flagstone terrace as he craned his neck to the work above. "She's done. Come on down." He must be a blacksmith. They were always built like that. "Let's get out 'o here 'fore dark."

Men swarmed down the ladders, which were then folded and put into two carts along with various iron bars and tools. The men scrambled into the carts themselves, and the horses trotted briskly out the gates.

She was locked in. Had someone found her secret passage? He wondered that her uncle would allow her nursery to be made into a prison, even sick as he was. Did Van Helsing rule here so completely? She must feel so alone!

He drew his power as the sun sank toward the trees, and after the sear of pain, he snapped into reality in the tiny dressing room on the fourth floor.

Ann sat on her bed, crying. She sensed his presence, though, for she looked up and wiped her cheeks with a handkerchief. He strode into the room. "What has happened? Why has your uncle allowed this . . . this desecration?"

"My uncle is dead," she said in a dull voice.

He sat beside her on the little bed, careful not to touch. "I'm sorry." She must leave here now. She had no choice. "Van Helsing ordered you locked up?"

"No," she said, and managed a tiny smile. "Squire Fladgate and Mr. Steadly were the ones who insisted. I . . . I went into the village to try to convince the squire to invalidate Erich's special license. They thought I helped you escape. Someone grabbed me, and I got away and then I touched several others accidentally, and . . ." She trailed off.

"Not a good day, on the whole." He wanted so to hold her and comfort her, maybe because it would comfort him to be able to give her some kind of solace.

She shook her head. "They brought me back, accosted my uncle. It's my fault that he—"

"His days were numbered, perhaps on one hand." He saw the guilt in her eyes. He knew that kind of guilt only too well. No one could lift that guilt for you. So he didn't try again. "You must leave here." He hesitated. "I'm sorry to add to your burden but surely you must see it."

"It's too late. They've even boarded up my secret passage."

"That is not the only way out of here." He reached into his pocket. "Here are three letters. One is to my solicitor, one to my banker. They will take your affairs in hand. One is to a lady who is very influential in the ton. Her name is Beatrix Lisse, Countess of Lente." At that her eyes snapped up to his. Of course, she knew all about Beatrix. "She will set you up and find you a lady companion. She is kind and capable." He rushed on. "And this is some ready cash for the journey." He knew that if they had accused Ann of murder, London might not be safe, either. But Beatrix would provide. She would send Ann somewhere safe until the murders were forgotten.

"I cannot take these things," she whispered. "Erich will never let me go."

"*Erich* does not have a choice," he growled, thinking how very satisfying it would be to put his fingers around that dandy's throat and squeeze.

"I don't want another death on my hands," she warned, as though she knew what he was thinking. Her voice was small, but firm.

Stephan sighed. The image of Van Helsing gasping vainly for breath receded. He put the letters on her night table. "I don't need to kill him. He is a coward. He thinks you are friendless. When he sees you are not, he will cease to be a problem."

She didn't look like she believed him. "What . . . what of you?"

Ahhh. What of him? That was the question, wasn't it? He

would do his duty by his kind. He could have no role in this woman's life. He was vampire. She was human. But he said the weak thing. "I will come to London when I can." He looked away when he said it.

Ann looked up at Stephan Sincai as he stared at her bookshelves, unseeing. Did he mean what he said? Would he come back? Did he . . . feel for her? The emotions churning in her had no name. Fear, yes, sympathy, of course, but also longing . . .

The room wavered around her as the pieces fell into place. She understood him like no other man. He was complex and difficult. He was good and had done bad things and was planning to do more in the name of good. He suffered and was strong. He could be tender and fierce. She liked him intensely. And then there was the longing to be with him, and the other longing that came in erotic dreams so strong she had had her first climax, sterile though it was.

My God! The conclusion was inescapable. She loved him. That was what this feeling was! She had known him only a few days, and yet she had known him for millennia.

She took in a breath and let it out. Could a man like Stephan care for her? She searched her memory of him. Some new recollections dropped into place; an interlude in Lapland fighting for the Danes, a vision of the translucent towers of Mirso Monastery along with the despair in Stephan's heart as he headed down the mountain toward it.

And then the memories from Mirso bubbled to the surface. Rubius, his daughters, the terrible suffering, the sexual use, the punishments, the pressure to eliminate emotion . . . Her mouth opened. Breath hissed into her lungs. They told him such torment was the price of entry to Mirso? *This* was the power they had taught him, this fierce sexuality unconnected to any emotion? Horrifying!

More horrifying still was the fact that he had let them do it. He had submitted willingly. Such was his guilt, his desire to atone. For what? He had let Asharti go in an act of forgiveness and charity. For this he had been so punished? For this he should be treasured. Yes, Asharti was evil. Yes, she had created vampires willy-nilly and made them into an army that threatened the world. They should have monitored her better. Rubius could have done that. Why blame Stephan? Why did Stephan so blame himself?

He tore his gaze away from the bookcase and gave her a smile he meant to be reassuring.

But Ann's mind was awhirl. How could he want to return to Mirso where he had suffered so? Would Rubius and his daughters ever give Stephan peace? They had made him into a killer that they could use again and again. Stephan thought his nightmare would end with Kilkenny and company. Ann wasn't so sure.

And she wasn't sure a man who had been through suffering like that could ever truly love her in return. He had been capable of love once. He had loved Beatrix. But now? He was examining her, uncertainty in his eyes. He must see she was in turmoil. She wanted to know what he was thinking more than anything else in the world. There was no way to do that. But she could feel what he felt about the experiences he had had since the night she had touched him in the cave.

It might kill her.

She didn't care. Before she could change her mind, she reached out and covered his hand on the counterpane with hers. He looked up, shocked. She braced for the shattering shower of experience.

It didn't come.

She felt his shock at her touch. She experienced his meeting with two of the Daughters. She realized he had washed his blood off her and been aroused by her naked body. She got a dose of his growing feeling for her. But his dismay at that emotion came through clearly, as well, his fear that his caring for her would make him fail in his mission, deny him redemption. She felt his resolve to complete his mission regardless of the cost, his certainty that it would kill him.

Stephan jerked his hand away. "Are . . . are you well?"

She blinked and nodded, as surprised as he was. "I suppose . . . well, maybe I already had all your experience and the essence of you. I just got the recent pieces; nothing I couldn't handle." She chuffed a laugh. "If I touched you every day, it just might be bearable." Was this what it took to live in the world? Touching the people she cared about often enough to not be overwhelmed? How had she gotten to twenty-five without knowing that? She could have comforted her uncle at the last. She could even perhaps have made love to a man . . . She drew her brows together, thinking about her mother.

"Has something disturbed you? You . . . you didn't remember the bits at Mirso, did you? The training?" His brows were drawn together. How dear of him. He wanted to spare her that.

"Most of them, I think."

He flushed to the roots of his hair. "Then you know how evil and dangerous I can be. That . . . that must be shocking for an innocent like you. I'm sorry."

"Don't be. I understand." She said it simply, from her heart. It was true. She did understand. She didn't tell him he shouldn't have submitted to the Daughters. It wasn't her place.

His gaze darted over her face. "But still you are disturbed. What were you thinking?"

She wondered if she could tell him what was in her heart. But could she not tell the man she knew so intimately anything? "I was wondering why my mother went mad when I was conceived. If she already knew and accepted and . . . well, accepted my father, why would . . . conjugal relations have driven her mad?"

"Perhaps she hadn't ever touched him before." His voice was a soft rumble in the growing gloom.

Ann looked out through the barred windows to the fading light. "Or perhaps she did not . . . accept him." Perhaps her mother did not *love* her father. Maybe that was what made touching Stephan different. She turned back and reached out to touch his hand again where it was laid along the counterpane. It was warm. The light hairs on the back of it scraped her palm. She felt a thrill wind down between her legs.

And that was all.

She grinned like an idiot as tears welled up inside her. She began to laugh and cry all at once. "Nothing. I felt almost nothing." Then the giggles swept her again.

He smiled at her tenderly as she laughed and gasped for breath. "I can't say I've ever been relieved to hear a woman say she feels nothing when she touches me."

"Well, not exactly *nothing* . . . " Suddenly the laughter died and she went wide-eyed. He was going to leave her to go fight Kilkenny and his horde. He might never come back. This moment, just before true nightfall, might be the last she ever had of him. "You have been very kind to me."

"Nonsense," he said brusquely.

She placed a finger to his lips. She thought she might faint from sensation, but not the sensation of his two thousand years of experience. If the reason her mother went insane during her conception was that she did not truly love her father, then Ann would be able to partake of physical intimacy only with a man she loved. That might well mean that Stephan Sincai was the only man with whom she would ever have the chance to know this part of life. She had tasted sexual pleasure without the joy of sharing she was sure it was meant to be. Now she wanted to know it all. If she missed this chance she might well live her life like a dry brown leaf blown in the wind. "I would ask a boon." She felt that he was attracted to her. He was beyond propriety, but he also had a chivalrous streak. He might let that get in the way.

"Ask it." But he held himself tightly. She knew he was afraid she would ask him to give up his mission, stay with her.

She would never do that. He believed completing that mission would make him whole. No one who loved him would ask him to sacrifice that. "You will go tonight to complete your mission," she said, looking at him steadily. "I ask one thing of you before you do." She saw him visibly relax. And suddenly she was shy. How did one ask this? "Would you . . . ? Would you consider having sexual intercourse with me?" He looked stricken. She rushed on. "It may be the only time it is possible for me. And to have missed the relations between men and women my whole life . . ."

She wanted him to make love to her? She said she knew everything about him. Didn't she know how dangerous that was? He could never trust himself with a woman again. Not after . . .

Stephan existed in some twilight of sexual pain. His cock had become an instrument of his own torture. But he embraced that torture. He was on his path. Sometimes he even produced a feeble glow, all on his own. Freya praised his efforts. Even Dee took grim satisfaction in his progress.

Dee had forbidden Stancie to use him during the daylight hours. "Stancie, this is a most dangerous time," Dee warned a pouting Stancie. "Too much restraint and you know what happens. Too little and he can hurt you. He is powerful now. Don't play with fire."

Stancie flounced out. Stephan knew she couldn't stay away. To tell truth, he was surprised when Stancie did not reappear that first day. Or the second. But he saw her getting more irritated, her temper more irascible, the crazy gleam in her eyes more desperate. On the fourth day, she let herself into the room, grinning slyly.

"So conventional, my sisters," she whispered, running her hands through his hair. "Truly timid. They are content to try to satisfy themselves by their own hands. Not me. They will be away for several hours. Plenty of time for me to have my fill of you. Soon you will go, and then what will I do?"

He would go soon? But he wasn't ready! He wanted to ask her about that, but her attention was elsewhere. She ran her hand over his rib cage. She caressed the crease between groin and thigh, then bent her head and licked at the great vein there. "Your blood is sweet, Penitent. I will miss you." The sear of pain when her canines pierced the vein was nothing compared to the other kinds of pain he had learned to suffer. She sucked and his cock swelled. He repeated the chants they had taught him, but it refused to soften. Was she holding him erect?

She did not bother with pleasuring him in any way. She simply straddled his hips and slipped him inside her, grinding her loins against him as she moaned her pleasure. She came almost immediately, having endured what for her was an unheard-of drought of three days. He held to his control. But she began again almost immediately, turning around so that his cock pressed at a new angle and she could squeeze his testicles. Stephan felt himself ramping up. She was relentless, banging herself against him, moaning her pleasure. Stephan began to feel the molten fire burn his loins, his bowels, his belly. She shuddered and contracted around him. There. It would be over now.

But it wasn't. She straddled his shoulders, her buttocks in his face, and let him lick her, while she pulled at his cock. "Yes, yes," she moaned. "Lick me." When she was roused again, she sat up and moved to hover over his cock, then plunged it inside her.

The feeling ramped up again. He was a volcano about to lose control. He needed her help to suppress his ejaculation, but she was focused only on her orgasm.

"Stancie," he said. "Help me." She rode him, banging against his hips. He knew it was worth punishment to speak thus to her. But she was beyond hearing. Where was her power?

He grunted with the effort to restrain himself.

Then the dam broke. He felt his balls contract. The molten lava surged up from his core through his cock in a pulse that tore a cry from his throat. The room contracted around them and then bulged out. A white glow pulsed out from him. Things seemed to speed up and then slow down. He saw the wave of power engulf Stancie. Her eyes grew round. Her lips pulled back over her teeth in some animal snarl. She might have screamed. He couldn't hear her. His hips arched up. The throb of his ejaculation seemed to reverberate in the contracting and expanding room. The shriek echoed in his mind. Pulse after pulse impaled Stancie as she writhed above him, not in ecstasy now, but in some kind of tortured, wrenching, psychic storm.

The last pulse of fluid from his cock pushed her off him. In horror, he saw her flung against the sideboard. Her eyes went blank, her mouth slackened.

The world bounced back into place. The room was filled to bursting with silence. Then he heard the low crackle of the fire. He managed to get up on one elbow. Stancie stared at the ceiling from the carpet just under the sideboard. Her gaze was blank. Slowly, she began to laugh. The laugh ramped up the scale until it was a shrieking gurgle. He made his way to her, took her shoulders.

"Stancie," he said sharply, shaking her, hoping to God that he hadn't done what he just thought he had. It was no use. She couldn't stop the shrieking laugh. And there was no one home behind her eyes.

◆ ◆ ◆

Stephan was still shaking when Dee dragged him into Rubius's private quarters. Freya trailed behind, crying.

Rubius looked up from a book whose leather binding was crumbling and frowned at the unexpected intrusion.

"It's over," Dee practically shouted. "Kill him. Kill him slowly, Father."

"What is the meaning of this, Deirdre?" Rubius asked, glancing to Freya, surveying Stephan briefly, and finally returning to Dee. Stephan was naked. He could only be grateful he was only partially erect. He tried to gather his senses, still not quite sure what had happened.

Dee took a breath. "It's Stancie. She's . . ." Dee glared at Stephan. "He . . . he lost control. He made her . . . crazy."

Rubius snapped his book shut. Maybe death at the Eldest's hands was Stephan's best hope. The memory of the empty look in Stancie's eyes and her maniacal laughter made him break out in a sweat.

"He deserves a week in the sun before he dies," Dee hissed, rounding on Stephan.

Stephan could make no defense.

"He didn't mean what happened, Father, I'm sure of it," Freya managed with a full throat. She sank into a leather wing chair and daubed her cheeks.

"I don't care." Dee turned to Rubius. "If you could see her, Father . . ." She trailed off as the Eldest stood. His habit stretched across his belly.

"Get hold of yourselves, both of you," Rubius snapped. "I shall see her, of course. But I can guess what happened."

"I want him punished, and punished, and—"

"And waste all our work?" Rubius tossed the book onto the chair seat and stalked toward Stephan, his eyes narrowing. Stephan felt as though a cold steel rod had been shoved down his spine. "How did this happen?"

Stephan wasn't sure who he was asking. He glanced to Dee. She only glared at him. Freya began to leak tears again. He took a breath. "She was . . . tutoring me privately." Was that what it was? Was that what they would think it?

"Alone?" Rubius asked sharply.

"Dee warned her," Freya said, trying to defend everyone at once.

Rubius's mouth turned grim. "How long had that been going on?"

"I . . . I don't know. Months."

Now the old man's eyes looked like robin's eggs, light blue and hard shelled. "And?"

"I . . . I lost control." He stared at the floor and hoped to god Rubius didn't notice that he was drenched with emotion, regret, fear.

"He must have been trying to harm her," Dee insisted. "How else would she go mad?"

Rubius sighed. He turned and poured himself a glass of wine and held it up to the light of the candles in the chandelier. It gleamed like translucent blood. "You know how it works, Deirdre. Her impulse is turned back upon her. She gets a blast of whatever she is."

"No, he must have—"

"You are not listening," Rubius snapped. "You could not be blind to the fact that Estancia was not balanced. The obsessive sex, the recklessness, the jealousy? I warned you to watch her. And yet I find she was allowed her way with the Penitent, without supervision, without support or restraint. She has jeopardized all our work." He waved the glass at Stephan as he took a sip. "Look at him. She's sapped his confidence. His emotion is out of control. She may have ruined everything."

"You can't be thinking of letting him continue on his mission?" Deirdre was outraged.

"Of course I can! Sit down. And Freya, stop blubbering!"

He waited for them to recover from their shock at his stern command and motioned Stephan to kneel on the carpet in front of the fire. "Now let's be clear on several points. Nothing will stop our mission, short of the Penitent's death. And I have no intention of killing him." Stephan could feel the Eldest's hard stare upon him, feel his inescapable will. "He has committed far worse crimes than losing control with Estancia."

Stephan shrank inside as guilt washed over him again. He deserved his fate.

"At least punish him. A week in the sun—"

"Would weaken him! There is no time!" The old man towered over the three of them. His bulk seemed to fill the room. He began to pace. "Our situation grows more serious. Kilkenny cares nothing for the Rules! He has penetrated the English government." Rubius rounded on Stephan. "Your penance is that you must kill Kilkenny and hunt down all he has made!" He turned to Dee and Freya. "Ready or unready, this Penitent becomes a Harrier in three days, and we send him out into the world to fight Kilkenny's army. Do you understand?"

"Yes, Father," Freya almost whispered.

"Deirdre?"

His eldest daughter met his stare for only an instant. "I understand." Her voice was like broken glass.

"Then take him back to his room, and work on correcting the damage Estancia has done. I want his emotions under control by the time we send him out."

Deirdre rose. "Get up," she ordered, and stalked toward the door.

Freya touched Stephan's shoulder as he rose. "He'll be ready, Father."

Stephan dared not look up at Rubius. He had never felt less ready, less worthy. He had driven this man's daughter mad today and the Eldest sublimated the anger he must feel

*to the cause of his kind. Somehow, Stephan must find a way
to follow his example.*

In three days they had patched up his control as best they
could. Dee had been unrelenting, while Freya tried to en-
courage him. She had been almost gentle with him. But they
had stimulated him relentlessly. He produced the glow, but it
was unreliable. He had blasted rocks and controlled his sexual release. Always the control he managed felt tenuous.
Stancie's eyes haunted his thoughts, accusing. But he had
made it through a session last night without the Daughters'
help to restrain him, and his glow had flickered a little more
brightly. Did one night mean he was ready?

Ready or not, here he was in the great central courtyard,
clothed, mounted on a strengthy stallion as dark as the night
around Mirso. The Source burbled over its rough stones. He
had a fortune in gold coins in his saddlebag. His horse
minced on the cobblestones, anxious to be off.

Around the courtyard stood troops of silent monks. Their
hoods concealed whether they were male or female. Why had
Rubius gathered them? Deirdre and Freya, ethereal in the
spring breeze, flanked a still and stolid Rubius.

"Go, boy." Rubius's voice echoed across a courtyard
silent except for the trickle of the Source and the impatient
clack of the stallion's hooves on the cobblestones. "You pay
for disobeying the Rules, beginning today. Your quest starts
in London. You will stop Kilkenny's blasphemy. Find the ten-
drils the brute has grown into the British government, then
trace them to their root. Send word back by the fastest couri-
ers of your progress."

Stephan nodded, once, hoping he seemed surer than he was.

"The refuge of Mirso is denied you until they are gone, to
the last one of them."

The ranks of monks shuffled nervously behind Rubius.

Perhaps they, like Stephan, thought that statement might be the equivalent of permanent exile. There was no worse fate for one of their kind. He pushed down that thought, just as he would push down all emotions. He would not fail. He wanted redemption and the refuge of Mirso too badly.

The wooden gates that stood four men high swung open.

Stephan wheeled the stallion and touched his heels to the horse's flanks. The creature sprang forward under him. The horse's iron shoes sparked against the cobblestones in the night. He glanced down, and saw Flavio, the closest thing to a father he had ever had, waiting at the gate. He saluted and got a tiny nod in return. He would see Flavio again. He vowed it.

Stephan couldn't make love to Miss Van Helsing. Her life or her sanity might depend on his refusal. Yet she looked up at him so expectantly, so shy. The shyness wrenched his resolve.

"If you'd rather not . . ." she stammered. "I . . . I quite understand."

"You must know I find you . . . attractive. But if I lose control . . ." How could she not realize? Perhaps she had not remembered Stancie. He straightened himself. "I could hurt you. You may not remember, but I drove one of Rubius's daughters mad."

She blinked. There was a long pause he found excruciating. "I remember that now." Her gaze roved over his face, examining him. "And what Rubius said about it. I'll take my chances." Then she smiled. It was a tiny, tentative smile. "I'll not be as taxing to your strength as Stancie."

That smile went straight to his heart. He was tempted. Surely he had enough control to hold back his own release long enough to pleasure a human woman.

But he was no longer the man to make love to her. "Making love" was not in his vocabulary anymore. What he had experienced with the Daughters was sexual acrobatic train-ing, nothing more. There was no caring. He had not cared . . . since Beatrix. And Beatrix had found him wanting.

He cleared his throat. "It isn't only that." How could he say this? But he had to find a way. It wasn't fair to let her feel rejected for herself. She deserved to be loved, to know physi-cal intimacy, and she had been so brave to ask for what she deserved. He could see her faltering even now. She thought he didn't want her. "No, no . . . don't misunderstand me. I . . . I want to. Very much." Zeus, what a cad he was! "It's me. I am not fit . . . anymore . . . to . . . You know this." He rushed ahead now, unable to stop himself. "What I did at Mirso . . . that isn't what it should be like. You deserve something bet-ter, someone who can . . . who will . . ."

To his surprise her features let go their anxious creases. "And who would that be? Erich? Or someone from the village on a bet? Jemmy, perhaps. That's it." She raised her brows and smiled again, ruefully this time. "I'm afraid you are the only likely candidate, Mr. Sincai. If you can't bring yourself to . . . well, I understand, but don't think I'll be throwing myself at the next male who walks through the door."

Bring himself to love her? He couldn't let her think he ex-pected loving her to be distasteful. Without thinking more, he gathered her into his arms. Of course he would give her what might be denied her the rest of her life. He kissed the top of her head, her hair tickling his lips. He wouldn't let it be like it was with the Daughters. If he could control his release, he could control the process as well. He would pleasure her ten-derly, as she should be pleasured. The pool of lava at his core the Daughters had raised to such excruciating effect was his burden. He would not let it be hers. It might be torture for him, but it was a price he would pay gladly that she might ex-perience pleasure. He took her by the shoulders and held her away from him. She was so slightly built. "I shall do my best to be worthy of your first encounter."

Wait—slightly built . . .

"There may be a bit of discomfort the first time." He cleared his throat. "I'm a rather . . . large man and you are a virgin after all."

"You won't fit?"

He smiled. She was so anxious. "No, I'll fit."

"Then I'd like to try." She was breathless. Was she already suffering?

He jerked his hands away from her shoulders "Did you get too much sensation?"

"No, no. It isn't that." She pressed her lips together over another secret smile. "It's just that no one has held me like that since . . . since I was very young. I . . . liked it."

Then, that was it. He was going to do this. Carefully. With total control. Regardless of his own torment. It wouldn't be like it was with the Daughters. He sent his senses out into the rest of the house. Mrs. Simpson was crying in the kitchen. Mrs. Creevy was in the library, drinking brandy. "Where is your cousin?"

"Erich is afraid of you. He left the house early this afternoon when the workmen came. He said he was going to find a safe place to stay for the night."

That meant Van Helsing thought Kilkenny would come tonight. Stephan pushed that thought away. He must focus if he was to give Miss Van Helsing the experience she deserved.

She was looking at him with those clear silver-gray eyes of hers, expectant. "Since I have already been so presumptuous, would it be too much to ask if I might use your given name?"

"Only if you will let me call you Ann." He smiled.

She nodded, shy again. "Stephan. How . . . how does one proceed?"

"Let me show you," he whispered, leaning in. He brushed his lips across hers.

Seventeen

Ann felt the brush of his lips like the shock of rubbing your shoes against the carpet on a windy day and then touching metal. It seemed to send a spark down to the spot between her legs. She leaned into him for more and he opened her mouth gently with his tongue. So surprising! So moist and . . . intimate. Was this what kissing felt like? It was different from the memories she had from Stephan, as different as seeing a painting of a flower and the real thing. A flash of fear shot through her. Would everything be so much more intense than she had remembered through Stephan? Maybe one really *could* go mad.

And then he gathered her into his chest. She smelled the warm scent of him, cinnamon, and under that the sweet exotic aroma of ambergris. His heart thumped against her breasts, so intimate, so vulnerable. She had never felt so close to another human being. The fact that he wasn't human was beside the point. He bent and kissed her neck, his lips brushing her throat and making her shiver in delight. Would he take blood from her? He sometimes did in the course of lovemaking. The Daughters had taken his blood regularly.

After his experience with them, would he be repelled by the act of sexual intercourse? That was what had caused his hesitation. She felt his uncertainty about his ability to have normal physical intimacy. He was as frightened as she was, maybe more. She resolved to make sex all it had not been with them, tender, giving. She knew what he liked. She could do those things. In fact, the very thought of doing them was making her wet and throbbing. It was only right to repay his generosity. If only he was not overcome by memories of his years with the Daughters, they could prevail.

It would be difficult to think if he was going to kiss her ears like that. It was difficult even to breathe. And then he was kissing her mouth. She gathered her courage and touched his tongue with her own. That must have encouraged him, for he probed deeper with his own, and she pressed her breasts against his chest.

"God, Ann," he said thickly, breaking away. "God, but I have wanted this."

"No more than I," she said as she bared her throat to him and he kissed it. "I have done a lot less of it than you. None in fact." He cupped her breast with his right hand and felt for her nipple through the cloth of her plain green gown. It was not hard to find. Her breasts had never been so tight and full. The stroke of his thumb across her nipple drew a little moan from her.

He broke away from her and cast about for a moment, before he said, "Would you prefer us to remain clothed? Perhaps you would find a man's body distasteful."

He preferred to be naked, and liked his women so as well. She knew that. She swallowed. She was a little frightened but her way was clear. "How could I find you distasteful?"

He took the lead in order to make her more comfortable about disrobing, she was sure. His eyes burned with intensity. The lips which had so recently been pressed to hers were sensuous and promising. He stood, ripped his neck-cloth off and tossed it away, then shrugged out of his tightly fitting black coat of superfine. She saw clearly that he was aroused, and that he was indeed a large man. His trousers bulged where they pressed his member against his thigh. She searched her memory, which meant she searched his, but he was strangely unconscious of his own body, so she was not certain what to expect. He pulled off his boots and stockings and stood before her, almost within touching range, but not. She wanted to touch him constantly now. She missed already the warmth of his embrace.

He ripped several buttons off removing his waistcoat of figured gray brocade. Then looked at her steadily and pulled his shirt over his head. She managed not to gasp. She had seen men's upper bodies; laborers working without their shirts, the blacksmith wielding his hammer over a hot forge. But those men were not Stephan. He was big all over, with muscled shoulders and thick biceps, just like in her dream. But the reality of him was more particular. Dark hair dusted his chest and pointed in a vee over his abdomen to parts below. Dusky nipples peeked out at his well-developed pectorals. The muscles were named in her anatomy book. But muscles in the flesh were far more exciting. Biceps, abdominals, and those delightful ones that went over the hip and girdled a man's most private parts—what were they called? Her head swam.

He looked apologetic as he unbuttoned his breeches. "Are you certain?" he asked, without a direct referent.

She nodded, smiling. If he knew that even now her thighs were sticky, he wouldn't have to ask. He pushed his breeches over his hips and stepped out of them. Freed, his erection was . . . impressive. It was fully erect, the tip reddened, the shaft swollen and veined. *That* she had never seen before. She knew all that was to go inside her, but that knowledge seemed very theoretical at this point. She felt a blush rising and lowered her head. Her fingers fumbled at the buttons down the front of her dress.

He knelt before her on one knee where she sat on her bed. "May I be of assistance?"

She nodded, and his hands came to her breast to slip each covered button out from its loop. His fingers were swift and certain. Her breasts pressed against his hands as she breathed. When he had unbuttoned it to beneath her waist, he took her slippers from her feet, handling them gently, and removed her stockings. Then he took her hand and stood up with her. He was so much bigger than she was. Her head came only to his chest. She had an urge to lean into him, to inhale the musky cinnamon scent of him. Instead, he slipped her dress over her shoulders. It pooled at her feet. He pulled at the ties of the short corset she wore in order to be able to undress herself. And then she was standing only in her shift. The thin linen was the only thing between them. He moved closer. His most male part touched her belly through the cloth.

Ann found that she was breathing hard. How long had she longed for this, feared it? She might end like her mother. But one night of pressing flesh to flesh seemed worth insanity. She reached up and took the pins out of her hair and tossed them to the carpet. Her hair fell heavily down her back. He bent and took the hem of her shift up over her head. She was naked. He put his hands on her shoulders. The only sensation she had was of her insides turning liquid.

"You are beautiful," he said. "Like a small and perfect jewel."

She looked up, startled. After all the women he had had, he thought *her* beautiful? He leaned down and swept her up in one movement. He placed her on her narrow bed and lay down beside her. He was touching her all along her length. There was just room enough for two. His erection pressed against her thigh. He brushed his lips along her forehead, down her nose. He kissed her mouth thoroughly, and she kissed back, moist and intimate. She found herself arching her breast into his chest. He dipped his head and took her breast into his mouth, tonguing her nipple and sucking gently. Ann thought she might faint, it felt so delicious. Was this what made one go mad? He turned his attention to her other breast. She moaned.

Somehow, when she was distracted, his hand had strayed to her thigh and now he cupped her mound of flesh with his palm. She knew she was wet, and that he could see her desire for him displayed plainly over her thighs. One finger strayed inside her, shocking her with new intimacy. "Shusssssssh," he murmured. "Relax and trust me. You will like this."

He slid his finger along her moistness while his mouth returned to hers. Her nipples still brushed his chest, and the sensation between her legs, on her mouth, and her nipples was driving her to distraction. But then he found a particular point of feeling between her legs she had never known was there, and the feeling ramped up into a whole new realm. She could have no thought but the feeling that grew and pulsed. It made her twist and moan aloud. He would touch her and then rest, and then rub her lightly again, until she was pulling him down to kiss him fiercely and bucking against his hand to find his fingers and the pleasure they gave again.

It seemed like forever that she was poised on some kind of precipice. No one could experience any more sensation than this.

And then she did. Her whole body contracted into some overheated well of pleasure and then shot her soul out of the bed, out of the room and into the night. Somewhere she realized someone was yipping in little moans, and a soft voice in her ear breathed soothing noises. Was this madness?

With a wrench her body jerked away, exhausted. Without her permission, tears welled up and she sobbed against Stephan's chest while he held her. This was so much more than the sterile contraction she had experienced at her own hand while she dreamed. When she could think again, she gasped, "What was that?"

"That was an orgasm, my love, and a good one, I should guess." He ran his lips over her hair, whispering to her.

"I thought it must be something entirely new. Well, that is as close to madness as I should like to get," she said, a little shaky.

"I would like to get you there often," he murmured.

"And how about your pleasure?" she asked.

"I shall hold mine in reserve."

She thought about that. He didn't want to ejaculate inside her. What had happened with Stancie made him afraid. And he was afraid that his experience with the Daughters would break through in the heat of his passion and horrify her. "Then I think I'm still a virgin, technically. That isn't fair, somehow."

"You should save that for your husband," he said. His voice was throaty.

"And what if this is only possible with you?" she asked pointedly. "Must I be denied?"

"You know . . . you know there is danger."

"I trust you." She said it simply.

He enfolded her in a crushing embrace. He started to say something, then couldn't.

God, she *did* trust him! He didn't deserve it. But he couldn't let her down. She had been so trusting that she had experienced one hell of an orgasm. It took not only trust but sensitivity to come like that. She was incredibly sensuous. And why not? Was not touching the sense that drove her life in many ways?

What surprised him was that the desire that even now made him rock-hard against her was not torture. The lava inside him simmered, but the sensation seemed a promise, not a threat. She wanted the whole experience. He could give her another orgasm tonight before he left for the lodge, perhaps more than one, without ever coming himself. Lord, only a few weeks ago he had serviced three insatiable daughters of Rubius almost round the clock without ejaculating. Surely he could manage to give Ann the tender experience she deserved as initiation to the world of sexual intimacy. That made him smile. He wanted to do that for her, to show her that ecstasy was only a distant cousin to madness. Of course, he didn't have the power of the Daughters to control him. But if he found himself close he could withdraw.

She would probably only want him to serve her once. After that, she would likely be sore from having her membrane broken. He only hoped she didn't lose all taste for the act. She was so tiny. He bent to her breast. She would be sensitive now. Only his tongue should be used on her breasts the second time, not his fingers. As he kissed her nipples, she ran her hands over his back and his shoulders as though she couldn't get enough of him. He tried to imagine what it was like never to have experienced intimacy of any kind.

Now her hands were exploring other parts of his body. She ran one down over his hip and around to stroke his buttocks. Then she put it between his thighs. She wanted to explore his genitals. He smiled as she scooted down so she could reach better. That put her mouth at his chest and she licked at his nipple, then sucked. She was intuitive, eager. He opened his thighs to her. Let her be in control here. That would reassure her. She cupped his balls. They were a handful for her small hand. She squeezed ever so gently and rubbed the stones inside his sac against each other. He swallowed. How did she know he liked that? After a moment, she caressed his shaft. The feel of her hand around him made him shudder. With her thumb she flicked the moisture at the tip of his cock over its head. God, woman! Tentatively, she moved her hand up and down the shaft. When he could not suppress a moan, she grew surer. How different from the curt demands of the Daughters!

"I want to be on top," she breathed. "Do you mind?"

All he could do was shake his head. He loved to have a woman where he could see her. He wouldn't let those endless nights when the Daughters rode him spoil this for Ann. He wanted to do this for her. He scooted under her and she straddled his loins. That opened her moist parts over the shaft of his cock. She rocked back and forth as though she knew exactly the way to drive him to madness. He closed his eyes once and considered chanting. But he could not keep them closed for long. In the gloom of the twilight room, she seemed to glow. Her eyes were luminous. Her slight figure, her heavy breasts hanging so delectably above him, made him quiver. All the while, she continued moving back and forth, sliding her slick parts along the shaft of his cock. She leaned back and lifted her hair off her back. Her breasts rose. Their nipples were pinched and taut. Her ribs showed over her smooth belly. Still rocking, she leaned over him, hands splayed on his chest, and bared her neck.

"Do you want blood? I give it freely." Her eyes were big, her voice throaty.

He shook his head and put both hands on her waist. "You have something else I want."

He lifted her. She knelt up. He took his own cock and tilted it, found her opening with his finger and left the head of his cock just at her entrance. "Now you control the pace. If we go slowly, you will open."

She nodded, smiling, and allowed him to settle her a little. He lifted her. She was so slight. He settled her a little more. She looked surprised, then pleased. She lifted herself and settled more. Up and down now. Soon she would come to the barrier of the hymen. Would she lose her nerve? He felt his cock press against it once, twice. She smiled at him and pushed herself down. A little gasp and a look of surprise was the only indication that her maidenhead was broken. He was inside her. He gathered her to him, and rolled over on top of her. She spread her thighs even wider. He braced himself to keep his weight off her. He slid in and out, shallowly and carefully, once, twice.

"Does that hurt?" he whispered. "I can stop, if you like."

"I want to feel you in me." She arched herself up, pressing her mound against him as he filled her fully for the first time. His hips moved of their own accord. He changed the angle to give her more pleasure. She moaned and his own sensation ramped up. *Tuatha, denon, reheldra, sithfren.* He began the mental chant, just to take no chances.

In and out. She began to writhe under him. She drew him down to kiss her, darting her tongue inside his mouth fearlessly. Without warning, she threw her legs around his loins and clamped him to her, rocking in counterpoint, taking him even deeper inside her. Then she let go, and he came out. His cock trembled above her.

"More," she whispered frantically. "More."

He thrust inside her, increasing the speed of his pumping to match her growing pleasure. She would come soon, he was sure of it. *Sithfren, hondrelo, frondura, denai.* He had control. She contracted around him with a moan of pleasure. The muscles of her womb milked at his cock.

And without warning, he exploded. His balls pushed a forceful stream of steaming juice out his cock. The world contracted into a single, blinding sensation.

No! He tried to pull out, late as it was. He could feel his semen spurting inside her. But she clamped her legs around his buttocks and clung to him as they came together.

"God, Ann!" She let him go and fell back limply to the bed. Was she conscious? Had he killed her? His hateful cock still spurted tiny droplets. It had been so long since he had come. He should never have risked it, risked her. "Ann!"

She opened one eye and a slow smile spread across her face. "Is it possible to have so much pleasure and not be mad?"

"Ann, are you all right?" He lifted her with one arm, cradling her against his chest, slipping his other hand around her head, rubbing one thumb over her cheek. "Tell me you're all right!"

"I'm fine," she said, nestling into his chest. "A little sleepy. Is that normal?"

He sighed. "Yes. That's normal."

"Can we rest a moment before we do it again?"

"Again?"

"Oh." She looked stricken. "Perhaps you only care to do it once? Or maybe once is all that's possible now that you've—"

"Shush." He put a finger to her lips. "I'm sure you can have more of the same if you like in a few minutes. Or several times. If you get sore, I can pleasure you with my tongue." To hell with Kilkenny. If he was here tonight, he would be there again tomorrow night. Was he not stalking Stephan even as Stephan was stalking him?

She thought a moment, looking at him. Her eyes were incredibly soft. "I might like that."

He clutched her to him. She was so precious. And he had endangered her tonight. "Why are you not mad?" he asked himself, not her. "After what I did . . ."

"What we did." There was a silence. "Remember Rubius said the magic worked by turning whatever energy the object had back on itself? He said Stancie had always been a little crazy, so she went crazier." She looked up at him. "I guess I wasn't crazy. Surprising, really."

"Then what was turned back upon you?" he asked, afraid to know.

She looked about to speak then thought better of it. "Someday I'll tell you."

He gripped her tightly and rocked. He had to go soon. But not just yet. They had a few hours. "Was it painful for you?" She hadn't seemed in pain.

"Not really," she said, surprised. "Should it have been?"

"Perhaps your membrane was already torn a bit. It happens with active women." He smiled down at her. "You seem to be forever climbing over rocks and such in the Gorge."

"Then I'm glad."

He had never known a woman so intuitive about pleasing a man.

Let alone a virgin. The thought crashed in on him.

"You don't think I was a virgin, do you?" She said it quietly. Was he so transparent?

But Ann could never have touched another man long enough to lose her virginity.

"Of course you are. Were. It's just that you did exactly what I like most. I . . ."

She smiled. She didn't need to say anything.

She knew him that well? He breathed and held her head against his shoulder.

He felt himself rising again. She must feel it, too. He shook himself mentally. Time enough for death and atonement. These hours should belong to Ann.

It was nearly dawn. Ann lay cradled in his arms, her white-blonde hair spread over his darker, coarser flesh. He watched her sleep, at peace with the intimacy of touching a man, naked body to naked body. They had done everything tonight. He had given her all of himself. She had come to orgasm again and again. As had he. She knew every secret desire and she had filled them, driving him to distraction time and again. She'd lifted her breasts to tongue her own nipples and used her hands on his cock. And she seemed to get pleasure from doing it. He had never felt that a woman was so much inside his mind.

It was almost frightening.

No, it was a gift. A gift he could not deserve until he had atoned.

Which meant he must leave her. He had never wanted so to shirk his duty.

And with that, he realized that if he did not leave her now, before dawn, he might never leave at all. He had his duty. His duty might have shown up at Bucklands Lodge tonight. The emotion he had spent—was still spending this night— and the sexual energy he had spent in all those orgasms would weaken him for the task ahead. He was never adequate to this task. Now, he must be even less so. To stay with her, pleasuring her night after night, was all he wanted, and it was all he could not indulge. He must leave her, and trust that she would use his letters to escape Van Helsing and the town.

"Ann," he whispered.

She turned in his arms like a sleepy kitten. "Stephan?" Her eyelids fluttered.

"I must leave, my love. If I don't go now . . ." His voice cracked.

She reached up to kiss his throat, suddenly very awake. "In all the . . . the chaos of today I forgot to tell you. I saw some of Kilkenny's followers at the tavern."

"At the tavern so openly?" He thought a moment. "Are you sure? How did you know?"

"Their scent. Unless cinnamon and ambergris has become a fashionable perfume. That and a certain electric expectancy in the air around them. Like how I feel around you."

"So." That meant it was tonight.

"I should tell you. They were women."

Women? He blinked once. They were not followers of Kilkenny. Ann had seen the Daughters. He felt his shoulders sag, weighted by their certainty of his failure. He wouldn't tell Ann who they were. Or why they were here.

"Go. I'll wait for you." She said it softly. He could see in her eyes she knew it might be useless. He treasured the fact that she said it anyway.

"Use your strength of character against him, Ann. Leave now, for London. Before your cousin returns." Would she? "I can't go unless you promise. I can't leave you here to him."

"I promise. Go and fulfill your destiny." Her eyes were soft, and full of tears.

He rose and pulled the coverlet up over her perfect, sensual nakedness. She would go. He must believe that. In London, she would learn to trust another man. She would touch him, and touching would make love possible for her. He felt a pang of emotion. Jealousy? But better that she find love in her life than be tangled with the likes of the Harrier. He picked up his clothing, but he did not dress. He liked to think he had given her the possibility of love. It was with him that she had found the way around her wonderful, awful gift. It was so little to give in return for what she had given him. Acceptance. Understanding. What woman, human or vampire, had ever shown him that? She was courageous. So much more courageous than she knew.

"You will be all right, Ann. You are strong. You just don't know your strength." He did. "You see the good in people. Even people like Jemmy Minks. You sort through the detritus of their souls and find the worth there. Use your strength." He drew the power. His throat closed on any more words. He was for Kilkenny, and he knew how that was likely to end. And if he won through, by some miracle, then he was for Mirso.

Either way, he would never see her again.

Eighteen

Ann watched the whirling darkness evaporate into the predawn dimness. Already the birds were chattering outside her windows. The room was empty, emptier than it had ever been. Stephan was gone, to engage in the fight of his life. A fight he believed he would lose.

Her insides felt like sodden earth, cold and heavy. She loved Stephan Sincai, and when he had reached his own climax this night, he had turned her love back upon herself, so she loved him twice as much as before; so much it was painful. That was what she couldn't tell him, not until he had completed his mission, for better or worse. She could never burden him with the guilt of having to choose between her love and what he thought of as his destiny. He would not be whole if he abandoned his task. And if he chose her over refuge? He would grow bitter, thinking about what he had lost. No one could build a future on that.

Future! She blushed at her own naïveté. She was thinking of a future with a man who was two thousand years old? If he lived through tonight, and if he returned to her, that did not mean there was a future for them. She would die in the blink of an eye and he would go on and on. Her blonde-white hair would become only white, her skin shriveled, and still Stephan would exist in the fullness of his manhood. There was no future where she and Stephan were concerned.

Stephan must know that even more clearly than she did. If he lived through his confrontation with Kilkenny, he would return to Mirso.

So he might never know she loved him. Had Stephan felt the magic she had felt being with him? He must, to have stayed from his purpose for so long. She sorted through her memories from him. He loved her. She was sure of that, because he was sure of it. But for him it was not the happy revelation it was for her. He thought of loving her as a crime which must be expunged. He believed what he had done would weaken him for his battle ahead. Guilt washed over her. Why had she not realized what she was doing to him?

She sat up abruptly and clutched the covers of her little bed around her.

Because he was wrong.

Images flashed in her brain; Rubius's admonishments, the principles of the training. No emotion. Suppression of sexual energy until it was channeled and transformed into devastating power. The Daughters' dreadful training techniques and how Stephan had suffered at their hands, and the demands of their lust.

They were *all* wrong.

And she must find Stephan before tonight to tell him just how they were wrong. It might be the only way to save his life.

The way ahead unfolded before her. Horrible events. Danger to her person and her mind. Danger she must embrace to reach her end.

And what was the end she craved? A world shared with Stephan. It seemed so impossible. They might love each other, but they were from two different worlds. It was absurd.

Well, she wouldn't think of that. First Stephan had to live. No, first she had to survive to tell him how. That meant facing Erich. She wouldn't just run away, leaving the servants to face him, and abandoning Maitlands and its tenants. Her resolve crystallized inside her, hard as a diamond. It was high time. She could never go back to hiding in her nursery, no matter what happened. Now she had something she wanted. If Erich stood in her way, then he must be vanquished like the dragon he was. Dragon or chimera? She would find out.

She threw off the covers and leapt out of bed. Stephan had shown her the way. If the worst happened and Stephan was killed and she wasn't, then she must take his advice. And now his advice served her purpose in another way. She sat at her writing desk. Mrs. Simpson would come with breakfast soon. She had to have the note for Jennings written and the others, as well.

Ann came downstairs in a plain, serviceable gown of gray-blue, not the one that Mrs. Simpson had brought up as Erich's gift. She would never give him the satisfaction of obedience. Mrs. Simpson was waiting for her in the main hall. Ann raised her brows in question.

Mrs. Simpson nodded. Jennings had done his part. Her hasty plan was in train.

Ann had her emotions almost under control. She would mourn for her uncle. There would be time for that. But just now she had to muster every one of her faculties, and that meant putting grief aside. The library was the only habitable room suited for the ceremony, according to Erich. She threw open the door. Inside, three men turned to look at her. Squire Fladgate frowned at her from his place standing by the fire. Mr. Cobblesham rose from his chair, beaming, as if a wedding

were a cause for joy in any circumstance. Erich was dressed
in his dandified finest, with primrose-yellow pantaloons, a
coat of blue superfine, a cream wool waistcoat stretched over
his paunch, and a cravat so high he could barely turn his
head. He stood by the sideboard, pouring himself a brandy.
Not surprising. His horror at her plain dress was almost
comical.

"What? Are you not wearing the gown I sent, Cousin?"
His voice had palpable outrage in it. "Do you insult me?"

"I have much to do today," she said calmly. "I have no
stomach for frills."

Mr. Brandywine, her uncle's steward, and his solicitor,
Mr. Yancy, were not here. Mr. Brandywine she had no doubt
of, but Mr. Yancy had to come all the way from Wells. Had
Jennings found him? Was he willing to undertake the journey? Erich strode forward to loom over her. "You may insult me but the result will be the same." He looked up to see
Mrs. Simpson bowing herself out of the room. "Simpson,
you are wanted here as witness."

Mrs. Simpson looked as though she might faint. But she
stepped back into the room.

"My, my," Ann marveled. "And Squire Fladgate as well as
Mr. Cobblesham to attend. I am quite honored." She let her
voice go hard. "And to think I am to be married even before
my uncle is laid to rest. Strange priorities, Mr. Cobblesham."

"We thought it best," Squire Fladgate chuffed.

"Such haste!" Ann tut-tutted. "Beware of wasted effort."

Behind her, she heard a scuffling in the hall. The door was
opened. Murmured greetings. Male voices. Two of them.
Thank God! "Gentlemen, should we not wait for our other
guests?"

"Guests?" Erich was suspicious. As well he should be.

"Think of them as the bride's party," she said kindly.
There was a good chance her gambit would fail. Perhaps
these "guests" would range themselves with Erich. But she

had never felt so . . . strong. Was it Stephan's faith in her? He might know her better than she did herself.

Polsham let Mr. Brandywine and Mr. Yancy into the library and withdrew. Mr. Brandywine was a short man, lean and energetic. Mr. Yancy, on the other hand, was tall, an elegant figure whose many wrinkles could not hide that once he had been a very handsome specimen. Each man carried a portfolio of papers. Mr. Yancy's was of leather. Both looked round the room and took in the situation before they focused on her. Mr. Brandywine's eyes were snapping with anger. Mr. Yancy gave her a slight smile. His old eyes seemed wise, even for one who had lived only seventy years. My, how her standards had changed of late!

"What does this mean?" Erich asked.

Ann took charge. "Mr. Brandywine, Mr. Yancy, I believe you know Squire Fladgate and Mr. Cobblesham. But let me introduce you to my cousin, Erich Van Helsing. And this is Mrs. Simpson." Mrs. Simpson looked as though she wished heartily she was elsewhere.

"Brandywine, I don't know that you belong at a wedding ceremony." The squire puffed himself up and tried to look consequential. "And Yancy, I hardly think these proceedings call for a solicitor. The license is in order, I assure you."

"Who are these interlopers?" Erich snapped.

"Mr. Brandywine is my uncle's steward, and Mr. Yancy his solicitor," Ann said smoothly. "I invited them here today just to clarify the situation. Do sit down, gentlemen, all of you, and you, Mrs. Simpson, please sit." She gestured at the comfortable wing chairs with which the library was provided. Mr. Yancy and Mr. Brandywine took their seats. Mr. Cobblesham resumed his. Squire Fladgate sputtered in indignation, but he sat. Mrs. Simpson perched nervously on the edge of her chair. Only Erich remained standing, looking mulish.

Ann sat in a wing chair upholstered in red leather. "Thank you, gentlemen. Now, to get to the point. Mr. Yancy, you are the keeper of my uncle's will?"

"Yes, Miss Van Helsing. I registered it this morning when I heard of his death. I have a copy here, if anyone would like to see it."

Ann watched Erich's eyes narrow. "Has the will been altered recently?"

"Lord Brockweir made some slight adjustments in it in the last few weeks."

Erich's expression went wary. "Are there any unexpected provisions in it?" he asked.

"None whatever, Mr. Van Helsing. There are some small bequests to servants and Lord Brockweir's favorite charities. But aside from those, the whole estate, including Maitlands and Bucklands Lodge as well as Lord Brockweir's own lands in Derbyshire and his town house in London and the rents and revenue thereof, and all the money invested in the Funds, are left to Miss Van Helsing."

"Not tied up in any way?" Erich asked sharply.

"No. With the exception, of course, that if Miss Van Helsing dies before she marries, they revert to the Crown. But you knew about that." Mr. Yancy's voice was so measured and logical. "I wrote to you some years ago at Ann's father's direction."

Erich looked like a cat who'd caught a mouse. He inclined his head in condescension.

"And why are they not tied up?" Ann asked.

"Because you are of age, Miss Van Helsing." Mr. Yancy's quiet voice was reassuring.

"Just so, Mr. Yancy." She glanced to Erich, who had a grim, determined look on his face. He must know his danger. She saw his eyes turn calculating. "And therefore I myself can dispose of the property as I choose?"

"You can," Mr. Yancy confirmed.

Erich looked wary. "Immediately?" she asked.

"Yes." Yancy's stentorian tones were most assured. God bless him! Just what she had hoped he'd say.

"*If* she's of sound mind." Erich said it as if he was throwing the card for a huitième on the table in a game of piquet. He glanced at the squire and Mr. Cobblesham. "According to one of your clerks, Mr. Yancy, the will says if Ann is not of sound mind, you continue the trust until her death or such time as she is married, in which case the fortune passes to her husband. I think we have had some very graphic demonstrations of late that Ann is hardly of sound mind." He sighed. "But it is a mark of my love and respect that I'm willing to take on that burden by marriage and care for her for the rest of her natural life."

And my money, Ann thought. But she gave no sign.

"Well, thank you for the news, Mr. Yancy." Erich rose. "I'll be in touch. Now if you'll excuse us, Mr. Cobblesham has other obligations today and would like to get on with the ceremony. Mrs. Simpson can show you out."

"Oh, there'll be no wedding," Ann remarked. "I have not agreed to marry you."

There it was. By the set of his chin, she knew Erich had not given up yet, though.

"He has a special license," Mr. Cobblesham protested. "And your uncle's blessing."

"Surely both you and Squire Fladgate realize that is of no consequence if the young woman does not consent?" Mr. Yancy asked, his voice hard.

"She did consent. I have witnesses. The fact that she's retracting now only proves her instability."

She didn't ask who he had procured as witnesses. He'd be able to buy testimony on the promise of his coming into her money. Mrs. Scrapple? Jemmy? Even the squire? She had no doubt potential witnesses to her "consent" would abound. "Mr. Yancy, I'd like you to draw up a settlement. I'm sure my uncle would not have wanted to exclude my cousin, had he had more opportunity to reflect. I should like to rectify that error. I think ten thousand in a one-time settlement and my uncle's secondary property in Derbyshire, the one that fronts along the river, would be generous."

Mr. Yancy nodded in agreement, a certain look of satisfaction on his face. "I'll see to it."

"Mr. Brandywine," she continued, "I shall be opening the house in London again immediately. Here is a letter to the Countess of Lente." Here she produced Sincai's letter. "She will provide assistance in procuring me a companion. I shall require the services of a full house staff. I expect to entertain. Could you also open an account with a London bank to provide for ready cash? Which do you prefer, Hoare's or Drummond's?"

"Drummond's," Mr. Brandywine declared, eyes gleaming now with a new sentiment. "I shall see to it at once. I will need your guidance on the crop rotation for the coming year as soon as possible, as well."

That was a nice touch. She almost wanted to hug him. "Of course. I believe it should be oats and rye this year, but I'm open to your suggestions, of course. And could I prevail upon you to find someone to accompany me to Tattersall's when I go up to London? I'd like to keep a carriage there, so I shall need to purchase some blood cattle."

"I know just the man. Colonel Wilton. Capital judge of horseflesh, and knows how to make his way around the pitfalls."

"This is ridiculous!" Erich almost shouted. "Why are you talking all this nonsense?"

Everyone turned toward Erich, who was flushed with anger. Her two supporters wore looks of studied curiosity. Mrs. Simpson smiled encouragement outright.

Erich gritted his teeth. "You can't buy me off with ten thousand and a paltry property in Derbyshire. The girl's loon. She needs to be tied up safely in a marriage. She terrorized the whole town only yesterday."

"I was upset," Ann said calmly.

"Who wouldn't be?" Mr. Brandywine chimed in. "False accusations, her uncle sick?"

"She . . . she—"

"I think she seems of very sound mind," Mr. Yancy observed.

"Simpson here knows that Maitlands can't even keep staff, people are so afraid of her."

Everyone turned toward Mrs. Simpson who flushed to the roots of her hair.

"It's true, isn't it, woman?"

Mrs. Simpson cleared her throat. "Some folks are superstitious, ignorant. Especially among the lower classes."

Ann had never been prouder of her. It was all she could do to keep her mouth still.

"I should think you two would be ashamed of yourselves, Fladgate, Cobblesham, promoting a sham marriage to an out-and-out fortune hunter." Mr. Yancy's eyes had gone remarkably hard. "Justice of the peace and spiritual guide are positions that come with responsibility. In fact, Cobblesham, isn't your living gifted by Brockweir? Which means it can be given elsewhere by Miss Van Helsing if she chooses."

Cobblesham blanched. "I . . . I thought her uncle . . . I mean, a special license . . . I had no idea the lady didn't—"

"Well, now you do," Mr. Brandywine said.

"There is still the matter of the accusations. She may have killed four men, or helped someone to kill them." This from the squire, trying to save face.

"I shall gladly answer Mr. Steadly's questions," Ann said. "And submit to his judgment."

"You can't stand to touch people!" Erich accused. "Is that normal?"

"I don't like to be touched, it's true." She couldn't get around that. Everyone knew it.

"Personal preferences do not mean a person is insane, Mr. Van Helsing, else you would be locked up for those pantaloons." Mr. Yancy frowned. "I think Miss Van Helsing has a very sane grasp of her situation, and it would take an action at law to try to prove otherwise. It is a case I should like to see a barrister try, as I'll assure you, you would lose. Now, Miss Van Helsing, what can we do for you in the most immediate sense?"

"You could escort these gentlemen out, if you would. I shall ask Jennings to bring Mr. Van Helsing's things to the tavern."

Erich looked from one to the other. Mr. Cobblesham rose hastily and made for the door without more ado. The squire's pace was considerably more measured, but he was clearly routed. As his two allies went out the door, Jennings and Polsham came in, and Erich knew this round at least was over.

"You have not heard the last of this." He pushed past Jennings and Polsham.

"Oh, I think she has." Mr. Yancy's calm voice chased him out the door.

Ann sighed as though a weight had been lifted from her shoulders. "Thank you. Thank you all." She looked up at the five people in the room. She hadn't been friendless after all.

"Damned grasping jackanapes!" Mr. Brandywine exclaimed. "Who does he think he is? Bad branch of the family . . ."

"On a practical note, I'm going to send to Bristol for some extra help for tonight," Yancy remarked. "They may arrive late, and they may look like the bruisers they used to be, but don't worry. Johnson is as trustworthy as they come and he'll bring some lads up to make sure that Mr. Van Helsing doesn't haunt the place."

He didn't have to say that, coming from Bristol, they wouldn't be subject to "superstitions."

"Did you mean it about the house in Grosvenor Square?" Mr. Brandywine asked.

"I did," Ann said. "It's time I faced the world and got out of my nursery." She saw looks of dismay cross her retainers' faces. "Of course, I shall want to take all of you with me. And . . . nothing can happen until after my uncle's funeral."

It hit her then, how alone she was, how much she would miss her uncle. But she managed a smile. "Unless you three would rather stay here and see the place put to rights. I shall need someone I can trust to supervise the whole. It's time we got this house out of dustcovers and the grounds put into order. And London is not to everyone's taste."

They started to speak, but she held up a hand. "No need to decide now."

"I'll take care of arranging your uncle's funeral," Mr. Brandywine said.

"I expect it will be a small affair," she said. He deserved more.

"Surely you jest, Miss Van Helsing." Mr. Yancy chuckled. "Lord Brockweir was well liked. And everyone within driving distance will want a look at the richest woman in the county, superstitious or not. It is your burden, my dear."

She thought about what she might or might not be doing in three days, when it came time for the funeral. She swallowed. "Then I'd like to do it right. Polsham, can you contact Mr. Watkins? I'll sponsor a supper and refreshments from the Hammer and Anvil, since there is no time to prepare the house. You and Mrs. Simpson will know what to order. Spare no expense. Mr. Brandywine can arrange for payment. Jennings, can you arrange for the procession from the house to the chapel? I shall provide the epitaph. And . . ." Here another thought intruded. There was the matter of Maitlands.

"Mr. Yancy, I want to make certain arrangements for Maitlands. Expect to receive a letter with instructions."

"You are a remarkable woman, Miss Van Helsing. I wish I could shake your hand," Mr. Yancy said. "I'll be in contact with the details of the settlement on Van Helsing." He bowed crisply and made for the door. The others followed.

The door closed. She allowed herself one moment of fear. It was all so much! But what was behind her was lost, and the only way to what she wanted most lay down that fearful road. She had no choice.

Now she must get to Bucklands Lodge before sunset.

Nineteen

Ann had told Mrs. Simpson she was taking the dogcart. Since Jennings had taken Erich's things into Cheddar Gorge, she had harnessed the Haflinger pony to the cart herself. The ten miles to Bucklands had been over good road until the last half mile. Now the narrow track wound through woods. The sun had set and evening gloom invaded the trees, making the way even darker. Full night was close now. She glanced behind her and clucked to the Haflinger. What did she expect to see? Shadows gliding between the trees? Bodies drained of blood littering a forest floor soggy with dead leaves?

But she saw nothing like that. Only fingers of mist curling through the tree trunks. She heard only the soft thud of the pony's hooves, the creak of the harness, and the shush of the wooden wheels on the damp earth of the track. Ahead was the lodge. She would be able to see it from here if there were lights on. But there were no lights. All around her was sinking into darkness. She dreaded approaching it. Every unfamiliar object in it would be drenched with the evil ones who had been there, the horrific deeds that had been committed there. Ahead was blood and pain and horror in the floor, the walls, every object, anything she might touch.

Was Stephan there? He had to be there. He knew Kilkenny would come looking for him there. Kilkenny and however many others. She shuddered and it wasn't from the dampness crawling along the forest floor. He would try to make her leave. And if she was right about how he was mistaken, she wouldn't be able to let him do that. She wondered if there was any way to make Stephan Sincai do something he didn't want to do.

The form of the lodge solidified in the growing gloom and the trees opened out. She pulled the pony and cart up the drive to the doorway and leapt to the ground. There was a stable out back, but she hadn't time to take him back there. She tied his reins to the decorative metal post set for the purpose to the right side of the portico, then patted his warm, moist hide and whispered that she would be back.

The windows of the lodge had been boarded up. Scrambling up the three steps to the front door, she saw nails scattered about where they had been used to nail the door shut. It was not shut now. It swung invitingly ajar, though bent spikes still protruded from its edges where it had been pried open. Did Stephan think Kilkenny and company would come in through the front door? She took a breath and pushed it open, relieved she didn't have to touch the knob. Nothing much came to her. A faint sensation of the workman who had nailed it shut, nothing more. It creaked open on darkness. Erich should have had it oiled. But if she were issuing recriminations, *she* should have brought a lantern. Her heart thudded within her. Could Kilkenny have already been here? Was she too late?

"Stephan?" she called out in a small voice. She cleared her throat and stepped inside, thankful that her boots protected her from the floor. "Stephan?"

A shadow loomed in the doorway off to her left.

"What are you doing here?" the familiar baritone rumbled.

She sighed in relief and ran to him. It seemed so natural to throw herself into his arms, to feel those arms circle round her. She felt the wash of fear he had experienced since he left her, the certainty that with all the emotion he had felt for her and his ejaculations, he had weakened himself so that the coming confrontation was hopeless. He wasn't happy that he had given in to his feelings for her. He thought he had let down his kind, that he had failed before he started. That was daunting. But it didn't change her own certainty. "Stephan, you're wrong about the power. It doesn't come from suppression."

He held her away from him. "You must go, Ann. You can't be here when they come." He turned her round and walked her forcibly to the door.

"Stephan, listen to me! Those women may have trained you that way, but it's only by opening yourself up that you are as strong as you can be. I know that."

"You're not making sense, my dear. You know nothing about it, and I don't want you to know." He swung the door wide and marched her through it.

"If only you'd—"

"Ann," he said sharply, turning her to him again. "Do you know what will happen here? Can you imagine?"

"I don't have to imagine," she said quietly. "I know everything you know about what happened here before."

That pulled him up sharply. He swallowed. "I had forgotten." He gathered himself. "Then you know why you can't be here."

"Just hear me out, and then I'll go."

"I'll do no such thing." His voice was stony flat.

"Then I'll go round the bend in the track and leave the horse, and walk back through the woods. I can be as stubborn as you are." She folded her arms and stared back at him.

Stephan looked around in the night for any signs of

intruders. He could see clearly when she could not. "Oh, very well," he said, exasperated. "Tell me quickly then."

It wasn't exactly enthusiastic, but she would take what he gave her. "Rubius told you that the power was anchored in your sexuality, and heightened by suppression."

"Yes. And he was right. It took me nearly two years, but I learned his lessons, and I did increase my power."

"But your power comes from connecting to your Companion. It has always been so. You know it and I know it through you."

"Yes . . ." He didn't see it yet.

"It is connection, openness, that makes you so powerful. You open that connection to the Companion. You could open yourself to other kinds of power and use them, too."

"You're talking nonsense, Ann. Their training *worked*. Empirical proof. Suppression made my Companion's power more forceful. Would that I had practiced a little more suppression of late." He looked disgusted with himself.

"I think they taught you suppression because they were afraid of you, Stephan."

He smiled ruefully. "Rubius and his daughters are very old, Ann. They are far more powerful than I am."

"They were looking for someone to be this . . . Harrier, weren't they?"

He nodded.

"Well, why didn't they take one of their devout monks and make him into one. Or her?"

He shrugged. "Who would volunteer for such a task?"

"So you think they chose you because they had something you wanted and they could force you to undergo years of what amounts to torture to get it."

His mouth was grim. "Something like that."

"Hardly admirable, are they? But what if they really chose you because you had more natural power than the others? What if the training was only to make you manageable?"

"I think it more likely they chose me to make an example of one who rebelled against the teachings of the Elders."

"All right. Both then. A rebel with too much power."

"Ann, you read too much into this. They had trained others before me."

"Unsuccessfully."

Now he was getting exasperated. "Only because they went too fast."

"Look," she said, her voice low. "You don't believe you will succeed tonight using their techniques. What have you to lose? Open yourself to all your power—"

"I've heard you out." He glanced out to the night-black forest. "Now go." There was an urgency in his voice that had not been there before.

Then she smelled it. Cinnamon and, underneath it, just a hint of ambergris wafted toward them. She felt a trembling excitement in the air as of the vibrations of a dozen insect wings. The pony tied off to the post shrieked a frightened whinny.

They turned toward the forest just as the shadows walked out from whirling pools of darkness. There were six of them. In front of the others stood a man with dark hair, not red, and pale skin. He was dressed simply, in buff breeches and riding boots, a simple, serviceable coat without adornment. His features were refined in that Irish way of straight, almost-prominent nose and eyes that promised that they crinkled when he laughed. This man hadn't laughed in a long time, though. His mouth, slightly wider than most, was set in grim purpose. He didn't look as she had expected. There was no sign of evil in his handsome open features. He bore no mark of Cain.

But Ann had no doubt who he was. Neither did Stephan. His hands tightened their grip on her upper arms and he thrust her behind him. "Kilkenny," he said bleakly.

Ann peered out around Stephan. Kilkenny stopped. The

others behind him spread out in a line. They were an odd mélange of young and old, workaday and elegant, plain and well made. All stared with dreadful purpose at Stephan as the red glow left their eyes. "And you must be the Harrier," Kilkenny said. His voice was shocking. It was not the Irish lilt they expected but a Scottish burr that echoed in the dusk. The man may have come from Irish stock, but he had been raised in the Scots Lowlands. "We've a score to settle, I believe."

"Yes."

Six! There were too many of them. That made the one word from Stephan so unbearable. If only he would take her advice! It was a horrible time for the test of an unproven theory. But he couldn't win out against six in any other way, could he?

"Let the girl, go, Kilkenny. She has nothing to do with this."

Kilkenny glanced to her. She could see his eyes were light, not quite blue, not quite green or even gray in the half-light. He nodded. "A human has no business here tonight."

She glanced along the line of vampires. Then her eyes returned to the one standing just behind Kilkenny. It was the creature who had killed Molly by draining her blood. A shiver went down her spine. Stephan thrust her toward the dogcart.

"Go," he hissed. "Go now."

She stumbled toward the cart. She didn't want to see what would happen here. What could she do against six vampires? She was five feet and not quite seven stone of human female. There was nothing she could do here except distract Stephan with fear for her welfare.

Ann scrambled into the cart and took up the pony's reins. No one else moved. Their gazes were locked together in a terrible tableau. She shook the reins over the pony's back. The beast darted down the track as though the devil was at his tail. It might be true. The cart jolted over the uneven

track. The palpable menace in the air receded. That was
Kilkenny's evil.

He hadn't looked evil, though. World-weary, tired but determined. Reluctant, even. That was how he had looked. The
pony slowed of his own accord as they left Bucklands behind.
Ann's heart did not. It pounded unevenly in her breast. What
was she thinking?

She hauled on the pony's reins. He almost sat back on his
haunches, he stopped so fast. She turned the cart around.
She couldn't leave Stephan to face six vampires alone. She
could not imagine waiting at home in her nursery for news
of the fresh murders at Bucklands Lodge and wondering
whether the bodies they found would include Stephan's. She
had to be here tonight, whether she wanted to see the horror
or not. She clucked to the pony. He took a few unwilling
steps, then reared in the traces, snorting. "Whoa," she said
softly. "Whoa, boy." He shook his head and snorted again.
He made it clear he was not going back to that smell of cinnamon and the red glowing eyes in the darkness.

Ann leapt down from the cart and started back down the
track at a run, holding her skirts up. God help that she was
not too late.

Too late for what? The breath pounded in and out of her
lungs in a rhythm with the thud of her feet on the soft earth
and the pumping of her heart. She didn't know. She only
knew she had to be there. The track curved in the darkness.
She had no time for curves. She veered from the road and
stumbled into the forest itself. Branches tore at her. The rising moon peeked through the trees. She pushed through the
verdant brush hoping she would not trip over some half-
buried log. The smell of rot and green life, damp stones and
wet wood, enveloped her.

Growls and shrieks of pain tore through the night. She
was too late! She pushed through a last dark wall of brush
and burst into the clearing in front of the lodge. The open

space was filled with wild thrashing. By the light of the
moon, she saw Stephan at the center of a whirl of bodies,
moving almost too fast for her to comprehend. She could
comprehend the smell of blood, though. Stephan was in his
shirtsleeves, and she could see the stains of blood splashed
dark across the white canvas of his shirt.

Her heart leapt into her throat. "Stephan," she whispered,
and then realized she had shouted it. One man stood off to
the side, watching the melee. It was Kilkenny. She could feel
the hum of power in the air. Red eyes glowed, including
Stephan's.

A body toppled out of the gyrating mass slowly, in counterpoint to the frantic activity. Its head rolled toward her, eyes
still blinking, mouth gaping. Ann shrieked and backed away,
blinking. But she could not tear her gaze away from the horror of the head until she heard a grunt of pain she recognized
as Stephan's. She searched for him in the melee. Another as-
sailant fell, headless. Now there were three and Stephan. His
shirt had been torn from his body. She could clearly see the
dreadful wounds there. His belly was slashed. A dozen holes
seeped blood. Her brain knew that he could heal such
wounds, but her heart simply clenched in terror that Stephan
could be so hurt. One attacker lunged out. Something glinted
in the moonlight. A knife! It found Stephan's throat. Blood
spurted. No one could survive that blow! He staggered back,
up the shallow stairs to the portico.

She darted forward against her will. Stephan! He glanced
toward her. Just that tiny lapse of attention, and one of his attackers lunged after him and got Stephan's head in his
hands. The brute began to twist. Another closed in with a
second long blade. It flashed again and again in the silver
light. Ann kept on running. No time for guilt. No time for
second thoughts.

As though time had slowed she saw him reach out a hand
to her as though to stop her, even as he strained in resistance

to the tall thug who grasped his head. They had him now. The third pulled back, gasping, then struck in for the kill from behind. Blood was everywhere. Stephan's blood.

"Ann!" she heard Stephan shout in a voice drawn out into an impossibly low rumble. She pushed up against the struggling mass of bodies and reached for that hand.

"Stephan," she shouted, or maybe she didn't. His touch almost burned her. She poured all her love into that connection, all her regret, but also all her will. She saw his eyes widen. It was as if they stood there, connected, and the man who twisted his head, and the one who raised the knife, and the other, attacking from the rear, weren't there, or if they were they didn't matter. It was only Stephan and Ann, joined by the touch of their hands. It didn't matter that the grip was slippery with blood. Their gazes locked on each other. Ann felt him open to her. Love, fear for her, anger at his enemies; all of it washed over her. Then she felt his power surge up and it was her power too, incredible, invigorating. It was Stephan and something else she felt, something that sang in his blood and rejoiced in living. She wanted to shriek in laughter or in ecstasy.

Stephan began to glow.

There was no other word for it. A faint outline of white surged out from his figure. It enveloped her hand in a tingling flow of life and energy. She had never felt so alive. The eerie white corona bathed the scene in light, making the blood shine black and the eyes of his attackers glow more purely red. Ann felt the power course through her and down, out into the earth. Indeed she seemed to feel a kind of rumble in the ground that echoed in her lungs.

Stephan swept the three vampires from him with one hand, the other still firmly joined to hers. They struggled up as he drew her into his body. The wound at his neck seemed to be closing, for the blood no longer spurted, but his body was still slick with it. The glow enveloped her and she felt strong, stronger than she could ever imagine. He looked down at her, tenderly.

"Ann." She heard the name echo, almost as though they were in her cave. The three vampires lunged. Stephan tore his gaze away from her and turned it on his attackers.

They stopped suddenly. For one long instant, their faces were frozen in surprise and horror. Then the power in the air ramped up. The corona expanded. A tearing shriek that was not made of human voices rent the air, and the three bodies . . . exploded. There was no other word for it. One moment they were lunging forward, and the next moment a shower of unrecognizable matter was shooting outward from the portico.

The glow faded. Shadows crept into the clearing again. The life and ecstasy faded, leaving Ann hollow. Stephan sank to his knees and she followed, leaning heavily against him. Blackness ate at her vision and she fought against the desire to gag or faint. Her stomach churned. Around them a semicircle of . . . of red slime radiated in stabbing rays like a sun. She saw Kilkenny beyond it with a horrified expression on his face. He fell to his knees, retching. Ann heard nothing but the ringing in her own ears. What had happened here?

Minutes passed. Ann shook her head and her senses rattled back into place. Stephan's chest heaved against her side where he cradled her against him. Somehow they had both collapsed on the stone of the portico. He hung his head. His dark hair curtained his face. The wound in his belly had nearly closed. The stab wounds were in various states of repair, from still bleeding to faint pink weals on his flesh "What . . . what happened?" she whispered.

He raised his head. His eyes still looked distant. His shoulders sagged. "I think you were right," he said in an exhausted voice.

"Has that ever happened before?"

"No. I melted glass once." A long pause. "I cracked

stones and . . ." Another pause. "I lit a fire in some leaves
and broke some rock." Silence. "But not this."

Footsteps sounded, muffled, in the damp earth. Ann
looked up. Kilkenny stood there, his heavy seaman's sword
drawn. He looked as white as his cravat. He raised his
sword. "I dispatch the evil one, in the name o' the future o'
our kind." His lilting Scottish burr was raw.

Stephan raised his head. "I'm not the one making vampires, Kilkenny." He was exhausted. Ann realized there
would be no repeat performance of his power tonight, with
or without her help, even though his wounds were healing.
His neck no longer even seeped blood, thank God. He let
her go, and staggered to his feet, hands on his knees, panting. She glanced to Kilkenny. He was fresh. In fact, he had
saved himself for just this eventuality. She wondered why
he hadn't struck Stephan's head from his body even now
with that heavy sword. "You are the one who is evil,"
Stephan accused.

"If the purpose be pure, the making of vampires is na
wrong."

Stephan managed a snort. "Pure! Like draining humans
of blood? That kind of pure?"

"We dinna drain blood." Kilkenny was stung to defend
himself. "We are the outcast, the hunted. All we want is to
establish a vampire homeland here; one strong enough to resist the tyranny of Rubius and Mirso. *Ye're* a minion of his
tyranny."

Ann was shocked. Kilkenny thought Stephan was the evil
one? "I saw the man who stood beside you tonight kill a
woman from my village," she accused.

"There have been killings all around here, man," Stephan
said. "Your followers were a band of killers."

Kilkenny narrowed his eyes. "Ye lie." But his mouth wavered. He raised his sword, but he was chewing his lip. *He
doesn't want to kill us,* Ann thought with surprise. *And he*

won't believe his followers would kill. What kind of evil is that?

A realization rolled through Ann. The man was idealistic. As idealistic as Stephan when he wanted to prove made vampires were as good as born vampires. *Well, now . . .*

"Come on, Kilkenny, let's make it a fair fight, hand to hand." That was Stephan's only chance. Kilkenny would never do it. Why would he give away the advantage of the sword?

"After what I just saw ye do? I'm thinking the sword is hardly equal to the weapons ye're wielding." Kilkenny looked wary, determined. Ann realized suddenly that he thought he was the one to die tonight. "Ye're an old one, after all."

Still she had to take Stephan's part. "He's injured, can't you see that?"

Kilkenny peered at Stephan, who was still panting, his breath ragged. The wounds might be healing, but he had obviously used up his strength.

The sword clattered to the stone. Ann cocked her head and knit her brows, considering. Was it possible . . . ? Could Kilkenny be . . . honorable? Before the two men could close with each other she scrambled up and did the only thing she knew how to do.

She stood between them and touched them both at once.

Kilkenny washed over her; his childhood as an outcast Irish immigrant in Scotland, the nephew of an Irish peer whose mother married down, growing up aristocratic but dirt poor, outcast from his richer relations, his resentment that the Irish were second-class citizens who could not even vote because they were Catholic, his participation in the Rising of '97 as a very young idealist trying to reclaim his Irish heritage, his realization that having lived in Scotland, he belonged to neither country, the journey to Marrakech as part of a tour of foreign capitals to gain support for the Irish cause, the enslavement by Asharti, the terrible things she did to him, being made vampire, the terrible things he did in her name when his courage failed him, his revulsion, his escape. And the fact that he remained an idealist.

All of vampire society was out to kill the vampires Asharti made, without regard to who they were or what they could contribute. For him, making England into a vampire homeland that could stand against Mirso was self-defense, both physically and mentally. He turned his self-loathing into a desire to create Utopia, where vampires and humans would live together as Scots and Irish and English couldn't seem to do.

She turned to Stephan, and saw his eyes blinking. She got only what she had not had from him since they last touched, the adrenaline rush of battle, the stoic refusal to acknowledge pain, the determination. She could only hope he was getting Kilkenny through her, at least an impression of him. And Kilkenny? She looked up at him and saw him blinking, too. Did he get what she had gotten of Stephan? He would see the idealism, the courage, the awful guilt for Asharti. Would Kilkenny blame Stephan for what he had gone through? Or would he recognize Stephan's suffering and the atonement as akin to his own impulses?

She waited in silence, trying to breathe and keep her own internal balance as she gripped each man's wrist. At last they stopped blinking.

"Well, gentlemen," she gasped. "It isn't quite as straightforward as you thought, is it?"

Kilkenny ripped his gaze from Stephan to look at her. "What . . . what are ye, woman?"

"No more strange than you are," she retorted. Then more gently, "You know me now, if you think about it."

She could see him thinking. He nodded. "Ye ha' the sight."

She laughed, and it almost turned to sobs. "You could say that."

"They were killin' humans, weren't they?" Kilkenny asked it softly. Sadness seeped into his eyes. Now, now they both understood.

Stephan straightened. "This doesn't change anything."

What?

"I dinna expect that it does," Kilkenny agreed. They began to circle each other.

"You're going to kill each other, when you're really just alike?"

"We're not alike," Kilkenny muttered. He pushed Ann out of the way as he slowly circled right. "Get back, woman."

"You're both idealistic. You've both suffered. You've both done things you weren't proud of." She looked from one implacable face to the other, incredulous. "You're both stubborn as hell!"

"He still makes vampires. That will be the destruction of our kind," Stephan muttered.

"But not willy-nilly. He thinks of it as a state one should aspire to and tries to pick only those worthy," she argued. They were crouched and ready to spring at each other.

"That's not worked out so well," Stephan growled.

Kilkenny flushed. "And ye're still the Harrier, bent on destroying the good and the bad together just because they're made not born. There were some good men who died here tonight."

Stephan ground his teeth and lunged.

The two men grappled with each other for purchase, trying to wrench an arm off to make a try for the head direct easier. Ann wanted to scream in frustration. Could they not *see* that this was pointless? Damn their eyes and their stupid pride! If she was bigger she would just pry them apart and shake them like a mother cat shakes her kittens.

But she wasn't. She looked around for a weapon. All she could see were the long spike nails used to board up the house scattered about the stone floor. She thought of stabbing either one or both, just to get their attention. But they probably wouldn't even notice, as intent on mutual destruction as they were.

Her anger boiled up into her throat. Men! These two were just too stubborn to give up their course. She would have expected better of them, now that she knew the depths of both their souls. Waste! Why couldn't they talk it over? Why couldn't they back down? How could she get them to just *listen* to her?

The answer, when it hit her, made her shiver. All the implications came raining down. And they didn't matter. She watched herself pick up the spike as in a dream. It was made by the blacksmith, the tip shaved sharp when it was still red with heat. She stood and turned to the assailants, letting her anger fuel her determination.

When she spoke, it was softly, but her teeth were gritted in frustration. "Will you stop, then, you two?" Their grunts of effort were her only response. Kilkenny got the weakened Stephan to the ground and was wrenching his arm. "Then I have no choice." She was really talking to herself. She raised the palm of her hand. There was no time for thought, only time to feel her stomach churn in rage. She stabbed the nail into her palm. A shock of pain made her gasp. She drew the point across her palm. Blood welled up in a line. This would stop their stupid wrangling. Then she walked to where the two men struggled on the stone floor of the portico.

Had Stephan healed all his wounds? No. There in his shoulder, a deep stab wound was still closing. And he was still smeared with blood. Enough, even if the wound closed? She bent, ignoring their struggle, and pressed her palm to Stephan's bare shoulder. His determination, his angst that he might fail, washed over her.

The two men both turned to her with a mutual gasp.

"Ann!" Stephan barked. "What have you done?" They rolled apart.

"She's infected herself," Kilkenny said in shock. He and Stephan scrambled up.

"And now I'm a made vampire, Stephan. Will you kill me, too?" She pushed her hand against Stephan's shoulder again, dragged her bleeding palm across his bloody chest while he stood there, sheet-white. "Or you, Kilkenny." She rounded on him. "Since I'm in love with a character so foul as the Harrier, surely I must be punished for it with death."

Both men took a step back from her fury.

It was Kilkenny who recovered first. "You . . . you did this for him?"

The fury drained away, leaving her shaky. She looked at her bloody palm, then up at the two men, horror writ on their faces. "Yes," she said simply.

Stephan felt the world fall away from him. He watched blood well from the wound in Ann's bloody palm. Her flesh was smeared not only with her own blood but with his. There was no going back, no starting over. She would be a vampire or she would die.

He looked to her face, furious an instant before, now big-eyed and uncertain. She had done this for him? She could love him that much?

"Ye're a lucky man, Harrier," Kilkenny said, his voice bleak. "To ha' a woman who will sacrifice everythin' for ye, an' even brave eternity. She's made it a little harder to hunt down all made vampires for Rubius, hasna she, then?"

"And you," Stephan countered, "still have your faith that you can identify men of goodwill and start a utopian society? It's just a little more complex than that."

"We Irish ha' always been dreamers." Stephan saw pain drench him as he tried to compass the depth of his failure. Then his features closed and he shrugged. "I should ha' followed my Scots upbringin' rather than my dreams. The Scots are nothin' if na dour."

"There was never an army, Stephan. He made twelve. He wanted a homeland. He thought he could control the spread, whether it was true or not. So Kilkenny wasn't the threat to the world of vampire and human Rubius told you he was. Rubius wants Kilkenny dead," Ann said, drilling Stephan with her stare, "because his dream was a threat to Rubius's own power. The Eldest used you."

"A common pastime," Stephan muttered. Rubius's daughters used him as much for their own pleasure as for their task. Asharti had used him to gain knowledge. She played on his sympathy to escape her just reward. Beatrix? Beatrix hadn't used him, except as an object of infatuation, but she never understood him, either. Only Ann accepted him for what he was and wanted nothing from him except . . . love. Ann didn't want eternal life. He knew that. She wanted his love. He stared out into the darkness. The moon lit the radius of sludge that had once been five of his kind. Made, true, but of his kind. He had executed them without a second thought.

He was not worthy of her love.

Ann seemed to read his thoughts. "They were trying to kill you."

"The four I killed in this house a week ago weren't trying to kill me. I surprised them."

"Rubius duped you, man," Kilkenny rasped. "We've both been betrayed by idealism."

Idealism . . . What was that? Stephan didn't know anymore. "I was a willing victim."

"Because you don't forgive yourself." Ann turned to Kilkenny. "Neither of you."

"Because I wanted an easy way to redemption," Stephan rasped. Forgive himself? He was unforgivable. His failings had cost others' lives and worlds.

"Hardly easy," Ann observed.

"She's right," Kilkenny agreed. Stephan realized he must know about the Daughters, through Ann. He was too tired and dispirited even to flush.

He gathered himself. "I let the one who made you go free. She killed, she infected humans to make her armies. I am responsible for your suffering, man."

Kilkenny shrugged, trying to pretend he didn't care. Stephan liked him for that. But Kilkenny's eyes went dead with memory. Stephan had seen what Asharti had done to him through Ann's connection. The Daughters were nothing to it, since Stephan had submitted himself to them. Kilkenny did not submit willingly. His sin was that he had done horrible things in order to please her in some twisted response to her dominance and mistreatment. That was what Kilkenny did not forgive himself.

Kilkenny mustered himself. "Hard ta foresee all the consequences of our actions."

"A fact which applies to *both* of you," Ann said, exasperated. She stood between them and looked from one to the other. "So, are you two done trying to kill each other?"

The silence stretched before Kilkenny nodded. "Take me if ye want me."

Stephan shook his head in disgust. He was going to let Kilkenny go. Mirso was well and truly lost to him from this moment on.

Kilkenny glanced around as though he had suddenly wakened and found he had been sleepwalking to a place he did not recognize. "Our purpose is gone. Wha' is left for such as ye and me, Harrier?"

Stephan pushed his hair back from his face. It was matted with blood. He couldn't think about purpose yet. He glanced to Ann. She was barely on her feet after the strain and excitement of tonight. And soon she would begin to feel the effects of her infection. She would need the blood of a vampire to give her immunity from the Companion. Lots of blood. She would become deathly ill. He had to make sure she survived, even if it was only to face the horrors of eternity. That was his purpose, now.

And then there was the problem of Kilkenny's twelve. That number might have grown.

"Did your twelve make others?"

Kilkenny passed a shaky hand over his eyes. "I thought not. We had a pact . . . Now I don't know."

"I suppose we will find out," Stephan said grimly. "But for now we must move on." He glanced to Ann. "After what happened here tonight, human society will be after our hides." Another thought occurred. "Two of Rubius's daughters are about. Perhaps you would find Scotland more congenial for a while."

"I doubt I shall find anyplace congenial," the man who belonged nowhere said bitterly.

Kilkenny too needed a purpose. "Perhaps there is a middle way for such as you," Stephan said. Kilkenny looked dubious. "Are we not looking for redemption? Perhaps it lies neither in adhering blindly to Rubius's Rules, nor in creating an ideal society out of whole cloth. Perhaps you have to begin with what you have, where you stand. It may be that you can only hope to make the world a little better. There is too much evil to be rid of it all at once."

"Wha' are ye saying, man?" Kilkenny looked exhausted, too.

"Only that you are a good man. I felt it. Perhaps you can do a bit of good in the world, not much, mind you, but a little."

"It's too late for me to take Orders." Kilkenny's smile collapsed around him. He probably once had a boyish grin that had the maids clustering round him. Those days were gone now.

"Then dispense justice where you can. Use your strength and the other gifts of the Companion in the service of good if you can find it." Stephan let no sympathy into his voice. The other man would not abide it.

"You mean I should wander the world like those broken warriors in Japan?"

"Ronan samurai." Stephan chuckled to himself. He knew a thing or two about Ronan samurai. He looked up at Kilkenny. "Yes. Start by finding the ones your followers made. Those are laid at your door."

Kilkenny's eyes danced about the carnage, the woods, the portico of Bucklands Lodge, considering. "Perhaps that is as good as any other plan."

"Perhaps even a plan is too much to expect just now."

Kilkenny turned bleak eyes on him. "Agreed. Just one deed, a little one, at a time."

"It might be all you can be sure of."

"And likely not sure of that."

"Just don't make any more vampires." Stephan laid the boundary.

Kilkenny raised his brows. "Not even for love?" He glanced to Ann.

Stephan breathed out. "Point taken."

Kilkenny turned to Ann. "Thankee for yer courage, miss. Ye saved a pair a' old warhorses from disgracing themselves tonight. I hope ye dinna live to regret it."

"Who can know?" She smiled and kissed him on the cheek. "That is too long to look ahead. I shall just look to the next small decision, and make it."

Stephan put his arm around her. She looked up at him with those trusting, all-seeing eyes. "You are wise, Miss Van Helsing, for one who has lived but a single lifetime," he whispered.

"Take care of her," Kilkenny said gruffly. Then he turned on his heel and strode into the shadows of the sycamores until he disappeared.

Twenty

Ann watched Kilkenny walk into the shadows through filled eyes. She had never seen a man so alone. Even the comfort of his ideals had been stripped from him. In some ways they had been his protection from what Asharti had done to him, and what he had done in her name. Now he had no refuge left. She and Stephan both understood the need for refuge.

She looked down at her bleeding palm and then up at Stephan. Her own refuge was gone forever, too. Why had she taken such a momentous step on an impulse? What kind of future had she let herself in for—outcast from all she knew, drinking blood . . . eternity, for God's sake? And where did God stand in all of this? Was she even one of God's creatures anymore, or had she crossed to the dark side?

Stephan smiled at her. Such a tiny, tenuous smile.

No, she had not crossed over into evil. She had crossed to Stephan's side. The last barrier between them had been cast aside. Whatever the problems ahead, what she had done was the next step on a journey she undertook when she found the courage to touch him in the cave. That had been an impulse, too, one that took her outside the comfort of her isolation. She would never regret it. Stephan's form began to waver around the edges. Her vision blurred. It was not just that her eyes were swimming with tears. She was hot, too, come to think of it. Extremely hot.

Concern darted into Stephan's eyes. He swept her up into his arms. "We need a safe haven. You will become very ill for a while."

"A refuge?" She closed her eyes and smiled. She was so tired. "We're short of those just now." But he was right. "The cave?"

He looked down at her and settled her in his arms. She must be very light for one as strong as he was. "It may come to that. But you would prefer someplace familiar to you, yet with more creature comforts." His eyes had that red glow in them she had come to find beautiful. She laid her head against his shoulder and felt the bulge of muscle against her cheek. Underneath the smell of blood was the wonderful cinnamon scent.

She felt darkness whirling up around her and then it was inside her head.

"This may be uncomfortable, but it will only last a moment," she heard him say. But it was far away. Then nothing.

Stephan pressed his translocation as far as he possibly could. He was surprised to see that he had made the crossroads at Sidcot, a good five miles from the lodge. Only a very powerful vampire could translocate so far, and weakened as he was from wounds and carrying Ann . . . Had her joining with him somehow increased his strength? His Companion still sang in his veins.

Good. Then he would press even harder this time and make it to Maitlands in two tries. He glanced down to Ann. Her sickness was progressing more rapidly than he would expect. She must have blood equipped with immunity quickly, before the Companion could wreak havoc on her body. She needed his blood.

Come to me! he called to his Companion. *Bring all the strength you have.*

The crossroads and the carriage that approached from Upper Langford were washed with the familiar red film as his eyes glowed with the power of the one who shared his blood. Darkness whirled up quickly, a searing pain ripped through him, and the darkness drained away, revealing the ruined Gothic arches of Maitlands Abbey stabbing the midnight sky around them. A night breeze made gooseflesh on his bare torso, but Ann was hot against his chest. The rooms of Maitlands were dark. He saw lights only in the servants' quarters and a dim glimmer in the distant chapel—no doubt the candles marking the vigil for Ann's dead uncle. But outside it was a different story. He spotted guards around the building, several carrying torches. To keep him out? To guard Van Helsing? The fool must know a few guards couldn't stop him.

Even as he watched, a horse trotted up the drive. It was Van Helsing. He knew the rider's identity long before one of the guards held his torch high and made his challenge.

"Who goes there?"

"The future owner of thish pile." Van Helsing sneered as he dismounted. "Give way."

"Well, if it ain't Mr. Van Helsing," another guard said as he sauntered up. Several others were also gathering. They seemed to be a surly lot, with several broken noses and cauliflower ears between them. "Whater you doin' here at midnight?"

"I've come to shee my coushin." Van Helsing was foxed.

"Well, she's hired us to tell you she don't want to see you," the leader of this unlikely band of protectors said. He grabbed Van Helsing by the shoulders to turn him around. The blackguard spun out of his grip, then staggered.

So, Ann had sent him to the right about. *Good girl*, he thought. *I knew you had it in you.*

"She thinks she's too good for me?" he muttered. He straightened in an exaggerated motion. "She's a loon!"

"Looks to me like a woman of sense if she don't want you haunting the place," one of the other guards remarked.

"Off with you, or the lads here'll make your head feel even worse in the morning than it's like to do from drink." The leader of the guards made a menacing move. Van Helsing flinched visibly, if a little late, in response.

"Very well," he said with exaggerated dignity. "I shall call on her in the morning." He glanced up to the house. "The bitch." He wavered, then leaned forward conspiratorially. "She'll have me in the end. I've got friends. They'll give her no choish."

"Let me give you a hand, fellow," a grinning guard said. Another picked up the horse's reins. Van Helsing struggled getting his foot into the stirrup. Two guards heaved on his buttocks and somehow he got into the saddle. He trotted down the lane, listing first to one side, then another. The guards returned to their stations, chuckling.

Stephan was not so sure he shared their confidence. Van Helsing's seat had been decidedly steadier trotting up than trotting out. The man was shamming drunkenness. It didn't matter. Stephan had no time for him. He could feel Ann shiver in his arms. His brows drew together in concern. The fever was starting already? Too soon! He had not much time.

He glanced up at the dark fourth floor and summoned his Companion.

When he flickered into the low-ceilinged room, he laid her on her narrow bed. They had made love in this bed. She had given him both her virginity and the hope that sexual congress with a woman, at least with one woman, was not a shameful torture but a hallowed gift. It was some kind of miracle he had not hurt her. And if he had been weakened for his horrible task by their lovemaking, still, at the moment of confrontation he had been stronger than he had ever been—also a gift from her. Together they had . . . what? He still wasn't sure.

He stared at her, silver hair haloed on her pillow, skin pale as parchment and gleaming with perspiration. She had been right about the power. Opening himself at that last moment had been even more compelling than suppression. Or maybe only opening himself to her. When he saw her there, he had hated the creatures around him for exposing her to this horror, knowing they would turn on her next. He had wanted to protect her more than anything he'd ever wanted. Perhaps she didn't need protecting. Or maybe together they were more than either alone . . .

God! What was he thinking? He shoved his hands in his pockets, as though to keep them from ever touching her again. She had given up *everything* she knew tonight and everything she was. The guilt of it ate at him. She couldn't know what eternal life would mean; the endless struggle with who and what you were, the repetition, the exposure to every horror man could concoct again and again, until belief in anything was well nigh impossible. Two thousand years of experience made one into a cynic even cynics would find harsh. She on the other hand had never been outside the neighborhood. She had lived her life in these small rooms. He had added becoming a monster to the burden of her psychic ability. New vampires were prone to madness when they could not cope with the terms of their new life and the power the Companion conferred upon them. Wasn't madness what Ann had been trying to avoid all her life?

He ripped her dress with a single tear and pulled off her half-boots. He unlaced her short corset. She seemed almost insensible. Then he threw back the covers and laid her gently between her sheets. Her shift was drenched with perspiration.

He felt her forehead. Burning hot. How could the infection progress so rapidly? Only in cases of infection by the blood of a very old and powerful vampire did such rapid onset occur. He might be two thousand years old, but that did not qualify him as old and powerful. He pulled the quilts up over her.

It was his fault. Touching him had sent her into the coma. If he had had the courage to stay away from her, she would not have found herself trying to warn him at the lodge . . .

Why? Why had she ripped her palm and pressed it to his bleeding flesh? He ran one hand through his hair in distraction. She knew what would happen! She knew everything. He sucked air into his lungs and went still. She did it for him. She said so. The air sighed out as he stared at her, tossing her head on the pillow. Her act had stopped him and Kilkenny from fighting. She was that selfless. He didn't deserve it! He didn't deserve her.

Forcibly he pushed away those thoughts. That way lay paralysis. Right now he had to get her his blood. He went to her dressing table and took up the little silver-handled knife she used to pare her nails. It would be too horrible for her to wake and find him tearing his own flesh with elongated canines. She needed a cleaner way to drink his blood. He caught a glimpse of his form in her nightstand mirror. God's breath! He looked like a bloody gargoyle. His shirt had been ripped from his body except for a single cuff and the tattered remnant of the other sleeve attached to his collar. His flesh was smeared with dirt and half-dried blood. His hair was matted with the sticky goo. He did not want her to wake and see such a horror hanging over her, but there was no time to clean himself. He could drain blood from a cut in his wrist into a glass and have her drink. Very clean, that. The blood might be mistaken for a cordial, anything but what it was. She moaned. She seemed to be worsening so quickly! Fear wound its way up from his bowels. There was no time for a slow drain from his wrist.

He sat beside her and felt for the pulse at the base of his throat on the right side. He thrust the knife deep into the artery then pinched the wound closed with one hand and tossed the little knife away. Still blood squeezed out through his fingers. He gathered her up with his other arm.

"Ann," he whispered to her. Then louder. "Ann!" Her eyelids fluttered. "You must do as I bid." Her eyes opened slowly. He saw them focus on him. A tiny smile touched her lips. "You need my blood." He was prepared to force her.

"Stephan," she whispered. Her body under the light shift was like a coal. She was slick with sweat. He held her to his breast. His hand on her slender neck helped her find the wound on his throat, and then he took his fingers away and let his blood spurt into her mouth. He made ready to hold her there when she struggled in revulsion.

She didn't struggle. She nuzzled at his throat, making a small sound of . . . of satisfaction, he would swear. One hand stole around his neck. She was kissing, sucking, her breasts pressed against him through the thin, damp shift. He threw his head back as he felt his loins tighten. He had never felt anything as sensual as Ann, rocking against his body in rhythm with the beat of his heart and taking his blood. As his body healed, she pulled harder at the wound. He felt as though she sucked his soul with his blood. His loins were enflamed into a full erection now. The wound closed under her lips. He felt it seal itself.

She sat back. Her eyes were clear. It would be brief. "You need more," he apologized. "The first infusion must be substantial."

She nodded. Of course she would already know how it worked. He took up the knife again and found the artery in the other side of his throat. Arteries were always the fastest. He waited for her to turn away, squeamish or horrified.

"If you can make this sacrifice," she whispered, eyes big, "the least I can do is watch."

He took a breath, plunged the knife in and held the wound closed. Still blood spurted between his fingers and sprayed her shift. She leaned in and first licked his fingers then as he freed the wound, she fastened on and gulped his life's essence and the blood that would share its gift of immunity with her. Again his genitals throbbed as she rocked against him, sucking. This time the wound closed faster. He must be regaining his strength. But the flow had been strong. She had gotten enough.

She sat back, flushed and clear-eyed. She'd need more soon, but he was strong enough for what lay ahead. He had fed several times in the last week. Thank Pillinger and the girls at the tavern for that. If she needed the last drop of blood in his body he would give it.

"Thank you," she said seriously, "for your gift."

"There will be more." Suddenly, he glanced down at himself, remembering his frightful state. Worse than the dried blood, his erection was subsiding only slowly. What business had he with an erection? She shouldn't see him like this. "Let me clean myself." He rose and turned his back on her hastily, knowing she must be horrified, hoping she hadn't seen her effect on him.

He froze and stared at the dried blood on his belly. He was making another vampire. Icy water seemed to well up around his heart. He had sworn to himself he would never do that after the debacle with Asharti. He'd also sworn to kill made vampires. But he had let Kilkenny go tonight, too. A year of sunlight on the battlements of Mirso would not be enough to atone. Yet he would be punished in a way far more terrible to him. The sanctuary of Mirso was lost. Rubius would never let him in. He would pay the final price for his rebellion.

Very well, he paid it.

He took a breath. He would not change the course he had taken tonight even if he could. Kilkenny did not deserve death. And though he trespassed against Ann and Rubius together by giving her his blood, he could not watch her die the horrible death the Companion meted out to those infected without the gift of immune blood. His eyes filled. He ripped his collar and the remaining shred of a sleeve from his arm. Chancing a glance back toward her, he saw her all-seeing gray eyes watching him. He dipped a cloth in her washbasin and scrubbed ruthlessly at his flesh. He must make himself less abhorrent to her.

He started at the soft touch at his elbow and turned to find Ann standing so near he could see the blood throbbing in the hollow in her throat. "Let me have Polsham bring up hot water. A bath would soothe you," she said.

He shook his head, a little too emphatically. "No one must know I'm here."

She held out her hand for the towel, smiling. "Then let me."

He felt his heart beating in his throat. She took his towel and motioned him to sit on the small stool. Then she dipped the cloth and wrung it out. She started with his back. She touched one shoulder with her bare hand while she moved the damp cloth over his flesh. Her fever had abated for the nonce, yet her touch burned him still. She said nothing. He sat ramrod straight, his muscles bunched as though that could deflect the softness in her touch. Inside, too, he clenched himself. She was ill, damn it! He would not let her touch lure him into a sexual response. Where was the training of the Daughters when he needed it?

The Daughters!

They would come after him, if not immediately, then after they had hunted down Kilkenny. Ann came around and knelt in front of him. She daubed at the blood from a scalp wound now healed that matted his hair. After they had killed him, they would kill Ann as well. She would have no protection against them. He was making her only to leave her to the tender mercies of Deidre and Freya.

Ann dipped the rag and washed his chest and belly. Stephan distracted himself from a desire to turn and take her in his arms with plans to protect her. They must go to the cave. The Daughters would surely look for him here. He must have time enough to give Ann full immunity.

And then he had to meet the Daughters. Better he sacrifice himself than have them find him with Ann. He hated to leave her alone in her new condition, but he could give her information, send her to Beatrix for help. Better that than that she face the Daughters. They must never know about Ann.

Twenty-One

Ann ran her hands over Stephan's body, marveling that the horrible wounds he had suffered little more than an hour ago were now no more than pink new skin. Some had already disappeared altogether. The feel of silken skin over muscle under her hands as she cleaned him inflamed her more than the fever had a moment ago.

She knew what was ahead of her; the sickness, the need for blood, the drag of eternity. She had experienced it herself, through Stephan. And yet, did one ever *know*? Would she succumb to the madness of the newly made when they realized that their state was irrevocable?

Perhaps. But strangely, that was not what preoccupied her. What she wanted to know was how she had found the courage to infect herself. In the heat of the moment, she had let her anger carry her to this most extreme of decisions without even considering the consequences. The anger had felt good. When had she ever been angry at her uncle, the servants? Even for Van Helsing she had only felt fear. The anger shooting out of her at the moment she pressed her hand against Stephan's bloodied shoulder was . . . freeing. In some ways, hadn't she always seen herself as a victim of her gift, confined and limited, unable to affect her own destiny? Victims didn't rail against their fate. They believed their submission was natural or inevitable.

But she didn't, at least not tonight. It was like passing through a gate. She felt it slap shut behind her, leaving her in unfamiliar territory on the other side.

The anger was not the cause of what she did tonight. It only freed her to do what she wanted to do. She wanted a chance to be with Stephan. She *knew* he loved her, had loved her for some time. But that didn't mean he would have chosen a life with her. They were too different.

Not anymore. Now they were alike. She had been willing to do the impossible to remove the barriers. Like the barrier of her humanity. Now she took his blood and felt its soothing call to her, however faintly yet. She took pride in the fact that he wanted her and his body could not hide it. She wanted him in return. He still might not choose a life with her. But she had done what she could to improve the odds.

She daubed at the blood in his hair. His eyes were closed as though he was afraid to look at her. That would never do. "What next, Stephan?" she whispered softly.

He was spared answering by a shriek of nails being wrenched out of new wood. It came from behind her secret door next to the fireplace.

Stephan set his mouth and stood. "I should have heard him," he muttered. Ann liked to think she knew what had preoccupied him.

The tiny door in the woodwork opened. Erich wriggled through it and stormed into the room. He had a stout stick in one hand. "Where are you, lightskirt?" He stopped dead when he saw Stephan. Shaking, he pulled out a cross. It gleamed in the candlelight. "You!" he breathed. "I thought you were dead."

"I'm not." Stephan rose. "What are you doing in a lady's bedchamber?" He loomed large in the darkness. His voice was a soft rumble, but one could not mistake the menace in it.

Erich held his cross out at arm's length. "Back, Undead! By all that is holy I adjure you." He raised his stout staff and began to retreat.

"Were you here to bludgeon her to death?" Stephan's voice was a growl now. "Do you inherit if she dies?"

"It goes to the Crown, Stephan," she said to distract him from the rage she could feel churning inside him. "He knows that."

"Then he came to force himself on you, hoping you could not refuse to marry him if you were mad. Either way, he deserves what he gets."

Erich was shaking. He held up the cross. "By all that's holy—"

Stephan lunged forward and snatched the cross from Erich's hand. "Fool! I have been a Jesuit priest in my time. And I was there with the Original of your paltry symbol nearly eighteen hundred years ago on Golgotha when the soldiers took Him down. You defile His name." Stephan raised a hand as though to strike Erich with the cross. Erich cowered and raised his club in defense. "You'll not threaten her further."

Ann stepped between them. "Of course he won't. He's going away." She turned to Erich. "Aren't you, Erich?"

"Yes, yes!" Her cousin nodded, trembling. "Away."

Stephan glanced at Ann, who hoped the pleading in her eyes could make him stop and think. "There has been too much blood tonight, Stephan."

Ever so slowly, Stephan let the tension flow out of his shoulders. They sagged. He turned away, his disgust with his acquiescence writ clear upon his features.

"Do you know what I suggest, Erich?" Ann continued, pressing on before Stephan could change his mind. "I suggest you help humans and vampires understand each other, wherever there is strife between them. You can become the expert on vampires, called in to explain one race to the other, when they rub against one another." Here she glanced to Stephan. "It can be a kind of atonement for the evil you have propagated hereabouts." She drew her brows together. "Why did you serve them, Erich? Was it money? Did they threaten you? Why?"

Erich straightened. "You have his blood, don't you? Your smell has changed." He drew himself up. "That's what I wanted. I wanted to be one of them—or rather, one of you. I want the power you have, the immortality. But Kilkenny would never countenance it. Said I wasn't of pure intent." Here he sneered. "As though they were worthy! They needed a slave who could do their business in daylight, that was all. They were never going to give me their blood. My consolation prize was your fortune. At least I would have lived my single lifetime in wealth and comfort."

"You have the property in Derbyshire, and a tidy income that can keep you in comfort," Ann consoled. "Retire there and contemplate for a while. Perhaps you'll think yourself well rid of your masters and their blood."

"To be faced with the thing you want most every day and be denied it! You have no idea how I've suffered," he hissed. "And how will I get the blood now?"

"Get a vampire to love you," Stephan said, his voice cold. "But you'll have to look elsewhere. We are unlikely candidates." His knuckles were white where he clutched the cross.

"I would go now, Erich," Ann said hastily. "My solicitors will be in touch."

"Thank her, Van Helsing," Stephan growled through clenched teeth. "She is the only reason you leave here alive."

Erich paled and backed toward the door. "I . . . I have friends."

Stephan took a single step toward the door. Erich turned

tail and ran, pulling it shut behind him. Ann had to laugh. "He will make a poor advisor on vampire lore," she said, sighing.

"He makes a poor human being in general."

Ann came to Stephan's side. She was feeling feverish again. She couldn't let him know that. After all he had suffered tonight he could not be constantly giving her his blood. "Where were we? Oh, yes. I asked you what was next."

"You will sleep until morning, and get what rest you can. Then I am afraid we must to the cave. Only there can I remain by your side and give you my blood as you need it."

That wasn't what she meant, but she couldn't press him now. She could see the distress in his eyes. He hadn't fully accepted yet what had happened, what she had done, what her action meant. She had to allow him time.

She smiled and nodded. "Lie with me and keep me warm? I feel a chill in the room."

She saw in his eyes he knew the fever was returning. They both knew he had to conserve his strength to make his blood last for the days it would take her to come to grips with the symbiotic partner who now shared her blood.

Stephan put his arm around her and led her to her bed. He turned her gently on her side, pulled off his boots but not his breeches and lay behind her, cradling her in his arms, his body curled around her. As he slipped the coverlet up around them, she began to shiver.

They'd need candles—lots of them, blankets. Stephan made mental lists to distract himself from the feel of Ann's body curled into his. Food? He'd steal from Mrs. Simpson's kitchen. He'd take her clothes and he'd borrow a shirt or two from Polsham. One trip to carry supplies, and one to carry Ann.

There would be a hue and cry when she was missing.

They'd find the pony and cart. They'd find the lodge and its horror. Would they think she'd died at the lodge? God willing, she'd be recovered and could return before they thought her a ghost or some other superstitious phenomenon. She'd be more alive than she had ever been, but these louts wouldn't notice.

How long until she had passed the worst of the sickness? Days perhaps. Then he would leave her to take care of the Daughters somehow. They were too old and powerful for him to kill. He would lead them away from here, away from Ann, before he challenged them. It would mean his death. When he did not return, she would be alone. But at least she would be safe.

Her rounded bottom curled into his loins and stirred them. He put down the erection ruthlessly. *God, man, the girl is sick with your blood, and you can't suppress your lust?* He chanted for control and got it. In the morning, just before dawn, she must have his blood again. He hoped they could both get a few hours' sleep before then.

Ann lay on the bed Stephan had made with a cushion of leaves over the cave floor and several blankets. She was shivering already, barely conscious, though he had given her his blood only an hour ago. The sickness was taking a fierce and furious course. He had never made a vampire, but he knew the process was usually much more gradual. Fear cycled in his belly.

He looked around. She should not have to suffer in such a damp, unfeeling place. Water glistened as it dripped from the stalactites and ran in rivulets to the central, gurgling channel that rushed through the center of the lofty room. Candles flickered on every rocky surface. Their warm and wavering light kept back the darkness in the echoing chamber, but they could not give warmth. He must build a fire.

He hoped the cave was big enough so that the smoke would not suffocate Ann. There was a draft from somewhere. That boded well.

It was his fault that she was in this horrible predicament. He knelt beside the stack of wood he had gathered from the forest outside. But his thoughts would not be distracted from the central question that drove his fear. Why was Ann's sickness so virulent? Stephan was only two millennia old. Not old enough for his blood to cause this kind of sickness.

He laid the fire and struck the flint into the shredded bark he had piled at the center. If his blood was powerful enough to cause this kind of sickness, would it be enough to save her from it? He blew on the sparks and watched them catch. Smoke curled up and was carried off by the draft. He turned to Ann. She seemed insensible, her head jerking from side to side as if in protest of the Companion's invasion. He must wait to give her blood again. He dared not drain himself. He was all that stood between her and death. He took a cloth and wiped her forehead gently. Could he bear to watch her suffer?

His fault.

He was a curse. He had never done anything in his long life but what it led to misery and irreparable harm. Beatrix, Asharti, Stancie, last night Kilkenny, and worst of all, Ann.

He hung his head.

His fault.

She opened her eyes because she heard his voice, calling her, commanding her to drink. She couldn't thrash against the pain anymore. The pain was a part of her. It was her soul, and if it was torn out of her, her soul would go with it. Stephan held her to his naked chest. He was bare to the waist. He had wounded his throat again to give her blood. She wanted to refuse it. He was weakening himself for her.

She shouldn't take more of his blood. But she was too feeble to resist. He bade her open her mouth. And something else bade her suck as well. Something inside that wanted his blood. Where had that feeling come from?

She sucked at his strong throat. A constellation of stars winked at her, golden and austere. Only slowly did they resolve themselves into the crystal surface of stalactites with candlelight winking off them. The blood coursed down her throat and the something in her that wanted the blood rejoiced. It seemed to be . . . singing, very faintly. There was a song of thrumming life coursing through her veins and arteries. For a single moment, the cave came into sharp focus and Stephan's flesh pressing against her felt real and near. She felt the blood throbbing in his body and . . .

And then the darkness claimed her again.

Stephan sat, motionless. Outside the sun was rising. He had replenished the candles and restocked his supply of wood early in the evening. Good thing. He might not have the strength for those simple acts now. At present he just sat, leaning against a huge rock, watching Ann. He couldn't give her more blood. He had to wait. He had almost drained himself to give her what she craved the last time. Still it might not have been enough for her. She had wanted more. His body would make more blood. But it took time, time Ann might not have.

The fire crackled and snapped. Its warm light flickered over Ann. She lay still under her blankets in this place of rock and water, hidden in the earth. So still. How long since she had been infected? Thirty hours? Thirty-five? He couldn't think. It had gone so quickly. Or maybe it had taken an eternity. Somewhere out there, the Daughters were waiting, but they hardly mattered now. Nothing mattered except giving Ann blood. He felt her drifting into the last crisis. And he had no more blood to give her.

Despair beat at the edges of his mind with dark wings. He hadn't always taken the right path in his life, or even looked for it. In the New World, after he had despaired of Beatrix and Asharti, he had let the Inca people perform human sacrifices to give him blood. He had pretended that he gave their lives meaning by impersonating a god. But they did not need him to worship. They were perfectly capable of finding meaning all on their own. There had been other times when he had tried to find the right way. He had trekked to Nepal and tried to be a spiritual leader instead of a counterfeit god. What good had that done? Had not the Chinese massacred nearly half his people? And what had he done but fight like a demon in return? His actions only added to the carnage. They didn't stop it.

His impulse to defend made vampires had ended in Asharti. His failure to love her as he loved Beatrix set her on her path. God! He turned his face to the ceiling of the cave. That simple movement made his vision waver.

Now he had tarnished Ann's life as well. Or caused her death.

The colors of the cave ran together, darkened. His head grew heavy and he nodded. Blackness . . .

Twenty-Two

Ann felt the singing more than heard it. It fluttered at the edge of her consciousness, urging her awake. Alive. She was *so* alive! Life seemed to be crowding down her veins. She was full to overflowing with . . . something else inside her. She should be afraid. She was not alone inside her body anymore. But she wasn't afraid. Nothing that felt this right could be fearful, could it?

She opened her eyes. A million sparkling coruscations leapt into focus. She gasped in surprise. Bright, incredibly detailed, the stalactites had a million subtle variants of color in them. And beyond the sparkling, pendulous stones were dim legions of others behind them. She realized they were hanging in darkness, but she could still see every one of them, marching back into the blackness that was still not black to her. What had happened to her eyesight?

The gurgle of the stream was loud in the cave, but behind it she could hear other things: the refolding of wings from a chamber somewhere that held bats, the dripping of the stalactites, the crackle of a fading fire, breathing. She turned her head.

Stephan sat, head drooping, back against a large stone to her right. There were smudged circles under his eyes. His dark curling hair gleamed in the light, but his features looked sharper than she remembered. The lines in his face were etched deep with exhaustion.

That was because of his gift. He had given her his blood again and again. And the being inside her that *was* her now had taken it with shameless greed, as much as he would give.

A horrid thought intruded. Had she killed him? But no, it was his breath she heard with ears that could hear sounds she had never heard before.

She sat up and the blankets fell away. The air in the cave was chill as always. She looked down. She was dressed only in her shift. She rubbed her hands across her bare arms and felt the tiny hairs that stood up there. She was . . . corporal. The feeling of her own physicality was almost overwhelming. She looked around. Everything was new and more intense. Yet she herself was more intense still. She was . . . strong and so *alive*! It was a feeling of . . . triumph, for lack of a better word—joy.

She crawled over to Stephan through the sand. She heard it shushing under her knees, felt its graininess. Stephan woke with a start as she touched him. The feel of his biceps under his shirt burned her and sent shocks down to her groin. The Companion in her blood surged. She smiled. He looked startled for a moment, then took her face in his hands and examined it as though his life depended on it. She felt the worry and the suffering he had undergone in the last hours. His shirt was loose and unbuttoned, and his pulse throbbed in the hollow of his throat. Whatever he saw in her face, it made him clutch her to his body. His heart beat against hers. She felt his heat, smelled his wonderful scent of cinnamon and ambergris. Erich had said she smelled that way too, now. The feel of Stephan's body against hers made her blood tremble in her body and pool in her loins.

"Thank God you're alive, Ann," he muttered as he kissed her hair. She could hardly breathe he held her so closely. It felt wonderful.

She ran her fingers through his hair and felt silken strands across her skin. She had begun to throb in time to the beat of his heart. But she wanted to see him. She sat back. "I think the thanks belong to you, Stephan. I only hope you've not weakened yourself beyond repair. I . . . I was so selfish and greedy."

He smiled at her tenderly. "Not you, my love, never you. But the one who now shares your blood knew what it needed. And what it needed, it took."

"And you, will you be all right?" She could not keep the anxiety from her voice.

"I am better even now." He smiled.

If this was better, she would hate to see him worse. "You look . . . tired." She smoothed the hair back from his face. He was such a beautiful man, both inside and out. His thigh against hers was warm. She began to throb.

He chuckled. "Only with worry. And that is now gone." A shadow darkened his eyes.

She wanted to wipe the shadow away. She knew what he was thinking. The Daughters still waited for him. "I . . . I feel so alive," she said, to distract him.

His eyes crinkled. "The blood is the life, my dear. Now you know what that means." But again the shadow crossed his expression. He gathered himself. "I . . . I'm sorry your life has been so changed. Not what you expected. Not what you wanted."

Ann straightened in his arms. Best take care of this right here and now. "How do you know it's not what I want?"

He looked surprised. But then he swallowed. "You don't know the burden . . . eternal life, the need for blood . . ."

"I'm not one of your ignorant, newly made vampires, Stephan," she said with some asperity. "I have your experience. In some ways I have already lived two thousand years." She saw she was not convincing him. "And reticence about drinking blood hardly seems a problem. To the contrary, my eagerness would have drained you."

"Living it is different," he whispered, looking away.

She had to give him that. A tendril of fear wound round her spine. Maybe he was right. "And . . . you don't think my mind is strong enough to bear it?" Insanity was her most basic fear.

He jerked back toward her. "No, it isn't that. You're the strongest person I know, to have borne the burden of your gift alone for all those years . . . But now I've burdened you with yet another trial." He seemed to want to say more but couldn't find the words.

"I took on the burden. This was not you."

He searched her eyes. "If I had not intruded on your life . . ."

Speaking of distraction, his smell, the sight of blood pulsing in the hollow of his throat, his body touching hers, were combining to make her almost dizzy. She pressed her breasts to his chest and closed her eyes. There was no denying she was wet between her thighs. "I feel so alive, Stephan," she murmured. "Is that not something to be treasured?" She should tell him how much she wanted him, but that seemed a trivial impulse when she had to convince him that she wanted the life she had chosen in that angry moment at the lodge, and that the responsibility was not his.

"That is the Companion," he said. "You will never be alone. And you and your Companion together are more alive than either of you by yourselves."

"It's wonderful," she breathed. "And the heightened

senses are wonderful." She brushed her lips across his col-
larbone. "To never have known this would have been a
tragedy." What would it be like to make love to Stephan
with her heightened sensibilities? She felt Stephan's nipple
through his shirt with one finger, shuddering with pleasure
at the thought. She glanced up, flushing in embarrassment.
Did Stephan guess her thoughts? Where had her breeding
gone?

Stephan smiled at her tenderly. "That impulse too is the
Companion." He brushed her hair from her face and ran his
thumb across her cheekbone as she flushed an even deeper
pink.

She was obviously feeling the first flush of life as he had
always known it. Stephan had never experienced that rapid
expansion of senses and the surge of life the Companion
brought the first time. But he knew it was almost overwhelming for humans when they changed. This was the time
when her struggle to accept could be made harder or easier,
depending upon her first impressions of her state. She
seemed positive. She was thinking about how it would be to
make love with all that heightened sensibility.

"Don't be embarrassed," he whispered. "The Companion
has an urge to life, and part of that urge is an increased . . .
sexuality." He ran his hand under her hair to cup the back of
her neck. His own Companion surged in response. The feeling seemed new as he thought about what was in store for
Ann. His genitals tightened and he felt himself swell.

"I seem to feel everything so keenly," she said, marveling, as she smoothed her palm over his chest and shoulder. He was certain her touch, even through the linen of
Polsham's shirt, would leave a bubbling burn behind it. "Has
it always been like this for you?"

He smiled, trying not to be distracted by the pressure of

her breasts against his side as she breathed. "How can I know? I was born to the Companion. But I see better than humans do and hear things they cannot. So I suppose the answer must be, yes."

She searched his face as though to memorize it. He knew what she wanted, though she would not voice her desire. Her Companion would be demanding it, just as his did now. He was fully erect, throbbing with desire for her. Traitorous body! He should be properly contrite for what he had done to her. He should be worrying about the Daughters.

The Daughters! They were out there, waiting for him. He must face them, to protect Ann. He would be killed. That was a foregone conclusion.

Then you should give Ann something to remember you by, something that shows her the good side of having been infected, that she might not lose her way in regret. Was that his Companion talking, wanting the ecstasy of sexual union so badly that it found any excuse to indulge? No, he told himself firmly. He was long past his youth, when his sexual needs had controlled his body. Control? Ann was running her small hands under his shirt now, across his chest, thumbing his nipple. He had spent two years under the tutelage of the Daughters learning control, yet at this moment he could hardly think coherently. He kissed Ann's forehead, knowing it took the last bit of control he had to do so only lightly. Now his control was all used up. There was no turning back . . .

Need surged through Ann like a rising tide. Universal forces were at work inside her body, moons and gravity, the earth and its molten core. She splayed her hands across Stephan's chest and felt the crinkle of each hair, the tightening of his nipple under her thumb. His heart pounded against her breast, his blood throbbed at her. She pulled lightly at his

shirt, and it ripped away. That made her stare! Was she so
strong? She felt a grin widen her mouth without her permission. Stephan ran his hands over her shoulders and bent
his head. She reached to kiss him. His lips were soft, but
their touch sent bolts of lightning through her spine. She
pressed her tongue inside his mouth. He tasted sweet and
moist, more sensuous than she could ever have imagined before today. It *was* day. The sun was shining somewhere,
though she did not know how she knew that.

What matter? She and Stephan were safe here in darkness
and candlelight, and she wanted him with every cell in her
body.

Wait! How could she ask a man so weakened to indulge
in the kind of exertions she was even now imagining? She
pushed back, examining his face. The smudges underneath
his eyes had faded somewhat, and what burned in their dark
depths said he was more than eager to exert himself. She
ripped her shift with one hand and pressed her bare breasts
against his chest. The hair teased her nipples into hardness.

"Stephan," she whispered frantically, "Stephan, take me."

She didn't want the tender exploration of their first encounter. She wanted his cock inside her, thrusting, his
tongue kissing her and sucking at her breasts. She wanted to
feel him ejaculate inside her, spurting again and again.
There would never be enough of him to satisfy her, but she
was willing to die trying to be satisfied. She pulled at his
breeches and the buttons popped away. She pulled them
down even as he pulled up her shift. She straddled his hips as
he sat against the rock, pulling his cock up straight and set-
tling herself on to it in two deep thrusts. They groaned together at the sensation of filling and being filled.

Hands on his chest, she moved her hips up and down,
once, twice slowly, then faster. He was panting, so was she.
He bit his lip. She heard him murmuring.

"Don't you dare try to keep control, Stephan Sincai!"

she whispered, leaning forward to take his lower lip in her teeth. "You know you can't hurt me. And I want the whole experience."

A grin flickered over his face and was gone, replaced by an intensity that might make her burst into flames on the spot. He wrapped his arms around her and pressed her to his body. They moved their hips in counterpoint. Their lips locked together. Her breasts were flattened against his chest. His tongue thrust in her mouth. The flood of sensations threatened to overwhelm her. The friction on her point of pleasure was almost unbearable. Had anyone ever felt so intensely? No human, surely.

Then all thought was banished as her world exploded. Shards of herself were mixed with the light and color that shot outward into the universe. It was if someone else was making the small cries she heard. She felt Stephan pulsing inside her as he grunted uncontrollably. On and on they arched and pulsed, shuddering in rhythm with the pull of life inside them. Finally, after what seemed like ages, there was a wrenching pull at her center and sensation whirled back down the scale. She collapsed upon his heaving chest. He wrapped his arms around her.

For a while she just lay there on top of him, her panting slowly subsiding, feeling him still inside her. No thoughts circled in her mind. Then tears welled up from nowhere and she was sobbing. He lifted her off his softening member and cradled her, but he didn't seem surprised by her tears.

"Shush," he whispered. "I know."

"It w-was so g-good," she managed. "I f-felt so close to you."

"The blood is the life," he whispered into her hair and that seemed to say it all.

But wait . . . He attributed all she felt to the Companion. Certainly the sensations had been far more powerful than when they had made love before. But to put it all on the

Companion was too easy, too dismissive. It wasn't just the urge to life. The sexual experience was good because she loved him and she knew he loved her. He must acknowledge that.

"I love you, Stephan." It was taking a chance to say that, but then, most women could not be sure the man they said it to loved them in return. They didn't have Ann's gift.

Stephan held her tighter, but he didn't say he loved her.

She raised herself on her elbows, loosening his embrace. Her brows creased in worry as she examined his face.

He swallowed. That was not a good sign. Then he smiled a tiny, deprecating smile. "I . . . I know about first loves, Ann. I was Beatrix's first love, as well. But those are not always the wisest or the truest loves. Even Beatrix admitted that she grew out of loving me."

Ann felt the outrage well up from the same place as the tears had come. "You grew out of loving her, too."

Stephan glanced sharply at her, as if to protest. But his words died on his lips, as they must if he was being honest with himself. He might have loved Beatrix Lisse at one point, but she *knew* he loved her now. He still cared for Beatrix. She knew that, too. But not the way he loved her. He had left his passion for Beatrix behind. That might be brutal, but it was true.

He shrugged. "The world is full of prices that must be paid," he said. "The fact that love died for Beatrix and me was a price. It doesn't change the fact I am your first love. It doesn't change the fact that there are other prices to be paid. I, for instance, have much to pay for yet."

She stared at him in disbelief. It was the drenching guilt she always felt when she touched him that stood between them now. He could not admit he loved her because he felt he was not worthy of happiness. Something so deep-seated might not be cured, but she had to try. "It is very arrogant of you to take the blame for everything, you know."

She could see by his expression that it hadn't succeeded. He shook his head. "I am not the only one who blames me."

"This Rubius? His daughters? Have you ever thought they might have reasons of their own for blaming you?"

"They hold the keys to peace, therefore who they blame is paramount," he murmured, his gaze sweeping the walls. "Though, of course, I'll never gain entry to Mirso now."

That stopped her.

It all fell into place. Mirso had been his dream, his hope. And she had convinced him to spare Kilkenny, forced him into making her vampire. *She* was the reason he would be denied the peace and atonement that he thought would finally free him from his guilt. Guilt drenched her like a bath of ice-cold water from the stream through the cave. This, this was what he felt every day of his life. She struggled to say something that might make him feel better, even if she did not. "Then . . . then you have already paid your price." That was stupid. He would pay the price of his lost dream every day for the rest of his life.

"There are still the Daughters, waiting in Cheddar Gorge," he said softly. "They have a shot they'd like paid."

More payment. She took his hand and pressed it to her bare breast. "Then don't go into the village. We could just go away. We'll go to France, or America, the West Indies, someplace far away. They have no hold over you."

He gathered her to him. "Perhaps you're right. Tonight, I'll get what we need from Maitlands, then we can choose where to go."

Was it that easy? She pressed herself away from him and searched his eyes. He was lying to her. He was making an excuse to go into Cheddar Gorge and confront them.

He was right. But not for the reasons he thought. He couldn't run away from them. They would keep looking for him to punish him for his "crimes." A life looking over your shoulder was a life half-lived. But he couldn't run away for another reason, too. As he said himself, they were the arbiters, the ones who judged him guilty. If he didn't face down that judgment, even reject it, he would never be whole again.

She would not let him go to face them alone, however. Together they were more than each separately. And then there was the fact that she loved him. Each time they made love, her feeling for him seemed to grow exponentially. She almost told him right then she was going with him. But it was too soon. She bit her tongue. There was almost a whole day to be lived through before he could go to them. Best save her arguments until the time to go was upon him. That way he could not think better of any promise he made to take her along.

She smiled and touched his face. "How will we spend the time until then?"

His eyes grew soft, then melted with another kind of heat.

God, but she was beautiful in the candlelight, and brave without doubt. She would make more of the gifts the Companion brought than he ever had. She would be fine without him.

He had no illusions of surviving his encounter with the Daughters. But if they let their guard down, he might be able to take them with him. Unless he had lost his power to turn their essence back upon themselves. Somehow Ann seemed immune to that power. There was so much he still didn't understand about it.

He touched Ann's white-blonde hair, examined her clear gray eyes, her fine translucent skin. Some might say her beauty was like fine porcelain, too delicate to handle. But they would be wrong. She had been strong, before. Now her Companion made her stronger still. In one way her beauty did not lie. It reflected an essence that was good and pure.

And that must be how she survived their lovemaking. What his power could turn back upon her was only her goodness.

No danger of that with the Daughters. But that was for

later. Now, he would take his time making sure Ann's memories of her first day as one of their kind were memories of love and pleasure. He gently put her from him and removed his boots, pulled his breeches off, and shrugged off the remains of his shirt. Naked, he got up and built up the fire. When he turned, she had removed the shreds of her shift. He smoothed out the blankets where she had lain next to the fire and beckoned her. Her perfectly formed limbs glowed in the firelight. Her slightly heavy breasts swayed as she came and knelt beside him. Her eyes were molten with desire for him.

She had already given him an incredible gift. She had brought the sexual act back to tender caring from the horrible training ritual it had become with the Daughters. He gestured to the blankets. "I think you'll find this more comfortable, my lady."

He lay down beside her and drew her down. "I believe it is your turn to receive." She had liked it when he used his tongue the first night, but then she had not had the Companion in her blood ramping up sensation far past anything a human could experience. He intended to show her the difference.

She lay back, smiling. "And will you hog all the giving for yourself?" she asked.

"For now." He dipped his head to her breast and tongued her nipple. She arched into him. The one thing the Daughters had given him was an almost infinite repertoire of sexual skills. He intended to set all of them to the task of showing Ann what it was like to have her Companion fulfill its urge to life. He had heard it said that the difference between sex as a human and sex for vampire kind was magnification of a hundredfold. He would ask her if that estimate was right later in the day . . .

Ann struggled up toward awareness from a dreamless sleep. She was warm. The fire still heated her back, though it had sunk to glowing coals. She was enfolded in Stephan's arms. The sun was setting outside the cave. She could feel it.

Well, if she wasn't mad now, she would never go insane. The sensations of Stephan's mouth on the moist folds of flesh between her legs, licking her point of pleasure while he stroked her breasts and kneaded them had been so intense, by rights they should have driven her mad. But with the new-found strength of her partner she had survived, nay even sought the sensations out a second time later in the day.

And she had taken her turn giving. She had Stephan's experience to draw on, after all. She smiled smugly. She knew she had given him exquisite pleasure, sure of just what he liked best. At first Stephan had resisted her request to use her mouth on him, said she should save that. For what? For whom? He still thought that there would be other men in her life. She knew why. He thought he would be killed by the Daughters. He thought her love was puppy love. Well, she couldn't disabuse him of that yet. And neither of them might survive the Daughters. In which case she wanted to have as much experience of love with Stephan as she could manage in the time left to them. In the end, he had yielded to her because his Companion bade him surrender. The wonder of silken skin, the throbbing in her mouth, the fact that he could not conceal the effect of her attentions had been a revelation. She liked to use her hands as well. Seeing him arch and spurt only confirmed just how much sensation she was giving him.

As she lay there, sated, her thoughts turned to her mother. To touch someone you loved, and who loved you in return, was nothing short of magic. It was a gift from God to know a man physically, spiritually, emotionally. She finally understood why the Bible called the act of lovemaking "knowing a man" or "knowing a woman."

Yet her mother had allowed the difficulty of the gift to

isolate her from everyone, including the man she married. She must have thought she loved him, to agree to the match. She must have *wanted* closeness. But her fear of knowing everything about her father got the upper hand. And what of her father? He'd known what her mother was before they married. Uncle Thaddeus said so. He must have loved her, to accept that burden. Yet her mother must have held back from giving herself over to the possibilities of love. If her mother could have mustered the courage to abandon her fear, could the tragedy of madness and suicide have been averted? A sadness came and sat in her chest, and then . . . relief. She wasn't doomed to repeat her mother's fate. She had the courage to love Stephan, to touch him, to let him love her, to abandon the refuge of isolation. She curled closer into his embrace. Then she let out the breath she realized she'd been holding, as guilt washed over her. How could she feel relieved at her mother's tragedy?

She bit her lip. Another breath. Not relieved at the tragedy. Relieved that she wasn't required to repeat it. *Don't lose your way in guilt,* she admonished herself. *That is the burden Stephan carries.*

She opened her eyes. Stephan was looking tenderly at her. She reached up and kissed his lips. They were slightly swollen. She smiled at him. She had done that. His eyes were serious.

"I know," she whispered, her voice husky with their lovemaking. "It's time to go."

He nodded, and his arms tightened around her in a crushing embrace that she returned. Then he let her go, and held her only by her shoulders as he kissed her forehead lightly.

"Yes," he breathed and rose.

She got up as well. "I do hope you brought some other clothing, since we seem to have ripped what we were wearing apart," she said, looking around. "Ahhh, very foresightful."

She descended upon a pile of clothing hidden in the crevice of a rock. She picked out a green gown, the most attractive of her small selection. She couldn't feel the person who had made it. She knew it belonged to her but that was all. Strange. On impulse, she touched a shirt in the pile belonging to Stephan. She got a very faint impression of the person who had ironed it. She picked it up and felt it with both hands. Alice. But she had to consciously open herself to know that. Polsham had worn it last. Then faintly, faintly, she felt hands at a loom.

She looked up at Stephan. "I can hardly feel the people who have handled this." It was hard to even form the words. "I mean I can if I try, but it isn't . . . overwhelming."

He examined her face. "Are you losing your gift?"

She turned and leaned down to touch the paper and string of a package he had bundled up to bring food up to the cave. She felt him, and . . . and Mrs. Simpson, and before that . . . maybe the butcher who had wrapped meat in it the first time. "It's still there," she said in a small voice that nevertheless echoed in the immensity of the cave. "But I have to listen to hear the others who have touched it. They don't . . . shout at me anymore."

"Maybe the Companion singing in your blood drowns them out a little."

She went still. There it was, a sort of humming she hadn't noticed since she first woke because it was always there. "It does. It *does* sing," she marveled.

"That's what others experience as vibrating energy when we enter a room," he said seriously. "Are you sorry things have changed?"

She smiled, and the smile grew into a chuckle and ended in a cascade of laughter. "I must have some new gowns made," she gasped. Indeed, the thought of all the things she might now do flushed over her. "I'll eat at hotels and turn the pages of borrowed books without using my stick, and sit in hired carriages. I don't have to be afraid of touching a new umbrella."

His eyes crinkled at the corners. "Freedom, indeed."

"You may well scoff, sir!" she protested, still laughing. "But you've no idea how shopkeepers look at one when one refuses to pick up the money, but asks them to select the right coins from one's reticule and put the others away."

"I don't," he said, smiling. Then he grew serious. "Life will be easier for you. I'm glad."

She felt the tug of his body, impossible as that was after all they had done today. But the time for lovemaking was over. She handed him the shirt and knelt to select what she needed from the pile of clothing, along with a bar of soap. She knelt at the edge of the narrow channel of the stream and splashed herself. The water was ice cold. Gooseflesh popped out over her body as she soaped. Good. It might focus her thinking for what was to come. She laved water over her face and rinsed the soap away, all without turning to look at him.

"Will you wash? It's cold but refreshing," she called over her shoulder as she slid into her shift. She shrugged into her half-corset and pulled the laces into a bow. Finally she pulled up the skirt of the green kerseymere dress, stuck her arms through the sleeves, tied all in place. She only turned when she was buttoning the two large decorative buttons that held the lot together. He stood with his clothes in one hand and his boots in the other. He had been watching her.

His long limbs laden with muscle, the point of his hip, his heavy sex, still full if not erect, struck her senses like a blow. He was . . . beautiful. She stepped aside as he passed her, knowing that touching him, as she longed to do, must be put aside. She had another purpose now.

She busied herself around the little campsite, stealing surreptitious looks to where he washed and dressed. She mustn't be taken by surprise. She had to stay close to him. He sat and pulled on his boots. The muscles bunched in his thighs. Ummmm. Stephan had opened a new world to her in more ways than one. In fact, the whole of her life at Maitlands Abbey now seemed like sleepwalking, half-alive. Now she had wakened, and the life and feeling running inside her would not be denied. She would not be denied. She was going with him.

Stephan glanced up at Ann. She was watching him, her eyes glowing. Now was the time. He would tell her only that he was going to the village and Maitlands to gather what they would need for their journey. He wouldn't tell her he was going to confront the Daughters. His heart clenched with despair and he pushed it down ruthlessly. There was a chance he could prevail, however small. He might be able to separate them. Could he say he needed additional training before going after Kilkenny? Could he lure one into sex? It seemed a sacrilege after the day he had spent with Ann. But it might be his only chance to live and return to her.

He was fooling himself. He was no match for even a single Daughter.

Leaving Ann without a final word to tell her how much she meant to him seemed a betrayal. But it might be even more cruel to confirm his love, then snatch the bliss he knew they were capable of achieving from her. She was betrayed by his past sins whether he told her or not.

Perhaps he was meant to die, without atonement. Perhaps hell yawned under his feet even now. Once, dying would have seemed a blessing not a penance. But now . . . it wasn't that he feared hell. He glanced again to Ann. Now he had glimpsed redemption. He didn't need Mirso. Loving Ann, protecting Ann, was all the purpose he needed in life. To have it taken from him was penance, indeed. The only thing worse would be to know he left her facing the

Daughters. That would be a hell worse than Satan's paltry fires.

He stood and shrugged on his coat. She hurried over.

"I must go now." He stroked her hair. "I shall be back."

"I'm going to make sure of it." Her hand gripped his shoulder. "I'm going with you."

He shook his head, managing deprecation. "Not needed. But if you wish me to get something special from Maitlands, write me out a list."

"Don't try to tip me the double, Stephan Sincai." Where had she learned that cant? She looked clear through him with those translucent gray eyes. "You're going to face the Daughters and I am going with you."

Couldn't he lie to her? She seemed to know what he was thinking, regardless of the fact that she said she couldn't read minds. He would have to count on her good sense, instead. "You can't come, Ann. They're old and strong. They'll want to kill you."

"Well, I don't think they'll be very happy with you, either, Stephan. The best thing we can do is work together. You saw what we did at the lodge."

"That was an accident, Ann. Our emotions were running high. Something . . . something sparked a connection, that was all."

"Well, let's do it again." She had set her mouth.

"I can't endanger you, Ann." For so many reasons. He called to his Companion. The darkness whirled up from the floor. He'd make a quick escape. He thought about the woods behind the tavern. The cave was bathed in a red film which turned slowly black.

At the last minute he felt something intrude upon his maelstrom of darkness, grab his arm and slide in next to him. Another Companion vibrated against his. Then the field collapsed in a shriek of pain and he popped into space directly behind the Hammer and Anvil.

Ann stood next to him, shaking the blackness from her vision. What? "You must go back immediately, Ann," he said, making his voice as stern as possible.

"No, Stephan," she gasped. "I'm coming with you. You *need* me against the Daughters. Maybe I'm a conduit that amplifies your power. I don't know. I just know the only chance you have against vampires so old and powerful is to open yourself and embrace the power we share."

"Ann, you helped me," he said in his most rational voice. "But now I can do it myself."

She looked up, all five feet of her, and shook his shoulders, though he did not move. "This is my fight, too, Stephan. I won't sit in that cave and wait for what happens. You can't expect that of me. I have too much to lose."

"*I* have too much to lose if you're harmed," he said through gritted teeth. "Even if I lived, do you think I could bear it if you did not?" He wanted to growl at her like the leader of a wolf pack. He wanted to shout, if that would make her obey. She crossed her arms. God, if the Daughters were in that tavern, they would feel his vibrations even now, and hers!

"I expect you to live with the possibility that you might have to, Stephan," she practically hissed at him. "Don't think you can shut me out. I'm part of this."

She was right about that. She had crept into his life until she was the most important thing, the best thing about it. He glanced to the tavern down the hill. Light spilled out into the darkness. He could hear the rowdy taproom, the ecstatic whimpers of the chambermaid as the boots slammed his seed into her in a closet upstairs, the baying of a hound at the approach of new patrons. But no vibrations.

"They aren't there, anyway, Stephan," Ann whispered.

She felt it, too. "Where could they be?" he murmured, distracted.

"Maitlands," Ann said after a moment. "Looking for you."

"Why not the lodge?"

"They'll have already been there," Ann said calmly. "That was undoubtedly their first stop. So they would cast around for another place for you to go to ground. They will have heard tales of me letting you out of the cell, that we're suspected together of the murders . . . They'll be at Maitlands, all right."

She was right. He stared at her hand where she clutched his biceps. He could tear himself away, take several steps— he was faster than she was—then draw the darkness. And find her at Maitlands directly after him if she could figure out how to draw her power. Hell, even if she didn't translocate, she could be there in thirty minutes if she stole a horse. It might be over by then. In which case she might run smack into the victorious Daughters.

"Damn it, woman! Can't you stay out of this?" he barked.

She shook her head, smiling ruefully. "No. Not anymore."

He stood there, clenching his fists. He was a vampire two thousand years old, with experience of women and humanity down the centuries, and he was powerless against this girl.

She smiled again, her victory twinkling in her eyes, and raised her brows in inquiry. "Shall we go, then?"

He hesitated. She set her lips and frowned in concentration. Then a wash of blackness swirled tentatively up around her knees. She was trying to translocate. He sighed. "Let me."

He called to his Companion and the darkness whirled around them both. He was going to take her into almost certain death. How could he protect her now? Damnation! But then, he was already damned. Now she was going to be damned with him.

"I knew you'd see the light," she whispered, gripping his arms now with both hands.

And the darkness overcame them.

Twenty-Three

Stephan blinked into space on the grassy lawn marred by jut-
ting pieces of masonry inside the ruined abbey walls on the
north side of Maitlands. The empty Gothic arches stretched
above them in the moonlight. The moon was waxing. Its sly
smile had grown into a knowing grin. Stephan's night vision
swept the grounds, expecting to see the guards who had
turned off Van Helsing the other night. He found only silence and . . . the vibrations of very old vampires.

He glanced to Ann. Her eyes were round as saucers. She
felt them, too.

"It looks as though you were right," he whispered, and
took her hand. He led her out onto the gravel drive at the
front of the house. Lights shone from several rooms in the
house, but out here the stars had come out and night wrapped
all in dimness. Several dark shapes lay in disarray on the
drive and another under the great fir tree in front of the
house. The smell of blood hung heavy in the air. He stalked
over to examine one shape. A guard, his throat slashed.

"Polsham, Mrs. Simpson," Ann whispered, frantic, and

took off at a run for the back of the house. Stephan ran after her, knowing what she would find.

Ann let herself into the kitchen, Stephan right behind her. The thick smell of blood was everywhere, mingled with garlic and beefsteak and the acrid scent of cooked chard. The Daughters must know they were here. They would be waiting somewhere in the house to feel his vibrations. Ann might be a surprise. Still, she was newly made. She would present no difficulty for vampires as old as Freya and Dee. Ann grabbed a candle and struck the flint in its holder, more out of habit than necessity, he suspected.

The light only revealed more clearly what they saw anyway. The two servants sat slumped over their meal at one end of the long kitchen table, their heads in their plates. The food, the plates, and the table were covered with gore. Stephan was surprised the Daughters had not fed, but maybe they had had their fill with the guards outside.

Ann gasped then made a dash for Mrs. Simpson. The sobs began as she lifted the woman's head carefully from the plate "Oh, oh no, oh!" she cried as she cradled Mrs. Simpson. The woman's eyes were all unseeing, her left cheek smeared with gravy and blood. Her white uniform was claret red where the great gash in her neck had flooded it. Stephan lifted the dead woman's head from Ann's arms and let it down gently.

"Sit over here." He simply lifted Ann at her waist and sat her in a chair at one corner of the chopping block. Then he laid Mrs. Simpson and Polsham out respectfully on the floor. Of course, that only made the wounds in their throats gape. The Daughters had not been careful. Behind him, he heard Ann whimpering.

He turned to her. There was blood on her hands, her dress. He grabbed a wet cloth from the great stone basin and wiped each of her hands. "Get hold of yourself," he said sternly, "unless you want to stay here while I confront them." Now that the Daughters must know they were here he would rather have her with him where he had some chance to protect her.

She gulped and shook her head, steadying herself. She was courageous, this one. His heart seemed to both expand and contract at once. Dear Ann. How could he risk taking her with him? How could he risk leaving her where the Daughters could catch her alone?

"They're waiting for us upstairs." He pulled her up and started across the kitchen.

"They . . . they know we're here?"

"Just as we know they are here." He gritted his teeth. They made their way up the back staircase to the great hall. He had a fix on the Daughters now. He stalked down the corridor and pushed open the library door.

They stood next to the great windows that gave out onto the night. The wind had come up and it was tossing the trees about. They wore diaphanous gowns, as they always had. The chiffon was laid over silk now, and neither the skirts nor the necklines were slit to the waist. But the colors were the same, black for Dee, white for Freya. Only Stancie's red was missing.

At Stephan and Ann's entrance, they turned slowly. Dee's eyes burned with hatred and triumph. Freya looked only sad.

"I said they would come."

Stephan and Ann both jerked toward the voice. Van Helsing stood with one boot on the andiron, a brandy in his hand. Dee's triumph and hatred were echoed in Van Helsing's eyes. The smug set of his mouth made Stephan want to break his teeth.

"Erich!" Ann exclaimed.

"What are you doing here?" Stephan growled.

Van Helsing raised his sandy brows. "Why, I am come to claim my bride, Sincai."

Stephan jerked back to Dee and Freya.

"Our servant deserves some reward for being so . . . useful," Dee murmured.

"You serve the Daughters, Erich?" Ann asked, incredulous.

"Correct." Van Helsing clicked his heels and bowed in military fashion, though it made his waistcoat strain across his belly. "Always have." He started to take a gulp of brandy then stopped, arrested, and peered at Ann with creased brows.

"We sent him on ahead to keep track of Kilkenny when your training was delayed. Kilkenny never suspected we would send a human," Dee sneered.

"I told you I had powerful friends, Sincai," Van Helsing remarked. He was still staring at Ann, though. Now outrage poked through his smugness. He stalked forward, staying just out of Stephan's reach. He turned on the Daughters. "You know what I want. After all my service . . ." His voice rose in an unattractive whine.

"And you shall have her, Servant." Dee was haughty. "When you have finished with her, she will deed you her property and you will kill her." Her words made a chill run down Stephan's spine. Could he not have found a way to make Ann stay in the cave?

"But now she's strong!" Van Helsing protested.

"And we are stronger." Freya sighed, weary.

"And what of the bedroom, will you be there to compel her, too?"

Dee shot him a look and held up her hand. He stopped in mid-sentence. No one pressed the Daughters. Dee went to where her cloak and a reticule lay over a leather chair. Bending to pick something out of the reticule, she tossed Van Helsing a small bottle. "Give her laudanum. You can have her whenever you like."

Laudanum! The one way to suppress the Companion! "Drug her," Stephan hissed through clenched teeth, "so this animal can have his way with her?" He could feel Ann's fear.

"Keep her as long as you like, Van Helsing." Dee shrugged. "Then cut off her head. I want no made vampires left behind. And you'd better not steal a drop of her blood or we'll serve you out the same," she warned.

"Have you two no souls?" Stephan growled. "You can have me. Punish me for making her, but let her go." He knew that was impossible. She was made. They would kill her.

"We'll punish you anyway," Dee snapped. "For your lapse with her, and for Kilkenny."

How did they know he had let Kilkenny go?

"We were watching in the wood," Freya explained.

God, they had killed him! The effort to spare him had been for nothing.

"No, not yet." Freya responded to the look of horror on his face. She took a long breath and let it out. "But we will. After we're done here, we'll hunt him down." She didn't sound happy about it.

"I'm only sorry we can't take you back to Mirso and mete out your punishment in front of the whole monastery."

"That's what this is about, isn't it?" Stephan asked, trying to keep his voice calm. "I'm to be an example to keep anyone else from getting any rebellious ideas. Isn't that it?"

"Essentially," Dee agreed. "You always were. You know, you had more natural power than anyone we had seen in a long time." She cocked her head, and smiled. "That, coupled with the history of open rebellion over the years, disregard of the Rules . . . Well, you had to be brought to heel."

"And did I not submit to . . . everything?"

"You submitted to training," Dee snapped. "But when it came to obeying the Rules? Once you were outside the influence of Mirso you didn't do so well, did you?"

They had him there. But he had to try. "I should think Rubius would want something more from his followers than blind adherence to Rules that were set so long ago. There is a morality beyond any of his Rules. If the Rules tell you to kill wantonly, then they're wrong."

Dee snorted. "You see, Freya? I told you he would not even bother to repent." She turned on Stephan. "Made vampires must be killed. We dare not upset the balance."

Freya looked away.

"And what of the guards and the servants?" Ann asked, her voice trembling with emotion. "They were innocents."

Freya shot Dee a reproachful look.

"Necessary," Dee snapped. "Steps to achieve our end."

Stephan began to gather himself, mustering control. He would need all his strength against the Daughters. He tried not to think about how futile his effort would be, or the fact that he had wasted that precious strength making love to Ann today. A shush of memory wafted over him; the confident certainty of her love in Ann's eyes, her touch, so wondrous to him and even more so to her as she ran her hands over his body, the miracle of sex transformed into lovemaking once again. No, he would not regret making love to Ann. He knew what the end was likely to be here. He would not shy from death. He only had to find some way to keep Ann safe.

"I have grown in power since Mirso," he said, trying to put a sureness into his voice he didn't feel. "You won't find me an easy target anymore. Let her go, though, and I will submit without a fight."

"Your mistake, Harrier." Dee sneered. "Your power makes it easier to dispose of you now. And Freya and I together will have no problems with you." She was enjoying this. Her eyes went red. She was prepared for any fight Stephan could make. He could feel her vibrations cycle up beyond feeling them. "Freya, help our servant here get Miss Van Helsing to swallow that bottle of laudanum."

Freya looked dismayed.

"The whole bottle?" Van Helsing asked, incredulous.

"As you said, she's strong now . . ." The red in Dee's eyes deepened.

Freya stepped forward, her mouth set, her own eyes going carmine. It was now or never. *Companion!* A red curtain descended over the room. Stephan gathered all his will and pushed it out at Freya, who wavered and stopped.

A blast of compulsion burst over him, almost knocking him to his knees. Wave after wave drenched him. Dee walked forward, her mouth grim.

"You think to challenge us?" The words echoed and boomed around the room as though they were the voice of a god. Slowly Stephan sank to his knees. His will couldn't reach Freya. "Freya!" Dee barked.

Freya's eyes went a deeper red as she advanced on Ann. Stephan's vision began to darken at the edges as he pushed against the compulsion Dee showered over him. He saw Ann's eyes go big, then blank.

"Give her the bottle, Van Helsing," Freya whispered.

Stephan threw his mind against the barrier that held him. He grunted and shivered. The blackness expanded until it seemed as though he saw Ann and Freya and Van Helsing at the end of a long tunnel. Van Helsing unstoppered the bottle and held it out. Ann raised a shaking hand and took it. She lifted it to her lips.

"No!" The shout was torn from Stephan's soul.

And then the blackness snapped shut upon the tunnel.

Stephan woke slowly. His head throbbed as though it had been bashed against a stone floor. He tried to remember. Dee had held him in a vise of will while Ann . . .

"Ann," he muttered and tried to raise his head. It slammed down on hard stone, as will came crashing down on him. Dee and Freya moved into his line of vision, hovering over him. Their eyes were crimson, and the color deepened to burgundy even as he watched. They wore the scraps of diaphanous fabric they had worn at Mirso, the ones split to the waist and down to their navels that gave them easy access to use of him. He was naked. He had seen that when he raised his head. The Daughters' faces glowed inhumanly in the light of a great fire he could see roaring from the corner of his eyes. He was sweating. Heat poured over him. He was in a dark place, lit only by the great fire. He lay on stone—a bench, perhaps? That made him shudder inside. Was he back in the bowels of Mirso?

"Well, Penitent," Dee murmured, moving a strand of hair off his sweating forehead. "Not penitent enough, were we? Father was right to doubt you."

"Let me talk to him . . ." Stephan managed. "Let me explain." Rubius would never forgive him, but it would buy him time.

"I told you we wouldn't take you to Mirso," Dee admonished. "Too exhausting for us to keep you under control during such a long journey."

"Then, where am I?" He raised his head and this time they let him. The space around him was vast. Columns and Romanesque arches disappeared into the dimness. He was chained to what looked like . . . a stone coffin, though it was not the chains that held him there.

"The old underground crypt of the abbey," Freya said, in a low voice. Her explanation earned her a hostile stare from Dee.

"Where is Ann?" Stephan ground out the words through gritted teeth. He was still at Maitlands, or near enough. If he could get away . . .

"Having the time of her life, I should think, albeit through a haze of laudanum." Dee chuckled. She rested her gaze on Stephan, almost tenderly. "As you will be shortly."

Stephan groaned, thinking about Van Helsing's pudgy hands on Ann, his wet mouth probing hers, the suffering she would endure, far worse even than rape. He had to find a way out of here! He *had* to stop Van Helsing.

Dee glanced to Freya. "Are you ready?" It was a challenge, as though she didn't trust her sister.

Freya took a breath and nodded.

Stephan felt his loins tighten. His cock began to throb.

God, they were going to bring him up and use him here? Now? He began to struggle against the compulsion even harder, trembling with effort. He couldn't go back to being used like they had used him, not after making love to Ann.

"No, no, my Penitent, there is no choice for you," Dee cooed as she ran her hands over his chest and down his belly to fondle the head of his cock.

Did they want to torture him before they killed him? Why didn't they tear his head off and be done with it? But he couldn't challenge them with that. He must stay alive to keep alive the possibility that he could help Ann. He swallowed.

They wanted to use him. Let them. It would only ramp up his power. If they made him climax he would turn their evil back upon them and they would end like Stancie. But madness would not declaw them, necessarily. They might still kill him and prevent him from going after Ann even though he would have had his revenge on them. He had better pray instead that they suppressed him. His power would increase until he could open himself to it as he had at the lodge and stab it out to hurt them, if not kill them. That might be enough to let him get away.

All right, he thought. *Let them think they've won. Go with them.* Already his body was alive with desire he had no wish to feel. He had to give himself over to it. He mustn't fight it. He writhed as Freya cupped his balls and squeezed, gently.

"We're not so foolish as to let you climax as Stancie did, poor dear," Dee whispered as she slid her fingers up and down his shaft. "We can control your release of power, too."

What?

"We can prevent your accessing it at all," she continued, smiling at his horrified expression. Her smile was as horrible as Stephan remembered. Fear shot through him. "And then when it begins to boil . . . remember the stain on the stone wall?"

"Dee?" Freya asked, as shocked as Stephan was. "You're not going to—"

"Decapitation is too easy, Freya. He has much to atone for, does he not?"

Stephan strained away, but there was no escaping Dee's hand, her breath on his neck.

"Dee, I—"

"Do your job, Freya," Dee hissed. "Obey our father. I am the eldest. Obey me in his absence. We must do this." Suddenly she smiled at her sister. "And enjoy it." She stared at Stephan. "I intend to."

She lowered her lips to Stephan's and thrust her tongue inside his mouth. He knew she wanted him to kiss her back. He did. God help him, for he couldn't help himself. But God must be busy elsewhere, for no help came.

Freya gathered herself. "Then I want to go first, Dee, before it becomes too painful for him." She held the translucent fabric aside and straddled Stephan. She lifted his cock and slid it inside her. The sensation should have put him over the edge. But he did not spill his seed. Dee was ramping up the feeling yet keeping him from his release. Stephan arched his back, groaning with the exquisite torture of the sensation. Already the quiescent lava in his loins began to churn.

He thought a chant. He had to keep the power from

boiling over inside him until he could think of a way out of this. He couldn't think about what might be happening to Ann.

Tuatha denon. Beluorga lefin. Argos pantid.
Bletherdon, hargarden, slitenger, shuit!

How long could he survive this?

Ann swam through a haze of dread that seemed to shroud her. Erich was carrying her upstairs. She was limp in his arms. She knew, somewhere inside, what he was going to do. He had told her once. Alice described it. But it didn't seem to matter nearly as much as she thought.

It was all over anyway. The Daughters had Stephan. Van Helsing had her. Over.

Erich kicked a door open. It swung aside. Burgundy velvet draperies. Bed hangings of the same. Brocade bedcover in red and gold that swam and danced. The faint odor of smoke from her uncle's pipe cascaded over her.

"Uncle Thaddeus's room?" she asked groggily.

"The room of the head of the household, my dear. Surely you see how appropriate that is now." Erich laid her on the bed and began fumbling at the buttons down the front of her dress. How like a fish he looked. A particularly repulsive fish who never used tooth powder. "What I'd like is to lick up some of your blood, but I daren't. Not while they're around. Of course, they'll go back to Mirso." Erich was mumbling to himself as he worked the buttons and ties. "But will they leave you alive? Perhaps I can persuade them. And they can say they'd know and come after me. But would they?" He pulled her dress over one shoulder then grasped her arm, practically wrenching her joint as he pulled her out of the sleeve.

At his first touch of her bare flesh she knew him. But it

wasn't like it was before, a shower of excruciating experience and a thrust of knowledge. No. It was rather like reading a book. The information was all there, pages flipping as she read, but not . . . visceral.

She saw his severe Germanic father who never thought he was good enough, the beatings. He had learned to be sly in order to avert his father's wrath. Always he lied, taking the easy way out. Lying with the local girls of the lower classes, wanting the power over them his father exerted over him. Losing his mother—the only example of kindness in his life, though her character was not strong and she indulged him with money they didn't have. Then being cast adrift when his father died, realizing the debts, that there would be no more money, that there had not actually been any money for years. The bitterness, the years as a wastrel gambler, learning languages in order to take advantage of people, pretending he was someone else, someone more important. His need to exert power drove him to new acts of sexual abasement, with whores and powerless women. But always he had hope. He was the only male Van Helsing. He lived on his expectations. If he could just get enough money together, he would go to England and hang on his British relations. Surely Ann's father would help him when he was the heir. But there was never enough money. Hearing that Ann's father was dead. Learning the terms of the will that blighted his hopes and left Maitlands to Ann. He took up drinking. Drifting into Romania, meeting a man who believed his lies about his vast circle of connections in England. The man took him to a village called Tirgu Korva. Meeting the Daughters. Promises, threats. He saw vampires as wonders of power—power he wanted for himself. Seeking out Kilkenny. Hoping to convince Kilkenny to make him. Disappointment and hatred when Kilkenny would not. How stupid he thought Kilkenny's ideals were! Hatred of Stephan, fear. Hatred of Ann for having what he could not.

She saw it all and absorbed it through the haze of the drug, along with the weakness, the petty vengefulness, the greed. But she also saw that those qualities were magnified by his situation. If his mother had lived . . . if she had been a stronger character . . . if only things might have been different for Erich.

Her eyelids fluttered as the book closed. Erich was still talking, more to himself than her.

"It might be worth the chance." He held her as he pulled off the other sleeve. "Of course, I'd have to leave. Sell out the property, or maybe rent it." He let her flop back on the bed and pulled her dress off by its hem, then her shoes. "I'll go to America. They'll never track me there." He stood and surveyed her. "With my laudanum-addicted wife? You're a bit of trouble. Still"—he chuckled—"there's nothing like a docile wife with a winsome body." He cupped her breast above her corset. His fingers dug into her flesh through her chemise. Someone moaned. "When I tire of plowing your cunt and making your anus bleed, I shall tutor you in pleasing me with your mouth. You'll kneel and suck my cock anytime and anywhere I choose."

He put his wet mouth over hers, filling her senses with the taste of rancid teeth and brandy. She tried to twist away. He chuckled—a horrible sound that echoed in her ears. He licked her cheek. His saliva seemed thick, almost like mucous. It made her stomach rebel.

He straightened, took a small knife from his pocket and cut the laces of her half-corset. Then he ripped her chemise and underskirt from her body, leaving her naked on the bed. She managed to raise her head. He was unbuttoning his breeches. They swelled over an erection.

Ann couldn't focus anymore, whether from the horror of what was about to happen or the laudanum. His face came back down over her, distorted as though by a nightmare magnifying glass. He was going to kiss her again, and then

the rape would begin in earnest. Thought was becoming difficult. So she didn't try anymore. His wet mouth descended
on hers. She gave herself to blackness.

Stephan rolled his head convulsively from side to side. Dee
was riding him, about to climax. Freya pinched his nipples
and ran her canines along his neck, her breath hot on his
flesh. The image of the black, greasy stain on the wall of the
room at Mirso seemed to fill his head. His body arched,
sweating. The sensation radiating from his cock had passed
from pleasure into pain almost immediately. Now the red hot
core inside him heaved and pulsed. They had both already
used him. He thought when Dee's muscles contracted around
him he might just explode like that other nameless would-be
Harrier. He had to find a way around that, some way to shunt
off the excess power surging inside him. He had to stay
alive, for Ann.

How long could he manage to survive this? They could
go on forever, he knew. Dee's frantic gasps turned to small
moans. He had not much time.

Ann. He would think of Ann. Not being ravished by Van
Helsing. No, he would think of their lovemaking, so tender,
so mindful of the other's pleasure. Dee contracted around
him, squeezing his cock rhythmically with the muscles of
her womb. His body arched even harder against her. *Ann.
Ann needs me,* he thought. *Ann understands me.* It was a new
kind of chant.

Somehow he made it through Dee's orgasm. She got off
him. His body collapsed against the stone of the coffin.

"Ummm," Dee said, as she shrugged on a silk robe and
went to stand even closer to the flames in the gaping
maw of the fireplace. "I thought he might be close that time.
Keep him roused, Freya, while I rest." Freya lay beside
him, her body pressed along his. She took his cock, still

painfully erect and needing, in her hands and began to work it.

Stephan could not help the small moan of protest that escaped him.

Dee picked up a glass from a large wooden tray sitting on the hearth and ladled spiced wine from a wassail bowl into it. "Perhaps you should suck him. That would be a more intense sensation."

"This is fine for now," Freya murmured into Stephan's neck as she rubbed her thumb over the head of his cock and spread the clear liquid leaking from it over the tip.

"I see you want to draw it out." Dee chuckled. "Very well. It has been a while since I was able to truly satisfy myself." Dee threw her head back as she stalked away in the darkness, stretching like a cat. She didn't let her compulsion falter, though. Stephan, disoriented and distressed as he was, had been waiting to feel their guard go down, even the slightest bit.

"I'm sorry," Freya whispered to him, as she circled his cock with her hand and pumped it. He groaned. "I really have no choice. Father thinks you are too dangerous to live."

"There's always a choice," he gasped, as the sensation rose again to the unbearable point. He had to bear it for Ann's sake.

"Not if you are my father's daughter, and you have been for three thousand years," Freya whispered. He felt her words in his ear, her breasts pressed against his side through the white chiffon strips that covered them, her thigh over his. Most of all he felt the molten core inside him answering the demands she made. It surged and bubbled. Why hadn't it been like this with Ann?

"You . . . you had to kill . . . innocent . . . humans?" he groaned.

He felt her hesitate. "That was Dee."

"So you . . . chose not to . . . to kill them." He felt like he was being torn apart.

Again the hesitation. Then she took her mouth from his ear. "Silence," she ordered, her voice clear so that Dee could be sure to hear it. Her hand slid along his cock more quickly. He arched again against the sensation pouring over him, gasping for breath.

Dee's face appeared over him. "Good," she murmured. "Excellent, Freya." She stalked around them. Stephan could hardly breathe, hardly see. His being was centered in his loins and behind their excruciating tightness was pooled the lava, waiting to be released, but not allowed release because of the tight bands of compulsion that bound him.

"I have brought some tools to increase his sensation," he heard Dee say, from somewhere distant. "A rod for his anus, some clips for his nipples, a ring for his cock. We could feed from him as well, as long as it doesn't weaken him too much."

"You . . . you planned for this?" Freya asked. The rhythm of her stroking slowed. Stephan breathed. "I thought we were going to help him if he couldn't kill them all. We never thought he would disobey—"

"Father told me it would come to this. I came prepared." Dee opened a small valise. Stephan saw it through a veil of desperation.

"Excuse me."

Van Helsing's voice came as a shock.

The Daughters jerked their heads up. Freya stopped stroking Stephan's cock. The lava in his groin sank to a simmer. Van Helsing? What was he doing here? Where was Ann?

"What is it?" Dee barked.

"Uh . . . Ann . . . I mean, it's the laudanum. Well, it put her out. She lost consciousness." Stephan couldn't see him, but he could hear the man's fear. He wondered if Van Helsing had imagined what he would see when he came down here to the crypts.

"And what of that?" Dee growled. "Get back upstairs. We have work to do."

"Well, but it isn't satisfying to have my way with her if she's unconscious." His pouty whine echoed in the immensity of the crypt. "It's, well, it's like taking a corpse." Apparently his grievance overcame his fear.

Dee and Freya just looked at him. "Wait a few hours. She'll come around," Dee said absently. She began rummaging in the valise. After a moment she looked up, apparently expecting that Van Helsing would be gone. "Get out," she said, her voice a low growl.

Stephan heard Van Helsing practically yelp like a kicked dog and his footsteps hurry away. The beast fed on his victim's fear and distress. But Ann was safe from that, for a few hours at least. Stephan's relief was short-lived. Dee held up two metal clips with serrated edges. She opened them like jaws and smiled.

"These will increase his awareness of his sexual sensation centers," she said, gloating. She took the little metal jaws and clamped them around his nipples. The teeth bit into tender flesh. A jolt of feeling went through him but it was pain, not pleasure. Surely this would act as a distraction from the stimulation, not add to it. Dee stalked back to the bag and took out two metal rods. The brands! She laid the ends in the coals of the great fireplace.

"Now, wash him, Freya. I think it's time for us to take turns sucking him."

He could last. He could. They could do what they would to him, and he would last. Van Helsing would not ravish Ann for hours. And somehow, in that time, he would find a way out of the clutches of his tormentors. They couldn't keep up their compulsion forever, could they?

Twenty-Four

Ann swam up through a haze of fog. She had been dreaming. Images careened through her head, horrible images of women with blood dripping from their mouths, and then she was one of them, and she was tearing flesh with her teeth. And then, in her dreams, Stephan was there. His voice was calming. He was saying something to her about the fact that she was strong now, and she had to use that strength.

Slowly, she began to be aware of her surroundings. She was in a bed. Red and gold brocade. It was scratchy against her bare back. The room was cold. She turned her head. No wonder. The fire had died down. And no one had pulled the curtains. They still looked out on night and tossing trees. But dawn was coming. She knew that. She wasn't sure how. It would be dawn in an hour or two. She felt heavy, as though she was under a load of blankets that were tucked too tightly around her so she couldn't move. Perhaps she didn't have to move. Maybe she would never move again. That should be comforting. And yet something poked at her, a sense of urgency she could not identify. How could she think with all the cobwebs in her head?

You're strong now, Ann.

That was Stephan's voice. Was it Stephan? Or was it her new partner, her Companion? There! That was it. She was changed. She was like Stephan now.

Stephan! She pulled her head around. She had to be strong for Stephan. She could hear things now, through the lamb's wool in her ears; the hiss of the coals in the grate; the branches of the lilac tree brushing against the window, and breathing accompanied by a soft burr. She blinked and tried to raise her head. It throbbed at her. The world spun. She lay back down.

Use your strength, Ann. The voice inside her reminded her of Stephan, but it wasn't exactly Stephan. *I am your strength.*

I need all the strength I can muster, she thought. *Give me strength.*

The world stopped spinning. The throb subsided. That was better. She could think more clearly now. It seemed as though the strength was in her blood, coursing through her body. She could feel it, pushed by her heart, surging out to her fingers and toes.

She tried raising her head again. She was naked, lying across her uncle's bed.

Erich sat in the chair in the corner by the fireplace. His receding chin was on his chest. He wore a brocade dressing gown and Moroccan slippers. A glass of brandy, slack in his hand, had spilled on his trousers. The burr came from his snoring.

It all came back. Erich was going to ravish her, and the Daughters had Stephan and meant to punish him, maybe kill him. Had Erich . . .?

She didn't know. Maybe she didn't want to know. She struggled to sit. That made the cobwebs start accumulating in the corners of her mind.

No. She couldn't allow that. She had to find Stephan. Now she knew what to do. *Companion,* she thought, as clearly as she could. *Whatever strength you have, I need it now.*

The answering surge along her veins made her feel alive. Anything was possible. That was a good thing, because she had to find Stephan. She looked around for something to cover her nakedness. The dress lying in a heap on the floor was torn down the front.

Where would Stephan be? Where could they have taken him? She got to her feet, a little shaky, and put one hand to her forehead. But the feeling passed. She slid quietly to the wardrobe and pulled it open. Her uncle's clothes still hung there. A dressing gown? It would drag on the ground and hinder her. She took one of his fine linen shirts and slipped it over her head. It was like to slip over her shoulders. So she tiptoed to the dresser and fished out one of his cravats. This she tied under her breasts like a belt. That would keep it on. What difference being clothed made she couldn't say. But she felt more able to face what might come.

She turned back into the room and took a breath. Erich might know where Stephan was. She hadn't felt his knowledge before, but maybe that was because of the laudanum. *I'm strong,* she thought. *And he needed their help to drug me. Well, they aren't here now.*

She took up her uncle's hazelwood cane and strode over to where Van Helsing snored. She could get an impression of what he knew by touching him, but that thought was repulsive. She poked his shoulder with it at the same time she called to her Companion. He snorted in surprise and turned his bleary eyes up to her, even as a red film dropped over the room for her.

"Where is he, Erich?" She asked it matter-of-factly.

He practically crawled up the back of the wing chair trying to retreat. But the red eyes her Companion gave her forced him to answer. "The . . . the crypts."

A shudder passed through her as she realized how similar the dark stone of the crypts would be to that stone room in which he had suffered for so long. All that was missing was the heat, and if they put that long cold fireplace to use . . .

Very well. That was her destination. She shook her head to clear the last of the cobwebs.

"You . . . you were supposed to be drugged," Erich accused.

"And so I was," she answered, looking around. "But you fell asleep, and apparently the laudanum wore off." She returned to the dresser and pulled out a pile of neatly folded cravats. These she tossed to Erich. "Now, lie down on the bed and tie your feet to the bedposts."

His wide-eyed surprise turned rebellious for an instant. Ann smiled as she let her eyes go red again. His mouth went slack and his eyes emptied. She watched as he tied himself to the bed. She tested the knots, then tied his hands to the posts next to the headboard and pulled them tight. "That should keep you from interfering," she breathed. Then she hurried from the room at a trot. She might be rushing to her death, but choices were gone. She had to help Stephan. He might not believe her, but she thought that together they might be able to win through. Even if they couldn't, what could she do but try?

"You can't leave me here," Erich shouted after her.

But she could. She was glad to leave him. He had tortured women, cheated honest people, and preyed on anyone he thought was weaker. Well, that wasn't her, not anymore.

She heard a choked sob behind her as she closed the door.

Now there was no one left to hear him.

Stephan felt his control weakening. They had unlocked his chains. He couldn't hold out much longer. He was so tired and the molten core at his center surged against his will harder than ever. He could practically feel it splash and bubble. Chanting seemed useless at this point. He had endured everything. Periodically they would let him take a gasping breath or two of rest, but that was only so that the sensation could be brought back renewed and even more virulent. A tight band of gold at the base of his cock seemed to constrict him, inflame him. They had sucked him until he wanted to scream. They had fed from him several times to maintain their own strength, and Dee made wounds on his body as Stancie once had. Dee had probed his backside as Freya sucked him. And Dee had branded him. But he healed. He always healed.

If it wasn't for Ann, he would welcome the conflagration. He longed for the torment to end. But he couldn't desert Ann. It had been so many hours. Was Van Helsing ravishing her even as he writhed here on this coffin?

Stephan panted as Dee lay back on the stone lid of the coffin herself and bade him insert his cock between her spread legs. The band around the base of his cock made him even more aware of his genitals. He thrust inside her as he bent to suckle at her breast. She pulled the fabric that plunged from shoulders to waist aside. He tongued her nipple as she arched up into him. She compelled him to move faster inside her. Freya watched. Stephan looked up at her from under his lashes. She had been looking more and more unhappy over the last hour. Her eyes were red, her lips set, but they were set in a frown.

"Pay attention, Harrier," Dee barked. "Be more assiduous in your attentions. He is near to finishing. We must keep the pressure on now."

"And what if he combusts and burns us up with him?" Freya asked sourly.

"We'll feel the final intensification. His vibrations will go off the scale. At that point, it's unstoppable. We pull away, that's all." She thrust her hips in counterpoint to Stephan.

Stephan felt the room begin to spin. The lava in his loins and belly surged.

"He's very close," Dee said, panting herself. "Roll over," she commanded. "Lick me. Freya, suck him, hard and fast."

"Dee, he's been punished enough. Let him go."

Stephan could hardly believe his ears. He rolled over, a sick feeling surging over him. He struggled against the burning in his core. He pushed frantically against their will. He had to hold out. He had to, for Ann.

"Don't you go soft on me, Freya, or Father will punish you as you've never been punished. How can you desert him at a time like this?" Dee straddled Stephan's shoulders. Her folds opened and he had no choice but to suck at her. "Now get over here and push him over the edge." After a long moment, he felt Freya's hands on his cock and then her mouth. *God! Please God in heaven, or Companion, or whoever might help. Help me now!*

Ann slid into the darkness of the crypts she knew so well. Caves and crypts had been her places of solace and refuge for so many years that they held no terror for her now. But now the smell of dust and damp stone was overpowered by the scent of cinnamon and ambergris. She heard gasping and grunting, moans. They were torturing Stephan. It made her feel sick inside. She set her jaw and slipped up behind the next huge pillar.

Peering around the pillar, she saw a sight that nearly stopped her heart. Stephan was laid out over a stone coffin, naked. The taller of the two Daughters, the one Stephan had called Deirdre, straddled him. Stephan licked her, even as he gasped and struggled. It was her moaning. Stephan's back was arched. He strained with every muscle. Sweat gleamed on his body. The other Daughter, Freya, sucked on Stephan's cock. Their eyes were burgundy red. Stephan writhed against them. Ann could feel not only their vibrations, but a horrible swelling throb in the air. It came from Stephan, she was sure.

"Soon, now," Deirdre called to her sister behind her. "His control of the forces inside him is fading. Get ready to jump back when the cycle becomes inevitable. We must be out of range when he ignites."

Ignites? Dear God in heaven!

Her heart jumped into her throat. She could barely breathe. She had to think. What to do to help him? Compulsion practically hung in the air. They were bottling him up inside and stimulating him until he was going to just . . . burn up? Her mind rebelled. She searched her memories of his experience, looking for whether he thought this could actually happen. And she found the stain on the wall in the room at Mirso Monastery. He thought that was what had happened to others the Daughters had tortured before him with their horrible training. And now they were trying to kill him in the same way.

She wanted to just dash to his side. But she had to be careful. The Daughters were strong. What to *do*? There was no time!

Before she could think, the shorter one he had called Freya raised herself from where she was working Stephan's erection with her mouth. She shook her head and stepped back. Ann could see the painful arch in Stephan's body ease a little, and the throb of energy that made her spine tremble edged down a notch.

"Freya, get back to it!" Deirdre said sharply. "We're almost there."

"I can't do this." Freya's voice was flat. She didn't look at her sister, or at Stephan.

Stephan had stopped licking Deirdre, as though, when her attention shifted to Freya, he had been released.

"Damn you, sister!" Deirdre got off Stephan's shoulders.

"What a time to get tired! There's no time to feed from him to renew yourself." She shouldered Freya aside. "I'll rub him. All you have to do is keep up your end of the compulsion." Deirdre sat at Stephan's hips and clasped his cock roughly in one hand. As she moved up and down on the shaft, she stroked the tip with the other thumb. Stephan immediately arched up again with a cry wrenched from his gut. His eyes went instantly red. Around him there grew a . . . corona of energy, like the glow of whitish light that had enveloped them at Bucklands Lodge.

"No, Dee. You don't understand. I *can't* do this." Freya just stood there, still. Then her eyes faded from burgundy through carmine to crimson and then back to dark pools in the dim light of the crypt.

Ann felt Deirdre's rush of rage as a physical wave of power. "Then don't!" she spat. "I'll do it myself. And you can tell Father why you had a change of heart about obeying him."

Ann saw Freya slump. "I can't please everyone," she murmured, as though she was surprised by that fact. Ann had no trouble hearing her, even in the immensity of the crypt. "Or there'll be nothing left of me."

"Your purpose is to serve him, serve the Elders, to serve our kind." As Deirdre's attention focused on Freya, she had stopped rubbing Stephan with the same intensity. The throb in the air slowed, and Stephan's writhing abated somewhat. The glow faded ever so slightly.

"I've served him for three thousand years," Freya said, her voice still dead. "My sentence is up, don't you think?" Now she turned her gaze on Deirdre.

But Deirdre jerked her head back around to Stephan. "No you don't," she said, through clenched teeth. "One of us still knows something of duty." She began to work his cock with fierce intensity. The throbbing that was Stephan cycled up again until it echoed in Ann's lungs. He groaned. The corona leapt out around him.

Freya turned and wandered toward the stairway that led up to the garden.

The throbbing was a drum that beat in Ann's head, accelerating, getting louder. Stephan cried out, the sound seeming torn from his throat. The corona of light intensified and grew until it engulfed Deirdre.

"He's past the point of return," Deirdre shouted in triumph to Freya's retreating form. "There's no way to stop it now." Indeed, she stepped away from Stephan, who continued to writhe in agony. The glow did not abate, but gleamed brighter and brighter until it was painful to look upon. To her amazement, Stephan's body lifted off the coffin lid about six inches and just hung there, twisting. His hoarse cries echoed against the stone and were thrown back in torturous confusion. Ann wanted to stop her ears.

Instead, she staggered forward into the flicker of the dying fire in the huge grate. "Stephan," she cried. "Hang on until I can touch you!"

"Ann!" Stephan gasped. "Stay back!" His last word turned into a growl of pain.

Deirdre turned back, unsure what was happening.

Ann couldn't think for the thundering throb of power in the air. She only knew she had to touch him. "Remember the lodge," she managed, even as she stumbled and fell.

"Too *late*!" His body was a bow. Muscles stood out in relief as he twisted in pain. His body gleamed with streaming sweat. "You'll burn with me. Get *back*!"

Ann scrambled up. She was so close. "I won't be hurt."

Deirdre lunged around the end of the coffin.

Ann stood still for a single second over the twisting figure on the coffin. Stephan looked at her, all his fear for her reflected in his glowing red eyes. "Can't hold it," he growled through gritted teeth.

Ann smiled down, her attention only for him. "Don't hold it. Trust me." And she placed both hands, palms open, on his shoulder.

The shock of power that shot through her was like lightning. Every muscle in her body contracted. All the pain of Stephan's last hours washed over her and through her. The room went red. Ann felt her hair rising out around her in a halo. Her Companion sang and its voice in her blood turned into a choir whose song soared with incredible strength.

The glow surrounded both of them. Deirdre stepped back, in horror or in awe. Ann tried to breathe and realized she was shrieking. But she didn't take her hands away from Stephan's flesh. "Let go. Let go. Let go!" That's what she was shrieking, or maybe only her mind was shrieking and she was making no sound at all.

She saw the horror in his eyes as he realized what he was doing to her. She managed a grin, though it might have resembled the rictus of a corpse. His horror turned to confusion. He looked wildly around. He was still trying to hold the energy back, trying to protect her. But he wasn't screaming anymore. Then his eyes returned to her and steadied. She wasn't shrieking anymore, either. They stayed like that, locked together in light for a second or an hour, who knew? The light faded a little. It seemed to drain out through her feet.

And then she saw acceptance in his eyes. She felt it through her hands. He thought he would kill them both. But he accepted that she would have it no other way. He let go.

Power shushed around them, through them, but it didn't carry pain. The throbbing slowed. Stephan settled back onto the lid of the coffin. Ann's feet grew heavy. She settled with him. With a shock she realized that she must have been suspended, as he was, in the piercing corona of light. The light had faded, but a glow remained around them. Stephan's eyes held wonder, relief, and . . . peace. He loved her. A moment of peace was handed back and forth between them before it faded into the close, damp air of the crypt. She saw Stephan's eyes register the intrusion of a thought. Ahhh, there was still the matter of Deirdre.

Ann turned slowly to face her.

Deirdre's eyes were no longer red. They were just wide with shock. She stood like a pillar of salt on the floor of the crypt. Ann could feel the power still humming around her and Stephan. If she touched Deirdre, what would happen?

But it was not her place. She looked back to Stephan. The glow had faded to a thin line of light that delineated his form. His erection was faltering. He was full, but not as painfully rod-straight as he had been. She had not noticed before the gold ring round the base of his cock. And his nipples had vicious little metal clips attached to them.

Stephan put his left hand over hers, where she still pressed her palms into his shoulder, and sat up on the coffin lid. Quietly, she released the clips from his nipples. The gold band dropped, clinking from his cock. He watched her without a sound.

His body tensed. His head raised, eyes snapping with intensity, as he looked up and past her. He was making a decision about Deirdre. His eyes went hard. She moved a hand to his bicep, not wanting to lose the touching yet. Then his brows creased. He looked from her to Deirdre and back again. The hardness drained from his expression. He took a breath and let it out, shaking his head. "Not worth it, Ann," he murmured. "She's not worth killing."

In that moment, she was prouder of him than she had ever been.

"So you can use her to diffuse the conflagration." Deirdre had found herself. She stalked toward them, eyes burgundy-red. The compulsion wielded by a very old vampire, the

Eldest of the Daughters, cascaded over them. "So I'll have to remove her."

It was Deirdre who lunged for Ann's arm. But Stephan grabbed Deirdre's shoulder and pushed her away. At his touch, the corona flashed up. Deirdre held to Ann. They were a circle of coruscating power. Ann felt her Companion surge in her veins. The room was shot with red.

"You'll never let it go, will you?" Stephan growled, his eyes red-black and angry. Now he let go of Ann and took hold of Deidre's shoulders with both hands. He thrust her from him, flinging her through the air. As he did, he released his power, just let go.

Deirdre burst into flames. They didn't start at one point and spread. They didn't start all over and grow. One minute she was in the air, her red eyes snapping with anger, and the next she was a glowing ball of flame, with no eyes at all. By the time the burning orb hit the ground there were only broken bits of charcoal to scatter on the floor. Flames licked at them and flickered slowly out.

The shock of it froze Ann. Stephan stood transfixed, shaking with rage. The only sound was Freya's cry.

"Dee," she sobbed. "Dee." Freya came running across the stone floor under the shadowy arches from the direction of the stairs up to the garden. She threw herself down among the bits of charcoal, looking about her frantically as though Deirdre might still be there somewhere. Ann watched, unable to gather enough of her wits to say anything. At last her body moved of its own volition to Stephan. He put his arm around her and tucked her in against his side as she hugged his naked body.

Freya's sobs slowly subsided. She rocked back on her heels, tears streaking her cheeks, and looked up at them. "Aren't you going to kill me, too?" She asked it without a real objection to that outcome, just curiosity.

Ann felt Stephan shake his head. "I didn't want to kill

her," he rumbled. A breath shuddered in and out of his chest. "If you don't have any designs against us, why should I want to kill you? You were the only one who had a shred of kindness for me." He tightened his grip on Ann's shoulders.

"You might as well kill me. I have nowhere to go now." Her voice had gone flat again.

"Go back and tell him not to bother sending anyone against us. The result will be the same." Stephan was leaning heavily on Ann now. She realized how exhausted he must be.

"I can't go back there. Not after this. Not after what I did."

Ann almost said something, but she bit back any impulse she might have to interfere. This had to be Stephan's call. How he felt about this last of the Daughters, how he reacted now was part of his journey, not hers.

"He isn't forgiving of failure."

"He will want atonement," she agreed, her voice soft with contemplating what kind of atonement her father might require.

Would he leave it at that? Ann waited. When he didn't say anything more, she chanced a glance upward. He was chewing his lip.

Stephan straightened. "No. You must go back to tell him that you will not atone. That is the only way you can survive being his daughter. There is no crime here." He took his arm from around Ann and stepped forward. She let him go. "You refused to participate in something you thought was wrong. Right and wrong transcend a father's orders. They transcend the Rules. Why should you feel guilty? Why should you atone?" He raised her from where she knelt. "Go to Mirso, Freya. Tell him. Then walk away."

"Away from Mirso?" Her voice was small and frightened. Dust from the floor and smears of charcoal, stained her white dress at the knees. "Mirso is the only refuge for our kind."

"Perhaps there is no such thing as refuge," Stephan said

softly. "Maybe that is the final truth about our condition, our tragedy."

"A tragedy I probably deserve." She heaved a sigh.

"Forgive yourself, Freya. There is time to survive this and become whole. We are eternal. You have all the time in the world."

She looked up at him. "There are some burdens that are too heavy to survive and become whole." She straightened. "I'll tell him, though. I'll consider it my penance. But I'll tell him about Kilkenny. The balance between our kind and humans is still in danger. There are still made vampires out there."

Stephan turned to look at Ann. "Not all made vampires are a threat to us, Freya. Can't there be degrees of good and bad?"

Freya gave a bitter chuckle. "I am the last person you can ask that question."

"Then let Kilkenny go . . ."

Freya's eyes darted about the crypt. "I . . . I don't know."

"Will you train another Harrier if he asks you?" Ann couldn't help but challenge her. That might be the real danger.

"No." The shake Freya gave of her head was a bit more certain. "I can't go through that again. Not that he might not find someone else to do it. But it would have to be an old one, as we were." She looked up again at Stephan. "In some ways, you were exactly what he had been looking for, for centuries. You are incredibly powerful. Even still you may not know how powerful. Your only fault was that you were an independent thinker." She smiled ruefully.

"You are, too," he said. His voice was kind as it rumbled through the darkness.

"I hope that's true," she said. She looked at Ann and back to Stephan. "We never realized that a sensitive like she is could both increase your power and ground you to keep it from destroying you. We had our plan so carefully outlined."

She shook her head. "Find a naturally powerful male, increase that power through sexual stimulation and control, then teach him controlled release. We created a perfect weapon. And of course, if we both increased his power and stifled its release, he could be destroyed. We discovered that accidentally." She gave a chuckle without a shred of mirth in it.

The stain on the wall. He had very nearly become another stain tonight.

"I thought sharing the power would diminish it," Freya mused. "And emotion? Emotion was supposed to sap your strength. Who could have guessed it was by sharing and giving in to emotion that you would realize its potential? That's what you did, didn't you?"

Stephan nodded. "It took all the courage I had. I thought I was killing her."

It was Freya's turn to nod. "I felt the emotion in the air at the moment you decided." Again she glanced between them. She sighed. "You've climaxed with her, haven't you?"

He nodded. "It didn't hurt her."

"Because she isn't crazy."

Ann was a bit tired of being talked about in the third person. "And we cared about each other. It was the healing experience it was meant to be, not hurtful."

Freya raised her brows, considering. "I wouldn't know about that. For us it was always just a job."

A job their father gave them. That was the saddest thing Ann had heard her say.

Freya looked down at the bits of charcoal smoldering at their feet, a lost expression on her face. "Well . . ." She turned slowly, and without another word walked toward the stairs up to the garden.

Twenty-Five

They watched her go. Ann was feeling a little lost, as well. Where to go from here? What happened after torture, and death, and glowing power, and risking everything in one leap of faith and trust? Slowly the reality of their surroundings sank in. She was barefoot, clad only in a man's shirt. Stephan was naked. They were down in the crypt of the abbey with dead bodies strewn all over Maitlands above them. And the sun was rising.

Stephan looked down at her. "We can't stay here," he said. "They'll blame us for the murders."

"It was never a refuge anyway." Still, the thought of leaving it behind was daunting. Where would they go? And was there even a "they" to go anywhere? Did he still think her love was a childish infatuation she would grow out of?

"Oh, dear!" she exclaimed. "I left Erich tied to the bed."

Stephan stumbled to the coffin in front of the dying fire and picked up a pair of breeches from a pile of clothing on the floor. She watched him pull them on, and shrug the shirt over his head. He was exhausted by his ordeal. But he had a

murderous look in his eyes. Gathering boots and coat, he
started across the crypt.

"Don't you dare think of killing him, Stephan Sincai,"
she called out. "I don't want his blood on our hands."

He set his mouth without looking at her and she followed
him up the stairs. At the branch in the passage, he paused,
not sure how to get up to the house. They must have trans-
ported him down here. She pushed past him. "This way
leads to my uncle's room." They burst through the passage in
the fireplace to find Erich still splayed across the bed in brocaded dressing gown, trousers, and slippers. His eyes went
wide when he saw them. Ann's sharp hearing caught carriage wheels and horses' hooves crunching on the gravel in
the drive. A shout of dismay indicated that someone had discovered the gutted bodies of the guards.

"So, Van Helsing," Stephan said through gritted teeth.
"You want to play with vampires. Dangerous work, that."

Erich whimpered and pressed himself into the bed as
though he could somehow sink right through both mattress
and floor to escape. Stephan leaned over him, a grim look on
his face. Erich shrieked. The smell of urine flooded the room
as a dark stain appeared on his breeches.

"Stephan!" Ann said sharply.

Stephan glanced back at her and then ripped the cravat
that tied Erich's right hand to the bedpost as though it were
string. Ann let out her breath. It was the work of a moment
for him to rip the others, as well. He grabbed Erich's arm in
a grip Ann knew too well. "Come with me, you cowardly
weasel." He thrust his boots and coat under his right arm,
and marched Erich out the door and down the stairs. Erich
sniveled in fright.

She heard Jennings shouting to someone—the butcher de-
livering in the early morning? Dear Jennings at least was not
dead. They were going to send the butcher's boy for reinforcements. It would not be long until the place was teeming

with interlopers, and Jennings and the butcher might be in at any moment. Stephan was hauling Erich to the kitchen.

Ann wasn't sure she could bear to see Polsham and Mrs. Simpson again, but she daren't leave Erich entirely to Stephan. She stayed just inside the kitchen door, her back to the wall, where she couldn't see their bodies.

Stephan went to where a great block held the kitchen knives.

The front door banged open. "Polsham!" she heard Jennings roar. "Mrs. Simpson! Are you all right?" Feet were running down the hall. Several pairs.

Stephan did not seem perturbed at all. He set down his coat and his boots on the table, took a long boning knife from the block and dragged Erich over to the two bodies. Erich had begun to sob. Stephan bent over the bodies, and when he rose, the knife was bloody. He wiped the blood on Erich's shirt, then took Erich by the wrist and bent again.

The shouts were getting closer.

Stephan handed the knife calmly to Erich. His eyes went red, and Erich slumped, his face vacant. "Whenever you think of hurting someone, you will become impotent," he said. "Repeat."

"Whenever I think of hurting someone, I'll become impotent," he murmured.

Stephan grabbed his clothes and strode to Ann. He was gaining strength. One arm was around her bottom in a trice, lifting her against his chest. The darkness whirled up. Jennings appeared in the doorway, gasping, visible only through the deepening black. Then all was gone in a searing moment of pain.

They popped back into time and space inside the cave. Several candles still guttered, shedding a dim flicker in the darkness. The damp and cold was a sharp contrast to the heat of the crypt. Stephan put her down, staggering a bit.

"Let him explain the knife!" he said through gritted teeth.

Ann suppressed a smile. Stephan thought the magistrates would do the job she wouldn't let him do. But she wasn't so sure. Erich had been cutting the rope from a box of wine brought up from the cellars even as Jennings had been coming in the door. Jennings would have been preoccupied by the corpses of his friends. She rather thought that Erich might be able to pull off an explanation that he had only just gotten free from where Stephan had tied him up as he killed the other two. She had no doubt that someday, down the years, she might encounter Erich again, up to his eyes in some scheme to make money off innocent people. He wouldn't take her advice to act as liaison between vampire and humans to foster understanding. Perhaps he'd use his imperfect knowledge of vampires to gull humans into believing he could exorcise their nightmares with crosses and garlic. For a price, of course.

She didn't forgive Erich for what he had almost done. He might have bungled it by falling asleep, but she had no doubt he would have tried to rape her if he could have. But his blood on her hands or Stephan's was a guilt she couldn't afford to indulge. Maybe she should feel guilty for the fact that Erich might escape retribution. Though Stephan's curse, if it held, was punishment enough. She hoped the curse would prevent Erich inflicting himself on other women. But either way, taking responsibility for anything he might ever do was a trap from which she had to walk away. She had seen too clearly what guilt had done to Stephan.

"I'm sorry we couldn't wait to get more clothing for you," Stephan apologized as he pulled on stockings and boots.

"There was nothing there I wanted."

"We'll get you some ravishing clothes in Paris."

"Is Paris far enough?"

He looked thoughtful as he shrugged himself with difficulty into his well-cut coat. "Probably not. The runner and that idiot of a squire will ache to believe we were in league with Van Helsing."

It began to sink in that she would never see Maitlands again. But she had known that from the day she resolved not to marry Erich.

Her tristesse must have shown in her face. Stephan took the distance between them with two strides and took her in his arms. "I'm sorry about Maitlands."

She looked up at him and smiled, as much because his impulse to comfort her pleased her as she was proud that she had anticipated this contingency. "At least it will be useful. I drew up papers with Mr. Yancy after I refused Erich's kind offer, just in case things did not work out. Or perhaps just in case they did. I told him that if I left for a time, Maitlands was to be turned into a school for girls where they teach something besides needlework and watercolors and playing the pianoforte. The money from the estates will fund the whole. They have to find a body to declare me dead and have it pass to the Crown. I think it will be safe."

Stephan raised his brows. "I am impressed. And you know," he continued seriously, "if you want to have it back in future years, you can come buy it up in a generation or two. Money is never a problem for our kind."

That took her breath away.

There it was. All the huge consequences of being "one of his kind" hit her at once. She felt her knees go weak. A generation or two? Money never a problem, even though she had not a shilling to her name at the moment? Sucking blood, boredom, a need for sex—would it become a preoccupation? How would she avoid the moral abyss that engulfed so many of them? Was she up to this? How could she be, who had never left her nursery?

She felt her gaze darting over his face. She had no control over her expression. He must be seeing all her doubts, all her uncertainty.

His eyes flashed horror, followed by resignation. His shoulders slumped almost imperceptibly. "I'll see you're established. There is, of course, no . . . obligation on your part."

What was he saying? She felt so overwhelmed she wasn't sure. He would help her. Without obligation. There was no obligation between them? Is that what he thought? After what had just happened between them? Had what he felt about her changed?

With a shock, she realized that even though he was touching her, she didn't feel his experience washing over her. Was she losing her gift entirely? How many times had she prayed for that? But now she *wanted* that disability. It was part of her and she would be bereft without it. She reached up and grabbed his face in both hands, staring into his eyes.

A sharp breath took her. There it was. All she had to do was focus on it. On him. Oh, he still loved her all right. He thought what he'd just seen in her eyes was her getting over her infatuation with him.

God, but he was maddening!

"I am *not* Beatrix!" she practically shouted. She tossed her hands in the air and pulled out of his grip. "Lord, what do I have to do to prove my love is real?" She paced across the sand floor of the cave as a candle guttered and went out. "I just faced down the Daughters of Rubius with you because I *love* you. I stood beside you and joined to you when you thought it would kill us both. Doesn't that earn me the benefit of the doubt?"

She thought that would get a rise out of him. It didn't. He stood, quiet. Another candle guttered. "I don't doubt you think you love me, Ann." His voice was quiet too, in the immensity of the cave. "I'm the only man you've ever touched.

But life is long, how long you've no idea yet. There will be other men. You'll touch them, too. First loves don't last."

"You're saying no first love has *ever* lasted?" She folded her arms. "None? Never?"

"Well, no, I don't mean to be absolute . . ." He looked taken aback. Good.

"Then you must think *your* love for me won't last. Because I can feel you love me. You practically burn with it." She also knew he felt he'd love her forever. The damned stubborn brute just wouldn't act on that. For fear. For fear of what? She couldn't quite make it out. She had to make him tell her.

A flush crept into his cheeks. He cleared his throat once, but nothing came out.

"Sorry, Mr. Sincai. That's the consequence of understanding you better than any other woman ever will. No hiding." She let her voice have an edge. She wasn't going to let him go until he told her what the barriers to loving her were. She couldn't overcome them until she knew what they were. She didn't say anything. She just waited for him to speak.

"My . . . my case is special." The words were practically torn from him. All right. That was a start. She didn't say anything. She didn't ask questions. It was up to him. She had told him she loved him. Wasn't that enough?

But maybe he couldn't feel how strong her love was the way she could feel his. She was the sensitive one, after all. Was she punishing him because he was not like her? She began to feel a little guilty.

Guilt! It was his guilt that stood between them, wasn't it? He thought he wasn't worthy. He hadn't forgiven himself. Hadn't he banished guilt as he gave advice to Freya in the crypt? He must have known his advice could apply equally to himself. She thought about that. Yes, she felt that in him. He knew.

But there was knowing intellectually and *knowing* in your

soul. Still, she couldn't tell him. She dared not prompt. It was up to him. All she did was raise her brows.

Stephan stood there in the cave as she raised her brows in inquiry. His insides churned. She deserved better than he was. He would disappoint her in a thousand ways. Look at her! She was courageous beyond belief to have ever touched him. She was willing to go to her death for him, and hell and hades; he was not worth that. And how her delicate looks belied her strength of character! She had even made him spare the despicable Van Helsing. What greater proof of a magnanimous nature did anyone need?

And now she was waiting. Waiting for him to tell her why there was no hope for this first, pure love of hers. If he told her, was that kindness? Should he just lead her along, let her come to leave him on her own? Wasn't he pushing her away even as he had pushed Beatrix away by telling her she would leave him someday? That . . . that was his fault, a sin, a sin of pride that he always told the truth. But God damn it, if she knew him through and through as she said she did, then she would know that about him! She would understand that truth was not something he could ignore.

He took a breath. He had to tell her why he was a special case. "I think you'll find some men are less worth loving than others." He tried to make his tone light.

She said nothing. He peered at her in the gloom as the candles went out one by one.

Very well. She wasn't satisfied with that. "I have made horrible mistakes in my life. Mistakes others have paid for."

She looked like she didn't understand.

Damn her! "I drove Beatrix away," he said through clenched teeth. "I made Asharti. I couldn't love her. I drove her crazy. She tortured, killed, made thousands like Kilkenny. I let a civilization make human sacrifices to me. I let another get massacred by their enemies because I wouldn't make them strong like I was by sharing my blood, even though they pleaded. I couldn't kill the Irishman. I couldn't even atone for my sins. Don't forget, I killed innocent made vampires at the lodge right along with the ones who had committed atrocities, almost without a second thought. And I ended in making you . . ." His voice trailed off, his passion drained away.

He glanced up. Ann's clear gray eyes watched him. There . . . there was no judgment in them. "You're sorry for that?" she asked calmly.

"No!" He shook his head convulsively. "Of course not. But . . ."

She raised her brows again.

He shook his head. She was going to pull it out of him. Make him say it . . . "If you knew other men, you'd know what I'm talking about. I'm not . . . good. Not like you are."

"Oh, yes. The other men I touched, say the squire, and Jemmy Minks, and my uncle. They were all far better than you are. Lord, my uncle wanted to give me to Erich, Stephan. I could have hated him for that but I loved him because I understood why." A look of alarm passed over her face. "For God's sake, you might just think I'm serious. You know I know all that about you, the Mayans, Tibet, Beatrix, Asharti. Don't you know I think your struggle to find the right path is one of the most admirable things about you, that I love you for it?"

"But I *failed.*"

"Not yet." She let a little smile cross her lips and uncrossed her arms. "You're still alive, aren't you?"

"Oh, yes. I'm still alive."

"I see the weight on your shoulders," she said softly. "You tried to lift that weight from Freya today. But no one can lift it for another. I can't lift it for you."

What was she trying to say? Freya? What had he said to

Freya? That he didn't blame her. That she shouldn't feel . . . guilty. Breath hissed into his lungs without his volition. Was that what Ann meant? But Freya had an excuse. She was the old devil's *daughter*, for God's sake, and had lived with that overpowering personality for three thousand years. Freya had reasons. But what excuse did he have for his crimes? Wanton ignorance? Stupidity? He took a step back from her. "I'm not worth your love, Ann." He rushed through the words. "Someday soon you'll realize that. And I always tell the truth, even though that's what pushed Beatrix away. Beatrix came to the same conclusion eventually. She did grow out of me." The anguish rolling up in his gut made him want to turn away from her, to run into the dark reaches of the cave and hide himself.

"So you've told me," Ann said matter-of-factly. "I consider myself thoroughly warned."

He let his gaze rove over the stone and the rushing brook and the guttering candles, almost frantic. When finally he let his gaze return to her face, she was looking thoughtful.

"Very well, let us talk truth. I suppose the truth is that you think me shallow and cowardly to have stayed in my nursery for ten whole years. I expect I don't have enough experience for you. You think you'd tire of me, even though you want me quite badly just now."

He rolled his eyes. She wasn't playing fair. "You can't believe that."

"As easily as you believe I couldn't keep on loving you knowing what I know about you. Easier, in fact. I know everything about you. I love what I know. I want to have a chance to keep on loving. Is that so wrong?" Suddenly all her role-playing washed away. Her face collapsed into raw need. It was almost frightening. "Can't you try to believe that if it's just *possible* that some first love somewhere has lasted, mine might be the next one? You trusted me tonight. I saw it in your eyes," she whispered. "You threw yourself into the abyss with me."

He stood, frozen. "As you did."

She nodded, big-eyed. "Is this so different?"

God, but he would toss himself into the abyss without a thought if it would save her an instant of pain or a moment of jeopardy. She was asking him to believe in her enough to let her love him. That he could do. But she was also asking him to forgive himself enough to believe himself worthy of loving. Ahhh, an abyss indeed. Could he have as much courage as this slender, ethereal girl? God help him, he had to, or he was condemning her to unhappiness for certain.

"I'll try," he said. "God knows, I'll try." He stepped to her and took her in his arms. He was afraid he might crush her, but he knew she was strong now. Strong with the Companion's song. He had to trust to that. He knew she would feel his commitment. It burned inside him even now. He wanted to be worthy of her. He was willing to brave the abyss to make her happy.

She looked up at him, tears in her eyes. "Take me to Paris," she said. "I want new clothes. Then I want to see Peking and Katmandu, with you."

He kissed her and felt the fire leap into his loins. Not the pain the Daughters inflicted, but the sweet burning for Ann that would drive him to give her pleasure in whatever way he could for as long as he could. He would protect her from her folly in trusting him. If she believed in forever, he would give it to her. His Companion pulsed in his blood. He could feel the throb in her throat as he covered it with kisses.

They were the same. They loved. They had forever. He had already given that to her with his blood. He would make it into a gift she would treasure.

The blood is the life.